Keithan Quintero AND THE PEGASUS AIR RACE

(A Story from the Future)

FRANCISCO MUNIZ

Hidden Spark
BOOKS

KEITHAN QUINTERO AND THE PEGASUS AIR RACE
(A STORY FROM THE FUTURE)
Book 2
Copyright © 2020 by Francisco Muniz

First Edition

Front cover illustration by Andros Martinez
Front cover concept design by Francisco Muniz
Interior illustrations by Francisco Muniz

ISBN 978-1-7360694-3-1 (hardcover)
ISBN 978-1-7360694-4-8 (paperback)
ISBN 978-1-7360694-5-5 (ebook)

www.hiddensparkbooks.com

I dedicate this book to

5J3PV3J-hW

Don't miss the beginning of Keithan's adventures in

Keithan Quintero and the Sky Phantoms
(A Story from the Future)

AUTHOR'S NOTE

This book makes reference to the author's edition of *Keithan Quintero and the Sky Phantoms (A Story from the Future) – Book 1*, published in 2020, and in which minor changes were made after revision of the first edition. No changes whatsoever were made in relation to the fictional events and outcomes presented in the original version of this book's prequel.

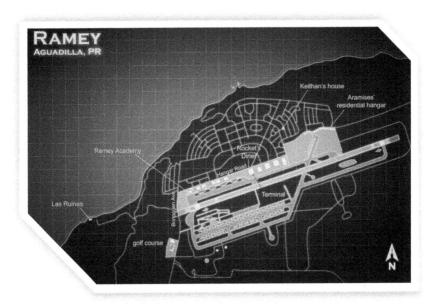

San Juan

Cidra

Aguadilla

Jayuya

Ponce

Cabo Rojo

CHAPTER 1

The presentation began at 1:30 p.m., and right away, the crowd gathered at the east side of Ramey Airport started cheering. Finally, after so much anticipation, and with only two days left for the event that promised to bring hundreds, if not thousands, of air racing aficionados, the official racecourse of the 2055 Pegasus Air Race was now being revealed.

Reporters and pro air racers with their crews formed the crowd that now stared with amazement at the many images that showed the different landscapes of the Caribbean island of Puerto Rico, where the race was going to take place. Such images captured the beauty of the island, but moreover, the challenge it also involved for the race, with over a hundred hover rings that would be raised at different altitudes and angles for the competitors to fly through.

All of this was being projected on the bloated surface of the embellished white airship that hovered a hundred feet above Ramey Airfield, though it was impossible to see from the top of the airship's wide envelope. That was where twenty-six-year-old Agent Brave Gala stood. She could see half of the crowd far below immersed in the presentation. Nobody below knew she was there. If somebody did spot her, he or she would probably ponder how she had managed to get there, for the small aircraft she had arrived in remained invisible to the naked eye. It so happened its stealth capability was so advanced it made the craft worthy of its name: Sky Phantom.

Gala was all set to carry out her mission. She was clad in a semi-armored black jumpsuit and calf-high boots, comfortable enough for all the flexibility she required. Her dark curly hair was short enough to stay out of her face. The flexed screen on her left sleeve remained in standby mode for communicating, and on her right forearm, she wore a gauntlet, which she had already attached to a cable that came out of the Sky Phantom.

Gala pulled at the cable one last time to make sure it was well hooked. All the while, she kept her feet firmly separated shoulder-width apart to keep the strong wind up there from making her lose her balance.

"Here we go," she murmured to herself before taking a deep breath. And without hesitation, she jumped off the airship.

Nobody witnessed her stunt. She fell backward, down the opposite side of where Pegasus's presentation was taking place.

Right away, Gala's pulse quickened in excitement mixed with terror. She remained in total control nevertheless. As a Sky Phantom knight, she was well trained for this sort of thing, so she kept her right arm stretched upward with her gauntlet and felt the abrupt pull on her shoulder when the cable tensed. Still, her gauntlet kept sliding down the cable, lowering Gala, only now at a much slower pace. Otherwise it would have dislocated her right arm if not ripped it out of her shoulder. But with the cable tensing, Gala slammed against the bloated surface of the airship's envelope.

"Ungh!"

Gala now hung halfway down to her destination, the ground still nearly 350 feet below. She couldn't help feeling a low level of vertigo, so in order to control it, she remained focused on her mission.

Soon she appeared below the lowest part of the envelope. It was then that Gala was able to see the airship's gondola. Unlike most of them, which were small and attached to the bottom of airships to carry passengers, this one was incredibly large, so much that it looked more like a mansion hanging from its roof and made of a series of circular modules with curved glass windows.

There was only one way to get to it, and that was through the balcony with the golden balustrade in front of Gala, which, to her luck, seemed to be unguarded. The big challenge was reaching it since Gala was currently hanging nearly thirty feet away from it due to the wide curve of the envelope above her.

Using her whole body, she swung herself back and forth, her right shoulder starting to hurt. It took a few seconds to gain enough momentum, and once she swung herself close enough to the balcony, Gala detached her gauntlet from the cable and stretched both arms forward. A gasp escaped her the instant she was freely suspended in the air—right before her gloved hands grabbed the golden railing.

A deep sigh of relief escaped her, and she pulled herself up and landed on the balcony. She had to take a moment to catch her breath before she pressed the flexed screen on her left forearm.

"Phantom Base, this is Agent Gala. Do you copy?" Gala said with a low voice, holding her forearm close to her mouth.

"We copy, Agent," a male voice replied through a tiny speaker next to her flexed screen. *"What's your status?"*

"I just made it to the airship's gondola and am about to enter it," Gala reported. "I'll contact you again once I complete the mission."

"Roger that, Agent. Good luck."

Just as Gala put her communicator in standby mode again, she heard the loud and excited cheers of the crowd in the distance. So far, it seemed the presentation was still going on as expected, but it made Gala realize she was running out of time. Already, twenty-five minutes had passed since it had started, and Gala needed to complete her mission before the presentation ended.

At least phase one had been accomplished. Gala had gotten into the Pegasus airship without being seen. Now it was time for phase two.

Gala passed through the opening beyond the balcony and stepped into a circular room that screamed luxury and wealth. It made Gala feel as if she had just stepped into a museum, or maybe inside a palace. The arched, gilded colonnade that stood high at each side of the room was quite impressive, as well as the varied collection of humanoid robots that accompanied them on top of black pedestals. The furniture was quite impressive too, though unlike the robots, they looked more like they were from another era—made of red velvet and decorated with golden Victorian ornaments. These were oriented toward the center of the room, where a wide round table stood accompanied by the large hologram of a white winged stallion bust that hovered low over it.

Despite the elegance and magnificence of the place, Gala did her best to not get distracted. She moved across the room, taking in every detail, focusing on spotting any surveillance cameras or movement. She remained particularly suspicious of the robots on the pedestals, wondering if they were watching her. Whether or not they were, there was no doubt that somewhere in that room was some type of surveillance.

Gala kept pacing across the room, her steps muted by the royal red carpet. She was nearing the other end when, all of a sudden, the wide metal door that stood there slid open, and a group of people came into view. There were five figures in all, three men and two women, all much older than Gala and dressed in expensive-looking suits. They had been talking among themselves but froze at the unexpected sight of the African American female agent in black standing merely ten feet away on the other side of the doorway.

Gala also froze when she saw them, but her eyes, now wide, instantly locked on the bearded figure with broad shoulders who stood at the front. She recognized him right away by his extravagant white suit, golden epaulets, and matching buttons. It was the very man she had been ordered to find: the CEO of Pegasus Company, Captain Giovanni Colani.

"Who are you?" said the man with a deeply puzzled look and in a clear Italian accent. "How did you get inside my airship?"

Gala didn't respond. Instead, she sprinted forward like a predatory feline and threw her arms at Colani. It happened so fast the rest of the group only had time to gasp before Gala grabbed Colani by his blazer and pulled him hard into the room. She let go of him and slammed the panel at the side of the doorway. The metal door slid shut behind her and locked. Shouts and thumping of the men and women on the other side followed.

"Help! Security breach! *Security breach!*"

Gala ignored the muffled shouting and surveyed the room a second time. Once she was sure there was no other way to get in, she faced Colani again.

"Move back!" Gala shouted. "I said *move back!*"

Colani had his hands up and staggered backward. Gala could tell the man was scared. She could see it in his eyes while she kept her gauntlet pointed at him. Little did Colani know, she had no intention of hurting him. Her gauntlet was nothing more than a gadget, not a weapon, but Colani didn't need to know that.

"Listen," Colani said, daring to speak, his voice shaky. "I-I have no idea who you are or if someone sent you. Just ... just tell me what it is that you want."

Gala was straightforward. "Information. All the information about your true plans with your air race."

"True plans?" said Colani, his eyebrows furrowed.

There was a loud bang on the door, then another, and another. It sounded as if someone was hitting it with a sledgehammer. Gala knew she didn't have much time left. She narrowed her eyes at Colani.

"Don't make me ask the hard way."

She moved her gauntlet closer to Colani's chest.

The banging on the door became much louder, its sound echoing in the room.

"Tell me!" Gala yelled, eyes full of anger. "I already know the truth about your camera drones. The only piece of the puzzle missing is what you really intend to do with them the day of the race. So for the last time—"

She didn't get to finish the sentence as an explosion behind her knocked her off her feet. The next thing she saw was a pair of bulky figures marching into the colonnaded room. They pushed aside the bent chunks of the metal that had been the door. Gala's sight cleared and saw that the figures weren't human.

They were robots, nearly seven feet tall, with sleek white-and-gold coverings and faceless heads that had nothing but a round red lens at its center.

"Fermala!" Colani shouted, pointing at Gala. *"Lei è un'intrusa!"*

The robots grabbed Gala by her upper arms before she was able to get up. Their hydraulic fingers locked instantly. Right behind them, Colani's companions hurried into the room along with more people. Colani, now in full control, straightened his blazer and approached Gala.

"It seems the tables have turned, stranger," he told her with a deep look. "It's *you* who should be giving information now. So start by telling me who sent you."

Gala hissed but didn't stop looking directly at Colani.

"*Who* sent you?" Colani insisted.

He waited for a few seconds but still got no answer.

"As you told me, stranger, do *not* make me ask the hard way."

Both of them kept staring challengingly at each other, Colani waiting for an answer, Gala testing his patience and waiting for the first chance to turn the situation to her advantage again. Meanwhile, everyone else waited with intrigue.

Unexpectedly, Colani lowered his gaze. Gala didn't know what the man was staring at.

"No matter," Colani said. "We'll figure it out once we scan *that.*"

Gala looked down at the small flexed screen with the digital insignia on the left side of her chest: a winged triangle slightly inclined to the right and with a tiny circle surrounding each of its corners. Her mission was over, she realized. She needed to get out of there fast. No matter what, she couldn't let Colani or anyone else there know what her insignia represented.

Out of options, Gala had to improvise. She took a deep breath and released it. "All right," she said.

Colani addressed his robots. "Remove her gauntlet weapon."

The order ended up being a mistake. Gala wriggled free as soon as the robots loosened their grips to carry out the order. She crouched in one swift move, then pushed herself off and rolled forward. The momentum brought her quickly back on her feet. Colani got out of the way in fear of being attacked, exactly as Gala had expected, and right away, she broke into a run.

"Don't let her escape!" Colani shouted, but it was no use since no one had been guarding the terrace at the other end of the room.

Only the elegant furniture and the round table at the center stood in Gala's way. She jumped onto the table and passed straight through the hologram of the winged stallion before she landed on the other side of the table, never reducing speed.

She could hear everyone hurrying after her, but Gala got to the terrace fast. Her eyes were fixed on the cable that still dangled beyond the balustrade. It was nearly thirty feet away. Gala realized her last steps would require maximum speed to reach it, not to mention all her strength.

"Fermala!" Colani bellowed from inside the room. But just as he did, Gala leapt onto the railing and jumped off, letting out her loudest cry.

"HEYAAA!"

The cry allowed her to channel all her energy. She kept going—ten feet, fifteen feet, twenty feet in the air, away from the terrace and toward the dangling cable. She threw both arms forward, hoping against all hope to reach it as she fell. Her whole life seemed to flash before her eyes in that horrifying moment, leading to the very instant in which she would plunge to her death.

Miraculously, both gloved hands caught the cable, and with a swing of her right arm, she locked the gauntlet to the cable and stopped her fall.

The incredible stunt made everyone who witnessed it gasp. One by one, the men and women who had run after her appeared behind the terrace's balustrade, their eyes now wide and their jaws dropped in disbelief, Colani among them. He and the others, including the two robots, could only stare as Gala, who was hooked to the cable with her legs dangling, pressed a switch on the gauntlet with her free hand and began to ascend.

Gala didn't bother to look at Colani. She kept looking straight up as she approached the airship's envelope. She could hear the CEO shouting out orders over the whining of her gauntlet's winding mechanism, and already she knew what to expect. Colani's security officers would be hurrying to the top of the airship from the inside to catch her. But by the time they got to the top and came out through a series of hatches that opened outward, Gala was nowhere in sight.

Four officers with black side caps and raised electroshock guns moved down the top surface of the envelope, cautiously stretching their necks while looking down the side of the airship, searching for Gala.

"Where'd she go?" asked one of the men, looking from one end of the airship to the other.

His companions looked puzzled too. They stared at each other as if wondering if they had heard correctly about the situation. Had she jumped off the gondola's terrace and gone *down* the airship instead of up? That would have been logical.

It turned out the four armed men were too late to see Gala hurry to safety as soon as she had reached the top of the airship. They were about to report their failure to Colani when an intense blue-and-white flame ignited nearly ten feet away from them.

And like a shooting star in broad daylight, the flame blasted away.

In seconds, Gala was flying at top speed in her Sky Phantom, away from Ramey Airport and low over the open sea. She was heading west, the burning exhaust the only thing visible about her craft, along with the cone-shaped cloud around the fuselage as a result of the supersonic speed.

Gala's destination soon came into view on the horizon: the isolated island of Mona preceded by a white forest of helical structured wind turbines that jutted out of the sea. Mona, despite being known to the rest of the world as an ecological reserve, also happened to be the location of the Sky Phantom Legion's secret base.

Still flying low, Gala went around the wind turbines and entered the base through an opening in the island's limestone cliff. The opening led her to the base's docking bay, an advanced technological environment that gave a completely different perspective compared to the natural habitat the island projected outside. There, Gala landed the Sky Phantom.

Several people in high-tech black uniforms turned their heads when Gala deactivated her craft's invisibility cloak. The Sky Phantom seemed to materialize out of thin air, revealing its elongated elliptical fuselage and vertical amorphous wings, which, like the rest of the craft, were made of a semitranslucent metallic material.

"Agent Gala," called a tall man in uniform from a distance. "The lieutenant colonel is waiting for you in Sector 5."

"On my way," Gala responded while she climbed down the craft.

Sector 5 was currently one of the most heavily guarded rooms inside the base. Gala reached it at the end of a corridor. The room was actually a cave full of highly advanced technology, with numerous tubes running like arteries all over its rock walls and workstations, which were oriented to the center of the room. It was at the center where Gala found Lieutenant Colonel Lanzard. A group of technicians in lab coats accompanied him.

"Ah, Gala. You made it," the colonel said over his shoulder in his deep voice. He was a man of medium height, with a square jaw and a strong appearance despite his white crew cut hair and pale wrinkled face.

Gala nodded to him, yet her attention went quickly to one of the two octagonal glass chambers that stood past the colonel and his company.

"What's going on?" she asked as she halted next to Lanzard.

"We're still trying to figure it out," Lanzard responded.

He kept his hands behind his back while looking at the object inside the octagonal chamber. Gala recognized it as one of two Pegasus spherical drones that the Legion had secretly captured a month ago, and of the two, the only one that was intact. It was about six feet in diameter, with an exhaust nozzle at its rear and a lens at its front. The drone rested on three independent stands, and it had a series of wires that hung from the chamber's iron top and connected to its chrome surface like electrodes.

"Look at its lens," Lanzard told Gala. "See it blinking?"

Gala nodded.

"It activated a few hours ago."

"By itself?" Gala asked.

"Yeah. We think it's either trying to reboot itself or to send out a signal."

"And you're not allowing it."

"That's right, which is why the lab engineers have all those cables connected to it. They're sending a constant charge to interrupt whatever it is the drone is trying to do. Anyway," Lanzard turned to face Gala and folded his arms. "Did you get to interrogate Colani?"

Gala did her best to hide her frustration. "I reached Colani but didn't have enough time to get information out of him."

"What happened?"

"A couple of his robot guards showed up. I barely managed to escape, sir."

Lanzard nodded but looked as if lost in thought. Meanwhile, Gala stared at the colonel, struggling to read from his expression if he was upset or disappointed.

"Well, it was worth a try," Lanzard then said. "It seems now we have no choice but to proceed with our original plan."

He turned to leave, and Gala followed him.

"Sir, with all due respect, you can't possibly be referring to the plan that involves the … the …"

"The boy? Yes, I am," Lanzard said matter-of-factly, still walking. "I haven't stopped considering it, if that's what you're wondering. Especially since we need to be more subtle now."

Gala couldn't help but hiss in disbelief. "Sir, we don't have time for subtlety. We should act with urgency before anything happens. And to rely on a mere boy—"

"That boy, Agent, might be the only chance we have left to get information—*the* information we need from Colani."

This time Lanzard stopped and turned to face Gala, forcing her to do the same.

"The failure of today's mission most likely warned Colani and his people that someone is on to them," he said. "We can only hope Colani at least won't suspect a thirteen-year-old boy."

"How can you be sure the boy you refer to will help us?"

"Because he has no choice," Lanzard said, a hint of slight satisfaction visible at the corner of his mouth.

Gala tilted her head and pursed her lips. She had no idea what the colonel meant. Aside from that, there was something else she was dying to ask.

"Sir, who is this boy?"

Lanzard didn't hesitate to reply. "His name is Keithan Quintero."

CHAPTER 2

B ouncing knees, accelerated heartbeat, chest expanding and contracting in deep breaths. These were natural responses of Keithan's eagerness to feel the adrenaline rush during the exercise he would soon be doing in the air. He had been waiting for this all day. It was exactly what he needed to distract himself for a while from the troubling secrets that had been revealed to him yesterday. Keithan knew he would need to deal with that matter, especially since he would need to reveal everything to his best friends too. But Keithan also needed a break from the stress it had been causing him, which was why he did his best to enjoy every second at the moment.

Keithan wasn't piloting this time, though. Neither were any of his pilot classmates. Like them, he waited quietly in one of the rows of aluminum and leather seats, which, instead of being fastened to the floor, were attached individually to the ceiling by mechanical arms. The small diamond-shaped transport aircraft that carried the six pilot students continued ascending over twenty thousand feet. It shook slightly every once in a while from the turbulence outside, but it didn't bother Keithan. This was normal, and as a level-five pilot student of the Air Racing Program, he was well trained to remain in full control and alert under much worse circumstances. Next to him, however, his friend Genevieve Donnelly seemed to look otherwise.

"Boy, I hate these exercises." Genevieve exhaled audibly while she checked her chest straps and harness for what was probably the tenth time.

Keithan turned. Aside from noticing displeasure in his friend's words, he also sensed slight fear in them.

"Why are you worried? It's not like we haven't done this before," he told Genevieve with a smirk.

"I know, it's just … it's not the same feeling as when we're piloting."

"Well, it shouldn't be. Today is skydiving."

Genevieve, whose smooth dark skin now revealed tiny beads of sweat, took a deep breath and let it out slowly, doing her best to calm down. She was so nervous she even rechecked the band holding her round afro puff at the back of her head, as if that was as important as her skydiving gear.

Keithan couldn't help chortling. He ran a hand through his jet-black hair, which still had the orange stripe he had painted on it a few days ago, and resumed focusing on what they would be doing soon.

The skydiving exercise was a requirement for every pilot student at Ramey Academy of Flight and Aeroengineering. It provided them with the real experience of simulating an emergency bailout from an aircraft and landing safely on the ground. Still, that didn't stop Keithan and some of the other students from enjoying it as the extreme and exhilarating sport it was. Right in front of him and Genevieve sat the Viviani twins, Owen and Lance. They kept nodding their heads in anticipation. Seated behind Genevieve, with an expression of full alertness, Aimi Murakami kept tapping on her armrests with her fingers. The only one Keithan couldn't see was Gabriel Ortiz, who was seated right behind him. Yet Keithan was sure Gabriel was as nervous as Genevieve since the boy had also expressed in previous exercises his slight fear of being dropped at twenty-five thousand feet.

The diamond-shaped aircraft had no windows for them to look outside, which by now made Keithan feel like being inside a can of sardines with his classmates. He continued waiting quietly. He had just begun to wonder how much longer he would have to wait when the pilot's voice came from the small speakers on the sides of each of the students' headrests.

"Twenty-four thousand feet, people," the man reported.

The students raised their gazes to the front, Keithan craning his neck to see over Owen's head.

Next to the pilot's seat, Professor Alexandria Dantés stood up and turned to face her students. She was dressed in her customary gray flight suit, which distinguished her from the students' blue-and-gray ones, and she had her light-brown hair tied up at the back of her head.

"All right, everyone," Dantés said in her pronounced British accent as she stepped forward. "We're approaching the drop altitude. Helmets on."

The students, who had been holding their racing helmets on their laps, did as they were told. There was no need for a briefing since Dantés had already given it to them right before takeoff.

Keithan pulled his silver-and-metallic-orange helmet over his head, instantly muffling all sound around him. He kept his visor raised and turned on the helmet's integrated communicator. Soon after that, he locked the chin pad into place and raised his gaze again toward the professor.

Not once did Dantés look at him, and Keithan knew very well why. She had been avoiding making eye contact with him ever since he had found out about her deep secret. It had happened by accident a few days ago. Dantés had turned out to be much more than a professor and a flight instructor—she was an agent of a top-secret group of fighter pilots known as the Sky Phantom Legion.

Finding out about it, however, had only been the beginning of Keithan's problems. For that reason, he had done his best to stay out of Dantés's way even though it was only a matter of time before the professor would approach him to take care of the matter.

Professor Dantés was now holding on to a lever on the left wall while she checked a small screen next to it that showed their current altitude. A few seconds later, she addressed the students again, but this time through a tiny microphone attached to her right ear.

"Drop altitude reached," Keithan heard her through his helmet's

integrated communicator. *"Everyone, activate your altimeters and confirm communication."*

"Racer One: Viviani, standing by," Owen said.

"Racer Two, Viviani, standing by," his brother, Lance, followed.

Genevieve was next. *"Racer Three: Donnelly, standing by."*

Keithan slid down his tinted visor and locked it. His head-up display appeared instantly on it, showing him the digital altimeter in neon green. It marked 25,000 feet.

"Racer Four: Quintero, standing by," Keithan reported to the professor.

Once the last of the students had confirmed, Dantés pressed a button next to the lever she was still holding. There was a buzz, and the mechanical arm behind each student's seat retracted.

Keithan felt an abrupt pull as his seat rose backward and then swung him forward, leaving him facedown. He clutched his solid-frame restraint with both hands and crossed his legs, holding the rest of his strength in his neck to keep his head from hanging.

"This is it," he thought out loud while releasing a puff of air.

He and Genevieve exchanged glances, though they could only see their reflections on each other's visor. Keithan could still tell how nervous his friend was due to the tight grip she kept on her armrests. He nodded to reassure her that everything would be all right.

A long crevice appeared below them. It expanded as the metal floor opened at the middle, doors extending downward. It revealed an endless fog of altocumulus clouds moving slowly below the aircraft. Only the strong battering of the wind outside could be heard now, enough for everybody to enjoy the suspense of the moment before Dantés spoke one last time.

"See you at the drop zone."

And with that, she pulled down the lever.

There was a click, and Owen and Lance dropped from their seats and out of the aircraft. A second click, and Keithan's and Genevieve's frame restraints opened upward and dropped them as well. The next instant, Aimi and Gabriel were dropped too.

The six students dropped like loose packages straight into the first level of clouds, only to reappear below them in seconds. Whether or not Genevieve and Gabriel were panicking, Keithan didn't know, but now wasn't the time to worry about them. It was time to enjoy the exercise, to feel the complete freedom of the free fall.

With his knees bent and his arms crossed against his chest, Keithan screamed at the top of his lungs while he front-flipped over and over again, gradually gaining speed. Seconds later, he stretched his arms wide to control the fall and remain facedown. There just wasn't a better feeling than this. It was total freedom to feel the wind against him while experiencing the rush and exhilaration of falling toward the earth without any restraints.

Even better was entering another level of clouds. Right away, Keithan felt their moistness, like being sprayed with cold water all over his body. He checked his digital altimeter as soon as he got out of the clouds—it was just about to reach the 5,000-feet limit, which meant his parachute would come out automatically.

Four ... three ... two ... one ... he counted in his head.

The altimeter reached 5,000 feet, but Keithan kept descending fast. The chute hadn't opened.

Keithan quickly searched for his classmates all around him in the sky. They were still free falling too. He couldn't see their faces since they were hidden behind tinted visors, but they were also moving their heads from side to side, as if wondering why nobody's chute had opened yet. Had Dantés forgotten to synchronize them with their assigned altitude limit? Or had she done it on purpose?

There was no reason to panic yet. Everybody knew what they had to do. The students reached to their sides and pulled their cords. Their parachutes deployed, slithering out of their backpacks like rapid snakes before they opened, forming giant red mushroom-shaped blossoms as they rushed down against the air.

Only two parachutes hadn't opened yet: Keithan's, and about twenty feet away, Owen's. Keithan didn't know about the twin, but he hadn't deployed his chute on purpose. He'd dared to make the exercise more challenging and intended to keep free falling to 1,500 feet.

Then he realized Owen's intention: the boy wanted to be the last one to deploy, and he was challenging Keithan.

Keithan checked his altimeter again—3,027 feet. The temptation was too much. He accepted the challenge and held his right hand near his waist, close to his pull cord.

Having just reached their maximum acceleration—or terminal velocity, as they also called it—Keithan and Owen remained falling, stomachs down but facing each other. They held their right hands near their cords like two gunslingers ready to duel, waiting for the other to draw first.

Keithan narrowed his eyes. He looked back and forth from Owen to his altimeter. He didn't even dare to blink. At the same time, he fought against the strong wind rushing against him to remain in a stable position.

Two thousand feet.

They seemed to have reached that altitude in less than ten seconds, and in even less, Keithan and Owen would reach their 1,500-feet limit.

"Pull. *Pull!*" he murmured impatiently at Owen, but his opponent was still as stiff and determined as Keithan was.

Fifteen hundred feet.

It would be suicide if they didn't deploy now. The earth below was rushing up fast, a wide composition of green, brown, and white grid patches mixed with the curvy and wiggly lines of numerous intersecting roads.

It was now or never.

Keithan had no choice. He gave in and accepted defeat, quickly grabbing his cord—but right before he could pull it, his parachute shot out on its own.

"What the blazes?!"

He saw the same thing happen to Owen's.

Keithan felt the strong pull, which forced his legs to swing forward as his body straightened up, abruptly reducing speed. His chute blossomed like a giant umbrella, and it only took a few seconds before he realized who had deployed it for him.

"*I thought I was clear in the briefing. This was* not *to be a competition,*" said the angry voice of Professor Dantés.

CHAPTER 3

Far on the ground, inside Ramey Academy, several students—pilots and aeroengineers—gathered in front of the concave wall of glass windows that faced the airfield. They were watching the six pilot students from the level-five Air Racing Program descend. One of the spectators, seated in his custom powered wheelchair and wearing the aeroengineer's orange-and-gray uniform, was thirteen-year-old Fernando Aramis. Fernando held his digital binoculars pressed to his eyes. He quickly recognized Keithan among the skydivers by his metallic-orange helmet, which matched the colors of their *d'Artagnan*: the racing aircraft the two of them had built together.

Even through the lenses of the digital binoculars, Keithan looked like a tiny action figure dangling from his parachute. It would take a few more minutes before he touched the ground. Then he and his classmates would surely head back to the academy, which would finally give Fernando the chance to confront his best friend.

Keithan might have been evading Fernando since yesterday afternoon for some reason. He might have even been evading talking to him in the classes they took together, which was so unlike Keithan. But whatever the reason was, Fernando had had enough. He would get some answers today, no matter what.

——(-o-)——

The last several hundred feet in the air were all about enjoying the coastal scenery below while carefully controlling the parachute toward the drop zone. Already Keithan could make out most of the details of Ramey Airport, to the point where he could have counted each person and aircraft out at the airfield, only there were so many today he wasn't going to have time before he touched the ground.

There was much activity going on down there related to the upcoming Pegasus Air Race, especially at the far east side, where the giant airship of Pegasus Company hovered.–All over the airfield, Keithan could make out crews of people and robots putting up glossy posters of the winged stallion logo of Pegasus. A few large banners that included the names and faces of each of the sixteen air racers were being put up too. A line of raised teardrop flags was already set at either side of the main runway, each with the white, black, and gold colors distinctive of Pegasus. And to the south of the runway, Keithan spotted a series of grandstands that were being built in addition to the ones that had already been raised for the qualifier tournament that had taken place last weekend.

Nevertheless, aside from all the activity going on down there, it was the metallic spherical drones overflying the airfield what kept Keithan wary while he descended. He found it hard to see them now as the camera drones that would be broadcasting the race, and all because of what he had learned about them no more than twenty-four hours ago. The spherical drones from Pegasus were more than what they appeared to be.

Now close to the drop zone, which was a mere white circle painted on the grass next to the west end of the main runway, Keithan bent his knees and braced himself. It was a successful landing, almost in perfect synchronization with Owen, who landed a few feet away from him. Spectators at a distance applauded when they saw the two boys touch ground, which was customary every time pilot students from Ramey Academy executed the exercise.

Keithan proceeded to take his helmet off while his parachute finished deflating behind him. He shrugged at Owen, letting him know there was no point in trying to figure out who could have won.

Owen, the mirror image of his twin brother, with pale pink skin, short black curly hair, and a jock-type body, gave Keithan a deep stare with puckered lips in response. It could only be interpreted as a to-be-continued look, and it was enough to show Keithan how much he despised him. Not that it mattered much to Keithan, who actually found it amusing, especially since Owen and his brother, Lance, used to try to challenge Keithan in the air whenever they had the chance, but so far they hadn't accomplished beating him at anything.

High above them, their classmates descended. Keithan and Owen pressed a button on their chests straps, making their chutes repack automatically and clear the area.

Harley Swift, Professor Dantés's assistant, approached them from behind. As usual, the young redheaded man with big aviator shades was mounted on one of the academy's circular hover platforms, which he controlled from a console in front of him. A pair of digital binoculars dangled from his neck.

"So, Mr. Viviani and Mr. Quintero, that was quite a performance up there," Swift told them as he stopped his platform in front of the two boys. His comment sounded more sarcastic than sincere.

"How did I do?" Keithan and Owen exchanged glares after asking simultaneously.

"How did you *do?*" Swift repeated. "Well, considering your lack of judgment *and* recklessness during the exercise, I'd say not too well. Don't be surprised if Professor Dantés wants to talk with you two when she arrives, so don't go too far. Ah, here she comes."

Swift nodded toward the runway before he resumed to looking up with his digital binoculars at the students who were about to land on the drop zone.

Keithan and Owen watched Dantés's diamond-shaped craft about a mile away. It was already moving down the runway, but it hadn't yet touched the ground. Instead, it kept hovering low with its antigravity plates, which provided a much smoother landing. The craft had just passed the airport's terminal and the big hangars, gradually reducing speed, when Keithan noticed what was about to happen.

A flock of five of the Pegasus spherical drones were hovering low on the right side of the main runway, and they were about to cross in front of the still-moving craft.

"Um, Mr. Swift—" Keithan started to say, but it was too late.

The five drones crossed right in front of the diamond-shaped craft's path, but the last one didn't make it in time and—CLANK!—hit the rear of the craft.

Both Keithan and Owen jumped.

"Whoa!" Keithan cried.

Shouts of horror in the distance followed as people at different parts of the airfield witnessed the drone fly out of control before it smashed against the pavement. The thing was in pieces almost instantly. Meanwhile, the aircraft continued moving though sideways now, its pilot struggling to keep it from hovering off the runway.

"What happened?" exclaimed Swift from his hover platform at the sound of the commotion. He didn't need a reply. He saw it as soon as he turned. "Oh, my—!"

He kept looking back and forth from the accident to the students he needed to watch as they landed. His headset rang, forcing him to press a button on its side.

"Professor! Are you all right?" he spoke into the microphone attached to his headset, his voice slightly shaky now.

Keithan turned to him.

"What happe—?" Swift was cut off, forced to listen. "Yes, of course," he then said. "I will. Right away, Professor."

He ended the call and turned to watch Genevieve and Gabriel, who were the last students about to land. Once the two touched the ground, Swift gestured for the students to gather around his hover platform.

"Listen up," he said aloud. "*Quintero*, pay attention!"

Keithan jumped. He was still gazing at the commotion on the runway.

"As you've witnessed, there's been an emergency with Professor Dantés's craft," Swift explained quickly. "She needs to deal with the matter, but she gave me direct instructions to escort you back to the academy immediately. No questions asked. So, Gabriel, Genevieve, repack your parachutes and let's go."

Professor Alexandria Dantés was a highly experienced pilot, but that didn't stop her from feeling as if her heart had climbed up her throat while her companion, veteran fighter pilot Mark Garricks, struggled to keep the aircraft from hovering off the runway. Fortunately, after a few intense seconds, the danger was over. The diamond-shaped craft came to a stop. Still, Dantés didn't lose her tight grip on her seat. She waited until she felt the slight thud of the landing gear when it touched the ground once the antigravity mechanism was deactivated. The sound was the only assurance that it was safe to remove her seat restraints. And so, once Dantés heard it, she got up and marched down the craft's side ramp.

Mark followed her, though at a slow pace. He couldn't wait to see what the damage had been, either. Unlike Dantés, however, it was hard to see how upset he was about it since most of his face remained hidden under his bushy brown mustache and the pair of wide shades that covered his eyes.

Both he and Dantés headed straight to the rear of the craft.

"Great," Dantés hissed, standing with her hands on her hips while staring at the craft's vertical stabilizer—or what was left of it.

Just as she had expected, the Pegasus drone had smashed against it, taking off its top half, along with its rudder, hinges and all. Mark had done nearly the impossible to keep the craft from hovering out of control without a rudder.

"Professor, this wasn't my fault," he remarked, scratching his head. "I assume Pegasus will cover this, right?"

Dantés looked over her shoulder at the big chunks of metal parts that had been the drone, which lay scattered about a hundred feet away. There were people already rushing in its direction.

A siren from the north alerted Dantés of a large yellow vehicle with black and white stripes that was coming in her direction. A small emergency crew in neon-yellow bodysuits held on to its sides like firefighters.

"Are you folks okay?" shouted one of the men when the vehicle stopped and he and his companions jumped off.

"Yeah," Mark answered, grimacing.

"Are there others inside the craft?" asked the same technician, who was now at the front of the group.

"No. Professor Dantés and I were the only ones on board."

The small crew gathered around the damaged area of the craft, ready to come up with suggestions for moving it out of the runway. Dantés, however, was already one step ahead.

She turned to Mark. "Contact the academy. Tell them to bring a tow robot to pick up the craft and return it to the hangar bay. I'll meet you there for a full report."

Mark seemed to hesitate. "Wait, where are *you* going?"

Dantés was already heading to the area where the drone had crashed. "I'm going to have a serious talk with those guys from Pegasus."

She did her best to remain composed despite the intense anger boiling inside her. She kept her eyes narrowed and her lips tightly pursed while she marched straight toward the group of people who were now gathered around the wrecked drone. They were all Pegasus representatives, as evidenced by their black side caps and matching shirts with the gold Pegasus imprint.

"Keep a perimeter, people. Don't let anybody who's not from Pegasus get near," one of the men was saying to the rest. "I'll need at least four of you to hurry up and pick up the rest of the parts scattered on the runway."

Two of the figures noticed Dantés approaching. They quickly tried to block her path, raising their hands in front of them, but it didn't work. They were no match for the professor's cold, intimidating attitude.

"Who's in charge here?" Dantés asked. She ignored the two figures, passing between them as if they weren't even there.

The rest of the group, which summed up to ten, turned to her, perplexed.

"I-I am," stammered the man who had been giving out orders. He seemed to question his own authority at the sudden sight of the woman who had barged into the area.

Dantés, on the other hand, wasn't even the least bit intimidated by the tall alpha male. She didn't hesitate to stop right in front of him and fold her arms.

"Would you mind explaining to me *why* a flock of your camera drones crossed the main runway at low altitude during the authorized landing of an aircraft?"

"We're still trying to figure it out, Miss ..."

"*Professor* Dantés."

"Professor Dantés," the man went on. "The Pegasus auto drones were just doing their usual overfly. It's part of their programmed surveillance routine around the airfield."

"Don't you think they should have been able to detect the proximity of any flying craft?" Dantés insisted. "No craft or object should be flying low over the runway during an authorized landing or takeoff. You people are lucky there weren't students in my aircraft when it happened."

"Students?" one of the men repeated, a look of surprise instantly on his face as well as on his companions'.

"That's a transport aircraft from Ramey Acade—" Dantés didn't get to complete the sentence, as one of the other men stepped in to hand a small data pad to the man in charge.

The tall, bulky man took the pad and quickly straightened up when he saw the figure on the pad's screen.

"Mr. Cola— I mean, *Captain* Colani," he said, his tone now sounding nervous.

Dantés noticed the rest of the group froze as well while they stared at the man with the data pad. He was now speaking to none other than the CEO of Pegasus Company.

The captain's voice was loud enough for everyone to hear. *"What's the situation, Mr. DeVille?"*

"Um, one of our drones accidentally hit a landing craft, sir," DeVille replied. "So far, everything is under control, but we're still working on—"

"Was anyone hurt?" Colani cut him short.

"No, sir. The drone got most of the damage. I'm actually in front of the woman who was on board the aircraft that was hit."

The man flipped the data pad, and Dantés found herself now facing the figure on the screen. Right away she recognized the distinguished features of the Pegasus CEO.

"My most sincere apologies, Miss," Colani addressed Dantés in a calm tone. *"I honestly didn't expect something like this to happen. My drones should have been able to detect any approaching craft on the runway. And they shouldn't have been flying so low. Clearly it was a minor miscalculation."*

Dantés raised an eyebrow and tilted her head. "Miscalculation?" she repeated skeptically. "Minor?"

"Yes. They are auto drones, after all," Colani went on.

Dantés stepped forward, clearing her throat. "Pardon me, Captain, but what if one of those drones repeats a mistake like that during your race tomorrow? What if it gets in the way of another aircraft and puts a pilot in danger? Or worse yet, the spectators, who will be nearby as well?"

The crew around her raised their eyebrows. They didn't seem to believe the tone of voice Dantés was daring to use against the Pegasus CEO.

Colani, however, didn't seem affected by Dantés's tone. *"We're taking every precaution to prevent that from happening, Miss, considering that there was another dangerous incident in my airship about an hour ago. But rest assured, the Pegasus Air Race will be carried out with the best and maximum safety precautions. No one will be put in harm's way. I promise you."*

Dantés kept her eyes narrowed while she studied the man on the screen. She was trying to find something deceptive in his expression, something that could tell her that Colani wasn't being completely honest. But so far the man's expression hadn't given any hint of that.

Still, Dantés didn't trust him. She didn't *want* to trust him, and with good reason. Giovanni Colani had a secret plot behind his upcoming race—Dantés knew that much already. As a secret agent of the Sky Phantom Legion, she had done her homework on the man. And even though she didn't know what that plot consisted of yet, she and the rest of the Legion were almost certain it was not for something good.

"Once again, my most sincere apologies for what happened," said Colani, wanting to put an end to the matter. *"As for the damage to your aircraft, I take full responsibility. Pegasus will cover it. Please allow my people to help you with anything you may require for your craft. DeVille?"*

The man holding the data pad hesitated before he answered. "We will help, Captain." He raised his gaze back at Dantés and nodded with a smile, a smile that Dantés could tell wasn't genuine.

CHAPTER 4

I t was 4:15 p.m. when Keithan got to number one, L Street: his home. Usually after classes he would meet with Fernando and either go to Rocket's Diner for burgers and shakes or to Fernando's residential hangar inside Ramey Airport. Today he'd decided to do neither. Just like yesterday, he'd chosen to avoid his best friend, and the truth was he hated himself for doing so.

Keithan had so much to tell Fernando since yesterday afternoon. The problem was Keithan still couldn't find a way to break it all down to him.

He had arrived at his home about half an hour ago, and he hadn't yet bothered to change from his flight suit into casual clothes. He hadn't also bothered to turn on the holographic TV or the stereo system, either. The last thing Keithan wanted was any distractions. He wasn't even in the mood to see or hear any news. He had enough news in his head already, the kind that had kept him deeply distracted, but more than that, worried.

Keithan was now in his living room, seated on the red faux-leather sofa and leaning forward, facing the glass doors that led to the terrace. He was staring at a fancy invitation card he held in his hand.

A printed golden frame decorated the card all around, and at the top of the frame was the chrome winged stallion bust logo of Pegasus Company. Keithan read the invitation silently for the third time.

Dear Mr. Keithan Quintero:

Captain Giovanni Colani, CEO of Pegasus Company, cordially invites you

and your father to a formal dinner party on his private airship next Friday,

April 30, 2055, at 7 p.m.

More than an invitation, it seemed like an award, even a privilege. Keithan could already imagine the look on his friends' faces at the academy when he told them about it. They would most likely think he was pulling their legs. Who would believe he'd been personally invited to an exclusive dinner party by one of the most innovative and powerful men in the aviation industry, the only man whose house floated among the clouds and inside an airship?

Yet, as fascinating as it seemed, Keithan still wasn't sure if he should accept to go to the dinner party. He wanted to have a nice time along with the Pegasus CEO. As the man had suggested when he gave Keithan the invitation, to talk about Keithan's mom, particularly about her acclaimed career as a former air racing champion and her victories—not to spy on Colani, as the Sky Phantom Legion was forcing Keithan to do.

"It'll be the ideal opportunity to find out what Pegasus is up to," Lieutenant Colonel Lanzard had told him. But from his tone, it had been an order rather than a suggestion, one which Keithan felt obligated to obey.

Tomorrow, Keithan thought while rereading the date. *The night before the grand Pegasus Air Race.*

If only things were as simple as Keithan had thought nearly a month ago, when he and his friends found out their hometown airport would be the venue for the famous air race. Back then, Keithan had been determined to be in the race, all in the hopes of becoming the youngest air racing champion in history. Unfortunately, his dreams had been shattered the day of the qualifier tournament when he was told he couldn't participate because of his age. More specifically, because of the simple fact that he hadn't been represented by a licensed flight instructor.

Still, that wasn't what made things so different and complicated now for Keithan. Professor Dantés had meant for him to be taken out of the tournament because she and the Sky Phantom Legion had uncovered a possible threat behind the upcoming race. A threat that, according to Dantés and Lieutenant Colonel Lanzard, involved spherical drones that had been weaponized, not to mention a mysterious plot that not even the Legion knew the details of yet except for its name: the Daedalus Project.

At least one thing was certain in Keithan's mind despite all that: Whatever the Daedalus Project was, whatever threat it could involve, he needed to warn his best friends about it. Keithan was trying to figure out how exactly he would break it all down to them when the doorbell sounded and made him jump. He picked up the invitation, which had slipped from his hand and fallen on the floor, and hurried to the front door.

"Fernando," said Keithan, surprised.

The boy with spiky blond hair, who was seated in his custom motorized wheelchair, ignored Keithan's reaction. "We need to talk, Keithan, and you know it."

Keithan hesitated. He opened his mouth to reply, but Fernando went on.

"I waited for you after classes yesterday. I even made my mom wait a few more minutes in front of the hangar bay, assuming you might want to leave with us. Couldn't contact you, either, because I know you lost your wrist communicator last weekend. Then today you ignore me the whole day. What's going on? Are you in some kind of trouble or something?"

Keithan sighed, remembering when they had last spoken. It had been yesterday afternoon, back at the academy. The two had been heading to their last class of the day when one of the hall monitor robots had halted Keithan to escort him to the headmaster's office. As expected, Fernando had assumed Keithan had gotten into some kind of trouble. There didn't tend to be any other reason for Keithan to be summoned by Headmaster Viviani.

Keithan didn't know how to begin explaining everything that had happened since then. For the moment, he simply stepped aside and gestured for Fernando to come inside.

"What's going on?" Fernando asked again, moving his wheelchair forward.

Keithan rubbed his forehead. "Fernando, there's, um, something you need to know."

His friend leaned forward, becoming impatient.

Keithan decided to start with the good news. "I-I met Captain Giovanni Colani yesterday at Headmaster Viviani's office."

He gave a slight smile, as if this were the only news he had to tell him. At the same time, he showed Fernando the invitation.

Fernando's jaw dropped, though his confusion was still noticeable. "Are you *serious?*"

Keithan nodded. "He actually went to the academy to meet me because he found out that I, you know, the son of former champion Adalina Zambrana, had tried to participate in the Pegasus qualifier tournament. That was why the headmaster summoned me to his office yesterday."

"And Colani—Giovanni Colani—invited *you* to have dinner with him in his airship?" Fernando looked in disbelief from the invitation to Keithan and again at the invitation. "That's so cool, but … that doesn't explain why you've been avoiding me."

Keithan was still struggling to continue explaining. "I know. It's just that—"

"Don't get me wrong, this is impressive and all. I mean, not even my dad, who's been working on his Daedalus Project *for* Pegasus, has had the chance to meet the CEO."

Keithan flinched. "He hasn't?"

"No. Anyway, you still need to explain why—"

"Hold on," Keithan, said. "Your dad still hasn't met Colani?"

"At least not in person," Fernando clarified. "As far as I know, he's been dealing with Pegasus most of the time through Drostan Luzier and that old guy who is always accompanying him. You know, the one with the red-lensed glasses and the weird white mustache."

Keithan frowned. "Hmm. You wouldn't happen to have a clue yet what the project is, would you?" He took a shot at Fernando by asking this, though he was sure what the answer would be.

"Not yet," Fernando told him. He handed Keithan back the invitation. "Dad's still keeping the project well hidden inside his private workshop. Anyway, whatever it is, he should be finishing it if he's scheduled to reveal it this Saturday at the air race."

"Finishing it" didn't necessarily mean a good thing to Keithan. All the more reason to give in to the urge to tell Fernando what he needed to tell him. Still, he couldn't bring himself to do it. Then he got an idea.

"You know, we could try to find out what the Daedalus Project is without your dad knowing about it," he said with a mischievous expression.

"Huh?"

"Think about it," Keithan insisted. "We could sneak into his workshop when he's not around and—"

"Keithan, what are you talking about?" Fernando cut him off. "It'll be impossible. Even when Dad isn't there, his MA robot is guarding the workshop. Besides, why are you changing the subject?"

Keithan didn't answer right away. "I'm just … curious, I guess," he lied. "I mean, what is it with your dad and all the strict secrecy—even from his own family?"

"It's part of his contract with Pegasus, you know that," said Fernando, now beginning to get irritated. "He can't reveal it until Saturday. Now, if you're not gonna tell me what's going on with *you*, I might as well leave."

Fernando moved his wheelchair and opened the door, but Keithan halted him.

"Fernando, wait! There's … there's something else—something very important you need to know."

Fernando turned with a perplexed and slightly irritated look. "So *tell* me already!"

This was it, Keithan knew. Once he told Fernando everything, there would be no turning back. His best friend would be sucked into all the trouble Keithan was already in.

Keithan took a deep breath. "It's about your dad's secret project with Pegasus, the Daedalus Project. The ... Sky Phantom Legion found out about it, and though they don't know your dad is involved in it, they, um ..."

"Wait a second," said Fernando, fear now noticeable on his face. "The Sky Phantom Legion?"

Keithan held his breath before he answered. "They think the project is part of a possible threat behind the Pegasus Air Race."

CHAPTER 5

I
f it was hard enough for Keithan to explain everything, it was even harder for Fernando to believe it. Keithan did his best to give him every detail of what had happened to him yesterday afternoon. It took a while, especially since Fernando required a few minutes for everything to sink in even after Keithan was done explaining.

"So let me get this straight," said Fernando, still looking as bewildered as he was at the beginning, "not only were you invited to a dinner party by the Pegasus CEO, who went to the academy to meet you, but you were then interrogated about your meeting with him by Professor Dantés and the lieutenant colonel of the Sky Phantoms? Then the two took you to their secret base because they have evidence my dad's project could be part of a threat behind this Saturday's race?"

"I didn't tell them your dad was working on the project—I couldn't," Keithan clarified. "Still, they found out about the project somehow, and Colonel Lanzard is convinced it's being built for some threatening plot."

Keithan knew it was a lot to take in, but Fernando had a right to know since it involved his father.

Fernando couldn't help shaking his head. "Nuh-uh. That can't be true," he insisted. "They gotta be mistaken. Dad would *never* build any of his inventions for evil purposes. He's not a criminal—worse still, a *terrorist.*"

"I know he isn't," Keithan said right away. "That's why I didn't tell

Dantés and Lanzard about your dad's involvement; I wasn't gonna get him into trouble. Still, they seem to have enough evidence to believe Pegasus is plotting a threat of some kind with the Daedalus Project. Which is why I think we should try to find out what your dad is working on—before the Sky Phantoms find out."

They kept on talking about all this on their way back to Ramey Airport, though this time they weren't headed to the academy, but to Fernando's house. Fernando and his family lived in one of the few residential hangars located at the northeast of the airport, far from the terminal building, as well as from the control tower and the main hangars. Keithan and Fernando passed the terminal and were now moving behind three twin-fuselage airliners that were parked in front of several large hangars. All the while, they paid little attention to what was happening all over the airfield regarding the preparations for the race.

Finally, they reached the residential hangars. Fernando's was one of the last ones, number H11. Curiously, while the others were similar in design, with their low arched roofs, Fernando's residential hangar was more elliptical. More than that, it resembled a giant weathered armadillo carapace. It was particularly segmented into three main divisions, its middle section covered from side to side with a grid of glass roof panels.

Keithan and Fernando were approaching the hangar but stopped about forty feet away from it when they noticed its main front door closed. In front of it was parked the scarlet minivan with transparent door surfaces that belonged to Fernando's mom, along with Keithan and Fernando's orange-and-silver racing aircraft, the *d'Artagnan*, which was attached to it. Yet what caught Keithan's and Fernando's attention most was that right next to the minivan and the *d'Artagnan* was another vehicle: a fancy roadster sports car with covered spherical tires and a sleek body, which Keithan and Fernando recognized right away.

"Drostan Luzier's car," Fernando said. "Looks like we're not gonna be allowed to enter the hangar for the time being."

They had no choice but to go to Fernando's dad's office instead, which was located at a small igloo-shaped annex at the left side of the hangar. As they headed in that direction, however, the large main door of the building began to rise with a grinding sound. Halfway up, Fernando's dad walked out with two figures: one, the pale-faced arrogant-looking Drostan Luzier, who was dressed in a fancy white suit; and the other, the old guy with red-lensed glasses and shiny white handlebar mustache who seemed to accompany Drostan everywhere.

Keithan could barely stand looking at Drostan Luzier, even from a distance. Up until a few weeks ago, he had admired the man as the racing champion and celebrity that he was. Drostan was the champion of the last two Pegasus Air Races and would be defending his title again this year. But all the admiration Keithan and Fernando had had for him had dissolved the moment the two of them had gotten the opportunity to meet him a few days ago, only to see just how full of himself the man was.

Drostan Luzier, whose long golden hair and flawlessly pale skin seemed to shine like porcelain in the afternoon sunlight, emanated a strong aura of overconfidence, as if he already knew he was going to win the Pegasus Air Race this year. The guy had just put on a pair of shades and was now addressing Fernando's dad. Meanwhile, Fernando's dad, a man with long raggedy gray hair, which he had tied back in a ponytail, wore his usual clothes stained with black grease. He nodded to Drostan nervously with his head slightly bowed.

It wasn't until Drostan and his older companion got into their car that Keithan and Fernando approached Mr. Aramis.

"Hey, guys," said Mr. Aramis, beaming. "Sorry I kept the hangar closed till now. I was doing the last private demonstration of the Daedalus Project to Luzier and his senior advising aeroengineer."

"How'd it go?" Keithan asked.

"Great. It's practically complete. All it needs is a few adjustments they recommended. It won't be a problem with the help of Emmeiseven."

"So can we see it now?" Fernando asked, figuring it was worth a shot.

"Sorry. Not yet, but soon," his dad assured him.

His smile told Keithan the man was enjoying keeping the project a secret. Still, Keithan couldn't see the slightest hint of malevolence in the man's expression, which he was glad about. He was still a bit concerned, though.

Mr. Aramis climbed into the scarlet minivan with the smart keys in hand. Keithan and Fernando proceeded to enter the hangar after the vehicle drove past and headed toward the right wall. There, Mr. Aramis detached the *d'Artagnan* from the minivan before he parked the latter farther away at the center of the hangar.

"There you go, guys," Mr. Aramis said as he stepped out of the vehicle.

Keithan followed him with his gaze. He had expected Mr. Aramis to go back into his private workshop at the back of the hangar, but instead, the man headed to his office at the side wall on the far left. As soon as the office door slid shut, Keithan made his move.

"Keithan, what are you doing?" Fernando said.

"Shhh!" Keithan replied. He was now cautiously hurrying toward Mr. Aramis's workshop.

"Keith— Keithan! You can't go in there!" Fernando cried in a whisper.

"I'm just gonna peek. I won't touch anything," Keithan said while still moving. He stopped right in front of the yellow PVC strip curtain that hung at the entrance of the private workshop. He gave one last glance at the office door before daring to push aside two of the PVC strips.

His heart accelerated with excitement and anticipation as he poked his head inside the workshop. Only the constant humming of an extractor could be heard. There had been very few occasions in which Keithan had been in there, though it had been months since the last time. Curiously, the place didn't look that different from how Keithan remembered. There were different kinds of machinery: from tube and metal panel rollers to a laser cutting machine and a big 3-D printer. Keithan also noticed all the power tools hanging on the wall as well as piles of spare parts and scrap metal that made the floor feel cramped.

The most recent addition in there was Emmeiseven, the six-foot-tall humanoid mechanical assistant robot that had been given to Mr. Aramis, compliments of Pegasus to help him speed things up on the Daedalus Project. Emmeiseven's smooth white coverings were now stained with black grease and soot. The robot stood in front of a worktable located at the center of the workshop, its back toward Keithan. Its gauntlet-like arms, which included a variety of tools, moved busily over what looked like a small yet very weird-looking engine.

Keithan couldn't make out what it was since the robot was blocking it from view. He swallowed hard and took his first step into the workshop.

He wondered if that could be it. Was that the Daedalus Project?

Keithan's heart beat faster. He felt like a spy in a movie who'd just managed to sneak into the lab of an evil inventor in an attempt to discover a secret weapon, and the robot was the inventor's henchman guarding it.

Keithan dared to take another step closer toward Emmeiseven. There was no way he could be heard over the humming of the extractor and the crackling of the robot's welder attached to its right arm. He was only six feet away and about to get a good look at the project when the robot's faceless head—a computerized helmet with a curved glass screen showing the words "Intruder Detected"—turned in his direction.

It happened so fast that Keithan froze like a mouse that had just been spotted trying to steal a piece of cheese. But even if Keithan had tried to run away, he wouldn't have had the chance, for in the next instant, the rest of Emmeiseven's body turned, and with a single long step, the robot stretched out one if its gauntleted arms and got a hold of Keithan.

"Arrgh! Let—go—of—me!" he cried out in pain. He tried to pull open the mechanical claw now enclosed around his left arm. "Let—*Help!*"

Emmeiseven was now dragging Keithan out of the workshop. All the while, Keithan shouted and struggled to set himself free. A shocked

Fernando started shouting for help too when he saw both of them appear through the strip curtain. He grabbed a piece of tube that lay next to him and moved his wheelchair as fast as he could to attack the MA robot.

It was then that Mr. Aramis appeared. "Hey! What's going on?"

Right behind him was Fernando's sister, Marianna, whose short brown hair with pink highlights bounced as she ran. She and her father hurried in the same direction Fernando was headed. Just then, Emmeiseven pinned Keithan against the top of a saucer-shaped concept aircraft, one of Mr. Aramis's inventions.

"That thing's attacking Keithan!" Fernando yelled, joining his dad and his sister halfway.

"Help! *Ungh!*" Keithan managed to shout just as the towering robot lifted one of its massive clawed feet and pressed it against Keithan's chest.

"Let go of him! That's an order, Emmeiseven!" Mr. Aramis yelled. He halted right behind the robot, his arms stretched to the sides to prevent Fernando and Marianna from getting closer. But still, Emmeiseven didn't obey.

"*Emmeiseven!*" Mr. Aramis shouted. "I order you to release him!"

This time, Emmeiseven obeyed. The words "Intruder Detected" faded from its head screen. At the same time, the robot loosened its grip.

Keithan slid down from the aluminum fuselage of the saucer-shaped concept craft and slumped to the ground hard. He grabbed his swollen forearm, feeling the blood slowly pumping back into his hand. His chest still hurt too, and Keithan raised his shirt to check for any scratches or bruises.

"Emmeiseven!" Mr. Aramis stepped forward, his tone and face full of authority and disbelief, unlike Keithan had ever seen him before. "You are *never* to threaten or harm anyone!"

The robot straightened up, lowering its arms and facing Mr. Aramis, though it didn't respond.

"Do you understand? Emmeiseven?" Mr. Aramis insisted. His

arms were still stretched to his sides in front of Fernando and Marianna. "Acknowledge order."

This time the robot responded in its metallic voice, "Order acknowledged." The same words appeared displayed in neon green on the curved screen where its face should be.

"Good," said Mr. Aramis with a sigh. "Now, return to the workshop and remain there. Acknowledge order."

"Order acknowledged," the robot replied, and with that the robot turned and marched away into Mr. Aramis's workshop.

Keithan, still horror-struck and breathing heavily, didn't dare take his honey eyes off from Emmeiseven until it disappeared behind the yellow strip curtain. All the while, he kept rubbing his left forearm, thinking that if the robot had gripped him a little harder, it would have easily crushed it.

Still seated on the floor, he turned his gaze at Mr. Aramis, who now stood looking down at him, perplexed, with his hands on his hips.

"Would you care to explain to me why this happened?" Mr. Aramis asked.

Keithan gulped. He glanced at Fernando and Marianna before looking back at Mr. Aramis. "I-I walked into your workshop, sir," he replied, fully embarrassed. "I know I shouldn't have, and I-I'm sorry. It's just … I wanted to get a glimpse of your project."

Mr. Aramis huffed in disbelief. "You know very well no one's allowed to go in there without my authorization. You all know that."

"I do, sir. I'm sorry." Keithan was unable to look at him now.

"Not only is it dangerous with all the machines I have in there, but I also assigned Emmeiseven to keep surveillance while I'm not around," Mr. Aramis added.

"Still, that was no reason for Emmeiseven to attack Keithan," Fernando interjected, moving his wheelchair forward. "Robots aren't supposed to harm humans."

"It could've killed Keithan, Dad," Marianna said, stepping in. She offered Keithan a hand and helped him get up.

"I know," her dad said with a frown. "That's what really concerns me. I never would've imagined Emmeiseven reacting so aggressively. Keithan, you sure you're all right?"

"Um … yeah. I'm just still a little shaken."

Sure that the danger was over, Mr. Aramis headed to his workshop to deal with the robot. Meanwhile, Marianna stared at Keithan as if he were a little kid who had just failed to pull off a prank and got caught.

"You know, sometimes I wonder if you just like getting into trouble," she told him. "You *sure* you're all right?"

Keithan hissed with a slight smile and nodded. He wasn't sure why, but seeing Marianna brought a warm feeling to his chest that seemed to calm him down. Seeing her even seemed to soothe the pain on his forearm a little.

"And what about you?" he asked her, shifting the focus away from his well-being. "How you've been since …? You know."

Marianna gave him a warm smile. "I'm good. Thanks for asking."

Keithan felt glad to hear that, considering the last time the two of them had seen each other had been in a room at Ramey Hospital while each of them sat on a bed and with their heads filled with wireless electrodes. It had all been part of the Sky Phantoms' plan to hide all clues that could reveal that both Keithan and Marianna had found out about the Legion's existence. While thinking about that, however, neither Keithan nor Marianna realized the unusual moment of silence between them, which suddenly was interrupted when Fernando cleared his throat.

Keithan and Marianna stepped away from each other simultaneously.

"So," Marianna said, "couldn't you just wait until Saturday for Dad to show us the project?"

Instead of answering, Keithan turned to Fernando, who sighed with a shrug and said to him, "You might as well tell her everything."

CHAPTER 6

The loud whining of Alexandria Dantés's metallic-red-and-black turbo hoverbike was more than enough to alert the people out at the airfield that she was riding it at top speed, even before anyone could see her shooting past. Dantés kept a straight path all the way from Ramey Academy, satisfying her need for speed in order to release the tension she'd built up as a result of having dealt with the accident in the afternoon. She continued eastward at over eighty miles per hour but decelerated as soon as she passed the arched terminal building and came to a stop in front of a tall hangar with no identification or number.

There, a man in a loose black jumpsuit seemed to be waiting for her. He walked out of the hangar's main entrance when he saw Dantés.

"Engine off," Dantés said into her wrist communicator right after she dismounted. The hoverbike's engine turned off instantly, and the bike, with its stand already out, touched the ground.

"Agent," the man called to Dantés with a courteous nod.

Dantés, still wearing her professor uniform, noticed the man approaching, yet she continued marching forward even after the man reached her, forcing him to turn around and follow her.

"Did the meeting already start?" she asked. She moved at a quick pace into the hangar.

"Not yet," the man told her. "All the other agents who were called are already connected through a private line, though. They're waiting for you."

"Good. Where can I reach them?"

"In the conference room."

The man pointed to a door at the right and halted. Dantés thanked him and continued on her own.

As soon as Dantés went through the door, she turned left and continued down a corridor that led to the conference room at the end. The conference room was windowless, with nothing more than plain navy-blue walls and a round table at the center with a black glass top. Eight high-backed chairs made of black leather surrounded the table, but none of them were occupied.

Dantés closed the door behind her and spoke out loud. "Private communication access code 253Q-Alpha."

The white neon lights in the conference room dimmed, and five rectangular holographic pillars rose from the black tabletop up to Dantés's height. Together, they formed an arc. Each one showed a different Sky Phantom agent, among them Lieutenant Colonel Lanzard, who had ordered the meeting.

The colonel, who was being projected in the hologram in the middle, spoke first.

"Agent Venus, glad you could join us," he said.

"Sorry for the delay, Colonel," Dantés replied. She had already pulled out one of the chairs and sat.

"Thank you all for making contact at such short notice," Colonel Lanzard continued. "As a main order of business, I want to report to those of you who don't know already that there was a failure in today's attempt to infiltrate the Pegasus Company airship in order to get to the CEO and interrogate him about his secret plans behind his upcoming race. As a result, we must acknowledge that Pegasus is now aware that someone is on to them. Agent Gala," he then said, "have there been any reports about the incident on the news?"

"None yet, sir," answered Gala, who was being projected at Lanzard's left. "It seems that Pegasus and its CEO have decided to keep the incident to themselves."

"All the more reason to mistrust them," Dantés commented.

"Not necessarily," interjected Theron O'Malley, who was being projected at Dantés's right. He was a broad-shouldered African American man with the major rank lines insignia on his shoulders. "It's possible Pegasus didn't reveal what happened because they can't afford that type of negative news with the air race coming up."

Dantés shook her head, unconvinced. Already she could feel the tension coming back to her neck. It frustrated her that the Legion still wasn't doing what needed to be done when she was certain they had enough evidence against Pegasus.

"Colonel, Major, and fellow agents," she said, placing both hands on the table and leaning forward, "regardless of whether or not we are certain of Pegasus Company's true intentions behind the race, we should implement the necessary measures and have the upper hand while we still have time on our side."

"What exactly do you suggest we do, Agent Venus?" Colonel Lanzard asked, his hands laced below his chin.

Dantés looked at every single member with narrowed eyes. "I propose—I *insist*—we stop the Pegasus Air Race from being carried out this Saturday."

The deep silence that followed allowed Dantés to carefully see the different reactions from each of the other agents, especially the colonel's. The man's wrinkled eyes and frown clearly showed he didn't approve. Yet it took Dantés a moment to realize the true reason of his silence: he was waiting for her to express her arguments for carrying out such a radical suggestion.

"You would agree with me on this if you understand the seriousness of the matter, which I am sure you all do, not to mention the fact that we're running out of time." Dantés was determined to be as straightforward as she could. "Pegasus revealed through the media a few days ago that it will have over a hundred of its spherical camera drones hovering all over Ramey Airport and throughout the whole island of Puerto Rico the day of the race. And we have proof with one of the drones that we captured that some—if not all of them—are weaponized. Now *that* Pegasus hasn't revealed."

"I agree," said Agent Gala after another short moment of silence. "There's also the matter regarding Pegasus's plan to reveal its so-called Daedalus Project, and as with the spherical drones, it could represent a threat."

"They have a point, Colonel," said Agent Matías, a bald man with a blond circle beard who was being projected to Lanzard's right. "We shouldn't wait until the day of the race to take action."

"*Then* it could be too late," Dantés warned.

Opposition, however, came right away. Dantés had been expecting it from the colonel, but instead, it came from O'Malley.

"Haven't you considered that by trying to stop the race from happening on Saturday we risk leading Pegasus to accelerate its plans, whatever they may be?" he said.

"Nevertheless," Agent Gala interjected, "as Colonel Lanzard stated a few moments ago, Pegasus already knows somebody is on to them because of today's incident."

Lanzard, who had been gently rubbing his left temple with two fingers, cleared his throat. "The fact remains," he said, demanding everyone's full attention again, "we still don't have the proof we need to determine Pegasus Company's true intention behind the race despite what we've gathered about the Pegasus camera drones and the so-called Daedalus Project. That said, we don't have enough sustained proof to stop the event from happening."

"What about Agent Ravena and his crew? Has there been any progress on their operation?" Dantés asked. She didn't realize how fast she had reacted. She turned to the redheaded man with green eyes and hawk nose who was being projected on the hologram to her left. He was the only person in the meeting who, so far, hadn't said a word.

Ravena's narrow gaze showed that he had been paying careful attention to the discussion, yet he straightened up at the mention of his name. He seemed to be about to speak, but the colonel went spoke first.

"For those of you who don't know," said the colonel, "Captain

Ravena has been posing as one of the pro air racers who will be participating in the race, and he is the agent who found out about the mysterious Daedalus Project a few days ago. Up to this point, his disguise has allowed him to be part of several activities regarding the upcoming event, which has also allowed him and his assigned crew, who are also Sky Phantom agents, to keep a close watch on Pegasus."

"My crew and I have been doing our best to find more clues about what Pegasus is up to," Ravena finally said. "Unfortunately, it's been quite a challenge. Pegasus's security remains tight during the activities that the other air racers and I have been invited to. Earlier today, it became even tighter below Colani's airship—no doubt because of Agent Gala's failed mission. Still, my crew and I will do our best to get to the bottom of all this and confirm if there really is a threat behind the race. Hopefully with enough time for the Legion to respond."

"That's why we should wait but remain ready for the time being," Lanzard pointed out.

No one seemed willing to counter the colonel's proposition, which made Dantés clench her jaw as she fought to control her impatience. Clearly the colonel wasn't considering her proposition of stopping the race before it began. The colonel and those there who supported him had strong arguments. But was that enough for them to take their chances when they could be right about their suspicions? She needed to try to convince everyone one last time.

"Then are we just going to wait for something to happen during the race? Just so we can remedy instead of prevent?" she dared to say.

"Not exactly," Lanzard countered. He still showed no worry on his face, as if he had it all figured out. "We still have one chance before the day of the race to try to find out what Pegasus is really up to. I know some of you have expressed to me that you don't approve, but I have no doubt it's an opportunity we can't let pass, especially after our failure today."

Right away, Dantés knew what the colonel was referring to, and right away she interjected. "Sir, we agreed—"

"We *agreed*," Lanzard cut her off, leaning forward, "that we would avoid using *him* as long as we could find the answers ourselves. That hasn't happened, and as you pointed out in this meeting, Agent Venus, we are running out of time. Now he has a chance—probably a much better one than any of us—to get the information we need from Colani."

"Excuse me, sir, but who are you referring to?" Ravena asked. He now looked as perplexed as Major O'Malley and Agent Matías. His interruption, however, didn't ease the tension hanging between the colonel and Dantés.

"Keithan Quintero, the thirteen-year-old boy who found out about the Legion a few days ago," Lanzard answered.

So that was it, then, Dantés realized, swallowing her frustration. It seemed Lanzard hadn't called the meeting to consider other options. He had already decided what their next move would be; he was simply informing everyone to prepare before moving forward with it.

"The boy is a pilot student from Ramey Academy," Lanzard explained, "and Giovanni Colani himself invited him to a dinner party on his luxurious airship tomorrow night. I ordered him to get information out of Colani, who shouldn't suspect him, considering he's just a boy. Now, Agent Venus …"

Dantés, who couldn't be any more tense and upset at the moment, raised her gaze again toward the colonel.

"I'm assigning you to this mission with the boy," the colonel concluded.

Less than a mile away from where Dantés was meeting in secret with the other Sky Phantom agents, Keithan, Fernando, and Marianna had just realized the challenge of their current circumstances. They definitely weren't going to get answers from Mr. Aramis about his top-secret project, at least not before the day of the race. To get answers before that, they were going to have to take a different approach, and most likely from another angle. But who knew if that would be twice as hard to accomplish?

Keithan couldn't decide what was more frustrating: the fact that he and his friends still didn't know what the Daedalus Project was, the fact that they were so close to it, or the fact that whatever it was represented a threat as the Sky Phantom Legion suspected. Still, only one thing was certain: he, Fernando, and Marianna needed to get to the bottom of this before the Sky Phantoms did, for Mr. Aramis's sake.

There was only one problem: despite how much Fernando and Marianna wanted to help, it was up to Keithan to solve this, and he knew what he had to do.

The three friends were now at the entrance of Hangar H11, gazing beyond the airport's main runway at the white bloated airship of Pegasus Company. The large machine floated low over the grassy area at the southeast of the airfield, behind it a distant orange-and-pink horizon with bright clouds. Tomorrow night, Keithan would have the privilege of being inside the airship. There, he would meet the very man who hopefully would clear up for him the whole mystery behind the Daedalus Project and the upcoming race. And maybe, just maybe, all his suspicions and fears could be put to rest once and for all.

CHAPTER 7

Seventeen hours before race day

Every student at Ramey Academy knew the morning protocol to follow at the hangar bay. Once you brought your aircraft for one of the yellow tow robots to park it in its assigned space, you were supposed to head to the main building and wait for classes to begin. Yet this morning, for some reason, students crowded around the wide entrance of the hangar bay. Keithan, Marianna, and Fernando noticed it right away as Mrs. Aramis drove the scarlet minivan in that direction.

"What's going on over there?" asked Marianna from the passenger's seat.

"I have no idea," Keithan said behind her.

As soon as the minivan stopped, Mrs. Aramis lowered the vehicle's side ramp for Fernando's wheelchair, and both boys got out. Keithan headed to the rear of the minivan. He was about to detach the hover trailer where the *d'Artagnan* was mounted on when a familiar voice called out to him.

"Hey, Keithan!"

Keithan spotted Genevieve approaching him with her close friend and assigned aeroengineer partner, Yari.

"It's not gonna do you any good bringing the *d'Artagnan* today," Genevieve told him.

Keithan and Fernando exchanged perplexed looks.

"Why do you say that?" Keithan asked the girls.

"All flight classes have been cancelled for today." This time it was Yari who answered. Like Fernando, the short, freckled girl with raven-black hair tied in a short ponytail was dressed in an orange-and-gray uniform.

"Why?" Fernando asked, moving his wheelchair forward.

"We think it might have something to do with today being the eve of the Pegasus Air Race," Genevieve said.

"Apparently Pegasus has taken full control of Ramey airspace," Yari added.

"Um, boys?" Mrs. Aramis called out from behind the steering wheel. "Hurry up with the *d'Artagnan*. I don't want Marianna to be late for school."

Fernando nodded to her and turned to Keithan. "What do you think?"

Keithan shrugged. "We could keep the *d'Artagnan* at the academy, just in case."

In the end, however, Keithan and Fernando decided not to, and so they let Mrs. Aramis take the racing aircraft back home. Both of them expected to see the pilot students in the hangar bay upset for not being able to fly today, but surprisingly, they all looked excited. The professors, on the other hand, didn't look so happy. Keithan could tell the cancelation of all flight classes had come up unexpectedly for them as well, which meant that those who gave the flight classes were going to have to make big changes to their lessons today.

"It's definitely not going to be an ordinary day," Keithan said.

He and his friends continued through the hangar bay, passing by the few aircraft that were parked at the sides and through the crowd of other students. They were still pondering why the flight classes had been cancelled when a husky aeroengineer boy with curly brown hair jumped right in front of them.

"Hey! Did you guys hear?" the boy exclaimed with bulging eyes.

The whole group stopped abruptly at Winston Oddie's sudden

appearance.

"*Winston!*" Yari cried, her right hand pressed against her chest as she glared at the boy.

"Did you guys *hear?*" the boy asked again, still excited. "All flight classes were cancelled today!"

"Yeah, we heard," Fernando told him.

"Oh, but do you know the best part?" Winston went on. He kept walking backward, clumsily bumping into other students, all the while allowing Keithan and the rest of the gang to continue forward. "They're letting us go at midday because of the final preparations Pegasus is doing throughout the airport for tomorrow's race!"

—(·o·)—

It had already been hard enough for the students to concentrate throughout the week during classes, what with the excitement of tomorrow's air race and everything. So with the addition of the morning news, it became almost impossible for them to concentrate. It turned out to be a bigger challenge for the professors to carry out their lessons, for how could they make their students pay attention when their easily distracted minds were already wanting to leave at midday?

Keithan was aware that he was also too distracted to pay attention during classes. However, it wasn't exactly for the same reason as the rest of the academy. Despite the excitement around him, he was worried about everything that was happening throughout Ramey Airport regarding Pegasus Company and its final preparations for tomorrow's race.

On the other hand, Keithan couldn't deny that deep inside, he was starting to enjoy the whole mystery and intrigue a little. In a way, it made him feel like a secret agent, for while the rest of the academy didn't seem to suspect anything about Pegasus and its main event, he knew something was amiss. Fernando thought so too, though he was still a bit more skeptical about it.

But there was someone else at the academy who knew something was amiss. Keithan suddenly remembered just as he was headed to his third and last class of the day, and he saw her in one of the hallways.

Professor Dantés.

The professor didn't look like she was having a nice day. Then again, she never did. But Dantés looked more serious than usual, and Keithan guessed he was about to find out soon why since she seemed to have spotted him from a good distance and was coming straight in his direction.

Great, Keithan thought.

Dantés's brown eyes were locked on him, making her look like a lioness about to jump on her prey. Pilot and aeroengineer students quickly moved aside at the sight of her. From a distance, it almost looked as if she were forcing them to move with her mind.

As for Keithan, he kept walking forward, wishing the professor would just pass him by and allow him to reach his classroom even though he knew that wasn't going to happen. He took a deep breath and prepared himself mentally.

"Quintero," Dantés said as she stopped right in front of him with her sharp chin held high.

"Yes, Professor?" Keithan responded as casually as possible. No way was he going to look intimidated by her in front of all the other students who were watching. Moreover, he didn't feel the need to worry. He hadn't done anything wrong ... at least not that he was aware of. Unless this had nothing to do with academy business, but with the secret Sky Phantom Legion, Keithan then realized.

"I'd like to have a word with you in my office—right away."

The professor's tone was almost robotic, but it still showed authority, which was why Dantés didn't wait for Keithan to reply. Instead, she moved past him and kept on walking, the sound of her calf-high boots echoing in the sudden silence of the hallway.

"Oh man. Not again," Keithan murmured with a sigh.

Just like the rest of the students who heard the professor, he deduced that the meeting wasn't going to be pleasant. It came as no surprise since he knew that being called to Dantés's office meant that you were either in trouble or were going to be. And already Keithan held quite a record of visits for having gotten into trouble on numerous occasions.

No sooner had Dantés left than Keithan heard several students nearby tease him.

"Oooo," some chorused in a low voice.

One pilot student girl who was a couple of years older than Keithan couldn't help commenting as she passed him by. "Busted again, eh, Quintero?" she said.

Keithan hissed, ignoring her and everyone else, and simply turned around to head to the professor's office.

The office was located above the academy's hangar bay area. Its door was open, but as soon as Keithan walked in, the glass door slid down shut behind him and frosted up. Dantés was at the other end of the room, still with a deep look and a clenched jaw. She was facing him and leaning against her glossy turquoise desk, which stood out from everything else there due to its organic shape. A holographic screen hovered behind her over the desktop, showing a rotating screensaver of the academy's crest: a chromed propeller with a copper spinner hub and its twin blades shaped like art deco wings.

"Come closer," Dantés ordered.

Keithan did his best to remain relaxed but wary as he moved past the many air racing trophies and medals displayed on the left wall. He stopped about four feet in front of the professor.

"I'll be straight with you, Keithan," Dantés began. "I don't like the reason I summoned you here one bit, but I had no choice since I'm under Lieutenant Colonel Lanzard's orders. I'm sure you remember him."

"Lieutenant Colonel Lanzard?" Keithan repeated. So this *did* have something to do with the Sky Phantoms. He felt a slight chill run down his spine as he realized where the conversation was going.

"Yes," Dantés continued. "He assigned me to prepare you as best I can for when you meet Colani tonight at his dinner party. So listen carefully." She started pacing around him. "As we expect, your being only thirteen should help you not draw any suspicion. That means your actions must reflect that as well. Do not give Colani any reason to suspect that you are on to him. Show as much curiosity as any other boy your age would, but get Colani to talk. However, and I mean this, be *very* careful about how you approach him. Remember, it's not just what you ask him but *how* you ask too."

"What should I focus on when I talk to Colani?" Keithan asked.

"The air race," Dantés said. "Persuasion is the key, Keithan. First, let Colani feel comfortable talking to you. Let him trust you. Then, slowly, cautiously, persuade him to tell you as much as he can about what he's planning to do tomorrow during the air race, with its spherical drones, his secret project, everything."

Dantés stopped in front of Keithan. "Now, it's probable you'll go through a high-security check when you arrive at Colani's airship, so you won't be 'wearing a wire' for us at the Legion to hear what happens in there. Despite that, I will need you to contact me if you find out anything that might seem suspicious or represents a threat—while you're still there or afterwards. As a precaution, one of our top agents is disguised as one of the participating air racers. He's backed up with a group that's disguised as his crew—also Sky Phantom agents. They should be able to reach you quickly and help you if something dangerous happens. Is that clear?"

Keithan gulped but nodded.

"Are you certain? This is very important, Keithan."

"I am," Keithan reassured her. "But, um … there's one problem, Professor." He showed her his left wrist. "I don't have a communicator anymore. Remember? The night my friend Marianna and I found out about the Legion? Some of your agent friends destroyed it before they took us for questioning."

"I know," Dantés said. "That's why the colonel ordered me to give you this."

She turned to her desk to pick up a small white box and handed it to Keithan.

Keithan's eyes widened. "Whoa! Are you—?"

"Serious? Very," Dantés finished the thought, her deep stare confirming it.

The clear top of the box showed a brand-new wrist communicator inside. It was actually the latest top-of-the-line model currently on the market, the very one everybody was talking about and wanted to have. It had the coolest sleek design in dark silver and electric orange, and it was still no bigger than any other wrist communicator out there. Among its usual features, which Keithan read from the package, it included a small flexed touchscreen, a tiny speaker, and an integrated microphone. Not to mention wireless access and more than enough data space for updates and additional applications. As for its new features, it included an integrated holo projector for 3-D GPS.

Yet the best part about the communicator almost took Keithan's breath away.

"A voice-recognition power-up synchronizer!" Keithan read on the box. Now he could power up the *d'Artagnan* with his voice right from the communicator. The box even included the external security device to install in the aircraft.

Dantés rolled her eyes, unimpressed. But Keithan didn't care; he kept staring in disbelief at the new gadget in his hands, feeling like a little kid who had just received the best birthday present ever.

"Keithan, I need you to stay focused on what's important here," Dantés said, demanding his full attention again.

"Oh, of course," said Keithan, keeping the boxed communicator on his lap. He didn't dare say another word as the professor, now with arms folded, stepped forward and leaned closer to him.

"Do *not* forget the main purpose for having that communicator," she told him. "If there's any reason you need to contact me while dining with Colani, simply press the number five for speed dial. Got it? Now, that said, do you think you're up to this? Really up to carrying out this mission tonight?"

There was no reason for Keithan to hesitate. "I am," he replied full of confidence.

—(-o-)—

Miles away, to the east of Ramey, the city of Old San Juan, well known for its multicolored colonial buildings and cobblestoned streets, was getting ready to be part of the grand Pegasus Air Race. Currently, its coast was the area with the most activity, as it had been selected as one of the main six points throughout the island of Puerto Rico to gather spectators during the race tomorrow. Just like in Ramey, long banners and holograms promoting the event hung all around, and people, mostly tourists and air racing aficionados, crowded the sidewalks while they stepped in and out of the numerous shops and took pictures of the historic architecture that surrounded them.

Agent Brave Gala had just arrived after a two-hour drive from Ramey. She looked at her surroundings and felt the urge to take a moment to relax and simply appreciate the beauty of the place. But she couldn't, not when she was on an important mission here.

Gala blended in easily with everyone around her. She had carefully selected a plain mint-green sleeveless shirt and a skirt to avoid drawing attention to herself. Her black pixie hair was covered in gel and combed backward. As for secret gadgets, she had brought a tiny communicator piece, which she carried inside her right ear, and a pair of sunglasses with a digital head-up display in its lenses, as well as a tiny camera integrated on its bridge. Both gadgets were linked to a secure channel for Gala to remain in contact with the Sky Phantom Base.

She continued walking down the cobblestoned streets. The heat of the day forced her to fan herself with one hand every now and then. She was heading uphill, toward the highest areas of the city, all the while pretending to be just another ordinary visitor. Her route eventually led her to a small plaza with a series of square garden patches and a fountain that stood in the middle. It was at this point that the agglomerated buildings ended, but Gala didn't stop there. She continued northward, in the same direction the plaza was oriented, until she reached the area where the space opened, revealing the full sky and the sea beyond the wide bright-green grass esplanade that ended at the front façade of an old stone fort.

It was at that fort, known as El Castillo San Felipe del Morro, where Gala had been assigned to go for her mission. She could see a crowd already there, which seemed to be growing as more people headed there too. It came as no surprise to her since the fort happened to be one of Old San Juan's leading tourist attractions. The sixteenth-century historic landmark had originally been built to guard the Spanish entrance to the Old San Juan Bay during the colonial era. Yet today, all of its history had become secondary, for the main reason people were gathering there was to see the Pegasus spherical drones that would soon be arriving to broadcast the race tomorrow.

Once Gala reached the fort, she settled herself at the top of the high stone wall of the left wing. Many other visitors were also settling nearby, some with digital binoculars and others with hover cameras floating next to them. Like Gala, they kept a safe distance from the ledge due to the strong winds that could be felt up there.

Sure that nobody was watching her, Gala pressed her communication earpiece and reported. "Phantom Base, this is Agent Gala. I've reached my assigned position."

"Copy that, Agent," the familiar voice of Lieutenant Colonel Lanzard replied through the device. *"We're watching the drones through our satellite right now. They're divided into five groups, each one headed out from Ramey Airport to a different destination."*

"How many drones in each group?"

"Twenty. You should be seeing the group headed your way any moment now. They'll be doing a flyby."

"Copy that, Base. Stand by."

Gala was set. All she had to do now was wait. She remained gazing westward, just like everybody else. She was ready to report whatever happened as soon as the Pegasus spherical drones arrived. It seemed like a simple job, but it also seemed like it was going to be quite a challenge gazing at the sky with the sun overhead and no clouds to block the intense heat.

Then, finally, the wait was over.

Francisco Muniz

"They're here! They're here!" someone shouted nearby.

Gala spotted them too.

Excitement took over the crowd. Onlookers started cheering and applauding while the new arrivals became clear in the distance.

The Pegasus spherical drones. They were flying low and very close to the coast, keeping a horizontal line formation, perfectly parallel with the sea.

"Phantom Base, my group of drones is arriving," Gala reported. "Get ready to receive transmission."

With the press of a button on the left side of her sunglasses, she began transmitting everything she was seeing to the lieutenant colonel and everyone else at the base.

"So far, everything seems to be under control," she said.

The metallic drones were flying fast. Suddenly, they released streaks of smoke, tracing the sky with black, white, and gold contrails. The reaction of the crowd was instantaneous, full of whoops and loud cheers. But they hadn't seen anything yet, for in the next moment, the drones changed their line formation into an arrowhead and executed a giant loop over the sea in flawless synchronization.

"Whoaaa!" the spectators cried in unison.

Gala dared not blink. She made sure the Sky Phantom base was seeing what she was seeing through her sunglasses. The twenty drones had just completed the loop, and quickly after that, they turned toward the excited crowd, still in perfect synchronization, and flew right over it, painting the sky above the city as a grand finale.

Not long after, Gala received confirmation of similar scenes witnessed in four other cities of Puerto Rico. They were the same cities that been selected as strategic points for the camera drones to broadcast the Pegasus Air Race tomorrow. Just like in Old San Juan, crowds had gathered in each of them. They, too, burst out with excitement when they saw the other drones arrive, from the summit of the bright-green mountains at the cities of Cidra and Jayuya, located at the center of the island, to the beautiful sandy beaches at the cities of Ponce and Cabo Rojo to the south and southwest.

A Sky Phantom agent was present in each of these cities, each of them with the same mission Gala had: to remain vigilant in the face of the Pegasus camera drones at all cost.

CHAPTER 8

Six hours before race day

"**S**on, are you ready?" Keithan heard his dad call out to him from outside his room.

"Not yet," Keithan responded.

He was almost done, though he was still struggling with his current look. Keithan had never gotten used to wearing formal attire. He had put on a fit midnight-blue suit with a stand-up collar and a black shirt with its top button open. He liked the clothes, but it made him feel so unlike himself, so stiff, so serious, and worst of all, so grown up. At least he'd compensated by wearing his power-strapped sneakers. He just hoped his father wouldn't mind.

Keithan was now combing his hair in front of the closet's mirror door. Meanwhile, he listened to Channel 2 News's field correspondent Rebecca Knight, whose image appeared on the holo screen projected in front of the bed. The young woman, whose glossy black hair shone blue with the sunlight, was reporting from the familiar north entrance of Ramey Airport.

"There is no doubt about it, ladies and gentlemen," Knight told the viewers, "the island of Puerto Rico has become the center of attention and the number one tourist destination as air racing enthusiasts from practically all over the globe have come to be part of the much-anticipated 2055 Pegasus Air Race tomorrow. Never in history has

Puerto Rico received so many visitors. It is overwhelming but exciting nonetheless. Locals seem to be excited about tomorrow's event too, and they have made sure to get good spots near the different strategic areas of the racecourse to be part of it all."

Images from different parts of the island appeared on the screen while Rebecca Knight continued reporting. Some showed the crowds of new arrivals who kept spilling out of the alternate airports with suitcases and backpacks, while others showed the many full hotels, villas, and beach houses that already displayed "No Vacancies" holographic signs on their fronts. Yet of all the places shown, Ramey was the most crowded, with hundreds of vehicles from all colors, shapes, and sizes, as well as camping tents close to the fences that enclosed the airport. Even numerous food trucks could be seen in different areas, their owners not wasting such a lucrative opportunity with so many people gathered there.

Keithan remembered how crowded the outskirts of Ramey Airport had been a week ago during the air race's qualifier tournament, but what he saw now on the news was more than twice as big a crowd. He could see part of what was going on out there at Ramey from the concave window opposite to his bed since his house was only a few blocks away from the airport. Like everyone there, Keithan couldn't wait for tomorrow. Yet he couldn't help imagining how cool it would have been if instead of being another spectator, he had been allowed to qualify for the race. The experience would have been much more different if he'd been one of the participating air racers.

"Keithan, we better get going," his dad said, bringing him back from his thoughts. "We don't wanna be late."

"Yeah, I'm coming," Keithan shouted back. He grabbed his brand-new wrist communicator and headed out.

He met his dad in the family room. Caleb Quintero was doing a last-minute check of his own attire in front of a mirror. The man was dressed in a trim silver suit with black shoulder and forearm patches and matching piping that ran from the neck to the bottom of the blazer. His usual stubble beard, which would have matched the color of his suit, was gone, exposing the man's still-young-looking face. He turned to Keithan, and right away he noticed the power-strapped sneakers.

"What?" Keithan reacted, letting his dad know with a pinched smile that he had put on the sneakers on purpose.

His dad simply rubbed his forehead and gave him an amused smile. "Nothing," he told him. "You know, son, you have to admit, having been denied the opportunity to qualify for the air race turned out to be something good. I mean, it led to Captain Colani noticing you and inviting us to his airship tonight. Many boys or girls your age would never get such an opportunity."

Keithan sighed with a shrug. "Yeah, I guess."

He still felt grateful and privileged for the opportunity even though he would have preferred being allowed to compete in the Pegasus Air Race. That is, if there was no threat behind the event, as Keithan was looking forward to confirming tonight. His dad, however, had no idea of the real reason Keithan had accepted the invitation to go to Colani's dinner party. The man didn't even know that a secret legion of fighter pilots had practically forced Keithan to do it, and Keithan had no intention of telling him, either. At least, not if it wasn't necessary.

"Well, we should be heading off," Keithan's dad said.

The two of them were about to head to the garage when the doorbell rang.

"Who could that be?" Keithan said.

He headed to the front door and opened it. He found a man dressed in black from head to toe on the other side. The man's gloves and chauffeur hat were also black. Even his thin mustache, which looked like a second set of eyebrows but under his nose, seemed to be part of his attire since it was black too.

Neither Keithan nor his dad knew him, yet Keithan noticed the small silver pin on the man's hat: a winged stallion bust.

"Good evening, sirs. I'm Antonio Cavaliere," the man said with a smile, his Italian accent very clear. "I will be your chauffeur this evening."

Keithan's dad hesitated. "Um, a chauffeur?" he said, looking at

Keithan, who shrugged in return.

"It was a last-minute call from the captain," Antonio explained. "He said it would be best if I came to pick you up, considering how crowded it is around the airport. This way it will be easier to enter it. Now, please, if you'll just follow me."

Never before had Keithan ridden in luxury. Antonio drove him and his dad to Ramey Airport in a fancy, low-hovering black limousine. The vehicle's inside was quite spacious. It included a little refrigerator on one side that also served as a counter; a holo projector on the ceiling, which according to Antonio could show every channel in the world; and leather seats so comfortable Keithan would have had no problem dozing in them if the trip had been longer.

Keithan, however, knew he needed to mentally prepare himself for what he was supposed to do once he met Colani. He reminded himself to stay calm and under control at all times to make sure Colani wouldn't have the slightest suspicion about him.

The limousine had no problem passing through the agglomerated vehicles on the outskirts of the airport or entering the airfield. Opposite the airport's north entrance, Keithan spotted Rocket's Diner, still open and fully packed with clientele. No doubt Mr. Rocket, the owner of the place, would be quite busy all night serving his famous shakes.

Finally, the limousine came to a stop. Antonio was courteous enough to open the door for Keithan and his dad from outside. The two of them stepped out and tilted their heads all the way back, for right above them now hovered the Pegasus airship.

It was quite an impressive sight from where they stood. The airship was so huge from up close it looked like a titanic whale hovering quietly in the sky. Keithan couldn't feel more privileged standing underneath it. He also felt his heartbeat accelerate, though he wasn't sure if it was from excitement or from the nervousness of being about to board it. Tensed cables held the hovering machine in place, and searchlights illuminated its underbelly and gondola, making it stand out even more than the full moon in the night sky. On the ground, Keithan noticed how tight security was. Dozens of men and women clad in black-white-and-gold uniforms carried small electroshock weapons on their waists.

"How are we getting into the airship?" Keithan's dad asked while still gazing up.

Keithan was just wondering the same thing when he heard Antonio behind him clear his throat.

"Gentlemen?" the chauffeur called to them. "This way."

He gestured toward a small hexagonal module that stood a few feet away. Its walls, as well as its roof, were made of glass and a metal frame. They revealed a figure inside the capsule. The small propulsors underneath the module's base made Keithan quickly realize the answer to their question.

"A flying shuttle," Keithan told his dad.

In front of it stood a metal detector gate guarded by two security officers. There, Keithan and his dad were asked to remove all metal items they had with them.

"Don't worry, young man," said one of the security officers. "Everyone who goes on board the airship has to go through this process."

Keithan hesitated before taking off his wrist communicator and placing it inside a plastic box. He was asked to remove his belt too, as well as his power-strapped sneakers. Only then was he allowed to step through the gate. A digital and life-sized X-ray hologram of himself instantly appeared at either side of Keithan. The second security officer took a moment to look at each one. Meanwhile, Keithan gazed outside the gate without taking his eyes off his wrist communicator, which the other officer was currently inspecting.

Seconds later, Caleb Quintero went through the same process. Once he stepped out to the other side of the gate, he picked up his belongings.

"Enjoy your dinner, gentlemen," Antonio told Keithan and his dad from the opposite side of the security gate. "I'll be waiting here to drive you back to your house."

Keithan and his dad thanked him and proceeded to follow the security officer, who led them toward the shuttle.

"Step right in and watch your step," the officer said invitingly.

The shuttle's glass door opened, and though Keithan had already noticed someone inside it, it wasn't until now that he realized that instead of someone, it was actually some*thing.*

"Whoa," was Keithan's sudden reaction, taking his dad and the security officer by surprise. He stopped right in front of the shuttle's entrance as he stared, frozen and with bulging eyes, at the robot inside. "W-what's that *thing* doing in there?"

"That's one of Captain Colani's serving robots," the officer remarked. "No need to fear it. It's programmed to pilot the shuttle up to the airship."

"No need to fear it?" Keithan murmured with a slightly nervous laugh. Surely the guy hadn't had any threatening experience with one of those things before. The robot looked similar to Mr. Aramis's Emmeiseven. Its faceless head was identical: nothing more than a computerized helmet with a curved glass mask.

The robot stood straight and unmoving, as if waiting for Keithan and his dad to enter. Still, to Keithan, it brought on a flashback of him being attacked by Emmeiseven.

At least, unlike Emmeiseven, this robot didn't have any kind of tools attached to its forearms. It was also much shinier and elegant, clearly an example of Pegasus Company's fancy inventions.

"You have nothing to fear about the robot," the officer insisted, gesturing for Keithan to climb into the shuttle. "By the way, Captain Colani has already been informed of your arrival. He's waiting to receive you."

"Come on, son. Let's not keep Colani waiting." Keithan's dad moved past Keithan and climbed into the shuttle.

Keithan followed, and the glass door slid shut behind him. He felt the floor tremble slightly after the robot activated the antigravity plates. And so the shuttle left the ground, gradually accelerating with a low humming. Both Keithan and his dad held on to the handrail and watched with full amazement as the lights of Ramey, hundreds of them as tiny as Christmas lights, became fully visible far below. They were spread for miles before the Atlantic Ocean, which also came into view like a rippled mantle spread far into the dark horizon.

Such a magnificent sight made Keithan pay no more attention to the silent robot piloting the shuttle. He became immersed in the ascent, feeling like a little Charlie Bucket traveling inside Willy Wonka's flying elevator. His dad, on the other hand, didn't seem to be enjoying the trip so much. Keithan noticed it by his dad's stiff posture, not to mention the fact that the man was holding on to the handrail with both hands.

"Good, we're almost there." Caleb sighed as he gazed up at the white surface of the airship. Still, Keithan noticed the nervousness in his father's voice. He did his best not to laugh or snicker.

The hexagonal shuttle was over a hundred feet high by now and still ascending. It slowly approached an opening at the bottom of the airship's envelope, from which a platform stood out. Once it landed on the platform, the glass door opened, and Keithan and his dad stepped out.

Giovanni Colani stood a few feet ahead inside the airship. The broad-shouldered man, whose black beard looked perfectly squared, was dressed in a black silk shirt under a well-tailored garnet suit adorned with golden epaulets. A man and a woman dressed in less flashy evening clothes accompanied him. The man, tall and fit, wore a dark-blue suit, and the woman, blonde and slender, wore a matching short skirt dress.

"Gentlemen! *Buonasera*. And welcome to my airship!" Colani bellowed over the loud sound of the wind. "I am so glad you came."

Keithan took a deep breath as he and his father approached him. He reminded himself not to get nervous, ready to shake hands with Colani.

The man and the woman at Colani's right moved past Keithan and his father to secure the shuttle to the platform.

"Young Keithan Quintero!" Colani said aloud, flashing his pearly whites from under his beard.

"Hello, sir," Keithan replied. He struggled to smile back as he felt the strength in Colani's handshake.

"And this is your father, I presume," said Colani, turning to Keithan's dad.

Caleb took the man's big hand and shook it. "Yes, sir, Caleb Quintero. Thank you for inviting us."

"It is my pleasure, Mr. Quintero," Colani replied jovially. "Welcome aboard. I apologize for having you both go through the tight security check on the ground, but we have to take every precaution, especially since yesterday afternoon, due to an incident that happened up here."

Keithan and his dad exchanged perplexed looks.

"What happened?" Keithan dared to ask.

"Oh, nothing serious, fortunately," Colani said. "Just, um … an extreme fan who somehow managed to sneak into the airship during the presentation of the racecourse. But it was all taken care of— *and* nobody got hurt."

Two new figures who Keithan recognized right away appeared from behind Colani. Keithan, however, couldn't help showing his surprise when he made eye contact with the one at the front, for it was none other than Mr. Perfect, the chisel-faced Drostan Luzier, who, as always, was accompanied by the silent man with the snowy handlebar mustache and curious red-lensed glasses.

"Excuse me, Captain Colani—"

"Ah, Luzier. I'm so glad you're here," Colani interrupted him before turning to Keithan and his dad again. "Allow me to introduce Mr. Drostan Luzier and his senior advising aeroengine—"

"Oh, we've already met," Luzier said spontaneously with a vague wave of his hand.

"You have?" Colani asked.

"At least he and I, a few weeks ago," Keithan clarified. "It was at the Aram—"

"At Ramey Academy. I remember," Luzier cut him off in his Dutch accent before he turned to Colani. "The day we went to give a presentation to all the students. Remember, sir?"

"Oh, yes," Colani replied.

Colani may have not figured out Drostan had just lied to him, but Keithan did. He remembered very well having introduced himself to Luzier at the Aramises' hangar a few weeks ago when the man and his quiet companion had arrived there to see Mr. Aramis's progress on the Daedalus Project. Just yesterday afternoon, the two of them had been at Mr. Aramis's hangar, and Keithan was sure the man had seen him and Fernando even though he had ignored them.

Keithan wanted to tell Colani about it, but after giving it a second thought, he figured it wasn't worth it, especially when Keithan could see Luzier and his companion didn't feel comfortable being there.

Fortunately for Keithan, Luzier said, "I'm sorry, Captain. I must excuse myself and my senior advising aeroengineer. We need to head back to our quarters below."

Colani raised an eyebrow. "You're not joining us for dinner?"

"I'd love to, Captain, but I need to rest. Tomorrow is the big event, after all."

Luzier didn't wait for Colani to reply. Instead, he nodded to the CEO and completely ignored Keithan and his dad. He even avoided making eye contact with either of them as he walked past them toward the glass shuttle at the edge of the platform. As expected, the man with the snowy white mustache and red-lensed glasses followed Luzier like a shadow. Keithan couldn't help wondering if the man spoke at all. *Maybe he didn't speak English*, Keithan thought.

At least watching him and Luzier leave was a relief. He hadn't been looking forward to feeling uncomfortable the rest of the evening while dining with such a person like Luzier.

Colani shook his head and returned his attention to Keithan and his dad. "Well, before we go inside, I have something for the two of you. I'd rather give them to you now to avoid forgetting about them."

He gestured to the blonde woman, who pulled out two golden

smart cards attached to black lanyards.

"They're VIP passes," Colani said. "To join me in my private cabin at the top of the grandstands tomorrow during the race."

"Wow! Thank you, sir," said Keithan, his jaw on the floor.

"Now, *avanti*," Colani said, gesturing for Keithan and his dad to follow him. "I hope the two of you are hungry. You won't believe the exquisite dinner that awaits us. And while we eat, we can get to know each other more. What do you say?"

Keithan couldn't hide his excitement. "That would be awesome, sir!"

The darkness of the night stood out by now at the airfield, but for Dantés, the entire site glowed like an emerald city while she gazed at it through the night-vision screen of her digital binoculars. The device also showed the exact distance in yards between Dantés's current position and her focal point, which revealed Keithan and his father now entering the airship's gondola.

It was official, Dantés realized, and there was no turning back: Keithan's mission had begun.

"He's in," Dantés said with a strained voice. She lowered her binoculars and turned to Agent Gala, who had just returned from San Juan and now stood next to her, clad in her high-tech black uniform. "Contact base. Report to the colonel that young Quintero has entered the airship."

Gala acknowledged the order with a nod and left. Meanwhile, Dantés resumed watching the tiny entrance at the Pegasus airship with her binoculars. She remained hidden in the shadow cast by the hangar behind her. Next to them was Captain John Ravena. He, too, was gazing at the Pegasus airship with a pair of digital binoculars.

Ravena gave a heavy sigh. "I can't believe our entire operation lies in the hands of a thirteen-year-old boy now. It should've been one of us inside that airship trying to get information out of Colani."

Dantés felt the same way, if not more frustrated by all this. She still couldn't believe Lanzard had insisted on dragging Keithan into this, considering how dangerous the mission could be. The boy and his father were entering the belly of the beast. And what if Colani found out Keithan was on to him? Worse still, what if Colani found out Keithan was working for a secret legion who wanted to stop the man's famous race? Now, however, there was nothing Dantés, Ravena, or anyone else from the Sky Phantom Legion could do but wait ... wait until Keithan contacted them and was out of harm's way.

"Let's hope the boy makes it count and gets the proof we need to stop Pegasus tonight," Dantés said. "No way am I looking forward to still not knowing tomorrow if there's a threat planned—"

Dantés didn't get to finish the sentence, for Agent Gala cut her off as she came out of the hangar, hurrying toward her and Ravena.

"We have a problem," Gala told them.

Both Dantés and Ravena turned around.

"What's wrong?" Dantés asked.

"There's a strange interference jamming our communications."

"What?" Dantés and Ravena exclaimed simultaneously.

"That's ... impossible," Ravena added, though not sounding too certain. "Our *safe* frequency too?"

"I'm afraid so," Gala said quickly. "Whatever it is, it's not allowing us to send or receive any type of communication."

Of everything else Dantés had been expecting to happen tonight, she had definitely not expected this. How could the Sky Phantom Legion, with the most advanced, stealthy, and secret technology in the world, lose all communications all of a sudden? Most of all, through their safe frequency?

She and Ravena wasted no time and followed Gala into the hangar. They reached the conference room at the far end, and right away Dantés and Ravena saw what Gala had just explained. Hovering over the middle of the round black glass tabletop was a holo screen that showed the words "STRONG INTERFERENCE DETECTED."

Silence hung in the room for a moment while Dantés and her

companions tried to make sense of it.

"Where's the source?" Dantés asked, her arms on her hips.

"No idea," Gala responded. "It seems to be cloaked."

The three of them were still staring at the holo screen when its image flickered and changed into that of a man clad in the same high-tech black uniform as Gala's and Dantés's. He was already speaking, but his voice crackled with interference.

"Agent— … copy?—Can you hear— … over."

Leaning over the tabletop, Gala tried to fix the transmission. She tapped different keys projected on the glass. Moments later, Ravena stepped forward to try.

"It's a strong sucker, that interference!" said Ravena, landing a fist hard on the glass tabletop. "It's well cloaked, and it's jamming all communications in Ramey. Cell communicators, internet, radar, you name it."

"Wait." Dantés stepped forward. "Only in Ramey?"

"Seems to be," Ravena remarked, still staring at the screen.

Dantés took a deep breath and held it for a moment. The last thing she needed right now was for things to get complicated while she waited for Keithan to contact her. The interference could be something temporary. But what if it wasn't?

"You think it's being done on purpose?" Gala asked the same thing Dantés was wondering.

Dantés tightened her jaw. "I'm not sure … but I have a strong feeling it could be."

CHAPTER 9

Five hours before race day

The fanciest dinner table Keithan had ever seen in his life awaited him, his father, and Colani at the very center of a circular room that opened to a balcony and the night sky. The table was draped in a golden cloth and set with dishware, silverware, and shiny glasses that looked more for decoration rather than for eating and drinking. Making the table more impressive still was the light that rested over it.

"Right this way, my friends," said Colani over the soft instrumental music that played in the background. He gestured for Keithan and his father to take two of the four red velvet chairs with golden ornaments while he approached a fifth and much taller chair at the other side.

"This room is also used as a conference room sometimes due to the limited space we have in the airship," Colani explained as he sat down. "However, as you can see, it has enough space for my collection of some of the robots I have designed since I started the company."

There were eight robots in total, four on each side of the room, and while Keithan's dad looked at them with fascination, Keithan could only look at them with concern. The last thing he had wanted this evening was to be in a room full of robots that looked just like Emmeiseven. He felt as if each of the humanoid machines were staring back at him despite their faceless heads. Each robot stood straight on top of a low black pedestal and between arched, gilded columns. Together, they looked more like sentinels than collectible statues.

"Are they activated?" Keithan asked Colani. Just like his worried tone, the question seemed to have come out of his mouth spontaneously.

"These? Oh, no," Colani said, "but a few others will arrive in— Ah, and here they are."

Four shiny, elegant-looking robots with sleek white-and-gold coverings and faceless heads that had nothing but a round lens in the middle came into the room. They brought a delicious smell while they carried different trays with food delicacies and drinks. Unlike Mr. Aramis's Emmeiseven, as well as some of the inactive robots on the pedestals near the walls, these had no gauntlets with tools. Instead, they had simple humanoid extremities decorated with golden ornaments, probably to look more appealing for the occasion.

One by one they brought the food to the table, and at the sight of it, Keithan and his father raised their eyebrows. Keithan even felt his nostrils widen as his nose took in the delicious smells: from the smoking steaks accompanied by different shapes of pasta to the platter of cheeses of all kinds. The fruit and vegetable salads also looked delicious and made the table look even more colorful.

"Gentlemen, don't be shy. I encourage you to try everything you see here. Mr. Quintero, I recommend the red wine, and for you, Keithan, the fruit punch, made by hand right here with fresh tropical fruits and a bit of mint to give it just the right kick. I bet it's unlike any other you have ever tasted."

Colani had just finished speaking when Keithan flinched abruptly.

"Whoa!" said Colani, startled.

"Keithan, are you all right?" said his dad, reacting the same way.

"Um …" Keithan hesitated. For an instant, he'd thought one of the serving robots had been about to grab him, though it had only tried to reach for the glass in front of him. His reaction made him accidentally hit the table from underneath with his knees, making all the china clatter.

"Oh! So-so sorry, Mr. Colani!" he stammered. He quickly looked at the robot standing beside him and noticed that it was still doing its job serving water on some of the glasses.

"It's all right, Keithan," Colani said.

"No. I-I really am," said Keithan, shaking his head.

"Don't *worry*," Colani insisted. "The robots are just here to serve us. You have nothing to worry about."

Keithan straightened up in his chair, completely embarrassed. He glanced at his father and gave him a slight smile to reassure him he was okay. Meanwhile, the four robots around them continued serving dinner, making the table look even more decorated than it already was.

As expected, Colani was the first to pick up his napkin and place it on his lap. Keithan saw his father do the same, and so he did it too. Keithan didn't know much about dining etiquette since he'd never been to a fancy dinner before. Thank goodness for his dad giving him a few pointers. The most important one was to watch his dad's every move during dinner when in doubt.

"You know, Keithan, you remind me so much of your mother when I first met her," Colani said with a smile. "She was so nervous too. I remember it like it was yesterday."

The man had already picked up his utensils to start eating. "She wasn't as young as you at the time, though," he went on. "She was in her late twenties, I think. Back in 2040."

"Wasn't that the year she participated in your air race for the first time?" Keithan asked.

"That's right," Colani said. "I had the honor of meeting her at the race's qualifier tournament. Mr. Quintero, were you there with her?"

"Mmm. No, sir," Keithan's dad replied quickly after swallowing the first bite of his sirloin. "Adalina and I weren't together yet. She and I met shortly after the race that year, I think."

"Oh, I remember when that made the headlines," Colani commented. "'Mystery Man Spotted with Air Racing Champion Adalina Zambrana,' and 'Mystery Man Turns Out to Be Professor of Mythology at University in Puerto Rico.'"

Keithan's dad couldn't have turned redder, and Keithan had to lower his head to hide his snicker.

"Adalina was such a remarkable young woman," Colani went on. "I remember people didn't take her seriously in the qualifier tournament at first. And I have to admit, *I* was one of those people. But as you know, Keithan, almost everybody underestimated her as an underdog. She really showed how great an air racer she was. And boy did she show us all!" He took a moment to smell his glass of wine and take a sip.

Keithan was already enjoying his plate of pasta with salad. Just as Colani had told him, his fruit punch tasted unlike any other he had tasted before. It was just right, so sweet, and at the same time, slightly sour—and minty.

Meanwhile, the conversation went on. Keithan was enjoying every minute of it, but he was still finding it hard to turn it cautiously toward what he needed to know—and what he'd been assigned to find out—about Colani and his secret plan behind tomorrow's race. He kept wondering how he could persuade Colani to talk about his secret project, but the Pegasus CEO knew how to maintain control of a conversation.

The man was now interested in knowing more about Keithan and his air racing background. Keithan kept the conversation flowing. He told Colani how much he had learned from watching videos over and over again of his mother air racing, especially those in the Pegasus Air Races she had won. Keithan even told Colani how his mother's racing aircraft had inspired him and Fernando when they built their *d'Artagnan* during their third year at Ramey Academy.

"The *d'Artagnan*? Like the famous musketeer?" Colani said.

"Yes, sir," Keithan replied. "She has some features very similar to the ones my mom's aircraft had. Twin forwarded arms with independent steering vanes, rear stabilizers behind the cockpit, even separate steering yokes."

"Wow! That's impressive," Colani said. "Did you gentlemen know Adalina was the first person to introduce an aircraft with forwarded arms and front steering vanes in my air race? It was quite innovative at the time, though much different than how forwarded arms are built today. *And* did you know Adalina helped me improve such a feature for other racing aircraft?"

Keithan, who was now savoring his dessert of French vanilla ice cream with sprinkles and smooth caramel on it, held a spoonful near his mouth when he heard this. "She did?"

"Oh, yes," Colani said. "After she became the first female champion of the Pegasus Air Races, I hired her as one of my advisors to help me with some of my designs, and … You know what? Come with me."

Both Keithan and his dad exchanged confused looks when Colani pushed back his throne-like chair and rose.

"Come on. There's something I'd like to show the two of you."

The man was already heading for the doorway. Keithan and his father hesitated, more noticeably Keithan, who hadn't yet finished eating his ice cream, but then the two of them stood up and hurried to follow.

—(·o·)—

Keithan and his dad got to see more of the inside of the airship on their way. Most of the spaces they passed, however, were narrow passageways, among them a steep set of stairs and aluminum catwalks that hung either from higher ones or from the wide and curved frames that shaped the bloated envelope. Still, everywhere they passed, Colani's fascination with luxury and classical style was evident. Keithan and his dad noticed it in the golden ornamental handrails, which reflected the low lighting above them, not to mention in the collection of vintage aircraft blueprints that hung on the walls in several rooms, all enclosed in fancy gold frames.

"Where are we going, sir?" Keithan's dad asked after they stepped out of a third catwalk and entered a narrow corridor with purple carpeting.

"We're heading to my favorite place inside the airship," Colani replied over his shoulder. "The designing room."

"Designing room?" Keithan repeated in a low voice. *Well, that was easy.* He realized this could be his chance to see if Colani had something that might be worth reporting to the Sky Phantoms.

"And here we are."

Colani stopped in front of a white door with a golden ornamental frame, but before opening it, he turned around. "You gentlemen are really going to like this. Especially you, Keithan."

The door slid silently to the side, and Colani allowed his guests to enter first. Keithan didn't know exactly what to expect, but when he entered, he found himself in nothing more than an empty dome-shaped room. It was made completely of dark-blue concave panels that had numerous tiny black dots on them.

"Um, sir? There's nothing in here," Keithan said.

Colani chuckled. "Don't let appearances fool you."

He closed the door behind him, and everything went black right before the many tiny dots in each of the panels started projecting neon-blue lights, which blinked rapidly all over the concave room.

Both Keithan and his father froze while they tried to figure out what was happening. The whole room now looked like a night sky but with a show of dancing blue lights that began to project very thin beams all around. Gradually, the beams started to synchronize, meeting among themselves to project different shapes. It was then that Keithan's eyes boggled.

"A virtual designing room!" he exclaimed, gaping.

It was as if they'd been transported into an entirely different space—a *virtual* space. The dark room no longer looked like a dome— now it seemed infinite and filled with floating shelves, machinery, and countless conceptual designs and schematics, all three-dimensionally projected in neon holograms. Together they created the illusion of being inside some kind of gigantic workshop.

"What do you think, gentlemen?" Colani asked, his hands extended low to his sides as if he had completed a magic trick.

"It's incredible, sir!" said Keithan, still gaping. He and his father turned around on the spot, looking at everything projected.

Colani moved to the center of the room. "This is where I come up with most of my ideas and develop them before I manufacture them. This room gives me no limits. I can create anything I want here, as big as I want it, and as complex as I want it. Let me show you. Computer, show library."

Both Keithan and his father stepped back when a 3-D sphere composed of infinite file icons appeared out of thin air in front of Colani. The hologram grew up to three feet in diameter. Colani made it spin with a swing of his hands about three times then made it stop.

Following that, he reached for one of its files, and in response, the sphere disappeared, and a three-dimensional design of what Keithan recognized as a jet engine appeared along with numerous schematics of the same design around it.

"This here, gentlemen, is one of the things I wanted to show you." Colani stepped aside for Keithan and his father to see better. "It's an original design Adalina helped me improve for the twin-fuselage airliners built by Pegasus. She and I worked on it for a couple of years, doing our best to make it much lighter but still as effective as its previous model."

"I remember this," Keithan's dad said, stepping closer to the image. "I even have pictures of you, sir, with Adalina during the public unveiling."

"And that's not all she helped me with," Colani continued. He turned back to the holographic image and said, "Computer, open all design documents involving Adalina Zambrana's participation."

There was a bright flash in the room, and a gallery of 3-D schematics appeared, floating in the room. There were over a dozen designs all around them now, from different conceptual racing aircraft to large commercial airliner concepts that had yet to see the light of day. For Keithan, it now felt like standing inside a virtual museum of aviation. Staring at it all with wonder, just like his father next to him, he could only wish Fernando and Mr. Aramis were here too. Without a doubt, this would have taken their breath away.

Colani took his time to briefly show Keithan and his father some of the aircraft concept designs. According to him, Keithan's mom had contributed to all of these, either during their initial phases or during their developmental ones. Curiously, among other designs Colani showed them, was a wide hover platform capable of carrying approximately twenty people. The design didn't seem impressive at first, but Keithan and his father raised their eyebrows when Colani explained the idea behind it.

"The purpose is to provide a new experience of sightseeing for tourists at famous landmarks," Colani explained. "Take, for instance, the Grand Canyon in Arizona and the ancient city of Machu Picchu in Peru. Imagine seeing such places from different altitudes, and all the while holding on to the railing of a hovering platform such as this one."

Keithan let out a whistle. "Is this already being built?"

"Not yet, I'm afraid," Colani answered. "I'm still working on a few safety issues with my engineering consultants. Plus, I'm still in negotiations with different governments to approve the project for permissions and funding."

Keithan made sure not to miss any of the other things Colani showed them. He looked carefully at every schematic and concept design projected in the room. All the while, he tried to spot anything that might seem suspicious or perhaps threatening in any way. So far, he hadn't seen anything of the sort, which reminded him once again of what he'd been wondering right from the start: What if the Sky Phantom Legion was wrong about Colani? What if the man wasn't actually planning any threat behind his air race as the Legion suspected?

At least one thing had been clear to Keithan: he *had* to find the answers to those questions tonight and report them as soon as possible to the Legion.

Disappointingly, Colani still hadn't mentioned a thing about tomorrow's race. The man was still caught up with talking about Keithan's mother and how great she had been. Despite this, Keithan reminded himself of what Dantés had told him at her office. "Persuade him to tell you as much as he can about what he's planning to do tomorrow during the air race, with its spherical drones, his secret project, everything."

Colani, who still stood at the center of the room, continued moving his hands around like a magician. He slid aside more hovering concept projects around him and opened new ones. These, the Pegasus CEO explained, were some of his most recent designs. He was about to open one of them when Keithan interrupted him.

"Wait! What about *that* one?" Keithan pointed at a digital file that had the picture of a familiar design.

"Oh, this one here," Colani said. "This is my latest innovation for this year's Pegasus Air Race."

Just like the rest of the files they had seen so far, this one didn't have a name. It only had an ID code. Colani brought it closer to them with a pulling gesture and touched it. The file opened, and a series of 3-D schematics popped out.

"I'm sure you folks are familiar with this," Colani said. "This is actually the first concept I made of the spherical camera drones that'll be broadcasting tomorrow's race."

Keithan beamed. Now he was getting somewhere.

He stared at the holographic design. The spherical drone looked slightly different than the actual drones that were already flying all over Ramey. This one looked like it was in its initial phase even though it also showed its main features, like its rotary propulsion system and the camera lens at its front.

Keithan approached the hologram and looked at Colani. "May I?"

"*Sicuro*," the man said with a nod.

Keithan extended his hands and slid aside schematic after schematic of the drone design. Then he stopped and zoomed in on the one he wanted to see. It was a clear cross-section of the drone, which revealed its whole inside mechanisms along with numerous text specifications. But just as Keithan had expected, the schematics didn't show any weapon hidden inside the drone. Not even the slightest evidence of a laser cannon like the ones that had been hidden in the two wrecked drones the Sky Phantoms had secretly captured. Keithan had seen them with his own eyes two days ago when Lieutenant Colonel Lanzard and Dantés had taken him to the Legion's hidden base.

His dad stepped closer. "What are you looking for?"

Keithan hesitated. "Just wanted to see its rotary propulsion system," he lied. "I heard rumors these things—the real ones—can change direction really fast while in the air."

"They sure can," Colani said, stepping in. "They're quite the little fliers, these beauties. They're also programmed to independently detect the racers and follow them at high speeds. Still, they're not fully independent. A camera crew, which will be located in each of the strategic points throughout the racecourse, will be controlling them to provide the best shots for viewers.

"You just wait and see, gentlemen. These innovative beauties are just a piece of the whole unforgettable experience I have planned for tomorrow's grand race!"

The way Colani said it showed how excited he was for tomorrow to come. His brown eyes seemed to reveal a little kid inside him, waiting for his big surprise to be revealed already.

Keithan's dad seemed to be infected by Colani's excitement, though Keithan knew it was more due to the intrigue Colani's words suggested. It was that same intrigue that was making Keithan anxious.

"*A piece of the whole unforgettable experience I have planned,*" Keithan repeated in his head. Whether or not the comment meant something good or bad, Keithan wasn't sure, but he knew he had to persuade Colani now.

Keithan's gut feeling kept telling him to just ask.

"Sir, are all the camera drones related to what William Aramis is working on with you?" For a moment Keithan didn't believe he had dared to finally ask the question.

Colani seemed to have done a double take. "Excuse me?"

"William Aramis? He's my best friend's dad," Keithan clarified. "Isn't he doing a top-secret project for Pegasus? You know, the one you're planning to reveal tomorrow in the air race?"

"Um, sorry, Keithan, but I have no idea who you're talking about," Colani said.

This time it was Keithan who did a double take. "You mean you don't know who …? What he's …?"

Colani frowned, shaking his head. "I've never met anyone named William Aramis."

Keithan felt at a loss, but suddenly he gulped, and his eyes widened at the dreadful realization.

Giovanni Colani didn't have a clue of what was being plotted behind his Pegasus Air Race.

—(-O-)—

The end of the night was drawing near. William Aramis realized it when he saw the time on the crusted steampunk-style clock that hung at the far wall of his private workshop. There were only two hours left before midnight. No wonder he felt exhausted. Still, William was determined not to leave the workshop until he made sure everything was set for tomorrow.

He headed to the left wall. There, he pulled down a lever and watched with pride as his top-secret project descended slowly into a steel safe underneath the concrete floor. Tonight would be the last night he would keep it there, since tomorrow he and Pegasus Company would reveal it to the rest of the world.

The Daedalus Project. William's latest and greatest work.

Once the project was fully underground, the safe's top, which was camouflaged with the same smooth concrete as the rest of the floor, sealed shut. A clink underneath followed, confirming it had locked.

"Almost done," William said to himself, rubbing his hands with satisfaction. He couldn't help yawning as he said it.

There was only one thing left to check, and so he turned to the MA robot, which stood to his right.

"Emmeiseven, show the unveiling sequence I uploaded to your

memory last Wednesday."

The MA robot, which now had all of its sleek white-and-gold coverings cleaned up for tomorrow's unveiling, was supposed to respond, but for some reason it didn't. Instead, it remained still with its gauntleted arms resting at either side. Even the front screen on its head, where its current status and other data were usually displayed, remained black.

"Emmeiseven?"

William repeated the command, only this time he added, "Confirm command."

Still, the robot didn't respond.

William exhaled, running a hand down his face. "I don't have time for this."

He so desperately wanted to leave already, especially since he had to wake up before dawn. He couldn't afford to deal with this unexpected problem in the morning, much less when he knew he wouldn't be able to rest at all if he didn't take care of it now.

William wasted no time and turned to his laptube on the worktable at the center of the room, along with the usual clutter of spare parts and tools. The laptube, a truncated cylindrical computer no bigger than a spray can, projected a holo screen on its top between two small projectors that stood out vertically at either end. Touching the screen with his fingertips, William tried to access a wireless connection with Emmeiseven's memory, but to his surprise, no connection was available.

Once again, another deep sigh escaped William as he fought his frustration. "I *really* don't need this right now!"

Not ready to give up yet, he grabbed a network wire and plugged one end into his laptube and the other to the side of Emmeiseven's head.

"Here we go. Let's get this over with," he murmured.

He accessed the robot's memory and opened the digital document he wanted to see. He wasn't ready for what he found next.

"What the …?"

The laptube's holo screen showed him the unveiling sequence he had uploaded into Emmeiseven two days ago, but somehow, it had been completely overwritten.

William looked from the laptube to Emmeiseven and back at the laptube. All the while, the robot didn't even blip.

"What's … *this?*"

William leaned closer to the holo screen. The sequence he was now staring at was nothing like the one he had designed. What it contained was even more puzzling.

"Phase One," he read. "Date of execution: Saturday, May 1, 2055. Targets—" He shook his head and leaned even closer to the screen in disbelief. *"Targets?"*

William scrolled down the digital page and immediately saw a list of names—people's names—he recognized right away. But that still didn't shock William as much as what he read below the list:

Requirement: Daedalus Project 23-9-14-7-19

"The Daedalus—?"

William didn't get to finish the thought, for in that moment, something struck him on the side of the head. He fell hard on his knees, though he managed to support himself with one hand while he reached out to where he felt the hit with the other.

Just then, the towering figure of Emmeiseven approached him. William instantly crossed his arms in front of his face, expecting the robot to attack him again. But this time, Emmeiseven swung one of its gauntleted arms over William's head and hit the laptube and different spare parts and tools that lay near it, sending them all flying across the workshop.

"NO!" William cried in horror as the laptube smashed against the wall.

Emmeiseven proceeded to grab the worktable with both metal claws and lifted it from one side as if it weighed nothing, right before throwing it against the opposite wall. More spare parts and tools went flying before clattering all over the floor. Soon after that, the out-of-control robot lowered itself and landed one of its wide clawed hands hard on the secret safe's concrete top on the floor.

William's eyes widened. Emmeiseven was trying to get to the Daedalus Project. William had no clue why, but he was certain it had something to do with what had been overwritten inside the robot's memory.

Shaking off the pain in his head, William grabbed a large wrench lying next to him, and with all his strength, he sprang toward the robot. But Emmeiseven was too fast for him. Despite having been standing with its back toward him, it seemed to have sensed him coming. Its torso straightened up abruptly and turned 180 degrees, all in one swift movement that allowed Emmeiseven to grab William's right wrist.

"Aaargh!" William shrieked, feeling the robot's strength, which forced him to drop the wrench.

His feet left the ground as Emmeiseven lifted him like a fish that had just been caught.

"Why ... are you ... *doing this?*" he struggled to say while still dangling.

Of course, the question was in vain. There was no point in trying to make the robot see reason.

With his face now level with the robot's head, William's eyes stared in terror as the curved screen now showed only three neon-green words flashing nonstop:

PHASE ONE INITIATED

William opened his mouth but never got the chance to cry for help. The last thing he saw was a clawed metal fist fly straight toward his face. Then everything went black.

RACE DAY

CHAPTER 10

It was supposed to be an unforgettable day at Ramey, considering it was the day many people had been waiting for. The day of the grand 2055 Pegasus Air Race! Yet for Keithan, the term "unforgettable" didn't mean something good, for even though he had been looking forward to this day, he couldn't stop wondering if the event was meant to go wrong, terribly wrong.

Such thoughts kept Keithan from sleeping much, to the point where he didn't even need his alarm, which he had set for 8 a.m. He had woken up two whole hours earlier due to his worrying, and he hadn't gotten out of bed yet. His legs were still hidden under the bedspread while he tried to contact Professor Dantés for the fifth time this morning. He'd been trying to contact her ever since he and his dad had left Colani's airship last night. He'd tried contacting the professor in every single way technology could make it possible—phone call, texting, online, but for some weird reason, nothing was working.

Frustrated, Keithan tried one last time, but once again he got no connection. His brand-new wrist communicator, which he kept on speaker, ended up sounding the busy tone after a few seconds of ringing. The main screen of the device showed him in bright orange letters the same words that had been appearing since they got home: "Signal Interference Detected."

Professor Dantés had to be waiting for him to contact her, and Keithan knew he was running out of time—the air race was meant to start in a few hours.

Maybe it's her communicator, Keithan thought. Still, that didn't explain why no type of communication was working.

He put his theory to the test. "Call Fernando," he said, holding the wrist communicator close to his mouth.

His friend's name, along with the contact number, appeared on the device's mini screen, but only for an instant before they were replaced by the "Signal Interference Detected" notice. The same thing happened when he tried contacting Marianna.

"Man!" Keithan grumbled and punched the mattress.

He had no choice. He had to get to the airport as soon as possible. He threw his bedspread aside before he jumped out of the queen platform bed and changed his clothes as fast as he could.

The last thing he put on was his brown racing leather jacket, and soon he was out of the house and on his hubless magnetic bicycle. He drank a bottle of pineapple juice with one hand while he pedaled with all his might. The sky was bright blue, with white bloated cumulus clouds that were only visible in the horizon far to the south.

Keithan thought about his dad on the way to the airport. Any moment now, the man would wake up and find one of the two gold VIP passes for the air race Colani had given them last night pinched with a magnet on the refrigerator and with a note on which Keithan let him know he'd already left.

Drops of sweat trickled down Keithan's forehead while he pedaled, forcing him to wipe them off with the back of his hand every now and then. Still, that didn't slow him down. If anything did, it was the huge crowd Keithan found as soon as he saw the airport's surrounding chain-link fence.

The outskirts of the north end of Ramey Airport was packed with air racing aficionados from all over the globe. There were people in vehicles and people on foot. It seemed that the crowd had multiplied tenfold overnight. Never had Keithan seen so many people at Ramey. It actually turned into a challenge for him, since he had a hard time making his way through the crowd even while riding his bike down the sidewalk.

"Excuse me! Coming through! Excuse me!" Keithan repeated aloud almost nonstop while still pedaling hard.

"Hey! Watch it, kid!" some people yelled at him.

To make matters worse, the only entrance of Ramey Airport open today was the one farthest at the west, facing Borinquen Avenue and Ramey's golf course. No wonder the vehicles that were bumper to bumper throughout Hangar Road barely moved. Keithan kept pedaling. Soon he passed Rocket's Diner on his right. A few minutes later, the golf course came into view as Keithan approached Borinquen Avenue. He could see it was much more packed with people—men, women, boys and girls, even a few pet dogs and cats that had already settled in with their masters to enjoy the day's event.

"Man! This is crazy!" Keithan said under heavy breaths while zigzagging through the crowd.

The airport's west entrance was now near to his left. As expected, the closer he got to it, the more agglomerated the crowd was. There, Keithan had no choice but to dismount his bike and continue walking with it beside him. The endless line of vehicles waiting to enter the airport looked like a narrow trail compared to the amount of people who were trying to do the same on foot. People were so close to each other that most of the little kids Keithan spotted were forced to remain on top of their parents' shoulders while they waited under the intense heat of the day. Surprisingly, nobody seemed to be complaining. Everybody looked excited to be there. That is, everybody except Keithan, of course, whose mind at the moment was only on his hopes of finding Dantés once he stepped onto the airfield.

It took approximately forty-five minutes for him to finally make it into the airport, and that was only thanks to his gold VIP pass, which granted him access through a small exclusive entrance. Once Keithan set foot on the airfield, he mounted his bicycle again and pedaled as fast as he could. He glanced at the checkered arch that was the start gantry. It had been raised in the middle of the runway and was accompanied by hundreds of flapping teardrop flags spread throughout the runway. He also glanced at the grandstands, which were starting to fill with people. Yet Keithan remained focused on heading straight to where he hoped he would find Dantés.

Past the line of main hangars and a pair of parked twin-fuselage airliners was the only hangar in the airport that wasn't identified with a name or a number. The building, made of low concrete walls and an arched aluminum roof with no skylight, stood a good distance away from where everything related to the race was happening.

"Let there be someone there. *Please* let there be someone there," he said under heavy breaths.

He pressed his brakes and skidded his bike to a halt right in front of the building's giant door.

"Hello! Somebody? *Anybody?*" he shouted, each time louder while he pounded on the door, but no one answered.

Fighting his desperation, he turned his gaze to the airfield. Loud music played out there while people gradually continued filling the grandstands located at the other side of the main runway. Keithan could see the grandstands already half filled, which worried him more since it meant he had little time left to warn Dantés and the Legion.

But what could he do? Where could he find Dantés and the Sky Phantoms if not at the hangar? No way would he find the professor out there among the crowd. He needed help, and he needed it fast.

Keithan started pedaling again. He rode eastward as fast as his strength allowed him and didn't stop until he reached Hangar H11.

He hadn't reached it yet and immediately exhaled in frustration when he noticed that its entrance was also closed. Had the Aramises left already? Still, with what little hope he had, Keithan rode his bike around the hangar and headed to the back, toward the residential half.

The door there was open to Keithan's relief, and so he let his bike drop on the patch of lawn in front of the house and hurried to the door. No sooner had he set foot inside the house than Laika, the Aramises' fully grown golden retriever, received him. Her barking came before she appeared, rushing toward him. She was wagging her tail very fast. Keithan hadn't even walked past the entrance hall and called for his friends when Laika landed her front paws on his blue shirt.

"Whoa! Easy now, girl," said Keithan, almost losing his balance. He couldn't stop Laika from licking his face until he grabbed her front legs and gently made her stand on all fours again. "Where are Fernando and Marianna?"

Laika seemed to have understood because she turned around and headed to the kitchen, where Keithan could hear several voices.

He followed her and found his friends seated at the dining table having breakfast. Their mom was in the kitchen too. She was a tall woman with long hair as blonde as Fernando's and dressed in weathered denim overalls. She kept moving around in a hurry, a cup of coffee in one hand while she continued serving.

"Keithan, dear," said Mrs. Aramis, suddenly stepping aside to avoid stumbling over Laika before she placed a plate of toast on the table.

Both Marianna and Fernando raised their gazes.

"Hey, guys," Keithan said with a lazy wave. He was still panting, what with all the riding he had done, not to mention Laika's greeting.

"Mm. Wan' s'me?" said Fernando, his mouth full of toast.

"Mom made waffles too," Marianna added, showing Keithan her plate. Like her brother, she was eating fast, as if wanting to finish quickly.

"We're in a bit of a hurry, but it's just because of the excitement of the race," Mrs. Aramis said. "We still have enough time before we have to leave."

Keithan considered taking a seat and grabbing a plate but shook his head instead.

"I'm good. Thanks," he replied quickly. "Listen, guys, I tried contacting you with my communicator earlier this morning, but for some reason I couldn't."

"See? There *is* something wrong with all the communications at Ramey," Marianna told her brother before she looked back at Keithan. "We don't know why it's happening. It started last night."

"We tried to call you too, Keithan, but there seems to be some weird interference blocking all communication signals," Fernando said. "We wanted to know how it went last night with Colani."

"Oh, that's right!" Mrs. Aramis said, looking at Keithan. She had finally taken a seat to have breakfast. "Fernando and Marianna told me you and your dad were invited to the Pegasus CEO's airship last night. How did it go?"

"Yeah. How'd it go?" Marianna said.

Keithan, who still stood in front of the dining table, scratched the back of his head. "Well ..."

"Did Colani show you his collections?" Fernando interrupted, sounding more insistent than his mother and sister. "I've heard the man has an awesome digital display of—"

"Um, guys, I'm afraid I don't bring good news about it," Keithan cut him off.

The three Aramises exchanged perplexed looks before they looked at Keithan again.

"What do you mean?" Marianna asked.

Keithan took a deep breath and exhaled. "It has to do with your dad's secret project ... the Daedalus Project. Giovanni Colani doesn't know anything about it."

His friends didn't react; they seemed to still be trying to make sense of what Keithan had just told them. Silence settled in the kitchen, disrupted only by the soft splashing of the water Laika was drinking from her bowl in a corner.

"What are you talking about?" Mrs. Aramis said. "How could Colani not know about the project when William has been working for him?"

"No, he hasn't," Keithan assured her. "Colani doesn't even know Mr. Aramis."

"What?!" Fernando and Marianna burst out in unison.

Keithan decided it was best to be straightforward. "The two of them have never met. Fernando, you said so yourself."

Both Marianna and Mrs. Aramis turned to Fernando, still looking confused.

"Whoa, Keithan! All I said was that they've never met in person," Fernando quickly clarified.

Keithan tucked in his lips in frustration. He knew he was wasting valuable time.

"Look, I know it doesn't make sense, but you gotta believe me," he said, more insistent now. "The Daedalus Project might've been started behind Colani's back. However, one thing we know for certain is that it was being supervised by the air racer Drostan Luzier, who we *do* know has been working with your dad. The question is, why would Colani not be involved in the project in any way? Especially since, as Mr. Aramis told us, it's planned to be revealed today, sometime during the Pegasus Air Race ... or before it." Keithan paused to look at each of the Aramises. "Think about it, guys, Mrs. Aramis. Doesn't all this seem too fishy to you?"

The three Aramises still looked at him with skepticism.

"Anyhow," Keithan went on, "since I left Colani's airship last night, I've been trying to contact Professor Dantés to report what I found out, but like with you guys, I haven't been able to—"

Mrs. Aramis cut him off. "Wait. Professor Dantés? Where does she fit in all this?"

Keithan hesitated. He'd been in such a hurry to explain everything to his friends that he had completely forgotten Mrs. Aramis didn't know the truth about what was happening—especially about the existence of the Sky Phantom Legion. Luckily for him, Marianna stepped in at the sight of her mother's deep frown.

"Yeah, about that, Mom," said the girl, giving Keithan a warning look. "The less you know, the better."

Fernando, who had taken his last bite of waffles, pushed his wheelchair away from the dining table and said, "Keithan, I'm pretty sure you're blowing all this out of proportion—and the You-Know-What Legion too."

Keithan rolled his eyes. He couldn't keep explaining anymore. He needed to take action now, and more than that, get results. "Fine. Let's go ask your dad, then. Where is he?"

A response didn't come right away.

"Yeah, where is Dad?" Marianna asked her mom.

Mrs. Aramis shrugged, taking her last sip of coffee. "Mm, actually, I haven't seen him this morning," she said.

"He must've gotten up early to prepare the project for the unveiling," Fernando suggested.

"So he must be in his workshop right now," Mrs. Aramis said. "He couldn't have left yet. Not when he wanted to show us the Daedalus Project first."

"Come on, Keithan," Fernando said. "Let's put all doubts to rest." He was now moving with his wheelchair toward the doorway behind him.

Keithan followed him, and so did Marianna and her mom. Even Laika joined them, despite now having the perfect opportunity to reach up to the table without being caught and snatch one of the waffles that had been left there.

Beyond the doorway, the five of them passed by Mr. Aramis's weird-looking aircraft prototypes in the hangar bay, among these a roughly built saucer with a small engine and vertical stabilizer at its top and the one that resembled a robotic spider with wings. Keithan and Fernando's *d'Artagnan* sat at the far end of the hangar. Curiously, the whole area was awfully quiet, which was unusual when Mr. Aramis was there. Still, Keithan and his friends continued moving toward the yellow strip curtain of the man's private workshop at the back. None of them were prepared for what they found on the other side.

The workshop was a total mess. Not just a mess, since Keithan and his friends knew how disorganized Mr. Aramis used to be in there, but much, much worse. It looked as if a tornado had emerged from the center of the area and unleashed its fury.

"What on earth …?" Fernando said, his words trailing off as he passed through the curtain.

Right behind him, Keithan and Marianna gaped in shock. As for Mrs. Aramis, she clutched her chest with both hands.

"Laika, stay outside. *Stay*," Marianna insisted, holding a hand in front of the golden retriever from the other side of the strip curtain.

Laika barked.

"What … happened here?" said Mrs. Aramis, still in shock. "William?" she called aloud. "William!"

Marianna, a worried look evident on her face, held her mother's arm with trembling hands. "He's not here, Mom."

Near them, Keithan stared at the mess, unable to say a word. He was also having a hard time trying to make sense of the scene. Tools, big and small, lay scattered all over the workshop floor as if they had rained down. Shards of the LED light bulbs of the lamps dangling low above them lay all over the place too. Not a single bulb had been spared. If not for the skylights high in the arched ceiling, Keithan and his friends wouldn't have been able to see a thing. Still, that was nothing compared to the strange sight of the large machines, which now looked far from operable. From the metal sheet roller to the tube bender, the 3-D printer and the nitrogen laser cutter, all of them were now either bent and had deep dents or had been torn apart like cheap plastic toys. It was so hard to believe that it looked more as if a beast had entered the workshop and smashed everything in there in an unexplainable rage.

A few sparks from a group of loose cables made Keithan and his friends jump.

"Ouch!" Keithan shouted when a spark landed on his left arm.

"Careful," said Fernando.

Keithan made his way slowly over the tools on the floor and approached the metal worktable that used to be at the center of the workshop. The thing now lay overturned against the right wall. More shocking still, it was bent like a half-open book, its remaining two legs now looking like twist ties.

"You guys didn't hear anything last night?" Keithan asked over his shoulder.

"Not a thing," Marianna replied while still looking around.

Fernando and Mrs. Aramis shook their heads.

"The walls that divide the hangar from the house have strong sound insulators," Fernando explained.

Of the three Aramises, Mrs. Aramis looked the most affected by the scene. Just like the rest of them, she was trying to make sense of what had happened, but her eyes had turned red and swollen. She bent down and picked up something from the floor.

"Dad's communicator," said Fernando, recognizing the remains of what had been the pocket-size device now in his mother's hand.

Keithan and Marianna stared at it too. Mrs. Aramis held on to it as if it were the last thing that was left of her husband. She reached into one of the side pockets of her jeans and pulled out her communicator to dial on it.

"Mom—" said Marianna, still holding her mother's arm.

"Hold on."

"But, Mom, you can't—"

"We *have* to call airport security, Marianna!"

"*Mom*," said Fernando, trying to bring his mother to her senses. "It's no use. None of the communications are working." He was already checking his wrist communicator to make sure he was right.

Still, Mrs. Aramis didn't react until she heard the busy tone in her device. Her hands were shaking, and her breathing had turned heavier and faster. Keithan feared she was starting to panic.

"Mom?" Marianna said.

Mrs. Aramis didn't reply. After a short moment of silence, she tucked her communicator back into her pocket and pulled out a smart key. And with an unexpected look of determination, she said, "I'm heading out to get help."

Keithan, Marianna, and Fernando could see she was struggling to avoid shedding tears despite her sudden change of attitude, but they didn't make any comment.

"I want you guys to lock the whole hangar as soon as I'm out in the van," Mrs. Aramis ordered. "Fernando, Marianna, check the door at your dad's office too. No one comes in and no one comes out until I come back."

"But—"

"No *buts*, Fernando," Mrs. Aramis said sharply over her shoulder. "No one comes in and no one comes out. *I mean it!*"

She had already passed through the strip curtain of the workshop, marching at a quick pace. Keithan and his friends stepped out of the workshop and saw an excited Laika following Mrs. Aramis, who was now hurrying to the scarlet minivan parked in the middle of the hangar.

"Not this time, Laika," Mrs. Aramis said, gesturing her to stay behind.

It took a few seconds for Laika to obey, and once she did, she headed back to Fernando, Marianna, and Keithan.

Just as Mrs. Aramis turned on the ignition, the giant door at the far end of the hangar began to rise, and as soon as it was high enough, the minivan accelerated in reverse.

A loud screech of tires followed when Mrs. Aramis forced the vehicle to do a tight 180-degree turn. Then she accelerated again.

Fernando, Marianna, and Laika remained unmoving in the middle of the hangar while they watched the scarlet minivan shrinking in the distance under the sunlight. Keithan, on the other hand, shook his head, not letting the confusion of the moment make him lose his focus. He and his friends had a lot to do now, and they had to do it fast. Keithan turned around and hurried back to the workshop.

"Go close the hangar door and everything else, guys!" he shouted. "Meet me back in the workshop! *Hurry!*"

He didn't wait for them to respond. He simply kept running until he reached the strip curtain.

Once inside the workshop, Keithan began to look for clues. There had to be something in there that could tell him what had really happened, anything that could reveal what had happened to Mr. Aramis. No way this could have been the man's doing, but whatever the reason, Keithan feared it might have been related to the so-called Daedalus Project.

Fernando and Marianna appeared minutes later. Marianna headed to the left side of the workshop while her brother stopped his wheelchair behind Keithan.

"Did you find anything?" Fernando asked.

Keithan nodded. He was crouched in front of the bent worktable.

His right hand rested on its metal surface, where four scratch marks stretched almost two feet. He raised his gaze and looked at the similar scratch marks around the room. On the walls, on the broken machines, on the bent nitrogen and gas tanks lying on the floor …

Like a creature with claws, Keithan was sure. Then it hit him.

"This had to be Emmeiseven," he said.

He looked at Fernando over his shoulder. Fernando, with a fist pressed against his mouth, simply responded with a nod.

"Guys, look!" Marianna called.

She was crouched at the other side of the workshop, pushing scrap parts aside, but then she rose and turned around. In her hands was a very familiar tubular device.

"Dad's laptube!" Fernando said. He quickly turned his wheelchair and moved it as best he could over the mess of tools on the floor. "Give it here!"

Marianna handed it over. "I don't think it'll be of any use now."

"Actually, it could," Fernando countered.

Keithan and Marianna stared, puzzled, while Fernando studied the laptube. Its black rubber casing seemed to have done little to protect it since the device was broken in half. It was missing one of its projectors too, but the cable that dangled from one of the ends turned out to be what caught Fernando's attention the most. He lifted it and showed it to Keithan and Marianna.

"What about it?" Keithan said.

"This is the cable to plug into Emmeiseven's memory," Fernando said. "It's an alternate connection to the robot's memory aside from its wireless access. I recognize it because it was designed exclusively for an MA unit robot. But look at this."

He raised the end of the cable to show them the unique five-pin connector design.

Marianna frowned. "So?"

She didn't see what Fernando was actually showing them, unlike Keithan, who reached out and took the cable.

"The connector; it's hanging loose from the cable," Keithan said.

"The only way this could have happened is if it was yanked out of its plug."

"Which means it might've been plugged into Emmeiseven before the laptube was broken," Fernando said. "And that means ..."

Marianna snapped her fingers. "We might be able to access the last commands Emmeiseven activated in its memory—before the laptube was broken!"

Keithan beamed. "Guys, that's brilliant!"

Almost instinctively, Fernando opened the broken laptube to try to reach its hard drive. Marianna, who didn't wait for his approval, helped him. Meanwhile, Keithan watched anxiously. To their luck, the hard drive was half loose inside and still intact, and seconds later, Fernando managed to pull it out.

"Aha!" he cried. He now held with his index finger and thumb a small cubic piece made of tiny green and silver parts.

"Do you have an adapter for it?" Marianna asked.

Fernando was already one step ahead. "Yup. Hold on."

Fernando, techie, resourceful, and genius as always, quickly opened a small panel on the side of one of his wheelchair's armrests and pulled out a cable, which he connected to the cubic hard drive. He flicked a switch on the other armrest, and a rectangular holographic screen flickered to life four feet in front of him.

"Let's just hope my system reads it," Fernando said, more to himself than to Keithan and Marianna.

Already he had taken out his data pad from the back of his chair and placed it on his lap. The device, which was connected wirelessly to his wheelchair, showed a digital keyboard on which Fernando began typing fast, working his magic. At the same time, numerous command codes grew from left to right in a cyan text on the deep blue background of the hovering holo screen.

"And ... got it!" Fernando exclaimed.

The image on the screen changed. Keithan read aloud the title at the top ...

"Daedalus Project 23-9-14-7-19: Unveiling Sequence."

He felt his heart accelerate as the intrigue intensified inside him.

Fernando leaned forward next to him, his eyes narrowed. "It seems to be a document that was uploaded into Emmeiseven's memory a few days ago. According to the data, it's the last thing Dad accessed from his laptube, but— Whoa! What's *this*?"

Fernando, who'd been scrolling down the image, suddenly stopped. Beside him, Keithan and Marianna stared, just as intrigued as him when they saw what was now on the screen.

"Phase One?" Marianna read aloud.

"What does that mean?" Keithan asked.

Like his friends, he stared at the holo screen without blinking, but his eyes boggled when he read what appeared below it. It was a list of names titled with a single word: Targets. Still, that alone wasn't what shocked Keithan and his friends—it was the fact that the names on the list were none other than those of the sixteen pro air racers who would be competing today in the Pegasus Air Race.

Now, more than ever, Keithan knew what he had to do. He turned to his friends with a deep look of dread and said it ...

"We gotta warn the Sky Phantom Legion ... whatever it takes."

Forty-one miles off the west coast of Ramey, the top-secret base deep inside Mona Island had just gone on high alert. Every Sky Phantom agent in there rushed to his or her designated area. The unusual readings on their radars had been the cause of the sudden urgency. It had automatically made Lieutenant Colonel Lanzard trigger the klaxons that now blared throughout the base. Red lights flashed in every room, office, and tunnel along with the loud sound. Yet it was the lieutenant colonel's deep, strong voice that confirmed to everybody that this was no drill. He summoned his elite force through every speaker inside the base.

"Phantom knights, report to bay area! Phantom knights, report to bay area!"

This elite group, always ready for action, consisted of highly trained fighter pilots clad in the most advanced flying unisuits the world did not know about. Each of these unisuits, which were made of strong but light black leather and matching carbon fiber fabric, included a flexible screen and micro projectors on the left sleeves that showed numerous digital keys and holographic readouts, which could also be synced to the pilot's aircraft.

The pilots, twenty-five in total, raced down the tunnels. Technicians, officers, and lab engineers quickly pressed themselves against the walls to allow them to pass through. Soon the elite force reached the bay, where much activity was going on, primarily around the line of super-advanced fighter aircraft that were being prepped. A set of high-tech black helmets already awaited the group on a long metal table, and one by one, each pilot grabbed one without stopping.

Thirty feet in front of them and the squadron of fighter aircraft, waited the very man who had summoned them. Lieutenant Colonel Lanzard was wearing his black tech suit with chrome shoulder patches and a silver aiguillette that hung from his right shoulder and under his arm. He stood straight with his hands behind his back and his feet separated shoulder width apart.

"Knights, gather around!" the colonel ordered over the noise of engines behind him. The twenty-five pilots did as they were told, each one holding his or her helmet under one arm.

"Listen up. Radarscopes have detected an anomaly overflying the Atlantic at approximately sixty miles northeast. We have no idea where it came from or what it could be. However, we do know the thing is moving gradually southwest, most likely heading to Ramey."

"How big are we talking, Colonel?" asked a tall female pilot with chestnut hair held in a tight bun.

"An absurdly large bogey," Lanzard clarified. "According to radars, it's bigger than a soccer stadium."

"And we haven't the slightest idea where it came from?" asked a male pilot in disbelief.

"That's one of my biggest concerns," Lanzard responded. "The giant anomaly simply appeared on our radars without a point of origin.

The worst part is that the thing somehow continues to disappear and reappear on our radars."

The knights raised their eyebrows. Some even flinched and exchanged looks that clearly showed they hadn't been expecting this. Still, they continued listening to the colonel's briefing.

"You heard right, knights. We are dealing with something that seems to have some kind of cloaking technology, perhaps somewhat similar to ours."

"Colonel, is there someone else aware of it? National Security, Air Force?" asked one of the pilots at the back of the group.

Lanzard shook his head. "Most likely nobody else has spotted it yet. So your mission is simple, knights: find out what we are dealing with and stop it from continuing its course—no matter what.

"Now, I want a small squadron of three knights to leave first. To this squadron, I need you to send a visual back here to base as soon as you find it. I want to see exactly what we're dealing with. Its strange behavior with our radarscopes is more than enough reason to consider it a possible threat. And no matter if its crew identifies itself, we will not, I repeat, we *will not* allow it to reach Puerto Rican airspace. You have permission to engage it if necessary. As for the rest of you, be ready to join them. Any questions?"

No one replied. Lanzard nodded with a determined expression.

"All right, knights, move out!"

With the approval of the ground crew, the first team of the elite force climbed into the cockpit of three of the Sky Phantom fighters. Their canopies sealed shut as the frameless edges melted into the semitranslucent fuselages. This made the three craft look now as if they had no cockpit canopy at all, for even those had no transparency when seen from the outside.

Meanwhile, from somewhere inside the bay, a motor came to life over all other sounds. A section of the high rock wall at the end of the bay began to open, slowly revealing the sea and the sky. One by one, the three Sky Phantoms that up till now had been hovering low and still shot out like bullets through the opening. None of their pilots heard their sonic booms, for in less than six seconds, they had already reached an altitude of five hundred feet above sea level and were far from the sound. And while maintaining a straight course at top speed and in a perfect V formation, the three Sky Phantom knights activated their fighter crafts' cloaking devices, instantly becoming what their names implied.

CHAPTER 11

I t had been far too long since the last time Alexandria Dantés had been in an event as big as the one that was happening today. She was standing in the crowd at the race's general public area at Ramey Airport, where the fun and the excitement were more than evident, like the contagious atmosphere at a carnival in broad daylight, in which people looked forward to seeing and enjoying everything.

All around, loud music played, and Alexandria could distinguish the intense smell of fresh buttered popcorn and cotton candy. Many people bought these and other snacks from the numerous tents behind the grandstands before they headed to their seats. Most of these people had been unable to resist purchasing the many souvenirs that were being offered too. Alexandria saw little kids with big smiles, carrying inflatable racing aircraft. Some of them even wore plastic helmets with cheap transparent visors and little plastic chromed wings sticking out at the sides—all while holding on to their parents' hands. As for the older kids and the adults, they carried colorful thundersticks in addition to the caps they wore with the distinguished chromed Pegasus Company logo at their fronts and a variety of T-shirts with flexed screens that showed the race's logo surrounded by animated racing aircraft.

Everything was quite overwhelming to Alexandria, and she had to admit it was somewhat intoxicating too. She couldn't deny it all reminded her of the days when she lived for this. When she had been an air racer herself, ready to give the crowd a great show. Deep inside her, she regretted those days were long gone.

But just as Alexandria started feeling that sense of longing, she shook her head. She couldn't afford to let herself be infected by the things around her. She ignored every seller who called out and gestured insistently for her to buy something. Unlike everyone else around her, Alexandria hadn't come to enjoy the show. She was on a mission, and her jeans and black shirt were only part of her disguise to blend in with the crowd as just another spectator and air racing aficionado. Because of that, she remained in her usual unamused character while she continued surveying the preparations for the upcoming race from behind her aviator shades.

She had been wandering through the general public area for nearly an hour now, but she still hadn't found anything unusual or suspicious. It worried her since it made her feel far from uncovering the truth behind the race. Adding to her worries was the fact that she hadn't been able to make contact with Keithan, whom she had hoped would have uncovered something about Pegasus and Colani. But it had been impossible with all the communications still disrupted throughout Ramey. She had waited for Keithan's call all night and earlier this morning, but she eventually gave up.

Now it was up to her and the rest of the Legion to find out the truth behind Pegasus and its race.

Suddenly, Alexandria heard someone calling out to her through the crowd, though not by her real name.

"Venus! *Venus!*"

She looked over her shoulder, and not far away, a blond man with a stubble beard came into view, struggling to get to her. Alexandria recognized him as another Sky Phantom agent despite his casual clothes.

"Agent Lynn," Alexandria said over the noise around them. "I thought you were supposed to be at the base."

The man exhaled, calming his breathing before he spoke. "Actually, I ... just got here from base. Lieutenant Colonel Lanzard ordered me to come since all communications are still disrupted here at Ramey. Are there any news yet about what's causing it?"

"I'm afraid not," Alexandria replied. "I can assure you, if this keeps up, I don't know if Pegasus will be able to proceed with its race—unless Pegasus is the one behind the communications disruption."

"Well, there's no time for that now. I'm headed to the racers' crew area, and you need to come with me."

Lynn hadn't yet finished saying this when he started moving again at a quick pace, clearly expecting Alexandria to follow.

"Wait. What's going on?" Alexandria asked.

"We now have something bigger to worry about, and we have to warn Agent Ravena and the rest of the crew."

At this, Alexandria reached out to Lynn's right arm and forced him to halt and face her.

"What do you mean 'bigger'?" she insisted, leaning closer to him.

Lynn looked around to make sure nobody was listening. Then he said in a low voice, "Base's radars detected a large bogey in the northeast headed our way, but our radars can't lock on it for some reason. It seems to keep disappearing and reappearing on our radars. Three Sky Phantoms were sent to intercept it."

The news took Alexandria completely by surprise, yet she managed to remain fully under control.

"Do you think the bogey could be related to the communications disruption here?" she asked, to which Lynn only shrugged with a look of concern evident on his face.

"What's our move, then?" she asked.

Lynn was straightforward. "First, we let Agent Ravena and his racing crew know. But whatever happens with the bogey, we stick to our operation. We are to keep watching Pegasus's every move here at Ramey during the whole event. Colonel's orders. As for Agent Ravena, he's air racing. Anything suspicious or threatening that any of the other air racers try, he still has orders to engage and let us know. Now, *come on*."

—(-O-)—

Miles away to the north, at 25,000 feet over the Atlantic, three conical vapor clouds with blue-and-white flames in their centers remained in perfect line formation while they flew northeastward at supersonic speed. It was all that could be seen of the currently invisible Sky Phantoms squadron. The leader, assigned the title of Phantom One, remained in the middle with his hands tight on the steering yokes. He kept looking back and forth from his radarscope to the intense blue sky outside his cockpit in the hopes of finding the mysterious bogey.

"Get ready to descend to fifteen thousand feet on my command," he said, addressing his two fellow wingmen through his helmet's integrated communicator.

"Roger that, Phantom One," his comrades replied.

In seconds, the three Sky Phantom fighters descended as if they were one through a thin layer of altostratus clouds. They were just settling at 15,000 feet when Lieutenant Colonel Lanzard's voice came through their communicators.

"Phantom One, this is Phantom Base. Have you spotted the bogey?"

"Negative, sir. Not— Wait a second."

Something had just become visible near the horizon, inside a giant white wall of cumulus clouds. It was a large gray silhouette, and it seemed to grow while the three Sky Phantoms approached it.

"Knights, bogey visible at twelve o'clock," Phantom One said quickly. "Confirm sight."

"Yes, sir," Phantom Two responded.

"I see it too, sir," Phantom Three followed.

Phantom One wasted no time to report. "Phantom Base, we've spotted the bogey ahead of us, coming our way. Stand by for visual."

"Copy— ...Phant—"

"Base, repeat."

"Cop— ...remain on—"

Static took over the lieutenant colonel's voice.

"How's this happening?" Phantom One grumbled even though he knew the familiar sound could only mean one thing.

"Knights, our channel frequency is being intercepted," he warned them. "It has to be the bogey. Stay sharp."

Phantom Two and Three acknowledged.

Phantom One flipped the trigger cover on each of his steering yokes without hesitation and kept an index finger over each one. Once again, he looked at his radarscope. For some strange reason, it still couldn't detect the bogey even though it was becoming clearer behind the wall of cumulus clouds. Meanwhile, the static coming from his communicator piece continued.

Then he started to make out an unfamiliar voice mixed with the static.

"Phantom Base, can you hear it?" Phantom One said without taking his eyes off the clouds on the horizon. "There seems to be a transmission intercepting our frequency. I can now make out a choppy voice mixed with the stat—"

But just as he said this, the static stopped, and Phantom One's sentence was held hanging when the small holographic image of a humanoid silhouette appeared in front of his head-up display.

"What the blazes ...?"

"Sir, what's going ...?" Phantom Three started to say, but just as it happened to his leader, his words trailed off.

The silhouette in the hologram spoke in what sounded like a Dutch accent. *"There is no need to remain on stealth mode. We can see you on our radars ... Sky Phantoms."*

The words were as shocking as the silhouette's mocking tone, which instantly brought a chill down Phantom One's spine.

That's impossible! he told himself in his head. *How could they have possibly spotted us?*

"Phantom Base," he said, struggling to remain focused, "are you receiving the transmission?"

He hoped to hear a confirmation from the lieutenant colonel, but instead, it was the silhouette who spoke.

"Yes. Your unique and advanced cloaking technology has finally been outsmarted."

"What are your intentions?" Phantom One dared to ask after a moment of silence.

The silhouette didn't hesitate to respond. *"Let's just say, for now, we just want you and the rest of the Legion to do exactly as we say."*

Phantom One narrowed his eyes and tightened his grip on his steering yokes.

"And what exactly do you mean by 'we'?" Phantom Three's voice interjected.

Pegasus, Phantom One realized, a feeling of dread suddenly running through him. "What makes you think we will comply?" he addressed the silhouette instead.

"The fact that we are prepared to take drastic measures if you don't. Now, you will allow our vessel headed your way to continue its course toward Ramey Airport. You are not to interfere in any way with the event that is soon to begin there and throughout the island of Puerto Rico."

"Sir?" Phantom Two called out to his leader.

Phantom One didn't respond, for at that moment he witnessed the large bogey they had been sent to find finally emerging from the clouds. The three Sky Phantom knights were still a good distance away from it, but Phantom One could tell right away Lieutenant Colonel Lanzard hadn't been mistaken. The craft was absurdly large, so large that it was hard to believe such a thing could fly. That thing out there, Phantom One figured, was the vessel the silhouette referred to, and its front clearly showed that it belonged to Pegasus Company, as it resembled the head and torso of a winged stallion.

"Rest assured," the silhouette continued nonchalantly, *"any move you dare to make, we will take down every … single … one … of the air racers participating in the Pegasus Air Race."*

Phantom One tightened his jaw. "Is that so?"

"We will gladly give you a small demonstration, just to prove how serious we are—and what we are capable of."

The silhouette nodded, right before it flickered and disappeared.

There seemed to be a short moment of confusion among the three Sky Phantom knights. Phantom One could only keep his gaze locked on the large vessel they were approaching, his index fingers still over his triggers.

Then an explosion to his right shook his craft.

"NOOO!" Phantom One cried, instantly pulling up hard. "Phantom Two, abort mission! Abort mission!" he shouted to the wingman to his left. "Phantom Three's just been taken down!"

"Copy that, Phantom One!" Phantom Two had already banked left.

Phantom One was setting his controls to make a teleport jump with his craft.

"Phantom Base, if you can hear this, we've been spotted, and we're under attack! I repeat, we are under attack!"

Whether or not the lieutenant colonel and the rest of the base heard him, however, Phantom One never knew, for seconds later, an intense light hit his Sky Phantom, right before the fighter craft burst into flames and exploded.

CHAPTER 12

"Hurry up, guys!" Keithan shouted over his shoulder while he ran.

His friends weren't far behind. Fernando moved his wheelchair with all his might while Marianna did her best to keep up. The three of them had just left Hangar H11 and were now headed toward one of the larger nonresidential hangars at Keithan's insistence.

"Mom's gonna have a heart attack when she gets back to our hangar and finds out that we're not there," Fernando said.

Keithan felt guilty for insisting that Fernando and Marianna come along, but after Mr. Aramis's mysterious disappearance, the three of them knew it was best to stick together until they found some answers—and help.

Soon they reached the hangar Keithan had led them to. It was no surprise for Keithan to find it still closed. Yet he still hoped somebody would be there. He didn't bother to pound on the large metal door at the front this time. Instead, he hurried to the right side of the arched building, looking for another much smaller entrance.

"Guys! Over here!"

He reached a seven-foot metal door with a small access panel. Keithan pressed his thumb on the panel. The red light blinked in response, and the words "Access denied" appeared below it.

"No answer?" Fernando asked as he halted his wheelchair next to Keithan.

Keithan pounded on the door three times but still got no answer. No one seemed to be inside the hangar, or maybe nobody wanted to answer. He looked at the whole side of the building, just as Marianna was doing not too far away. Somewhere nearby had to be a camera pointed at the door to which he could signal.

"This hangar doesn't have a single window," Marianna said while she approached.

Keithan took a deep breath and exhaled. "There *has* to be someone inside."

"Maybe they're at the race," Fernando suggested.

"Yeah," Marianna said.

Keithan shook his head. "All of them?"

Fernando and Marianna shrugged.

The three of them turned their heads to the rest of the airfield, where all the noise was coming from in the distance. At the other side of the main runway, past the numerous Pegasus teardrop flags, they could see the grandstands already full of people waiting for the air race to begin. Keithan couldn't help wondering how exactly he, Fernando, and Marianna could could start looking for someone from the Legion among the hundreds of people out there.

Then it hit him.

"One of the racers!" Keithan shouted.

Marianna and Fernando didn't seem to get it. They followed Keithan, who was running toward the front of the hangar.

"Keithan!" Fernando called.

Keithan stopped but didn't turn around.

"One of the air racers is a Sky Phantom!" he exclaimed, his eyes wide and still staring beyond the main runway. "I almost forgot about it! Lieutenant Colonel Lanzard mentioned it when he and Dantés took me to the Legion's secret base. Dantés also reminded me about that yesterday at her office."

"What are you talking about?" Marianna asked.

"One of the Sky Phantom agents has been disguising himself as one of the participating air racers to spy on Pegasus," Keithan went on explaining. "His crew too."

"Great. So we just have to figure out which of the sixteen racers could be the agent," said Fernando.

An amplified voice heard throughout the whole airfield interrupted them.

"Ladies and gentlemen, boys and girls, get ready for the event you have been waiting for ... the 2055 Pegasus Aiiiir Raaace!"

The entire crowd went wild, a combination of cheers and applause with thundersticks and horns. At the same time, an impressive display of daylight fireworks of different colors took over the sky, getting everyone's attention. Loud music followed, which seemed to be synchronized with the fireworks display.

"Whoa!" Keithan and his friends cried, gazing at the sky.

Below the fireworks display, the giant screen on the bloated side of the Pegasus airship came to life. It showed the chrome winged stallion bust of Pegasus Company.

Moments later, the music died down, and the announcer spoke again.

"We ask that everyone head to their respective seats, as we will begin the presentation of the air racers in just a few minutes."

Fernando turned to Keithan and Marianna. "We better hurry up. Do we have any clue about which air racer could be a Sky Phantom agent?"

Keithan lowered his gaze and sucked in his lower lip. "I ... don't know. It could be any one of them."

"No, it couldn't," Marianna interjected.

Keithan and Fernando shot her quizzical looks despite Marianna's look of determination.

"Look, the three of us spent weeks studying each of the air racers before the Pegasus qualifier tournament. We might not have a clue about which of the racers could be a Sky Phantom agent, but we might have a clue about who it *couldn't* be."

"Aaron Oliviera," Keithan was sure. "He couldn't possibly be a Sky Phantom. He just graduated last year from Ramey Academy."

"I agree," Fernando added. "He's only been air racing throughout the States since he graduated."

"So that's one off the list," said Marianna, starting her count by holding a thumb up. "Who else?"

Curiously, just as if she had been heard, the amplified voice of the race's announcer said, "Let's welcome our first air racer as he approaches the runway in his famous *Sky Blade*, Mr. Champion himself, and who for his second consecutive year will be defending his title. From the Netherlands, Drostaaan Luzieeer!"

Once again, the crowd burst out with cheers and applause.

Keithan, however, only tightened his lips at the racer's name. He spotted the man's sleek chrome racing aircraft coming up to the runway and slowly passing in front of the grandstands for everyone to see. Meanwhile, the airship's giant screen showed a much closer look at Luzier in his black-and-white uniform with gilded linings—the shot coming from one of the dozens of **spherical** drones that hovered low throughout the airfield. Luzier, seated in his cockpit with his canopy open, waved lazily at the crowd.

Curiously, the man's face didn't seem to show the slightest excitement of being there. He looked as if he were bored and didn't even care about the race. Despite this, Keithan could tell one thing for certain about the man ...

No way Luzier could be a Sky Phantom agent.

"That filthy traitor!" burst out Fernando.

He started moving his wheelchair toward the runway, but Marianna managed to grab his arm.

"Fernando, wait!"

"*Wait?* Are you kidding?" Fernando shot at her. "Marianna, that guy most likely is responsible for Dad's disappearance!"

"I know. We all do, but be reasonable. There's no way we're gonna be able to get to him."

"She's right," Keithan said. "We're still gonna need the Legion's help to do that."

Keithan understood Fernando's frustration. He, too, had seen

Luzier involved with Mr. Aramis in the Daedalus Project since the very beginning, which was one of the things he needed to tell Dantés and the rest of the Sky Phantoms.

Soon after presenting Luzier, the Pegasus announcer proceeded to present the next air racers who were starting to show up on the runway. The first was Italy's pride, Rosangela Sofio, in her four-wing racing aircraft, the *Fiore Veloce*. Then it was the Japanese rookie Daiki Tamura in his T-shaped racer with bottom rudder, the *Tsuki Furasshu*. Following Tamura, was the American John Ravena in his black forward-swept wings racer with twin red stripes, the *Apparition*, and right behind him was one of the crowd's favorites, the American goth racer who didn't seem to like any color except black (and perhaps blood red—but barely), Leeson Lancaster, aka the Vampire, in his famous fully black racing craft, the *Bat Fury*.

"Wait a second," Keithan said and pointed at the racers. *"Him!"*

"Who? The Vampire?" Fernando asked, his upper lip twitching up.

"No. The one in front of him, Ravena. I didn't study him."

"That's because he showed up unannounced at the qualifier tournament. Like you did," Marianna said. She was gazing at the runway with both hands over her eyes to see better. "If my memory serves right, he was presented that day as an air racer from Nebraska with a short history of air races there."

Something about the man's simple background didn't seem convincing to Keithan. He had a gut feeling there was more to Ravena than met the eye, especially when Keithan and his friends had studied every single one of the racers' backgrounds during Keithan's training for the qualifier tournament.

"Ravena … he has to be the Sky Phantom agent," Keithan murmured and turned to his friends again. "He has to be."

Neither Marianna nor Fernando said anything, and their expressions showed they were thinking the same thing.

"If he's from the Legion, his crew has to be too," Marianna said.

"We gotta get to his crew, then," said Keithan, fully determined.

He was about to start running when Marianna pointed to the west of the airfield.

"Uh-oh. Mom's coming," she said.

The three of them froze at the sight of Mrs. Aramis's scarlet minivan approaching fast. An official airport security vehicle was following it.

"You go," Fernando told Keithan.

Keithan jerked his head back in surprise. "What?"

"Marianna and I better head back home and help Mom. She's gonna need us there. Besides, there's not much time left."

"He's right, Keithan. The race is about to start," Marianna said.

Keithan glanced at the air racers. They were aligning their aircraft in front of the starting line.

"But wait!" he interjected just as Marianna and Fernando turned away. "I'll have to cross the runway. It's the only way I'm gonna be able to get to the crew area. How am I supposed to do that?"

Fernando shot a worried look from the approaching minivan to Keithan and the far west of the runway. Then he pointed in that direction. "Through there."

Both Marianna and Keithan turned in the same direction and saw what Fernando meant. He was pointing at the large start gantry from which the race starting lights hung. The metal structure arched over the runway about a half a mile away in front of all the racers. A few Pegasus officials were using it as their only bridge to access both sides of the runway.

"It'll have to do, Keithan. Now *go!*" Fernando told him. "Go find the Sky Phantoms and tell them to stop the race!"

Already he had turned around to head back to the hangar. Marianna was also about to leave, but before doing so, she reached for Keithan's hand and pressed it gently.

"Good luck," she told him.

Keithan pressed her hand in return and gave her a warm but concerned look. "You too."

Marianna forced herself to let go and ran after her brother.

Keithan should have started running too, but in the opposite direction. Yet he hesitated when he realized that he needed to come up with a good excuse to be allowed to cross the gantry. Pegasus officials wouldn't just let him do it, but Keithan couldn't risk telling them the truth. He could only trust the Sky Phantoms out there. He looked down at the gold VIP pass hanging from his neck and pushed the inside of his left cheek with his tongue. Slowly, an idea started forming in his head, and so he started running.

As far as Keithan could tell, he was the only person on this side of the runway. It seemed even airport security had their hands full on the other side. Keithan had to jump over the extended line of metal barricades decorated with numerous Pegasus banners. Nobody seemed to have spotted him until he reached the foot of the arched gantry.

"Whoa! Who are *you*?" said one of the two Pegasus officials standing guard there.

Keithan stopped abruptly. Panting, he raised his VIP pass to show it to them.

The two men leaned forward, and one of them said, "How did you get that?"

"Captain Colani himself," Keithan replied.

"Captain Colani?" the other official repeated. "But why are you on this side of the airfield? The event is—"

"I know. It's a long story," Keithan cut him off. "Listen, my name is Keithan Quintero, and I need to get to the other side and to the VIP area. This gantry is the only way for me to get there. *Please.* The race is about to start!"

He kept his best expression of desperation, hoping it would help persuade the two men, who so far looked more confused than skeptical.

"*Please!* Captain Colani is waiting for me," Keithan insisted. He glanced at all the air racers and back at the two men.

"He doesn't have much time," the second official told his companion.

The latter shook his head and turned to Keithan. "Come with me, quickly." He gestured for his companion to remain there and motioned for Keithan to follow him.

Keithan breathed a deep sigh of relief and started up the steps of the gantry. The structure, mostly made of metal tubing, started as a ladder that went approximately twenty feet up. Beyond that, it continued like an ascending catwalk. Three other Pegasus officials were near its middle. As expected, they were surprised at the sight of Keithan.

"It's okay. He has a VIP pass," said the man escorting Keithan. "I'm taking him to the VIP area."

He was gesturing for them to step aside so he and Keithan could pass when the announcer's voice was heard again throughout the airfield.

"Let's receive with a big round of applause now our host. The man who has made all this happen today, the CEO of Pegasus Company. Ladies and gentlemen, boys and girls, Captain Giovanniii Colaaaniii!"

The roar of the crowd was instantaneous when the image of Colani appeared on the airship's giant screen. One of the Pegasus camera drones captured him from the balcony of a small modular area that was shaped like a flying saucer, located at the top of the grandstands. Colani, dressed in his usual fancy pearly white side-buttoned suit and matching peaked cap, waved at the camera and proceeded to adjust a small microphone on the collar of his suit. A group of about fifteen or twenty people accompanied him on the balcony, all of them wearing expensive suits and day dresses and holding thin flutes with champagne. Among them, Keithan spotted the man who always accompanied Drostan Luzier. The man was easy to spot due to his red-lensed glasses and white handlebar mustache.

"Uh-oh," said the official in front of Keithan.

Keithan turned to him. "'Uh-oh' what?"

"You're not going to get there in time before the race starts. Colani's appearance is our cue. Come here!"

He and Keithan had moved past the other Pegasus officials and were now at the middle of the gantry. Yet instead of continuing forward, the man halted and gestured for Keithan to look at the two rows of racing aircraft facing them on the runway.

There was no doubt about it, the race was about to start.

Keithan gulped. He looked down and saw the rows of flashing red starting lights underneath the metal grid.

"It might be best if we wait here—at least until the race begins," the man next to him said over the noise of all the aircraft and the excited crowd. "Lucky you, eh, kid? You're going to get the best view!"

Keithan smirked slightly. He was now gazing at the air racers, all the while aware he had to hurry and get to the crew area. Yet Keithan couldn't find it in himself to move now due to the tension of the moment, not to mention the fear growing inside him as each second passed. Worse still when he realized the real threat hovering low at either side of the runway, multiplied by the dozen ...

The Pegasus **spherical** drones.

Now, more than ever, Keithan couldn't help wondering if any or all of those drones were armed with laser cannons like the ones the Sky Phantom Legion had captured. What if those things were meant to attack the racers before the race began?

Colani's voice brought Keithan back from his thoughts.

"Welcome, everyone, welcome!" the man bellowed, visible on the giant screen with his arms extended to the sides. "I hope you are as excited as I am today. A great race awaits us—an unforgettable race!" He lowered his gaze toward the runway. "To all you air racers, I wish you the best of luck, though there can only be one champion today. May the best racer win! Now, are you people ready?"

The grandstands burst out in wild cheers.

"Racers, are *you* ready?"

The reply came with the roar of each of the racing crafts' engines, getting the crowd even more pumped up. The hairs on Keithan's arms and the back of his neck stood up.

And so the starting sequence began.

"On your marks!" Colani bellowed.

Right underneath Keithan, the row of red lights on the gantry blinked five times at one-second intervals.

His heart accelerated. He looked back and forth from the air racers to the hovering **spherical** drones. He dared not blink.

"Get set!"

The row of yellow lights underneath the red row blinked next, also at one-second intervals.

By now, Keithan's breathing had become rapid at the intense anticipation. His gut told him to hurry and find the Sky Phantoms in disguise at the crew area, but still Keithan didn't move. Gulping, he gripped the metal railing in front of him hard.

This was it! Beads of sweat formed on his temples.

The third and lowest row of lights flashed bright green, and a loud beep sounded a second before Colani shouted the final word ...

"GO!"

With their engines deafening the airfield, the sixteen air racers shot off at high speed. No longer were they in line formation. They rushed straight in Keithan's direction. All the while, the grandstands exploded with excitement. The sixteen racing craft reached the starting gantry in seconds. Each one made a loud swoosh as it passed right underneath Keithan, who immediately leaned over the railing with wide eyes and mouth gaping open. He spun 180 degrees, still following the racers in the lead as they ascended and continued westward over the runway.

This was really it, Keithan realized in shock. The grand Pegasus Air Race had officially begun. But Keithan feared that wasn't a good thing.

CHAPTER 13

For a moment, Keithan couldn't resist feeling immersed in the event. The excitement was so strong that he imagined himself being one of the air racers, flying his *d'Artagnan* with full power. If only that had been true, he thought. He would have given so much for such an opportunity.

The cheers from the audience in the grandstands made the moment even more exciting. Just like him, everyone there followed the racers with their gazes as each aircraft banked left, heading south and slowly disappearing in the distance toward the first of the hover rings in the sky. The last of the aircraft were almost out of sight when a hand fell on Keithan's shoulder and brought him back from his thoughts to the top of the gantry, where he still stood.

"Come on, lad. Let's get you to the VIP area!" insisted the Pegasus official who had taken on the task of escorting him.

Keithan shook his head and quickly reminded himself of why he was there. He followed the man, carefully watching each step as he descended the metal gantry. He was ready to make a run for the air racers' crew area as soon as he reached the bottom, but it looked like it wasn't going to be an easy task with so many Pegasus officials and airport security officers down there. To complicate things, the man escorting him stopped at the bottom of the gantry to wait for him to step down.

"Stay close to me now," he warned, to which Keithan responded with a nod and a lazy smile.

Keithan had no choice but to play along until he could make his move and run away. The problem was the man now held him by the shoulder while he led him through the other Pegasus officials who kept moving busily all around. Both of them kept bumping with some of the other uniformed men and women, who didn't stop and kept talking into their communicator earpieces. The two of them also had to evade stacks of fiberglass crates that appeared on their way. Keithan grew more desperate as he continued moving. He kept looking to the far left while they approached the grandstands. He could see the metal barricades that enclosed the racers' crew area.

And so, running out of patience, he did the first thing that came to his mind: he crouched and reached for his power-strapped sneakers.

"What's wrong?" asked the man, forced to stop.

"One of my shoes' power straps loosened."

Keithan pretended to be working on his sneaker while he gave one last glance to the left.

"One ... two ..." he murmured. And right on "three" he sprang to the side and ran.

"Hey! *Hey*, kid! Come back here!" his former escort shouted. He hesitated before giving chase.

Keithan didn't bother looking back. He remained low while he kept running and zigzagging among the uniformed men and women all around him.

"Stop that kid! Stop that kid!" other officials soon started shouting, getting the attention of the airport security officers nearby.

Still, Keithan kept running toward the barricades. He leapt over small stacks of fiberglass crates. He even managed to evade the Pegasus officials who saw him coming their way and tried to grab him, fear and exhilaration swirling inside him. Keithan felt as if he were running desperately for a touchdown down a football field crowded with the opposite team's players.

Almost there, almost there, he repeated in his head.

The four-foot-tall metal barricades now stood a mere yard ahead, decorated with different Pegasus banners. Keithan reached them and landed both hands on one of them to push himself up—right before he swung his legs over it and landed on the other side. He used the momentum to continue running, but not without first looking over his shoulder to see the Pegasus officials mixed with a few airport security officers, who were also giving chase.

Finally inside the air racers' crew area, Keithan looked all around for John Ravena's crew. Fortunately, each crew wore either unisuits or shirts with the same colors of its racer, which made them easier to identify.

"Somebody, stop that kid!" kept shouting some of the Pegasus officials who had jumped over the barricades.

People from different crews who noticed what was happening seemed to hesitate while they tried to make sense of why a kid was causing such a commotion. Their confusion at least gave Keithan enough time to find the crew he was looking for. He recognized it on the fifth stretch marquee to his right. All of its members were wearing black polo shirts with twin red stripes on their sleeves, which resembled those on Ravena's racing craft. None of the men and women there, however, had yet spotted him hurrying in their direction. Their attention was currently on the different holo screens they had set under the stretch marquee, which showed them the race's progress.

Keithan was now a mere fifteen feet away from the marquee, almost out of breath. Still, he gave everything he had to reach it. Then two Pegasus officials surprised him from either side and grabbed him.

"No, wait! Let me go! Let me go!"

Keithan kicked and wriggled, trying to set himself free but to no avail. He was no match for the two large and heavily muscled men who held him by his upper arms. The men had no trouble restraining him while the rest of the officials who had chased after Keithan formed a circle around them.

"Easy. Hey! Easy now, kid. You know you can't be here," said one of the men holding Keithan.

Still, Keithan didn't stop struggling.

"Let me … go! *Please!* I need to talk to Ravena's racing crew!"

Keithan craned his neck to look at the crewmembers in front of him. They had finally taken notice of him, and some were now approaching.

"I'm … running out … of … time. *Please!*"

"That ain't gonna happen. Now hold still," said the Pegasus official who had escorted Keithan.

Just then, one of the members of Ravena's crew, accompanied by five more, stepped in. "Whoa. What's going on here?"

Keithan answered before any of the Pegasus officials could explain. "I need to speak to you in private. It's an emergency!"

The Pegasus officials still weren't convinced.

"Any of you know this kid?" one of them asked Ravena's crew.

The crewmembers shook their heads, still looking confused about what was happening. Meanwhile, Keithan struggled to set himself free from the two men's grips.

"I know who you are! I know who you *really* are!" Keithan shouted. "Lieutenant Colonel Lanzard told me everything about you. You're Sky Phantom agents!"

Both men holding Keithan exchanged confused looks before they turned to Ravena's crew again.

"What is he talking about?" asked the man to Keithan's right.

Keithan noticed the particular reaction of the men and women from Ravena's crew. Practically, all of them seemed to shoot Keithan deep looks with tight lips, as if telling him not to dare say more.

"Keithan!" someone called from over the commotion. Whoever it was was trying to make its way through the gathered group of Pegasus officials and airport security officers. "Let me through!" the figure insisted. She managed to push her way right into the center of the circle.

Keithan instantly beamed with relief at the sight of her. *"Professor!"*

Despite her casual clothes, which clearly showed she wasn't supposed to be there, either, Dantés marched straight toward Keithan as if she owned the place. Hard to believe none of the Pegasus officials dared to stop her.

"Take your hands off that boy," she demanded. It was hard to tell if it was her words, her tone, or her deeply serious look what made the two men let go of Keithan, but they didn't even hesitate. Both of them stepped away as the professor continued approaching. Keithan's freedom didn't last long, though, for Dantés grabbed him by one arm and dragged him away.

"Stay quiet and follow my lead," she whispered while forcing Keithan to move at her pace.

The Pegasus officials, still confused by Dantés's unexpected appearance, watched her take Keithan into the stretch marquee of Ravena's crew. It wasn't till a few seconds later that one of them reacted.

"Hey! Where do you two think you're taking him? Miss!" It was the official who had tried to escort Keithan to the VIP area.

Keithan looked over his shoulder and saw the man about to come after them, but some of Ravena's crewmembers blocked his way.

"It's okay. She's with us," said one of the crewmembers.

"Just keep walking," Dantés ordered Keithan, pressuring him to move faster.

"I need to tell you—" he whispered back to her, but Dantés cut him off.

"Not here. Wait till we're out of earshot."

Soon they reached the stretch marquee. Dantés led Keithan to the end where a small enclosed tent stood. Inside it, all the noise from the event was muffled, mostly due to the constant low rumbling of a generator coming from nearby outside, which was accompanied by the humming of an air conditioner.

"All right, Keithan. Don't even bother telling me how you managed to sneak into the racers' crew area." Dantés rested both hands on her hips and stared down at him. "Just get straight to the point. What's going on?"

Keithan, still agitated, said, "Professor, the race has to be stopped!"

"Why? What did you find?"

"There's a plot behind the race to attack the air racers!"

Dantés's hands dropped to her side.

"And that's not all," Keithan continued talking fast. "I don't know why, but the plot is somehow linked to the so-called Daedalus Project."

Keithan hadn't noticed the three Sky Phantom agents who had entered and stopped behind him until one of them, a blond man probably in his late twenties and also in casual attire, stepped forward.

"How do you know that?" he asked Keithan. His expression, the same as that of his companions, was full of confusion and deep worry.

Keithan was about to answer, but the amplified voice of one of the race's commentators outside interrupted him, quickly followed by loud cries from the crowd. He and everyone else in the tent turned their gazes momentarily to the entrance. Then Dantés turned to Keithan again.

"How do you know there's going to be an attack against the air racers?" she asked him.

"William Aramis, Fernando's dad," Keithan blurted out. "He's the one who was secretly working on the Daedalus Project, and he was getting help from Drostan Luzier, who was apparently providing Mr. Aramis materials endorsed by Pegasus—"

"Wait. Drostan Luzier? The air racing champion?" interjected the blond man next to Dantés.

"Yeah," Keithan reassured them, though still looking at Dantés. "The thing is, Fernando, his sister, and I got access to Mr. Aramis's laptube and found a secret file that he downloaded. It's somehow connected to the Daedalus Project. It revealed everything about the plot against the air racers, and for some mysterious reason, it requires the project."

Dantés and her three companions exchanged confused glances. Then Dantés shook her head and leaned closer to Keithan.

"Are you certain about all this?" she asked.

"Absolutely."

Dantés nodded, narrowing her eyes, and straightened up. "All right. I'm gonna need you to take me to Fernando's father right away."

She took Keithan by his left shoulder to turn him around, but

Keithan didn't budge. Instead, he grabbed her forearm and said, "We can't. Mr. Aramis disappeared. We fear he's been kidnapped."

"What?"

"I'll explain everything else later. Right now, you have to stop the race. If it's true, there's going to be an attack against the air racers, and it's gonna happen at any moment. You have to warn the air racers somehow—figure out a way to get them to head back to Ramey or something."

"The **spherical** drones," one of the other agents said, stepping forward. "Surely it'll be with those things that the racers will be attacked."

Everyone else inside the tent seemed to freeze. Keithan was aware of what the Pegasus **drones** could be hiding inside. The mere thought of it made him gulp hard.

"It would be the perfect move," Dantés said in a low voice, as if more to herself than to her companions. "Those things are spread throughout the racecourse and all over Puerto Rico, transmitting the race. If some or all of them are armed like the ones we captured, they could easily intercept the racers anywhere."

"But there's no way of warning the racers. Our private communication lines still aren't working here at Ramey," remarked the blond agent with the stubble beard. "We'll have to leave Ramey, find an area where we can contact—"

"Whoa, wait a second! Not even *your* communication lines are working?" Keithan interjected. "But you're the Sky Phantom Legion! I mean, you're supposed to have the most advanced technology the rest of the world doesn't even know about!"

"As you can see, kid, we're dealing with something we've never faced before, and no doubt about it, Pegasus is behind it." The blond agent returned his gaze to Dantés. "Whatever we do, Agent Venus, we must do it—"

The cries of shock from the race's commentators, along with those of the spectators' in the distance, interrupted him. It seemed like something serious had happened outside, and it made everyone inside the tent rush out and hurry to one of the holo screens hovering under the crew's stretch marquee to see.

"Whoaaa! Ladies and gentlemen, Daiki Tamura just hit one of the hover rings hard with his craft's right wing near the Arecibo coastline," reported the commentator while doing his best to keep his tone under control. "It doesn't look good; his racing craft seems to be out of control and descending. Pegasus drones are closing in to see if he bails out."

Keithan's hands flew to his mouth while he watched the horrifying scene on the screen. The T-shaped racer was diving fast toward the sea, its opponents racing past it.

"Wait," suddenly said the second commentator. "It seems Tamura is recovering ... he's trying to recover."

There were loud gasps from the crowds.

"And he makes it!" the first commentator cried excitedly. "Daiki Tamura manages to recover in his *Tsuki Furasshu* and is now ascending fast to catch up with the rest of the racers! What a stunt, ladies and gentlemen!"

Keithan and everyone around him sighed in relief, though in Keithan's case, not necessarily because Tamura had managed to recover and keep flying, but more because he'd thought the racer had been attacked. That, Keithan knew, was still a possibility, which was why he turned quickly to face Dantés and her companions again.

"Professor?" Keithan asked, expecting her to focus on what she needed to do.

Before Dantés could reply, one of her companions said, "We should send the Sky Phantoms to protect the racers."

"And alert home base as soon as we can," added one of the other agents who had been inside the tent.

"That's exactly what we're going to do," Dantés said. "Follow me."

Once again, she placed a hand on Keithan's shoulder and forced him to move along with her. Together, with the three other agents behind them, they continued moving under the stretch marquee where the rest of the crewmembers remained watching the air race transmission.

"Agent Lynn," Dantés said, addressing the blond agent, "I'll need you to alert all the other agents here about our current emergency."

"I'm on it," the man replied over the noise around them. He wasted no time and left to carry out his order.

"You two," Dantés said, looking at the other agents still marching behind her and Keithan. "Head to home base immediately and report everything to the lieutenant colonel. Tell him to send a squadron to protect each of the racers in the air."

"Got it!" both agents replied and immediately marched out of the stretch marquee.

"What about contacting the police?" Keithan asked as he and Dantés stepped out of the marquee in the opposite direction the other agents had left. "Shouldn't we let them know so they can help?"

"It's best if the Legion deals with this first," Dantés answered. "We don't want to create widespread panic."

Keithan noticed Dantés was leading him toward the exit of the crew area.

"And what are *you* going to do?" he asked her.

Dantés halted and turned around instead of answering, almost making Keithan bump into her. She reached for Keithan's gold access pass without even asking and yanked it off his neck.

"Hey!"

"Sorry. I'll be needing it."

Dantés turned around and gazed up at the saucer-shaped VIP structure above the middle of the grandstands. "I'm going straight to Colani and get to the bottom of all this once and for all—and stop him."

Keithan flinched. "Wha—? No. Professor, Colani is not involved in this, and there's no ti—"

Dantés didn't let him finish as she raised a hand in front of him. Her gaze, however, unexpectedly drifted to the sky. Keithan stared at her, confused. Then he looked up too.

"What in the world …?"

A gigantic machine at least four times the size of the Pegasus airship was coming in from the north. It was slowly descending from the sky and approaching Ramey Airport like a man-made island brought by the wind. No doubt it belonged to Pegasus, for its front reflected a solid representation of the company's logo: a stallion bust with incredibly large wings spread wide open behind it.

The people in the grandstands, who up to this moment had been fully immersed in what was happening in the race, began to notice the new giant flying machine. As expected, gasps soon followed, all at the wonder that was now stealing the show.

"Whoa! Ladies and gentlemen, we … we, um, have a surprise for you," said one of the race's commentators, his voice amplified throughout the entire airfield. His tone, however, revealed that he was also surprised by what he was seeing. "A new, much bigger aircraft from Pegasus is making its unexpected approach to Ramey Airport. Let's welcome it with a round of applause!"

The people in the grandstands cheered for the approaching machine, their applauses gradually growing despite the air race, which continued being projected on the large screens on the other side of the runway.

Keithan, on the other hand, remained dumbfounded next to a frozen Dantés, who also remained staring at the giant machine in the sky. Less than a mile away now, he could hear the flying machine's deep constant humming, most likely from its powerful generators, which inspired an all-consuming dread. Worse still, Keithan couldn't help being amazed by how much bigger the thing was compared to Colani's airship, which still hovered low to the left of the crew area and the grandstands. Colani's airship was dwarfed by the absurd size of the mysterious new ship.

Struggling to make sense of what was happening, Keithan managed to switch his gaze momentarily to the VIP area at the top of the grandstands. He wished he'd brought a pair of digital binoculars to get a glimpse of Giovanni Colani up there. All he could see were silhouettes of people behind the glass of the saucer-shaped structure above the rest of the spectators. He couldn't tell who any of them were.

"I really don't like this," he whispered, raising his gaze to the sky again.

"Me, neither," Dantés said. "That thing in the sky shouldn't be here." Her gaze hadn't left the approaching vessel.

Keithan turned to her and frowned. "What do you mean?"

"No less than an hour ago, home base detected a large bogey coming from the north. A small squadron of Phantom knights was sent to stop it from reaching our airspace."

"Maybe ... maybe they allowed it to pass, considering it's from Pegasus."

"Or maybe the squadron failed to stop it."

Keithan gulped at the professor's comment.

The vessel, with the sun overhead in a cloudless sky, was already casting an enormous shadow over half of Ramey. It seemed to be coming to a stop at approximately two hundred feet above the airfield. Its impressive front began to open. First its enormous stallion's head, which tilted upward slowly. Then the stallion's neck and chest tilted downward like a drawbridge. The vessel's interior became visible ... and what it revealed made Keithan freeze in horror.

What looked like hundreds of the Pegasus spherical drones hung like chromed Christmas balls in row after row of racks that stretched over a dozen levels deep inside the giant machine.

It was in that moment that Keithan realized that what the Sky Phantom Legion had feared, and what Lieutenant Colonel Lanzard and Dantés had warned him about, had come true. The worst thing about it was that none of the spectators on the grandstands and throughout the outskirts of Ramey Airport had a clue about what was really about to happen.

"Professor, I don't think that's just a flying carrier ..."

Dantés finished his thought. "No ... it's a Trojan horse."

Both of them watched as the scene unfolded. The arsenal of spherical drones detached from their racks and started flying out of the carrier, spreading over the sky like a swarm of agitated bees leaving their hive.

CHAPTER 14

"**E**ngine on!" Dantés said loud and clear while holding her wrist communicator close to her mouth.

The command made the only hoverbike parked at the end of the many food and souvenir stands behind the grandstands rumble to life and rise two feet off the ground.

"Where are we going?" asked Keithan, who had simply followed Dantés at her insistence.

The professor didn't reply. As soon as she reached her hoverbike, she leaned over it with one hand on the handlebar and mounted it.

"Get on!" she said.

Keithan did as he was told despite not having a clue about the professor's plan.

"Hold on!" Dantés cried over the bike's loud engine.

Keithan grabbed on to her waist and braced himself. With its engine roaring, they took off. Dantés rode the bike straight through the souvenir and food stands, honking insistently to force everyone nearby to get out of the way.

"Watch out!" Keithan cried at the sight of a group of Pegasus officials who were starting to block their way next to the grandstands. He expected the professor to slow down and find an alternate route, but instead, Dantés accelerated straight toward the officials.

"Are you craz—?"

"Just hold *on*!"

Dantés threw her whole body backward, forcing Keithan to tighten his hold on her waist. The hoverbike rose, its front higher than its rear, and passed right above the Pegasus officials.

"Whoaaa!" Keithan cried.

The officials' looks of shock below the bike were priceless. Soon they were out of sight as the bike continued hovering ten feet high over the numerous stacks of fiberglass crates. Airport security officers also gazed up, dumbfounded at the sudden sight of the hoverbike passing over them. But they didn't seem to bother trying to stop them, as there was a lot more to worry about right now with what was happening much higher in the sky. The absurd number of camera drones were still fanning out all over the sky.

And all the while, the air race went on.

Dantés lowered the bike to two feet off the ground and again pushed it to the max. She drove it across the runway, toward the north of the airport. Meanwhile, the race's commentators could still be heard doing their best to explain to the audience what was happening.

"Ladies and gentlemen, just like you, we are trying to make sense of what is happening," one of the commentators was saying.

"That's right, Mark," his female companion continued. "It seems we have more camera drones to provide more views of the race throughout the racecourse. Now, if you look at the screens, the race is still going on, and what a show, ladies and gentlemen!"

"It's no surprise: Drostan Luzier is still in the lead!" the first commentator said. "He just went through two hover rings with a single loop maneuver. And right behind him is John Ravena in his *Apparition*. He manages to pass through one ring. And right on his tail, still holding third place and keeping a strong chase, is the Vampire in his *Bat Fury*!"

Just as the commentator finished saying that, Dantés and Keithan arrived in front of the Sky Phantoms' hangar, which now had its main door half raised. Neither one had yet dismounted the hoverbike when a female Sky Phantom agent in a black full bodysuit rushed out of the hangar toward them.

"Captain Venus! So glad you're here! Your presence is requested at home base. A capsule is already set to take you—"

"I'm not going to base," Dantés cut her off. "I need a small team armed and ready to accompany me to the VIP area at the grandstands to detain Colani right now."

The agent hesitated. "Y-you can't, Captain. Colonel Lanzard gave strict orders not to take any action against Pegasus until further notice after what happened with our squadron."

Dantés shook her head. Keithan remained behind her, fully intrigued.

"What do you mean?" Dantés asked. "What happened to the squadron?"

The female agent leaned her head slightly the side and frowned at Keithan. Keithan could tell she was wondering if they should be talking about the matter with him there. But then the woman answered.

"The entire squadron was taken down by that very vessel now hovering over us." She pointed upward to the flying machine in the sky, which still had its front open. All around it, the swarm of new spherical drones seemed to be forming a giant rotating circle.

"And that's not all," the agent added with an unsteady voice. "Right before the surprise attack, home base received a transmission demanding us to stand down and allow the vessel to continue its course here. Otherwise every single one of the competing air racers will be intercepted and taken down too."

Dantés released a deep breath. "So that's how that thing managed to get here."

She gazed up at it with a deep look before looking back at the agent.

"That's why we have strict orders not to take any action, at least for now," the agent said.

"No," Keithan interjected. "You can't just do nothing. Professor ..."

"Quiet," Dantés warned him over her shoulder.

"But, Professor—"

"Keithan." She turned abruptly toward him, a look of worry deeper than his on her face. "Pegasus knows about us! Don't you see?"

Keithan's jaw dropped. He froze simultaneously at the shocking realization.

"We have no idea how this was accomplished," the agent reported, "but that thing managed to see and attack our squadron while it was in stealth mode."

There was a crashing sound behind. Keithan jumped.

"Ooooo!" the two commentators chorused in the distance.

Both Keithan and Dantés turned around.

"Fritz Kelleher just hit one of the hover rings while trying to beat Daiki Tamura to it!" the male commentator exclaimed. "It doesn't look good … and he ejects! It's official, ladies and gentlemen, Kelleher is out of the race!"

The reaction of the crowd followed, booing over a mix of cheers, thundersticks, and horns.

Keithan gave a deep sigh of relief despite Kelleher's accident. It seemed nobody out there was aware yet of the threat still developing behind the race.

"Our communications are back!" someone shouted from the hangar's main entrance. "Quick, Agent Venus! You gotta see this!"

Keithan turned around to see one of the other agents rushing up to them with a data pad in his hands.

"What is it?" Dantés asked.

The young agent halted in front of her and handed her the data pad. "It's an image from our radars. It seems the situation just became a lot more complicated."

Keithan wondered how it could possibly be more complicated.

He quickly checked his wrist communicator and noticed that it still had no signal. It appeared only the Legion had recovered its communications. He raised his gaze toward the data pad in Dantés's hands. The device's screen showed a green digital map of the whole island of Puerto Rico beneath a grid. Contrasting the almost rectangular shape of the island, however, was a red oval shape blinking over Ramey's location. No doubt it was the mysterious large vessel hovering high over Ramey.

But there were two other shapes blinking on the map, one slowly approaching the south-central coast of the island, the other also approaching but from the northeast coast.

"Home base just sent us that video feed," the young agent told Dantés and the female agent next to her. "Colonel Lanzard confirmed it. Those other shapes are two more of those giant vessels headed to the island. One is headed to the south checkpoint of the race, the other to the north checkpoint."

Keithan's fear started growing inside him once again.

"They seem to be positioning themselves in an attack formation," Dantés said while still looking at the data pad's screen.

"Now will you go to home base?" the female agent urged Dantés.

Far over the coastal city of Ponce in the south of Puerto Rico, the sky remained gray. It hadn't rained yet, but that didn't seem to worry any of the hundreds of spectators who were gathered there, mainly at the popular boardwalk known as La Guancha and where checkpoint three was located. Many other spectators were enjoying the race there, but they were watching it from luxurious yachts, which varied in size and had been gathered like exclusive VIP stands on the water.

Once again, everybody out there threw their hands in the air and cheered when they saw four more racers shoot past and at top speed over them. Oliviera's *Guaraguau* and Rosangela Sofio's *Fiore Veloce* were the ones up front, though not too far ahead of Tony LeVier's *Lightning Dragon* and Matthew McMillan's *Flying Blue Bull*, who were still putting up a fight to try to pass the front-runners.

Each racing craft shot flawlessly through a hover ring at a different altitude and banked hard to the left, continuing the intense race inland. They were all soon out of sight, which made everyone turn their heads to the west again and wait for the next racers, whose silhouettes were slowly coming into view on the horizon. The crowd was ready to root for them too.

Suddenly, some of the spectators' attention began to switch toward another, very different silhouette that was also approaching the coast. This one, however, was coming from the south and at a much slower pace than the air racers were.

Some people pointed at it in wonder while others raised their communicators and hover cameras again to take pictures of it. The flying machine was still hidden inside the clouds, but what seemed to keep everyone staring at it was the fact that it was absurdly large.

The silhouette's front began to become clear as it came out of the clouds. It was a giant chromed Pegasus bust with its wide-open wings stretched backward.

Gasps of awe followed. Confusion began to turn to dread in everyone when the winged stallion's bust began to open … right before a wide swarm of the metallic spherical drones flew out of the giant flying vessel, spreading high throughout the sky.

As that happened, another vessel appeared miles away to the north side of the island, approaching Old San Juan and where checkpoint five had been located. The crowd gathered near the massive high stone wall of El Morro and throughout San Juan Bay spotted the mysterious large vessel right away as it approached the coast unannounced. Unlike how it happened at Ponce, however, this other vessel could be seen clearly from far away since there were barely any clouds visible at the north coast of Puerto Rico. More than that, the mysterious vessel contrasted with the bright cyan sky. Yet its size was what kept everyone dumbfounded, for it looked as big as a small floating island made entirely of dark metal. And just as it happened at Ramey and Ponce, the front of the flying craft opened to release a swarm of innumerable spherical drones that flew out and covered the sky.

And still, the 2055 Pegasus Air Race went on.

CHAPTER 15

A ll hell was breaking loose.

That thought circled inside Keithan's mind while he hurried back to the Aramises' hangar. Everything happening today seemed unreal: the communications disruption throughout Ramey, Mr. Aramis's strange disappearance, the plot found inside Mr. Aramis's laptube to attack the competing air racers, even the three giant vessels that had arrived with hundreds of spherical drones. And now the unimaginable fact that the Sky Phantom Legion had been attacked.

And despite all that, what Keithan feared most was that things were most likely to get a lot worse.

There was nothing more he could have done to help Dantés and the rest of the Sky Phantom Legion, which was why he knew where he had to be now. He could see his destination ahead. The Aramises' hangar had its main entrance fully open. There, Keithan spotted Marianna, and to his surprise, his dad. The two were gazing at what was happening over the airfield, Marianna with her viewscreen headset and hover camera and Keithan's dad with a pair of digital binoculars.

"Hey!" Keithan waved his arms at them.

His dad gave a deep sigh of relief when he saw him. "Son, are you all right?"

Keithan stopped in front of him and Marianna but had to bend over with his hands on his knees to catch his breath before he could answer. "I'm … fine." Still panting, he raised his gaze at his dad. "When did … did you get here?"

"About fifteen minutes ago," his dad replied. "I went to the race's VIP area, and I was expecting to find you there, but I got worried when Colani told me you hadn't shown up, especially since I couldn't reach you through my communicator. So I figured you would be here. Marianna and Fernando told me about what happened to their dad and the plot against the racers."

"What's with all those drones up there?" Marianna asked. "And with that flying vessel?"

Keithan swallowed hard and straightened up. "It-it's all part of the attack, and there are two other vessels already flying toward Puerto Rico."

Both his father and Marianna looked at him, stunned.

"Are you serious?" Marianna said.

Keithan nodded and looked over his shoulder at the hovering vessel. "Whatever's gonna happen, it's not gonna happen only here at Ramey. Trust me, it's a lot worse than what's happening here."

He wanted to explain everything, but he needed to get everyone together.

"Anything new about your dad?" Keithan asked Marianna.

The question made his friend's worried expression return. "Not really. Airport security officers came. They checked Dad's workshop. Asked us a whole bunch of questions too, but they left in a hurry when all the spherical drones showed up."

"Guys!" shouted Fernando from inside the hangar. "Quick! Come over here!"

He was at his work area at the right side of the hangar next to the *d'Artagnan*. A rectangular holo screen was projected four feet in front of him. His mother was next to him, along with Laika, who remained with her front paws on the armrest of Fernando's wheelchair, also staring at the holo screen. Mrs. Aramis, Keithan noticed, still looked deeply affected by her husband's disappearance. Her eyes were still red and puffy, and she held a hand over her mouth.

"What's wrong?" Keithan said.

Fernando pointed to the holo screen. "Look. The whole thing with the drones is turning pretty scary."

Everyone gathered around him and watched the screen with full attention. Fernando had it divided into two viewports. The one on the left showed live footage of the Pegasus Air Race. Yet it was the one on the right, with the semitransparent logo of Channel 2 at the bottom right, that caught everyone's attention. It showed the blazing wreckage of what appeared to be a crashed aircraft along with the remains of two Pegasus camera drones in the middle of a narrow suburban street, just a few feet away from several houses.

"Oh my—!" Marianna gasped and covered her mouth with both hands.

A male news correspondent with a small microphone attached to his ear addressed the viewers at a safe distance from the burning wreckage.

"Residents from this community at the city of Ponce experienced the fright of their lives when an aircraft and two of the Pegasus camera drones overflying the area crashed on their street. We want to clarify for our viewers that, fortunately, there were no casualties. According to witnesses, the pilot of the craft managed to eject and escape in time."

Keithan and the rest sighed.

"Firefighters are on the way," the news correspondent went on. "As you can see behind me, police officers are doing their best to control the scene by preventing people from getting closer to the flames. From the details we've been able to collect, the accident occurred when the aircraft collided with two drones in the sky. Witnesses say there were a lot more drones overflying the area when the collision happened, though it's unclear why."

The camera moved away from the reporter and got a close-up of the wreckage. Keithan leaned closer to the image and narrowed his eyes, deeply intrigued. He focused on a twisted piece of debris barely visible within the flames and gray smoke. Suddenly, his eyes widened when he noticed something about the twisted piece.

"That was a military fighter aircraft!" he exclaimed in shock.

"What? You mean it's not one of the racers?" his dad asked.

"No way! Look at its symbol," Keithan insisted.

Everyone around him leaned closer to the holo screen, squinting. It was hard to spot it with all the smoke rising from the wreckage, but Keithan knew that symbol very well. He was sure his dad and his friends would recognize it too—a red horizontal stripe bisecting a white bar at either side of a navy-blue circle with a white star inside it—the official roundel of the United States Air Force.

The news correspondent didn't seem to have noticed it since he hadn't mentioned anything about it. Instead, he continued pondering the excessive number of Pegasus drones overflying the island when there had already been others settled over specific areas of the racecourse to broadcast the event.

"Wait a minute—" the news correspondent interrupted himself, instantly reaching for his earpiece and pressing it. "Ladies and gentlemen, I'm receiving new information...." His voice had turned shaky, and Keithan could see the man now struggling to hold his composure in front of the camera. "I-I've just been informed that two, no, *three* more collisions in different cities have been reported. It hasn't been confirmed if any of them involved civilian aircraft. What has been confirmed, ladies and gentlemen, is that it also involved more of the Pegasus camera drones."

Keithan felt chills running down his spine. He wondered if those collisions had really been accidents. More than that, why they were happening.

"I thought you guys said the racers were the ones to be targeted," Keithan's dad said with a deep look of concern.

Keithan exchanged the same look with his father before turning to Fernando and Marianna, who looked just as worried. Mrs. Aramis seemed to share the same expression too.

"Quick, check the other channels," Marianna urged.

Fernando clicked a button on his right armrest repeatedly, making the right viewport change channels fast. He stopped it on Channel 11, which was also showing breaking news about the recent crashes.

"… We fear the Pegasus Air Race is getting out of control," a female voice reported while the screen showed a shot of a column of black smoke rising from deep inside a thick wooded area. "Hundreds of the Pegasus camera drones continue to spread farther inland for some reason. Authorities have just confirmed that a small civilian aircraft collided with several of them. What's worse, several people claim to have witnessed the drones fly straight toward the craft, as if the drones had targeted it."

"What?" Keithan and Fernando chorused with bulging eyes.

"Why is this happening?" Mrs. Aramis said with a shaky voice.

Neither Keithan nor his friends dared to say anything else. Things were starting to get uglier—and not just at Ramey, but throughout the whole island. They continued watching the holo screen while Fernando searched more channels. It turned out nearly a dozen more were also covering the crashes.

"As you can see in the sky, there are way too many camera drones flying in the area," a female news correspondent addressed the viewers. "We urge all of you who are close to where these things are overflying to remain indoors."

"This just in," said a reporter from another news channel, "two military aircraft have been confirmed to be among the craft that have crashed."

"Oh, dear!" Mrs. Aramis gasped.

"So the military is taking action," Marianna commented.

"So it seems," Fernando said, "but they won't stand a chance, not with so many drones in the sky."

"And what about the air racers?" Keithan said, still trying to make sense of everything.

He reached out to Fernando's wheelchair and pressed a button on the armrest, instantly making the left viewport that was showing the race take over the whole holo screen.

Surprisingly, the event was still being broadcast as if nothing was wrong. The commentators continued narrating animatedly to the spectators' delight while the screen showed four of the air racers flying low and zigzagging with impressive skills within the green mountains deep inside the island. Hover rings at different altitudes awaited the racers at almost every turn, and with incredible precision, some of the racers managed to shoot through them, earning more points. Crowds gathered at the top of some of the mountains could be seen throwing their hands in the air when the racers flew by.

"Amazing maneuver by Rosangela Sofio!" one of the commentators said. "Oliviera imitates, doing his best to pass Sofio and take sixth place. They'll soon leave the island's mountain range behind before they head north, toward San Juan. Meanwhile, let's see how the leaders are doing … Oh! And it looks like they're only minutes away from reaching Ramey to complete the first lap! Luzier is still in the lead. Not a surprise, ladies and gentlemen. Ravena right on his tail."

"Oh no," Keithan murmured. He turned to Fernando and Marianna with a look of dread in his eyes, which his friends shared at the sudden realization.

Keithan, Fernando, and Marianna returned their gazes to the holo screen, which now showed the four racers in the lead flying low and at maximum speed in front of an overcrowded beach. Unlike at Ramey, only a few spherical drones could be seen hovering over the excited fans who cheered at the sight of the racers, clearly unaware of everything else that was happening in other parts of the island.

Keithan recognized the site. It wasn't far from the east of Ramey. At the speed the racers were flying, he knew it wasn't a matter of minutes before they reached Ramey—it was a matter of seconds.

Keithan broke into a run but not without first turning to his father and snatching the digital binoculars from his hands.

"Whoa! Where are you going?" his father said.

"I gotta see this!"

Soon Keithan was outside again. He halted just a few feet away from the hangar's main entrance then raised the binoculars and gazed left to the eastern horizon. Zooming in on the image on the device, he spotted four tiny shapes in the sky flying fast and straight in his direction.

"They're coming!" one of the race commentators said. "Ladies and gentlemen, boys and girls, the first air racers are already coming into view!"

The man's words made the already-pumped-up crowd in the grandstands stand up and look eastward.

Under different circumstances, Keithan would have braced himself to throw his fist into the air and cheer when the first air racers reached the airfield and completed the first lap. Yet now, an intense feeling of dread overtook him. It made him look high above him. It was then that he saw dozens of the Pegasus spherical drones break away from the circle high over the airfield. They were descending, though that wasn't what worried Keithan. What did worry him was that each of those things had its front lens pointed at the approaching air racers.

"They're gonna attack the racers," he said in a low, trembling voice.

He heard his dad and the Aramises reach him, and still Keithan kept staring back and forth from the spherical drones to the approaching racing craft. Just like when he watched all the racers take off, his heart rate accelerated, making him feel as if it were going to explode. At the same time, he tightened his grip on the digital binoculars while still holding them in front of his eyes. He didn't dare blink.

He gave one last look at the drones as they settled at a lower altitude. He could tell it was going to happen; he could almost sense it. The Pegasus Air Race was about to go terribly wrong.

Everyone around Keithan seemed to hold their breath. For an instant, the entire airfield seemed to have gone completely quiet too. Then, without any warning, the drones fired.

"Nooo!"

Loud gasps from the Aramises and his father followed. They, too, watched in horror as a horizontal shower of orange laser bolts rained eastward from the hovering drones and straight toward the approaching racers. Incredibly, the first two racing craft, Luzier's and Ravena's, broke hard to opposite sides to evade the attack. The other two weren't so lucky despite their pilots' quick reflexes. Just as they got to Ramey, the laser bolts hit them. Tony LeVier's *Lightning Dragon* was the first one to go down. It burst into a ball of flames before it hit the runway, where it disintegrated in the blink of an eye. Daiki Tamura's craft suffered the same fate, but he managed to eject right before his aircraft smashed against a hover ring and crashed, leaving a trail of debris in the middle of the runway.

Screams of panic and terror took over the entire area. The commentators seemed to be momentarily at a loss for words. They tried to narrate what was happening, but their shock was clear.

"The camera drones, people ... they've just attacked LeVier and Tamura!"

"It's ... it's ... incredible, ladies and gentlemen. The ... I can't— It's hard to describe."

"To everyone in the audience, remain seated. Please remain seated. Race officials are already on their way to deal with the matter."

Meanwhile, Keithan, his dad, and the Aramises remained petrified. They continued witnessing the developing chaos before their very eyes. Some of the **spherical** drones were still shooting at Luzier and Ravena, who were still in the air but leaving the airfield fast. A group of the drones had already shot after them.

Then everyone jumped when some of the drones exploded.

"Whoa!" Keithan, Fernando, and Marianna cried.

"What just happened?" Keithan's dad cried. "How did—? *Whoa!*"

More drones started exploding in midair. They looked like they were self-destructing. First, the ones that had fired at the air racers. Then the rest that had remained in the large circle formed in front of the large hovering vessel. One by one, they burst and dropped like flies all over the airfield. Ten. Twenty. Thirty ...

"What's happening?" Mrs. Aramis said aloud, hands pressed against her chest.

It took a few seconds for Keithan to realize the Pegasus drones weren't self-exploding. They were being shot at with small purple laser bolts that were appearing out of thin air.

"It's the Sky Phantoms!" he cried. *"They're here!"*

CHAPTER 16

The battle was on! It was inevitable. And too many lives were in danger now, not just those of the air racers. Sky Phantom knights gave it everything they had to take down as many of the spherical drones as they could. Even though they remained in full stealth mode, home base could still see them through their unique live satellite feed projected on the giant holo screen that hovered at the far end of the control room. The feed provided a clear aerial view of the dogfight: twenty-two Sky Phantoms versus the innumerable drones, together littering the sky over Ramey, along with their intense exchange of continuous laser bolts.

Also visible on the feed was the Pegasus airship, which so far remained still, hovering at the south end of Ramey Airport. Even more distinguishable because of its size was the intimidating dark vessel, which also remained unmoving.

From the very center of the control room, Lieutenant Colonel Codec Lanzard stood leaning forward with both hands resting on the main console. He watched the battle with narrowed eyes and careful attention.

"Don't take your eyes off the giant vessel, people," he said loud enough for everyone in the room to hear. "Make sure no shots or more drones come out of that thing."

"Sir, more air racers are approaching Ramey from the east," a technician reported from one of the console stations.

Lanzard had been expecting this, and so he pressed a button on his console and said, "Knights, more racers are coming your way. Be ready to protect them too."

"Copy that, Colonel," replied several voices through the console speaker.

Lanzard hadn't taken his eyes off the giant screen in front of him. Already he could see the challenge of his order, considering that the priority of the counterattack was to protect the civilians on the airfield and its outskirts. Nevertheless, the image on the screen made it obvious that his squadron was significantly outnumbered. There were just too many enemy drones in the sky. And still, that was nothing compared to how many more had to be dealt with throughout the rest of Puerto Rico.

Up close at the airfield, it was unbelievable to witness the chaos and panic. To Keithan, it seemed like a dream that had turned into a nightmare in the blink of an eye. The spherical drones looked like they had gone haywire. They filled the sky with laser bolts as they blindly attacked their stealth enemies, which returned fire nonstop. Every few seconds, a drone exploded in the air and crashed on the airfield. The people below at the grandstands and throughout the airfield screamed and ran for cover from the falling debris.

Keithan, his dad, and the Aramises, however, remained watching in shock in front of Hangar H11. They could see the terrified spectators in the grandstands dispersing like ants leaving a giant anthill.

"Quick! Everyone inside!" Mrs. Aramis shouted to them. She wasted no time and forced Fernando to rotate his wheelchair toward the hangar.

Keithan's dad grabbed Keithan by the shoulders and forced him to turn around too.

"Marianna! Come on!" her mom shouted.

A spherical drone crashed about twenty feet behind them. Its deafening sound was the only warning they got before debris flew in their direction.

"Watch out!" Keithan's dad cried.

He threw himself over Marianna and Keithan so fast neither Keithan nor Marianna saw him coming. The three of them landed hard on the asphalt just as a metallic piece of the crashed drone flew over their heads.

"Get up! Come *on!*" Keithan's dad cried. He pulled both Keithan and Marianna up and forced them to run.

Once they were all safe inside the hangar, Mrs. Aramis closed the wide entrance door halfway so they could still see outside. As for Fernando, he called out for everybody to gather around him. He turned on his projected holo screen to continue watching what was happening outside. As expected, the Emergency Broadcast System had been activated on almost every local channel. It was warning everyone on the island to stay indoors. Field correspondents from other channels and at different scenes throughout Puerto Rico also did their best to explain to viewers what they were witnessing.

Out of breath, Keithan, his dad, Marianna, and her mom watched the different channels Fernando had broadcasting simultaneously. They saw columns of black smoke being captured from different places throughout the island. This was just a sample of how bad the whole thing was turning out. Most of them were being broadcast from some of the checkpoints of the racecourse. And just like at Ramey, people were screaming and running for cover.

"Wait a second! The race is still going on?" Keithan said in disbelief when he saw the race's official channel still showing live footage of the race. "Quick, check how many racers are still in the air."

Fernando pressed a button on his armchair and made the viewport showing the race take over the whole holo screen. Some of the Pegasus drones were still broadcasting the race, following the racers from different angles, distances, and altitudes. The commentators were no longer talking due to what was happening, and the remaining air racers still flying were no longer competing but fighting for their lives. They zigzagged over and over again, executing their best maneuvers to escape the attacking drones.

"Oh my— Those are Aaron Oliviera and the Vampire!" Marianna cried, instantly recognizing their two racing craft.

"And look!" Fernando added, pointing at the screen. "Right behind them, Rosangela Sofio and— *Whoa!*"

He and everyone around him threw their heads back when they saw the racing craft flying last get hit by a shower of orange laser bolts and burst into a ball of flames.

"Is he ...?" Keithan's dad started to say.

"He ejected! He ejected," Keithan replied with a sigh just as he spotted a tiny shape shoot out of the flaming craft and release what appeared to be a parachute. He turned his attention to the bottom-left corner of the holo screen. There, a digital map of the entire island showed a line tracing the racecourse along with moving dots of different colors. The dots, as everybody knew, represented each of the air racers still in the air, and so far, Keithan could make out thirteen still flying. Yet while most of them continued following the racecourse, one in particular had moved away from it and was now heading deep inland.

"What is he ...?" Keithan murmured before he said aloud, "That's Luzier! He's leaving the racecourse!"

He had just said that when another dot left the course line and started moving in the same direction of Luzier's dot.

Keithan recognized that second dot too. "That's Ravena!"

"He must be going after Luzier," Fernando suggested.

"Is that a good thing?" Keithan's dad asked.

"I bet Luzier is trying to escape," Marianna said. "We believe he's involved in the attack."

"*What?*" Keithan's dad exclaimed.

Two loud explosions outside made everybody jump. They were followed by distant screams, which made a tense Laika bark from nearby.

"It's like a war zone out there," Mrs. Aramis said, looking

momentarily out the hangar's half-open entrance.

Keithan and his friends, still shaken by the explosions outside, tried to stay focused on the trajectory of Luzier's and Ravena's dots on the digital map.

"Luzier can't escape," Marianna said with a trembling voice. "If he does, everything's lost. Dad's whereabouts …"

"Someone needs to help Ravena stop him," Keithan said, though more to himself than to his friends.

His own words made him feel a sudden surge in his chest—the type of surge that emerges when fear and excitement mix. He could feel it growing inside him, intensifying, even accelerating his breathing, as if urging him to take action.

I should help, he thought. *I could help.*

He turned his gaze to the entrance. Slowly, he backed away from his friends and his dad. None of them noticed him as they remained deeply concentrated on the holo screen. None of them even turned to Keithan until the deep roars of the *d'Artagnan*'s engines rattled the walls and skylight windows.

"What the …? Keithan!" Marianna shouted.

Keithan barely heard her as the *d'Artagnan*'s three engines revved. The vibration was stronger from inside the cockpit while he strapped himself in and put on his helmet.

"Keithan!" Fernando yelled as loudly as he could over the noise. "What on earth are you doing?"

"What does it look like I'm doing? I'm gonna go help Ravena stop Luzier!"

"*What?!*" everyone shouted in shock. They were already hurrying toward the *d'Artagnan*. The weathered orange-and-gray racing craft, with its two crab-like arms extended forward, was now rising slowly and stirring ground dust beneath her.

Keithan swung one arm to the side repeatedly, gesturing for them to move away. "Guys, I can do this! I can go after Luzier!"

"Are you crazy?" Mrs. Aramis snapped.

"Set that craft down this instant, Keithan!" his dad shouted.

But instead, Keithan pulled back a lever to his right and made the cockpit canopy swing downward over him. As soon as it shut, the head-up display came alive, projected on the canopy's glass. He gradually rotated the *d'Artagnan* toward the entrance, which was open enough for him to fly out.

"Keithan, don't do it!" Marianna shouted, waving her arms desperately at him.

His dad waved too, though he looked more angry than worried. "Don't you dare!" His voice, like Marianna's, was muffled by the canopy's glass.

Keithan ignored them despite their efforts. He knew what he was about to do, and he knew he had to do it. He gave one last glance at Fernando to his left, who simply held his hands out to the sides, as if asking Keithan if he had lost his mind. Keithan tapped the side of his helmet in response, telling Fernando to try to contact him through his earpiece, which he hoped was working now.

"KEITHAAAN!" his dad and the Aramises shouted at the top of their lungs. Still, it was hopeless, for the roar of the *d'Artagnan*'s engines intensified when Keithan gave the craft full thrust.

And in that instant, the small racing aircraft blasted out of the hangar.

CHAPTER 17

Keithan kept a tight grip on the two independent steering yokes in front of him. He had to at the speed he was flying, which also kept his body pressed against his seat. He would have preferred a slower and more gradual takeoff, but not under the current circumstances. He'd intended to leave Ramey as fast as he could to get away from the invasion of Pegasus drones. He managed to do so by banking hard to the east soon after he left the Aramises' hangar. It wasn't until he reached an altitude of five hundred feet that he changed direction to the southeast, farther inland, still at top speed.

The land below rushed past him in a blur almost halfway to the horizon. Grids made of streets and houses mixed themselves with patches of different greens and browns from which light-gray highways snaked their way across. Then the mountains came, taking over the land with their vibrant greens and standing widely and dominantly, as if rejecting the notion that they were to be invaded by the grids of compressed civilization lying at their feet. These were the mountains where Keithan had last seen Luzier and Ravena head to from the racecourse's official map. He hoped to find the two racers soon, and he expected Fernando to help him. Unexpectedly, it was Marianna's voice he heard instead coming through the helmet's integrated communicator.

"—lost—mind?" was the first thing he heard her say over the annoying static.

Keithan rolled his eyes. He had been hoping she would be a little more supportive at the moment. "Yes, Marianna, I'm *so* out of my mind," he replied through gritted teeth.

There wasn't any point in trying to convince him to turn back, especially now when it would certainly be more dangerous to return to Ramey. Luzier and Ravena would also be trying to stay away from the spherical drones.

"You have— ...mount—"

"Say again?"

"—fl—over—mountain range."

Keithan shook his head and simply put all his attention on his flying. He banked left and pulled the yokes, making the *d'Artagnan* climb. He knew he would have a better chance of spotting the two racers from a higher altitude, like a bird of prey. He reduced speed too, that way he could see whatever flew in his direction better. The clear sky above him gave him another advantage, as it allowed the midday sun to provide more than enough light for Keithan to see. He just hoped the chase wouldn't lead to the south, where the weather looked completely the opposite: clouded and with a giant gray curtain of rain covering the land below.

"Where are you, Luzier?" Keithan murmured.

Far in front of him, he started making out a bunch of tiny dots in the sky. No doubt those were Pegasus drones. Below them would be several grandstands with panicked people running for their lives. As Keithan got closer, he also made out different shapes in the sky attacking the flying drones, most likely Air Force fighters trying to take them down.

Then Keithan spotted two other shapes in the distance. They were becoming more defined as they came in his direction.

"There you are!" Keithan cried, recognizing the two racing craft.

He braced himself to join the chase. Just as they were about to pass below him, he dived in a half roll, and as soon as the *d'Artagnan*'s orange crab-like arms and front steering vanes pointed toward the two craft, Keithan gunned the thrusters.

A rush of adrenaline came with the stunt. Keithan dared not blink, fearing to lose Luzier from sight. With his eyes narrowed and his face puckered up, he continued flying as gracefully and boldly as the two pro racers.

He was gaining on Ravena's black racer, close to twenty feet behind. And past Ravena, approximately twenty-five feet ahead, he could see the burning exhausts coming out of Luzier's sleek chrome racer.

Boy, these guys are fast! Keithan thought. He was having a hard time keeping up with the two racers even with the three engines of the *d'Artagnan* pushed to their maximum.

The most challenging part of the chase began when Luzier dived and forced Ravena and Keithan to do the same and continue flying among the rushing mountains. Keithan, still far from giving up, released a deep breath and concentrated harder. Now it was not just about speed, it was also about precision, skills, and control.

"I can do this. I can do this," he told himself.

"Keith— Keithan?" Marianna called.

"Hold on," Keithan said.

He couldn't afford any distractions. He needed to stay sharp on his every maneuver. His instincts guided him. He trusted them, just as he always did when air racing. And all the while, he felt like he was racing through a natural obstacle course, weaving at ubelievable speed through the mountains.

Judging by Luzier's maneuvers, he could tell the man was struggling to lose Ravena. Once, it looked like Luzier would make a sharp turn to the left, but unexpectedly, he turned abruptly right—too late for Ravena to follow. Keithan, on the other hand, managed to bank right and continue after Luzier. He accelerated with Ravena left behind.

"All right, Luzier, let's see what you're really up— *Whoa!*"

Keithan threw the *d'Artagnan* to the right at the sudden reappearance of Ravena's craft, which cut Keithan off as if to reclaim his position behind Luzier. Flying last again, Keithan continued doing his best to keep up. He executed evasive maneuvers like the two pro air racers, zigzagging over and over again, cringing every time he almost crashed into a mountain. Moments later, they left all the mountains behind. What remained from the land below now met with the open sea a short distance away.

"Um, guys?" Keithan said to his friends. "An update on where exactly I'm headed, please."

"*You're fl—southw— Uh-oh!*"

"Uh-oh? What do you mean 'uh-oh'?"

Inside Hangar H11, Marianna continued struggling to communicate with Keithan. Still, such a struggle was nothing compared to the inner one Keithan was causing her.

Why did Keithan have to be so stubborn? Her mind was a mixture of irritation and concern. To make matters worse, she also felt every muscle in her body tensing with each second that passed, mostly out of fear for Keithan's life.

Beside her, she noticed Fernando, their mom, and Mr. Quintero also tense by the way they, too, followed Keithan's live trajectory on Fernando's laptube. Luckily, the device could track down the *d'Artagnan* for miles, and from its small holographic touchscreen, it showed them a clear aerial view of where Keithan was flying. As a result, everybody ignored the bigger holo screen still projected in midair in front of them with the racecourse map and the live coverage of the chaos outside.

"Why is Keithan headed in that direction?" Marianna cried, pointing at the laptube's screen and unable to hide her frustration any longer. "He *knows* there are a lot of drones there!"

Once again she brought a hand to the microphone of the earpiece she had taken from Fernando and attempted communicating. "If you can hear me, Keithan, stop the chasing and come back home. *Please!*"

But static was the only thing she could hear now.

"I'm sending a text message to the *d'Artagnan*'s computer,"

Fernando told her, his fingers dancing over the laptube's projected keyboard. "Let's hope it goes through."

"And that Keithan doesn't ignore it," Mr. Quintero commented.

They kept watching the orange flashing dot that represented the *d'Artagnan* hovering over the west coast of Puerto Rico. It was moving slowly south toward the race's checkpoint at the city of Cabo Rojo.

Suddenly, everybody jumped when the loud, high-pitched hum of the Emergency Broadcast System interrupted the local channels' live coverage on the bigger screen.

"Attention! This is not a test! Repeat! This is not a test!" an urgent voice announced. *"Local and federal authorities have declared a state of emergency in all Puerto Rico. All civilians, seek shelter immediately and remain indoors until further notice. This is not a test! Repeat! This is not a test!"*

"Oh dear, Keithan ..." Mrs. Aramis said, her voice almost a whisper. She exchanged looks of dread with Mr. Quintero, who remained unmoving, gripping the back of Fernando's wheelchair.

Marianna could only imagine how Keithan's dad was feeling. Watching his only son risking his life out there in the middle of an aerial invasion that was spreading throughout the island. How dare Keithan do this to him!

"Darn it, Keithan," she murmured. "Stop the chasing and come back home ... before you regret it."

The air battle at Cabo Rojo came into view almost immediately beyond the *d'Artagnan's* cockpit—and it was *intense!* Happening beneath a curtain of heavy rain, it looked like a show of explosions and tiny laser bolts within a cloud of Pegasus spherical drones that hovered over the race's checkpoint and grandstands. The drones were firing nonstop in all directions. Some were getting hit hard and blasted out of the sky by returning fire that seemed to appear out of thin air—a sure sign that the stealth Sky Phantoms were out there putting up a good fight.

But despite how the battle looked from a distance, Keithan feared he was about to get a taste of it up close, and all because of Drostan Luzier. Most likely, the famous pro air racer intended to get rid of Keithan and Ravena by forcing them to fly into the middle of the air battle. Keithan, of course, considered turning away, but the thought of letting Luzier escape encouraged him to play along. On the bright side, flying through the air battle would only be a matter of seconds. All he and Ravena had to do was make it out of there alive.

"And here we go," Keithan said under his breath, bracing himself. Almost in perfect synchronization with Ravena's and Luzier's craft, he pushed his throttles and flew the *d'Artagnan* straight into the battle. Instantly, the heavy rain became deafening against the *d'Artagnan*'s fuselage. Orange laser bolts ripped past the cockpit canopy like tiny shooting stars, barely missing. And all around, spherical drones and hover rings fragmented and burst into flames.

To Keithan, it was like experiencing the most realistic 3-D air battle simulation game ever, except with no ammunition to fire back and with a one-life chance.

Now, more than ever, he put all his flying skills to the test. He continued executing extreme evasive maneuvers with quick reflexes. Every drone in his way, he evaded it without thinking, either with a roll, a knife-edge, or a zigzag maneuver, just like Luzier and Ravena were doing. But with every move he made, he felt as if his heart was going to climb up his throat. Never had Keithan felt so scared and thrilled at the same time while flying.

Then—*WHOOSH!*—the *d'Artagnan* made it out, right after Luzier's and Ravena's craft.

"Woooo!" Keithan cried with huge relief.

Hard to believe the *d'Artagnan* hadn't gotten a single scratch. Keithan once again focused completely on chasing Luzier, though the rain was making it a challenge for him to see. But first he gained on Ravena's aircraft from the right. Ravena saw him. Keithan gave him a thumbs-up, trying to show that he was there to help. He expected a response of approval from the Sky Phantom agent, but instead, the man, still doing his best to stay on Luzier's tail, waved an arm backward insistently, as if telling Keithan to go away.

"What? No way!" Keithan responded even though his mouth was hidden behind his visor.

No sooner than he said this than a laser bolt shot past between their two aircraft, quickly followed by two more.

"What the blazes?" Keithan shouted.

Keithan flipped a switch to his right, turning on his head-up display. A small virtual screen showing a rear view appeared on a corner of the canopy's glass, and Keithan looked at it in horror.

It revealed three metallic Pegasus drones flying right behind him and Ravena.

"Uh-oh."

Keithan hadn't questioned what he was doing up until now. He couldn't help wondering if this had been the dumbest thing he had come up with out of impulse and his constantly troublesome cockiness.

More laser bolts brought him back to the moment, making clear what he had to do. He had to outsmart the spheres and survive. Chasing Luzier would have to wait.

With an angry but determined puff, Keithan wrenched his wings' ailerons in opposite directions, along with the rear stabilizers, and sent the *d'Artagnan* in a radical spin, out of the spheres' line of fire. He kept at it for about three seconds, then stabilized the craft and did a horizontal loop that successfully positioned him behind the drones.

From there, he noticed the spheres were ignoring Luzier's craft and directing their attack at Ravena's. As for Ravena, he maneuvered as best he could to avoid getting hit. He twisted desperately left and right, but he didn't stand a chance. The spheres were too close to him. What happened next was inevitable.

"Nooo!" Keithan shrieked as a spray of laser bolts struck Ravena's craft, sending it on a steep spiral dive. He could only watch, horror-struck, hoping Ravena would eject in time. But it never happened. The Sky Phantom agent's cockpit burst into flames while still dropping. Keithan shot over it before Ravena's craft crashed into a valley.

The three **spherical** drones scattered as if having confirmed that their target had been destroyed. Their move allowed Keithan to see Luzier's racing craft up ahead again. And so, trying to shake up what he'd just witnessed happen to Ravena, he punched his thrusters and continued the chase.

Rain continued pounding on the *d'Artagnan* almost as loudly as the roars of her three engines. Much worse, it barely allowed any visibility, blurring both the land and the sky. But still, that was the least of Keithan's problems, for despite his chasing Luzier at high speed, Keithan was now the one being hunted. He realized it at the sudden reappearance of the three Pegasus drones on the screen of his head-up display.

"Oh boy," Keithan breathed with dread.

Now it wasn't a choice; he had to let Luzier escape. He banked hard to the left, breaking off the chase as an aggressive stream of laser bolts whizzed past the *d'Artagnan*. Knowing the drones' flying capabilities, it didn't surprise him to see them turn incredibly fast in his direction.

Fortunately, Keithan got an idea just as fast at the sight of a group of mountains looming ahead. He glanced at the rear-view image on the head-up display screen and said, "Let's see if you three can play *my* game now."

He plunged low and zoomed into the tight passage among the mountains.

A new race was on, and Keithan had selected its obstacle course. At least that was how he chose to see it to keep his hopes up over the terrifying moment he was experiencing. Just like when he'd been following Ravena and Luzier, he flew low, weaving among the mountains with the sharpest of turns he needed to execute. He kept so low he almost brushed against the tallest trees with the belly of the *d'Artagnan*. Meanwhile, his pursuers continued shooting at him. Yet nothing prepared them for what Keithan dared to do next ...

A Derry turn at one of the narrowest areas in the whole serpentine passageway.

It would have been a piece of cake to follow, or even imitate, without any risk at a much higher altitude, but Keithan had thought of exactly the opposite to his advantage. He didn't even have time to catch his breath. The stunt was a hard right turn that Keithan abruptly reversed with a roll under and a steep turn in the opposite direction. Even more impressive, he completed it with an abrupt and almost vertical climb just as he came face-to-face with a massive mountainside—and he did it all in an instant.

None of the spheres were able to match it. Keithan witnessed it as he craned his neck while still with the *d'Artagnan*'s twin front steering vanes lifted skyward. Two of the spheres crashed into different mountainsides and disappeared, each in a ball of flames. As for the third one, it almost suffered the same fate. Having been behind its former companions, it managed to arc over one of the mountains, almost shaving its treetops, but continued perpendicular to Keithan's direction.

"Ha haaa!" Keithan cried as he watched the remaining sphere fly away. He had just shot past the top of his mountain and had leveled the *d'Artagnan* again. Yet his celebration didn't last long, for moments later, he noticed the sphere had already found a new target. It was another racer who had unexpectedly drifted into sight. The dark-blue fuselage, along with the orange wings, let Keithan know instantly who it was.

"Aaron!"

Aaron Oliviera, the recently graduated student from Ramey Academy, and as far as Keithan knew, the youngest of the pro air racers who had qualified for the Pegasus Air Race. The two of them had spoken a few days ago when Keithan had tried to participate in the race's qualifier tournament. Just like Keithan, Oliviera had been looking forward to being in the race. And now he was going to be hunted down in it … but not if Keithan could prevent it.

More than a thought, it was a lightning reaction. Keithan did a half loop, changing his direction, and gunned the *d'Artagnan* toward the speeding sphere and Oliviera's racing craft. Keithan was about a quarter of a mile away, but he was gaining on them fast in a diagonal line.

The sphere had already started shooting, forcing Oliviera to execute evasive maneuvers. Keithan knew he wouldn't be able to protect him, but he swallowed hard at the realization of what he *could* do.

He could save Oliviera.

How Keithan got the guts, he never knew, but he kept his course straight toward the Pegasus sphere with full determination and awareness despite the growing fear that wanted to take control of him.

"I better not regret this. I better not regret this," he repeated to himself over and over through gritted teeth.

He did his best to keep the *d'Artagnan* steady, fighting the limits of her strength at full power against the wind.

"I better not regret this. I better … not … regret … *this!*"

Five seconds from impact, Keithan released both steering yokes and yanked up with all his might on a red lever between his legs. At the same time, he squeezed his eyes shut, and everything dear to him flashed before his eyes.

His goal to become a legendary air racer.

His sacrifices.

His friends.

His father.

The memory of his mother.

Then it happened. The *d'Artagnan* crashed into the Pegasus flying sphere, creating a thundering crash before the two exploded in a massive fireball.

CHAPTER 18

The orange dot over the digital map of the island disappeared, taking Marianna, Fernando, their mom, and Mr. Quintero by surprise. They all flinched before they froze, still staring at the laptube's screen. None of them seemed to be sure what to make of it, but as the seconds passed, it started to become clear.

"No," Marianna breathed. "It ... can't be."

Her heart seemed to contract so tightly it felt like it would stop beating. It made her clutch her chest. She fought to keep her mind blank to prevent herself from imagining a clear picture of the worst.

She turned to Mr. Quintero and saw the horror in his eyes, the blood red of their sclera filling with tears. His hands looked worse. They were shaking uncontrollably, as if the man wanted to burst out of his petrified body.

Beside him, Marianna's mom remained with both hands over her mouth and her eyes wide, which were filled with tears. She was also shaking. And then there was Fernando, who, to Marianna's surprise, showed no emotion. She didn't know how her brother managed it, but he seemed to have shaken off his shock and started working on his laptube, concentrating deeply. He looked back and forth from the device's projected keyboard to its holo screen, leaning forward and typing like a superfast automaton. Everyone around him watched.

A red dot flashed on the screen. It made Fernando pull his hands away from the laptube. Three seconds later, the red dot reappeared and continued flashing.

"He's alive!" Fernando shouted with a clap, almost giving everybody else a heart attack.

Both Marianna and her mom yelped, right before Marianna smacked her brother slightly on the back of the head.

"Ow!"

"Don't do that again!"

"But *look!*"

Everyone leaned closer around Fernando and the laptube's holo screen.

"That's not the same dot. Keithan and the *d'Artagnan* were orange," Marianna said.

"I know. This one's the emergency tracking beacon installed underneath Keithan's seat," explained Fernando, now beaming.

Mr. Quintero straightened himself. "What does that mean?"

"What does that mean?" Fernando turned to him. "It means Keithan ejected! The *d'Artagnan* must've been taken down, but he ejected!"

Marianna let out a deep breath just as she saw her mom's and Mr. Quintero's faces getting their natural colors back.

At least Keithan was alive, but Marianna still had the desire to strangle him the moment she saw him again.

Rocketing skyward gave Keithan the strong sensation of sinking into his seat. It didn't last long, though, since soon he started slowing. He came to a standstill at approximately one thousand feet, which gave him the sensation of sudden weightlessness an instant before he began to fall. But before he could gain speed, his parachute shot out from the back of his seat. The abrupt jerk that followed assured Keithan the parachute opened without any problem, and so, finally, he puffed with relief.

Now calmly descending, Keithan reflected on what he had just pulled off. He couldn't believe it. He had sacrificed the *d'Artagnan*—the very racing craft he and Fernando had built together and studied with—all to save Aaron Oliviera.

Whether or not Oliviera recognized the *d'Artagnan* before it happened, Keithan couldn't know, but he didn't care. Oliviera had escaped unharmed. Keithan could see him now speeding away, deeper inland.

Keithan lowered his gaze, and his heart dropped. Far below, he spotted where the remains of the *d'Artagnan* had fallen. All he could make out, however, was a column of black smoke roiling upward. At least, Keithan noticed, the remains had fallen on what appeared to be a pineapple field, far from any housing or other populated area. There barely seemed to be any housing for miles. The land below was nothing more than one giant valley spread toward a black lagoon that stretched horizontally to the south. It wouldn't have been much to look at if not for the impressive curvilinear crop signs looming below Keithan's feet.

The signs looked like giant carvings made by a much-advanced civilization. They covered an area almost the size of two football fields. Anyone who wasn't familiar with such signs would believe they had been made by extraterrestrial visitors as a type of communication marking to be seen from space. But Keithan knew well that that was nothing more than an old urban legend. Nevertheless, the crop signs made him realize where he was descending to.

"Lajas Valley."

All of a sudden, a low buzzing in the distance made Keithan raise his gaze again. It seemed to be increasing, but the fact that it sounded familiar, like a small jet engine, was what sent a chill run down his spine. And he saw what was making the sound with a double take to his left: a lonely Pegasus sphere flying at his altitude and headed straight in his direction.

Eyes bulging, Keithan looked back and forth from the sphere to the ground. He tugged desperately at the parachute's risers above his shoulders, not knowing what else to do. No way could he unhook himself when, according to the altimeter projected inside his helmet's visor, he still was 627 feet away from touching the ground. He looked at the sphere again. It seemed to have no intention of slowing down, and it was already positioned to attack. Keithan was a sitting duck, dangling helplessly from the parachute.

This was it.

His jaw clenched and his eyes shut tight, ready to meet his doom.

Then ...

Zzpt-zzpt—BOOM!

The blast made Keithan cross his arms in front of his face, just as a hot force, like a gust of wind, pushed him abruptly opposite to where he had last seen the flying sphere.

Now swinging, Keithan dared to open his eyes. He was still alive, in shock, but still alive. And the flying sphere that had been coming toward him was nothing but debris, now plunging earthward.

"B-but ... how ...? What...?"

Keithan looked all around him for an explanation that seconds later appeared at approximately twenty feet in front of him, as if out of thin air.

It was a Sky Phantom aircraft, and watching it up close, hovering in midair, Keithan beamed and shouted, "*Man*, am I glad to see you!"

CHAPTER 19

T he landing was nothing like the way Keithan had practiced many times at Ramey during his flight classes. Not only did he remain on his ejected seat all the way, but he also landed hard. At least it felt great to touch the ground despite how it felt to land on his butt cheeks, which continued hurting for quite a while.

Keithan was already on his feet. He had tossed his helmet aside and was currently examining his new surroundings, turning slowly on the spot. Just as he had seen while descending from the gray sky, the damp area showed almost no sign of civilization nearby. A few old utility poles aligned beside what appeared to be a road in the distance, but nothing more, not even a field of solar panels or wind turbines, which were usually found at wide-open areas such as the one where Keithan stood. As for the Sky Phantom craft that had saved his life, it had disappeared long before Keithan had landed.

Keithan accepted his current situation: he was alone, and he had to figure out a way to get back to Ramey.

He trusted Fernando was tracking his landing coordinates, but Keithan couldn't simply stay there and wait to be rescued. He still needed to find Mr. Aramis, and now more than ever he would need the Sky Phantom Legion to help him, which was all the more reason for him to return to Ramey as soon as possible. Therefore, Keithan started walking.

He was headed toward the only road visible in the whole valley even though it was far away. In the meantime, Keithan kept himself busy with his brand-new wrist communicator. He wanted to contact his dad and his friends with it to let them know he was okay, but the device's main screen showed he had no signal.

So much for the communicator.

At least the screen showed him the time: 12:21 p.m. At the press of one of the buttons on the side, the 3-D holographic GPS, along with Keithan's current coordinates and the weather readouts, came to life. The data hovered around Keithan's wrist like a semitransparent gauntlet. According to the compass, Keithan was moving southward.

Having landed on one of the giant crop signs, he could see curving patches all around him where the crops had been flattened. Such patches were so big it seemed like it would take him forever to reach one of the crop sign's borders. It actually took him about forty minutes, and by then Keithan was panting and starting to get thirsty. He had taken off his racing leather jacket and was carrying it in one hand. Still, he felt the weight of his sweaty blue T-shirt, which he kept peeling off as it continued plastering against his back.

He came upon the lonely road soon after stepping out of the crop sign. Keithan looked both ways and noticed that the road stretched far to the horizon in both directions. To the west, about a hundred feet away, he could make out a green reflective road sign mounted on two poles. He headed in its direction, looking forward to seeing what it said. Yet he regretted it halfway there when he was able to read the sign.

"RUTA EXTRATERRESTRE," it said in white lettering, which Keithan understood as Spanish for extraterrestrial route. At its top left, the sign had the white silhouette of a flying saucer.

Keithan huffed. "Great."

Just like the giant crop sign, the green road sign was nothing more than a tourist attraction inspired by local urban legends about UFO sightings.

Once again, Keithan looked around, not sure where to go. He considered continuing down the road, past the sign, to see where he would end up, but he noticed a glint far across the road, behind a group of hills. He narrowed his eyes, but still he couldn't make out what it was.

"It's worth a shot," he said with a shrug. He wiped the sweat from his forehead with the back of his hand, and gathering his strength, he crossed the road. He climbed up the nearest hill, though with some difficulty since it was slippery from early rain. Once at the top, he released a deep breath.

As if the crop signs hadn't been peculiar enough, what Keithan saw on the other side made him wonder if he had stepped—or landed—into the Twilight Zone: that mysterious dimension between science and superstition that he'd heard Mr. Aramis mention many times when talking about retro science fiction. Keithan was now staring at a wooded valley from which three ivy-covered lattice towers stood out over the treetops, each with the weirdest pyramids Keithan had ever seen. They appeared to be watchtowers of some kind but roughly built and weathered by time. Their pyramidal tops, which rested on rusted overhangs, were steep, slightly bloated, and made of spaced modular levels. And their surfaces, Keithan noticed, had numerous window slits that created linear and curvilinear markings, like hieroglyphs from a super-advanced civilization. Just as peculiar, the three structures were positioned close to each corner of a wide triangular platform that was also raised over the treetops but lower than the watchtowers.

"A vertical landing platform," Keithan said at the same time he realized it was fake.

It turned out Keithan was gazing at what remained of the abandoned UFO landing port that a group of locals and a former mayor of Lajas had started to develop near the end of the 2020s. According to rumors, it was to provide a safe and secluded landing area for "alien UFOs." Keithan found the idea ludicrous. Hard to believe, despite the strong criticism it had received, the project had gotten its initial construction approvals, though it wasn't long before the whole thing was halted due to lack of funding.

Thank goodness for Mr. Aramis, who always talked about all things related to legends and folklore about UFO sightings. Keithan even remembered Mr. Aramis talking about the time he and some of his old college buddies visited the site and sneaked their way in to explore it. That gave Keithan a similar idea.

He started down the hill, toward the raised platform. Yet a wrong step made him slip, and he slid down fast since there wasn't anything near for him to hold on to. He came to a stop at the bottom when he landed in a group of bushes.

"Argh!" Keithan cried in pain, reaching for his left leg.

Raising his back, he saw that a branch had ripped part of his pants and cut his thigh. It wasn't a deep cut. It wasn't bleeding much either, but it hurt a lot. Despite this, Keithan got back on his feet and kept walking. No way was he going to let that stop him, much less in this place.

Moments later, Keithan came before a tall chain-link fence that he would have climbed over if not for the barbed wire affixed at its top. But it turned out he didn't need to, for he found part of the fence missing not too far away, a hole big enough for him to crawl through.

"Hello!" Keithan hollered, holding both hands over his mouth like a megaphone. "Can anybody hear me?"

There was no response. All he could hear inside the wooded area was the chirping and buzzing of different birds and insects, accompanied by the rhythmic dripping of water all around. They seemed to contribute to the gloomy atmosphere maintained there by what little light made it through the crowns of the trees and the cold air that smelled of damp earth and grass.

Once again, Keithan checked his communicator and huffed. *Darn it! Still no signal.* Now would have been an ideal time to talk to Marianna. At least to hear her voice to distract him from feeling alone.

He kept walking through fern and foliage. He felt his shoes sinking two or three inches into the muddy soil, making it hard for him to accelerate his pace. He wanted to get out of there, as wandering through the wooded area beneath the watchtowers and the triangular platform gave him a creepy feeling.

The place looked like something between an old abandoned theme park and a junkyard, only there weren't any rides, not even pieces of what could have been one. Still, the place's theme was evident everywhere, mostly on the numerous graffiti and murals of flying saucers and alien heads that were painted on corrugated zinc panels and discarded vehicle parts. Faded signs of different shapes and sizes also showed it with their weird, curious messages like "WELCOME, ETS," "TAKE US WITH YOU," and "VISITORS' (FROM ALL GALAXIES) SOUVENIR SHOP," among many others.

Keithan even walked past several giant sculptures that looked like they had come out of a dystopian science-fiction movie. He wasn't sure if they were supposed to be crashed spaceships, teleporting machines, or both. Yet what was so impressive about them was how elaborate they were, not to mention the fact that they were made of all kinds of scrap metal parts, no doubt the works of a genius artist. They would have looked even more impressive if not for all the vegetation and wide spiderwebs covering them like they did everything else there, as if nature had reclaimed the area.

Keithan was climbing over some twisted and rotting metal pieces laying in his way when he heard a rustling of leaves to his right. It made him freeze for a couple of seconds before he jumped off the pile of scraps and crouched behind it. He turned off his holographic gauntlet so it wouldn't be spotted. The rustling was becoming louder, and now Keithan could hear it accompanied by the squishy sound of footsteps.

"Stay calm, Keithan," he whispered to himself, doing his best to control his breathing. He peered through the scraps and saw movement behind some bushes where the sounds were coming from. Then he noticed one, then two figures. They were coming closer. Maybe they could help him, but if they had bad intentions, Keithan needed to make sure they didn't find him.

Still crouched, he examined his surroundings. He could lose them anywhere under the trees and keep running till he could find a safer place. That is, if the figures didn't know the area too well, either. He could do it. The wound on his thigh still hurt, but it wasn't bad enough to stop him from running.

He looked again through the metal parts. The figures were coming from the side of the concrete base of one of the watchtowers, bright white beams extended from their hands. No more than thirty feet now stood between them and Keithan. Still, Keithan waited, ready to make a run for it if necessary. Then one of the figures hollered in a deep voice.

"Keithan! Keithan Quintero!"

Keithan had definitely not expected that. He didn't recognize the voice.

"Keithan!"

This time Keithan stood up, revealing himself. The two figures raised their light beams at him.

"Ungh! Would you mind?" Keithan protested, shielding his eyes with his right forearm.

Both strangers turned off their lights and gradually came into clear view. They were two broad-shouldered men clad in green camo trousers, rough-terrain black boots, and black carbon fiber shirts with only their left sleeves long and so tight they accentuated their muscles. One had dark skin and a shaved head. The other had tanned skin, a stubble beard, and a black cap that he wore backward. It didn't matter if they were soldiers or local hunters. Either way, Keithan was certain neither man was to be messed with.

"Are you Keithan?" asked the man wearing the cap backward.

Keithan hesitated. "Yeah?"

"We're here to take you out of this place."

The same man gestured for him to follow, but Keithan knew better than to go with two strangers. It didn't matter if they knew his name.

"Um, who are you, exactly?" he dared to ask, ready to run in the opposite direction.

"Don't be afraid." The man with the cap pressed what appeared to be a mini screen on the left side of his chest, making a digital insignia appear. It took some effort for Keithan to make it out from where he stood, but he recognized it. It was a silver triangle slightly leaned to the right, with tiny circles in each of its corners and a stylized wing attached to its right.

"You're Sky Ph—!"

"Shhh!" The man with the cap cut Keithan off and looked at his companion over his shoulder. "Getting anything?"

The other man was staring down at his left sleeve, the long one, which Keithan noticed was glowing with different readouts.

"Nothing so far," the man replied. "No electronics detected for a mile radius aside from the boy's wrist communicator and his power-strapped sneakers. Sensors aren't detecting any suspicious movements, either. We're good to go."

"Good." And with that, the man with the cap backward drew out a very familiar pen-like device, which he pointed at Keithan.

"No— *Wait!*" Keithan shouted in horror, but before he could make a move, a tiny dart shot out from the gadget and landed on his left shoulder. "You bast ..."

His words trailed off, for in that instant, he felt the dart's effects take control of his body. First, his muscles became heavy. His eyes followed, turning all blurry at the same time his mind drifted away. Then the rest of his senses seemed to shut down.

Keithan didn't even feel hitting the ground right before he lost consciousness.

CHAPTER 20

An electric shock made Keithan wake up with a fright and sit bolt upright on the floor. Soon after that, he crawled backward at the sight of the two agents who had found him in the woods.

Both men had been crouched at either side of him but quickly stood up.

"Whoa! Take it easy. It's all right," said the man with the shaved head.

"You're safe, kid," added the one with the black cap backward.

"*Safe?*" Keithan exclaimed, his honey eyes fixed on the small Taser in the hand of the bald man.

The man noticed Keithan's eyes and put the Taser back into the holster on his belt. "It was just to give you a light zap to wake you up. That's all."

The other guy stepped forward. "Sorry for bringing you like this, but we couldn't show you how to get here."

But where exactly was here?

Still agitated and on the floor, Keithan turned his head in all directions, trying to figure out the new room he was in. It was small and circular, like an empty water tank, its curving iron walls black with floor-to-ceiling lines of rivets. Keithan felt around with his hands. The floor was cold but rough under his hands, like concrete. The ceiling, however, was something else entirely. It was one transparent dome with reinforced steel frames that Keithan expected to reveal the sky beyond it but instead revealed a jade-gray underwater view with fish and algae.

Slowly, Keithan got on his feet. He gave a second look above him to confirm what he'd just seen. It wasn't an illusion, the room *was* underwater.

"W-where ...?"

"Still in Lajas, inside one of the Legion's old stations," the bald man said. "Now, come. You're expected at the control room."

Both men were now leading Keithan down a sewer-like tunnel dimly lit by lines of cyan strips that stretched along either side of the floor. The moisture could be felt in the air, but at least it didn't smell like a sewer.

Along the way, Keithan continued doing his best to figure out where exactly he had been taken. "One of the Legion's old stations at Lajas," said Keithan to himself as one of the men had told him, "and somewhere deep underwater." The more Keithan thought about it, the more he wondered if it was true. He couldn't help thinking about how risky it would be to have a Sky Phantom station in a city so well known for its fascination with UFO sightings. Not to mention the many old urban legends that promoted such things.

Then it hit him. The Cartagena Lagoon! The only lagoon in Lajas and the very same one Keithan had seen while descending with his parachute. Keithan remembered hearing about legends related to the place. According to accounts from locals, there were people who claimed to have seen strange lights in the middle of the lagoon late at night. Some described them as dancing lights of different colors beneath the dark water's surface, while others had claimed that such lights shot out of the water without making a sound or a splash and disappeared into the night sky. Yet to Keithan, it all made sense now: this Sky Phantom station he had been brought to was hidden deep at the bottom of the Cartagena Lagoon.

Fortunately, the tunnel wasn't too long. Soon after it curved right, the entrance to the control room appeared.

"You said I'm expected," Keithan said while still following the two agents. "May I ask by whom?"

"Agent Venus," the man with the cap backward replied over his shoulder. "She's the one who saved you while you were dropping with your parachute."

Keithan frowned. "Agent Ve—" Then he remembered. Professor Dantés! That was her code name!

He entered the control room and saw his professor at the other end. Her back was to him. She almost looked unrecognizable in her black Sky Phantom knight uniform. Yet it was Dantés's stance what gave her away, with her feet separated, her hands clasped behind her straight back and shoulders, and her hips slightly leaning to the side.

She and four other Sky Phantom agents in matching uniforms were watching a wide collage of over a dozen holo screens. Each screen showed them a different channel's coverage of the current invasion of Pegasus drones throughout Puerto Rico. There was more activity going on at both the left and right walls of the room. Technicians in black uniforms and with tiny microphone headsets monitored different maps projected on their console stations.

"Agent Venus," called one of the men escorting Keithan.

Dantés turned. A slight look of surprise seemed to betray her composure when she saw Keithan. She seemed about to hurry up to him but held herself back. She took only a couple of steps, forcing Keithan to walk up to her.

She looked at him up and down, as if scanning him. Then she said quickly and in a somewhat casual tone, "You all right?"

"Yeah," Keithan replied with a shrug, imitating her casual tone. He could tell the professor was trying to hide her deep concern but without success.

Dantés cleared her throat. "Good."

She kept nodding while staring at him. As for Keithan, he tried to come up with a way to thank her for saving his life. The uncomfortable silence between them didn't help, though.

"Um …" he started to say, rubbing the back of his neck, but at that exact moment, Dantés spoke too.

"You do realize you are lucky to be alive, right?"

Keithan lowered his gaze. Thanking Dantés was going to have to wait since he could tell she wasn't done with him.

"Hundreds of spherical drones out there," Dantés told him over her shoulder, "hunting down all the air racers in the sky and everyone else getting in their way. And as if that wasn't enough to keep us Sky Phantoms busy, I spot *your* racing aircraft take off from Ramey and get into the middle of the aerial battle."

Keithan opened his mouth to explain, but once again, Dantés cut him off.

"You and I are going to have a *serious* talk. But not—"

"There's a new coded message from Mona base," interrupted one of the technicians at the console station on the left wall, loud enough to get everyone's attention. He remained facing his holo screen. "The last of the air racers have been escorted to safety by Air Force fighters. Six racers in total are now safe."

"Six … out of sixteen?" Keithan whispered with dread, hoping against all hope Aaron Oliviera was among the six who had survived.

He glanced at Dantés and the other uniformed men and women in the room. It was impressive how none of them revealed an expression of concern or fear. Not even with a twitch at the corner of an eye. These people really knew how to stay in total control at all times, Keithan thought.

"Anything else?" Dantés asked the technician.

"Yes, Captain," the technician said. "Lieutenant Colonel Lanzard just ordered all Sky Phantom knights in the air to retreat and return to home base or nearest stations."

"Finally," Dantés exhaled.

Keithan, on the other hand, shook his head and turned to her. "You're leaving the fight?"

"Our mission was to protect the racers in the air. We protected as many as we could."

"But the spherical drones—"

"Look for yourself, Keithan," Dantés shot at him. She pointed at the many live images of the flying spheres on the collage of holo screens. "We took down as many of those things as we could, and we are still incredibly outnumbered. Almost thirty to one. If you aren't still convinced ..."

She turned to the technician working at the console station at the right side of the room. "Minimize all current holo screens, and give me a full-size satellite image of the island with all enemies and bogeys detected."

Instantly, every single holo screen floating shrunk as if it had been sucked into nothingness, right before a new giant holo screen appeared on the same space.

Keithan's jaw dropped when he saw the image. It was a high-definition view of the entire island of Puerto Rico with its different shades of green, brown, and gray covered by an excessive cluster of magenta dots. Clearly, the dots were the innumerable Pegasus spheres. They were spread all over the island like a virus and keeping a dense concentration mainly over the northwest, mid-south, and north coasts: the same areas where the three colossal flying carriers had arrived. More shocking still was what it all meant: the Pegasus spheres had taken complete control of Puerto Rico's airspace, as if having formed a blockade to hold the entire island hostage.

Staring dumbfounded at the map, Keithan wondered for the first time what he should have wondered at the very beginning: Why? Why was this happening? What was the real purpose? The more he thought about it, the less sense it made to him. He couldn't come up with an explanation.

"Almost unreal, isn't it?" Dantés said, her eyes on the map too. "The entire island is now at the mercy of Pegasus. Worse still, the Sky Phantom Legion too."

That last part made Keithan turn to Dantés.

"Pegasus knew about the Legion before all this happened," Dantés explained, noticing his shock. "And we have no idea how."

"You mean before the attack?" Keithan was now more confused.

Dantés nodded. "Pegasus revealed themselves to us by somehow intercepting our highly encrypted communications. And not just that. They demanded that we not interfere with the arrival of the flying carriers, or else they would attack the air racers."

"Then the carrier in the northwest attacked and shot down one of our squadrons before the Legion would comply," added the bald burly man behind Keithan. "After that, all hell broke loose."

It took Keithan a moment for everything to sink in. Yet he felt something about the professor's explanation was amiss. According to her, the attack against the air racers was planned to happen *if* the Sky Phantom Legion had tried to stop the flying carriers from reaching Puerto Rico. That didn't match with what he and his friends had found in the hard drive of Mr. Aramis's broken laptube. Based on the mysterious file in the hard drive, the attack was meant to happen all along. And Mr. Aramis ... was he responsible for that? *He couldn't be,* Keithan thought. *Fernando and Marianna's dad? He would never do such a thing.*

Keithan shook his head, refusing to think he could be wrong, and looked at Dantés again.

"What do you plan to do?" he asked her.

"We don't know yet," Dantés said with a deep sigh. "We should try some communication with the enemy and parley. At least try to persuade them to remove the spheres from the island and move the battle away from civilians. We're waiting for Lieutenant Colonel Lanzard's next orders. Rest assured, we *will* stop Pegasus. It's personal now for the Legion." She paused and faced Keithan with a menacing look, one that was all too familiar to Keithan. "In the meantime, do you mind telling me why the *hell* you were flying in the middle of all this with your *d'Artagnan*?"

The words struck Keithan like a slap to the face. They were so unexpected he hesitated. He wasn't even sure what was worse: the angry tone in which Dantés had asked or the penetrating stare she kept focused on him. Now *that* was the professor from Ramey Academy he knew.

"Just tell me, tell *us*," Dantés insisted.

It was such an uncomfortable feeling for Keithan, seeing the uniformed men and women in the control room now staring directly at him too, waiting for an explanation. Even the technicians at their console stations would have been staring at Keithan too if they hadn't needed to stay sharp and continue monitoring what was going on outside through their holo screens. Still, Keithan reminded himself of why he had taken off with the *d'Artagnan*, and so he regained his confidence and spoke.

"I went after the air racer Drostan Luzier. He's involved in the whole invasion and more. So I chased him while he was trying to escape." *There. I said it.*

He expected to see at least some looks of comprehension, but instead, the Sky Phantom agents shared skeptic expressions.

"Drostan Luzier?" repeated the big man with the cap backward. "It can't be."

"Well, he used to be with the Pegasus CEO in almost every public appearance," interjected another male agent nearby. "But ..."

"Luzier is dead, Keithan," Dantés said matter-of-factly.

"*What?*" Keithan exclaimed. "No!"

"I'm afraid so," Dantés said. "He was one of the racers shot down by the flying spheres."

"It was confirmed minutes ago on the news," added another agent.

He gestured to one of the technicians at the stations, who nodded in response and brought a small viewport to the bottom of the island's map for Keithan to see. The viewport showed the breaking news report of Luzier's death after being attacked by the Pegasus spherical drones.

Keithan shook his head slowly while he watched the report, speechless and still not believing it. Drostan Luzier, his only hope to find out what had happened to Mr. Aramis, dead. The evidence was right there in front of Keithan, an amateur video footage of Drostan's racing craft lying in the mountains, completely deformed, like a broken tin toy, its cockpit in flames. Yet to Keithan, it still didn't make sense.

"How is it possible?" he said, more to himself than to everyone around him. "Why would the spheres attack him when he was behind the whole thing?"

"If what you say is true, don't think it's strange he was probably betrayed," Dantés told him. "But that means he couldn't have been the real mastermind behind everything that is happening. To me, there's only one person who could have organized all this, and that's the very same man who owns all those spheres, as well as the flying carriers: Colani."

Keithan turned to her. "No. It wasn't Colani," he assured her. "He would seem like the logical suspect, but I'm almost certain it wasn't him."

"And what could you possibly—?"

"The Daedalus Project," Keithan cut her off.

The entire control room turned deathly quiet. It was clear every single Sky Phantom agent and technician there had heard those words before.

"It was planned to be used for the invasion, but Giovanni Colani didn't know about it," Keithan explained. "Apparently the project was developed behind his back."

No one around him seemed to know what to say. Keithan went on explaining.

"Professor, that's what I wanted to tell you last night, when I got home from Colani's airship, but no communication was working at Ramey. Then, earlier today, at the crew area—"

"What's your point, Keithan?" Dantés said, her expression now of deep concern.

"My point is the Daedalus Project might be the key that holds the answers to everything that's happening—and it's linked to Drostan Luzier, not to the Pegasus CEO. That's one of the reasons I went after Luzier."

A heavy hand landed on Keithan's shoulder and forced him to turn around. It was the burly bald agent. He leaned closer to Keithan and said with a worried but hopeful tone, "Kid, by any chance, do you know what the Daedalus Project is?"

Keithan puckered his lips, looking straight back at him, and shook his head.

The man couldn't help huffing his disappointment.

"But I know where it is," Keithan added before giving one final look at Dantés. "We gotta get back to Ramey as quickly as possible."

CHAPTER 21

" **A** s quickly as possible" would have been in a Sky Phantom aircraft. That, unfortunately, wasn't a choice to get back to Ramey with so many Pegasus spheres overflying the place. Instead, the trip had to be on land, in one of the Legion's raven-black vehicles, distinctive for its twin spherical tires, one at the rear, the other at the front, and the driver's cabin, which was isolated from the passenger's. Inside the latter, sat Keithan and Professor Dantés, strapped and facing each other in opposite seats.

Keithan, glad to finally be able to speak to the professor in private, took the opportunity to explain to her with as much detail as possible everything he and his friends had found out about Pegasus and the attack against the air racers. More importantly, he told her everything he knew so far about the Daedalus Project and Mr. Aramis's involvement in it, which had led to the man's strange disappearance. Dantés listened intently all the way.

As their ride continued north toward Aguadilla as fast as traffic allowed it, the two of them also saw the terrible damage the flying sphere attack had left throughout the island. Crashed spheres lay almost everywhere like abandoned scrap metal. Some were still in flames in open green fields, on top of houses and other buildings, even in the middle of roads and highways, forcing drivers to turn abruptly to evade them. One sphere, Keithan saw, had landed on the hood of a car and made it collide with two other vehicles. Other spheres lying on the road were getting kicked and pounded by angry people armed with hammers and metal tubes.

There were also a few wrecked U.S. Air Force fighter aircraft. These were surrounded by firefighting units who were doing their best to put out the flames.

"Thirty minutes to reach Ramey," said the agent who was driving, his voice coming from the speakers behind Keithan's and Dantés's seats.

The closer they got to Ramey, the worse things looked. Cars, trucks, even RVs, seemed to have been abandoned on both sides of the road at odd angles, some with their doors open, others lying on their sides as they had fallen—if not driven—into ditches. On top of that, people were still running down the main road that led to Ramey, terrified and panicked and trying to get as far away from the airport as they could. And then there was the National Guard, both on foot and in their six-wheeled tank-type vehicles, doing their best to control the chaos on the outskirts of the airport. No doubt the National Guard would already be inside the airport too. About a dozen soldiers in camo fatigues blocking the main entrance suggested it.

Keithan feared they might not let them enter judging by their rigid stance and intimidating long weapons.

One of the soldiers stepped forward and raised a hand at the sight of the raven-black vehicle gradually reducing speed in his direction.

"Don't worry. This vehicle has full clearance to enter," Dantés reassured Keithan, as if having read his thoughts.

How exactly could that be possible under the current circumstances? Keithan had no clue, but sure enough, the group of soldiers stepped aside and allowed the vehicle to pass.

Soon Keithan saw Hangar H11 up ahead. Once the vehicle parked in front of it, he rushed out and ran toward the building's entrance, which was still half open. There, he found Marianna and Laika. Marianna was gazing skyward at the giant Pegasus carrier and the swarm of drones with her headset and its matching globe-shaped camera, which hovered over her left shoulder. She removed her headset at the sight of Keithan and ran toward him. She looked angry but also as if she was about to burst into tears. She couldn't match Laika's speed, though. The barking golden retriever shot past her and got to Keithan first.

"Hey, girl! I'm all right. I'm back," Keithan told Laika, gently trying to brush her aside so he could continue.

Just as he straightened up again, Marianna surprised him by throwing herself at him in an embrace. Keithan raised his arms to hug her back, though not as strongly as Marianna was. Marianna kept her arms locked around his neck, making it hard for Keithan to breathe. Still, he didn't struggle to loosen himself from her grasp. Instead, he took in her familiar and soothing scent, which reminded him of spring flowers and sweets.

They held each other for a few seconds. Hearing his friend sniffling, however, made Keithan pull himself away a few inches.

"Why are you crying?" he asked her.

Marianna's expression morphed abruptly despite her red and swollen eyes.

"Why am I crying? Are you *serious?*"

"Um ..."

"We thought you'd been killed!"

"But ... my seat's tracking beacon. It was activated. I checked."

Marianna released a loud grunt and pushed herself away from him.

It wasn't until that moment that Keithan noticed his dad with Mrs. Aramis and Fernando behind Marianna. His dad was shaking his head, but he stepped forward and pulled Keithan into an emotional hug. He would have kept Keithan in his arms longer if not for Dantés, who stood a few feet away from them.

"Professor?" Caleb said over his son's shoulder. "*You* brought Keithan back to Ramey?"

"Yeah, um ... it's a long story, Dad," said Keithan, noticing his father's weird stare toward the professor, most likely because of her highly advanced black uniform. He glanced at Dantés and noticed her deeply serious gaze. Then he glanced past her and noticed the raven-black vehicle that had brought them leaving.

"I'm sorry, Cal— I mean, Mr. Quintero," Dantés said. "Your son brought me here because he says he has something important to show me regarding everything that's happening, and we haven't much time. Keithan?"

Keithan nodded. "Right. Come with us, Professor."

He gestured for Fernando and Marianna to catch up to him while he hurried ahead into the hangar.

"Hey," said Fernando, slapping hands with Keithan while pushing his wheelchair. "So glad you're all right. Did you hear about Luzier?"

"Yeah, and I still can't believe it," Keithan replied. "I thought the guy was behind all this. By the way, I'm so, *so* sorry about the *d'Artagnan*."

"Yeah, well, let's … let's just be glad *you* made it back. Now, what's going on with Dantés being here?"

"Yeah, why is she here?" Marianna asked, keeping up with them.

"She saved my life at Lajas after I ejected from the *d'Artagnan*," Keithan told them in a low voice even though the three of them were out of earshot from the adults behind them. "Don't worry. I'll explain everything later. Right now, we gotta find out what the Daedalus Project is and show it to Dantés. She and the Sky Phantoms might be able to help us find your dad."

The whole group went all the way to the back of the hangar, toward Mr. Aramis's ruined workshop. One at a time, they went through the yellow PVC strip curtain. Laika, however, remained obediently at the entrance.

"Whoa," Dantés exhaled at the sight of the wreckage inside.

Keithan went straight for the little cube lying on the floor next to Mr. Aramis's broken laptube and showed it to Dantés.

"This is the hard drive I told you about, Professor. So far, it's the only thing that proves Mr. Aramis's involvement in the Daedalus Project."

"And where's the project?" Dantés asked.

Keithan turned to Fernando and Marianna with a questioning look, hoping they would help him out.

"It could still be here."

Mrs. Aramis's response took everyone by surprise. All eyes turned to her. She, however, was staring deeply at the floor.

"What makes you say that?" Keithan asked her.

It was Marianna who answered. "Dad's safe."

Marianna was now staring down at the floor too.

"The safe … of course!" Fernando cried. He pointed at the center of the workshop's floor.

Keithan lowered his gaze and noticed the crevices there. He started clearing the area. Marianna and Dantés joined him. Together they pushed aside scattered tools, scrap metal pieces, and other stuff till a whole rectangular area on the floor became fully visible. Chunks of concrete were missing from it as if somebody had hit it with a sledgehammer.

"Looks like someone tried to open it," Keithan guessed.

"How *do* you open it?" Dantés asked.

"From there." Mrs. Aramis pointed to an access panel on the wall at the other end of the workshop.

Everyone hurried toward it. Fernando, who managed to get in front of it, pressed it with an index finger, making a digital keyboard appear.

"Mom, please tell me you know the password," he said.

Once again, everyone turned to Mrs. Aramis, but she shrugged and said, "I-I'm sorry. I don't. Your father tends to change it. I do know he tends to relate it to what he's keeping inside the safe, either directly or indirectly … as an easy way to remember it, I think."

"So, if the Daedalus Project's in there, maybe the name itself is the password," Marianna suggested.

"Really?" Dantés said with a frown. "I mean, wouldn't he have chosen a less obvious password?"

"It's worth a shot," said Keithan, not wanting to overthink it. "Try it, Fernando. Type in 'Daedalus.'"

Fernando leaned closer to the digital keyboard on the access panel and typed, but when he pressed Enter …

- INCORRECT PASSWORD -

The words flashed in red and made everybody huff.

"I knew it couldn't be that obvious," Dantés said.

"Wait," Marianna said. "The complete name of the project included a series of numbers. Fernando, Keithan, do you remember? It was in the file we found inside the hard drive."

There was a moment of silence. Then Fernando began to recite, "Twenty-three … nine … fourteen …"

Everybody stared at him while he continued concentrating.

"… seven … and … *nineteen!* Daedalus twenty-three, nine, fourteen, seven, nineteen! That's it!"

Keithan chortled. "How could you have possibly remembered that?"

"I'm an aeroengineer student. I have to memorize codes all the—"

"Are you sure that's the code?" an anxious Dantés interrupted, clearly wanting to hurry things up.

"Yes," Fernando replied.

"Then go ahead. Type the whole name," Marianna urged.

Everybody watched Fernando type on the access panel, but Fernando halted after adding the third digit next to the name Pegasus.

"Darn it!"

"What? What is it?" Keithan said.

"I can't type the whole thing. The panel has spaces for a maximum of ten characters."

"Well, then, just type the numbers," Dantés told him.

Fernando did exactly that and pressed Enter.

- INCORRECT PASSWORD -

Everyone couldn't help huffing in frustration louder than the first time. Keithan even scrubbed his hands down his face, though he wasn't growing as impatient as Dantés seemed to be. The professor glowered and kept her jaw clenched.

This time, a warning appeared on the digital panel and made everyone lean closer.

- CAUTION -
FAILURE TO TYPE CORRECT PASSWORD
A THIRD TIME WILL SHUT DOWN
SYSTEM COMPLETELY.

"Well, that's not good," Keithan's dad said. No sooner than he said this, Dantés turned around and marched toward the yellow strip curtain.

"Professor," Keithan called. "Where are you—?"

"We don't have time for this," Dantés shot at him. "I'm going after Colani with the rest of the Legion."

"We can do this!" Keithan insisted. "Professor, *please!* We *can* figure this out. We just ... we need to think harder. Mrs. Aramis."—he turned around—"you mentioned your husband tends to change the password to something related to what he keeps inside the safe, right?"

"Yes," Mrs. Aramis said.

"So it's probable the password is indeed related to the name Daedalus and the numbers."

Dantés seemed to be about to interject.

"Just hear me out," he said, raising a hand at her while looking at the others. "Now, to what else can we relate the project?"

"To Pegasus, obviously," Marianna said.

"And to air racing?" Fernando suggested.

"Hold on," Keithan's dad stepped forward. "Daedalus. Pegasus. Two names derived from Greek mythology. Daedalus is known as the most famous inventor, craftsman, and architect in all Greece. Pegasus is the legendary winged horse."

"Yes. So?" Dantés said. "What else could they have in common?"

"And with air racing?" Mrs. Aramis added.

"Perhaps something about ... flying?" Keithan said almost subconsciously.

"Well, Pegasus flew," Marianna said, "but Daedalus ..."

"He also flew!" Fernando exclaimed at the sudden realization.

Next to him, Keithan's dad snapped his fingers. "That's right! The story of Daedalus and Icarus!"

At this, Keithan shook his head and said, "Okay, now I'm lost."

He expected Dantés to be lost too, yet the professor remained still, her eyes narrowed and her arms crossed as if deeply considering what they seemed to be unraveling.

"Keithan, we read the story in our first year at the academy, in our English class!" Fernando reminded him.

"According to the story, Daedalus and his son, Icarus, were imprisoned in the labyrinth that Daedalus built for King Minos of Crete—the famous labyrinth that also imprisoned the minotaur," Keithan's dad explained as quickly as possible. "To escape captivity, Daedalus built two pairs of wings made of wooden frames and feathers adhered with wax for him and his son. But Icarus died because he flew with the wings too close to the sun, which melted the wax—"

"Whoa! Hold on," Fernando interrupted. "Pairs of ..."

Everyone waited while he murmured the numbers again.

"Twenty-three, nine, fourteen, seven, nineteen ..."

Then it seemed to hit him, and so he raised his gaze and said, "I think I know what the password is."

He didn't wait for anyone's approval. Instead, he turned again to the access panel on the wall and typed. Everyone around him watched silently, intrigued.

"Um, Fernando ..." Keithan said.

"Trust me," Fernando responded. He held his index finger over the Enter digital key as if suddenly having second thoughts.

"*Wait*," Marianna said. She quickly put on her viewscreen headset, which she had hanging from her neck, and drew out her globe-shaped hover camera from one of her pockets. "I wanna record this. Ready!"

Fernando pressed Enter.

Everyone held their breath. Keithan almost cringed. The suspense was overwhelming. Then ...

Click!

The typed password vanished along with the digital keyboard on the panel's screen. A green check mark appeared, just as the rectangular marked area on the floor behind them unlocked and started rising.

CHAPTER 22

"Wings." Keithan couldn't believe it all depended on such a simple word. Just as Fernando figured out, the word had been right next to the name of the project all this time but written as a cipher.

"A letter-to-number substitution cipher," were Fernando's exact words. "It's when each letter is simply substituted by the number of its corresponding position in the alphabet. In this case, 23: W, 9: I, 14: N, 7: G, and 19: S."

Keithan, his dad, Dantés, and the Aramises watched the rising safe reach its maximum height with a heavy clunk. Marianna's round hover camera still hovered over her left shoulder, capturing the moment. The safe now stood like an iron monolith at the very center of the workshop, twelve feet tall and six feet wide. Its double metal doors began to open outward. Keithan felt his heart racing in anticipation. The moment seemed almost unreal, as if the doors were about to reveal a new dimension, or worse, Mr. Aramis's darkest secret. Yet at the sight of what was inside the safe, Keithan only raised an eyebrow and wrinkled his nose.

It didn't look like anything threatening. Just as the password suggested, it was a pair of wings, the kind that the mythological Daedalus would have built if he were in this day and age. The wings looked like sculptures standing vertically, approximately four feet tall and two feet wide. They were sleek, with small twin curved channels on their back edges but no ailerons. One wing stood in front of the other, yet together they blocked from view the device which they seemed to be attached to.

Everyone approached Mr. Aramis's invention, fully intrigued. Keithan and Dantés stepped the closest, cautiously studying it.

"What exactly is it?" Keithan's dad asked, staring over Dantés's shoulders.

"Looks like a drone," Mrs. Aramis said, craning her neck.

"It's not a drone," Keithan and Dantés responded simultaneously, neither of them taking their eyes off the object.

"This looks more like it's … made for riding," Keithan added.

Marianna leaned closer. "How can you tell?"

Keithan and Dantés pulled the wings aside like a pair of doors to reveal what they were attached to. Everyone tilted their heads, still trying to figure out what they were staring at. It was a small board made of two circular platforms that were connected by twin tubes, each one with an antigravity plate attached. The bottom platform also had an engine with an exhaust nozzle and a pair of airflow vents. Tiny rivets covered the whole thing, giving it a roughly built look. Yet it wasn't until Keithan managed to see the other side of the thing that he realized what it really was.

"Oh my gosh!" Keithan exhaled.

"What?" Fernando asked, leaning forward from his wheelchair.

Keithan grabbed hold of the thing and brought it out of the safe. Surprisingly, it didn't feel as heavy as it looked. Still holding it vertically in front of him, he rotated it for everyone to see: two foot mounts with bindings attached to the two circular platforms.

"Guys, this is a winged jetboard!" Keithan said, awestruck.

The others' reaction was swift, mirroring Keithan's.

Keithan felt the urge to get on top of the thing and turn it on to try it out. He could just picture it: zooming out of the hangar with it and taking the thing for a spin in the sky. This was definitely something he hadn't expected to find. A jetboard … a winged jetboard. *Mr. Aramis, you're a genius!*

"This is *it*?" said Dantés, abruptly bringing Keithan back from his daydreaming moment. Not only did she still look confused, but judging by her tone, she was more upset and frustrated by what they had found. "*This* is what Mr. Aramis was working on in top secret for Pegasus? What does this have to do with the sphere invasion? The air race? *Colani*? Why would this thing be a threat compared to everything else that's happening?"

Keithan scratched his head. He, too, was trying to make sense of everything now. "Well, the hidden file in the hard drive of Mr. Aramis's laptube specified this thing was a requirement."

"He's right, Professor," Fernando said. "The file showed that it was planned to be used for the invasion and the attack against the air racers."

"Yes, but how, exactly?" Dantés insisted, still irritated.

The more they thought about it, the more confusing everything became. Moreover, if the project was still there in Mr. Aramis's workshop, but Mr. Aramis …

A soft hissing pulled Keithan from his thoughts, breaking the momentary silence inside the workshop. The sound seemed to be coming from over their heads.

Frowning, Keithan shot a look at Fernando and Marianna before the three of them raised their chins to look at the glass ceiling above them.

"Oh no," Fernando said with dread.

Over twenty feet above them, they found Emmeiseven hanging upside down like a bat, staring down at them with its faceless head. Then …

"Watch out!" Keithan shouted just as Emmeiseven released its grip from one of the ceiling's curved beams.

It seemed to have been waiting for the right moment to drop. The intimidatingly large robot surprised them by landing with a heavy clank in the middle of the group. It straightened itself with its claw-like hands open.

Everyone staggered backward.

"What the blazes?" Dantés exclaimed.

Fernando cried out, "That's our dad's— *Whoa!*"

Right at that moment, Emmeiseven snatched the jetboard from Keithan's grasp with a swift swing of its right gauntleted hand. It rotated its torso 180 degrees with the same movement to face the PVC strip curtain.

"No!" Keithan cried. He sprang straight toward the robot with his arms forward and jumped on its back, wrapping his arms around the robot's neck.

"Keithan, don't!" his dad shouted.

He and Dantés sprang forward to help, yet even together they weren't a match for Emmeiseven. The robot, still with the jetboard under one metal arm, swung its free arm and stopped Caleb midway, clutching his left shoulder.

"Argh!" Caleb cried.

Dantés managed to grab the robot's arm with both hands, but Emmeiseven simply flung her and Caleb backward several feet against two broken-down machines. As this happened, Mrs. Aramis did her best to protect Fernando and Marianna by standing in front of them with her arms stretched to the sides. It was the best thing she could do while they watched the fight in horror.

"Keithan, let go of it!" Marianna shouted, but Keithan kept his arms locked around Emmeiseven's mechanical neck.

He didn't know why Emmeiseven wanted the jetboard; he just knew he couldn't let the robot escape with it.

"Aaargghh!" he cried as Emmeiseven's claws gripped his waist. The pain forced him to let go, but the robot didn't let go of him. It pulled Keithan off its back and swung him hard against the floor like a rag doll.

"Ungh!"

"Keithan!" cried Fernando and Marianna.

Keithan's dad and Dantés were already back on their feet, struggling to figure out what to do. As for Keithan, now sprawled on his back, he released another loud cry before the robot landed a metal clawed foot on his chest and pressed. Keithan tried gasping for air. His eyes grew wide in terror at the sight of Emmeiseven's free clawed hand closing into a fist, about to strike him.

"Help ..." he barely managed to breathe.

There was a red flash and a whoosh above him, right before Emmeiseven's head disappeared. Its now headless body twitched and shook at the same time oil and sparks shot out of the numerous wires and tubing now dangling on its neck. It continued twitching for a few seconds before it dropped the jetboard and collapsed to the side.

Keithan reached for his chest, dazed and breathing heavily. Luckily he wasn't bleeding, but his shirt now had two ripped holes that stretched from his left clavicle to his lower-right ribs. For the second time today, he thought he had been about to die. A deep sigh of relief escaped him as he realized he was still alive.

Raising his gaze, he was shocked to see Marianna now standing in front of him. She still wore her viewscreen headset, and her camera still hovered over her left shoulder, but she was holding a three-foot-long red wrench with both hands.

"Y-you did that?" Keithan said between heavy breaths.

Marianna couldn't respond. Panting, she dropped the wrench and removed her viewscreen headset before offering Keithan a hand to help him up.

Keithan took it, and once on his feet again, he turned around to look at the now-still body of Emmeiseven.

"Marianna, that was awesome!" he told her while still rubbing his chest.

The robot's head lay several feet away. Its glass front was now cracked and broken. Keithan frowned in anger. He wished he'd been the one who had knocked Emmeiseven's head off. It would have made him feel a whole lot better.

The others were already gathered behind him and Marianna. They were also staring down at the broken MA-7 unit.

"I knew that thing was bad news since day one," Fernando said.

Keithan chortled, though it made the muscles on his chest hurt more.

"So that was how Pegasus intended to get the project," Marianna said. "Emmeiseven was just waiting for somebody to open the safe."

"Wait a second," said Dantés suddenly, stepping forward. "This is one of Pegasus's robots?"

"Yeah. Well, it was Dad's mechanical assistant robot," Fernando clarified. "Drostan Luzier and some guys from Pegasus brought it several weeks ago to help our dad with the project."

Dantés bent down and picked up the robot's head.

"Um, what are you doing, Professor?" Keithan asked.

"Getting to the bottom of this." Dantés was now examining the head. "If this robot was working for Pegasus, it might hold some answers about the whole purpose of the project. Fernando, is there a way we can connect this head to a computer?"

Fernando hesitated. "Uh … I-I think so, but only if you take its hard drive out since the head's main outlet is broken."

Dantés nodded, still staring at the robot's head. She grabbed the loose parts dangling from the bottom and yanked out its entire internal mechanism. She started disassembling it, tossing aside metal pieces and wires. Keithan and the rest watched until Dantés said, "Aha!"

In her hands was Emmeiseven's hard drive. It was twice as big as the cubic hard drive Fernando had taken out of his dad's laptube. It looked a lot more complex too: dodecahedral and covered all around with an elaborate labyrinth of circuitry made of silver-and-gold lines.

"Quick, Fernando. Work your magic," she told him.

Fernando took the hard drive and connected to it a small cable he'd pulled out of a small panel on one of his wheelchair's armrests. He had the holographic touchscreen projecting in no time. He started typing on the digital keyboard displayed on the data pad now resting on his lap.

"See if you can—"

"Found it! Look," Fernando said before Dantés could finish.

Everyone around him leaned closer to Fernando's holo screen. The thing now projected what Keithan could only make out as an agglomeration of computer codes floating on a dark background. In the middle of the screen, a framed neon-green text that Fernando had enlarged stood out:

MA-7 Unit
Last login: Sat May 01, 2055 00:45:22
Shadow File: Daedalus Project 23-9-14-7-19
Phase: Two
Last loaded command: Steal Sky Phantom aircraft while in flight and deliver to Pegasus.
Requirement: Daedalus Project 23-9-14-7-19
Status: Active

Keithan's dad and Mrs. Aramis may have been completely at a loss, obviously because they didn't know about the Legion, but Keithan, Fernando, Marianna, and Dantés did understand how serious—and bad—what they were staring at was.

"You gotta be kidding me," muttered Keithan, still focused on the highlighted text. He turned to Dantés with dread.

Despite the fear in the professor's eyes, Keithan could tell she was still confused by what they were staring at. He, too, found it more confusing than everything else they'd found out so far, even after rereading the loaded command still highlighted inside the displayed frame.

"So that's it, then," he thought out loud. "That's what all this is about."

"Getting a Sky Phantom craft," Dantés finished for him.

"W-what's a Sky Phantom?" asked Keithan's dad, exchanging a perplexed look with Mrs. Aramis. No one answered.

"But that's impossible," Fernando said. He raised his gaze to Keithan, Dantés, and Marianna with a questioning look. "Emmeiseven? Programmed to fly the Daedalus Project to steal a Sky Phantom craft? Not even the best pilot in the world could accomplish that. Not even your mom if she were alive, Keithan."

Keithan looked back at the robot's headless body lying in front of them. "Maybe Emmeiseven could. I mean, look at it. Its white coverings:

sleek, aerodynamic—a totally unnecessary feature for a mechanical assistant robot, don't you think? Unless … it was meant to fly too."

"But how could it steal a superfast fighter aircraft like a Sky Phantom—and in midair?" Fernando insisted.

Keithan turned his gaze to the winged jetboard lying next to Emmeiseven's body. "With a matching superfast and highly maneuverable flying device … like that one."

Silence followed for a moment.

"But I thought the Sky Phantoms could turn invis—"

"Not to whoever is behind all this, I'm afraid," Dantés said quickly before Marianna would reveal any more to Mrs. Aramis and Keithan's dad. "My … *colleagues* and I found out about that the hard way. So I fear I have to agree with Keithan. Perhaps that robot could do the job with the winged jetboard."

"You mean like the way cowboys used to catch up to trains back in the Old West to rob them?" Marianna said.

"Yeah. But in this case, in the sky," Keithan said.

"Excellent analogy."

The new and unexpected voice made everybody jump and turn abruptly on the spot.

Just when Keithan and the others thought things couldn't get any weirder, they found themselves staring at a ghost. At least, that was Keithan's first thought at the sight of racing champion Drostan Luzier, who, still in his racing uniform, now stood in front of the workshop's yellow strip curtain. Worse still, Luzier held what Keithan recognized as a fist energy pulser: a small handgun with separate twin barrels, one on each side of Luzier's horizontal fist.

And the man had it pointed straight at him.

CHAPTER 23

Nothing could have prepared Keithan for this chilling moment, mostly because he'd never imagined himself experiencing it. It was one thing to see a villain surprising a character with a handgun drawn in a movie or a TV show. But having one pointed at him, right there and right now, made Keithan freeze in terror. This was no joke, no act, either. Luzier had a real weapon in his hands, and he didn't seem hesitant to use it.

It shouldn't have surprised Keithan and the Aramises seeing Luzier there, at least since his involvement in the Daedalus Project was no secret to them. But seeing Luzier back from the dead? That wasn't only surprising, it was spooky too. The man didn't look his best, though. His golden hair was all sweaty and plastered to his head, and his racing uniform no longer looked impeccable, as it was all muddy and tattered. Still, Luzier kept a perfectly straight posture.

"You!" Keithan exclaimed in shocking disbelief. "H-how is it possible?"

"We saw you crash in a wooded area deep inland," Fernando said, also shocked. "It was all over the news."

"You only saw my aircraft crash," Luzier corrected them in his Dutch accent and with an expressionless face. "It was the perfect diversion for me to buy more time."

"I thought you were nothing more than an air racer," Dantés said. She was the only one who didn't seem intimidated by either Luzier or his fist energy pulser, which the man kept pointed forward. She stared at him with narrowed eyes. Luzier, however, gave her a smug smile.

"You're not the only one with a double identity, Alexandria. Or should I say ... Agent Venus?"

Keithan raised his eyebrows and turned to Dantés. The professor's self-confidence and cold stare had vanished.

"That's right. I know a great deal about you and your secret legion," Luzier went on while staring directly at Dantés with his haunting sky-blue eyes, which looked like those of a feline and were so hard to read. "And I must say, of all the Sky Phantom agents, fancy seeing *you* here. It's ... how best to describe it? Perfect?"

Dantés frowned. "What's that supposed to mean?"

"Hmm, nothing important. Now—"

"Wait!" a trembling Mrs. Aramis dared to interrupt, holding up her hands. "What have you done with my husband?"

Luzier didn't answer.

"Please," Mrs. Aramis insisted. "We need to know."

She kept her hands up even though they were shaking. Keithan noticed she couldn't hold back the tears running down her cheeks.

"He's still alive," Luzier said, though his attitude showed no empathy.

Everyone gave a deep sigh. Keithan felt a heavy weight of relief instantly spread through his chest.

"That's all you need to know for the time being. Now,"—Luzier raised the separate barrels of his fist energy pulser again—"I want everybody to step away from the Daedalus Project—except you, Keithan."

Keithan glanced at his dad and Dantés with a double take. "Huh? Why?"

"You're coming with me."

"*What?*" everybody cried.

"*No.* Mr. Luzier, you can't—" Keithan's dad started to say.

He'd just taken a step forward but froze when Luzier pointed the weapon at him.

"H-he's my son, Luzier. I can't let you."

"You don't have a choice. Now, step back."

Still, Keithan's dad didn't move.

"*Step back!*" Luzier thundered.

Twin pulse shots followed. Marianna and her mom yelped. Keithan jumped and looked at his dad, expecting the worst. To everyone's surprise, his dad wasn't hurt. The two pulse shots Luzier had fired had only left two holes on the concrete floor, mere inches away from Caleb's shoes.

Out of the corner of his eye, Luzier must have seen Dantés about to make a move because he quickly swiveled his gun at her.

"*Don't* even try it!" he warned her, his fingers tight on the grip's multi-finger trigger.

"All right!" Keithan shouted and raised his hands in front of him. "I'll go with you, Luzier! Just … just don't hurt anyone, okay?"

He dared not take his eyes away from the fist energy pulser.

"Okay?" he repeated.

Luzier, now with a deeply menacing look, nodded in response. His gaze, however, remained fixed on Dantés, who stared straight back at him with fiery eyes and tightly puckered lips.

"Pick up the Daedalus Project."

Keithan did as he was told. "Now what?"

Loud gasps escaped Marianna and her mom when Luzier turned the energy pulser toward Keithan.

"No!" Keithan's dad stepped forward, his hands still up. "Take me instead. Please!"

"That's not going to happen, Caleb," Luzier replied.

"Then take *me* instead," Dantés said, her hands also up. "He's just a boy, Luzier. We can't let you—"

"*Shut up!*" Luzier roared.

He moved behind Keithan and pressed both of his fist pulser's barrels underneath Keithan's chin, forcing Keithan to throw his head back.

"All right! All right!" Dantés said.

"It's okay. I-I'll be fine, guys," Keithan managed to say over his fear. At the same time, he struggled with the pressure under his chin. He didn't know what else to say. He just needed to keep Luzier calm.

Luzier forced him to start moving backward and toward the yellow strip curtain, all the while pressing the twin barrels harder under Keithan's chin. Yet he made Keithan stop close to three feet in front of the curtain.

"Oh, I'll be needing all the evidence related to the Daedalus Project too." This time, he turned to Fernando. "Young Mr. Aramis, I'm sure you know what I'm referring to."

Keithan managed to look at his best friend, and so did everybody else. Fernando was so nervous he didn't seem to know how to respond, or whether or not he should.

"Your father's laptube and the MA-7 unit's hard drive," Luzier specified.

Hands trembling, Fernando unplugged Emmeiseven's hard drive from his wheelchair. He placed it on the floor and sent the dodecahedral piece rolling toward Luzier.

Luzier picked it up. "And the laptube?"

This time Fernando didn't move. He gazed at Dantés instead.

Don't give him the hard drive. Don't give him the hard drive, Keithan wanted to tell her. He thought of all of Mr. Aramis's inventions and concept designs that the thing surely contained, among them things Mr. Aramis might have not revealed to anyone yet or probably needed not to be revealed at all, especially to someone like Luzier.

"Here," Dantés said suddenly.

She reached into one of her pockets and pulled out the small cubic piece.

"What's that?" Luzier said.

"It's all that's left of Mr. Aramis's laptube," Dantés told him. "Its hard drive."

"It is," Keithan reassured Luzier, his head still held back.

Luzier stared suspiciously at the cubic piece while slowly placing Emmeiseven's hard drive in one of the pockets of his racing uniform.

"Bring it to me. Slowly," he told Dantés.

Neither of them took their eyes off each other. Dantés took each step as if she were walking on thin ice, keeping the hard drive close to her stomach.

"That's close enough. Put the drive on the floor and step away," Luzier ordered.

Dantés swallowed hard and placed it a foot away from the man's boots. She was starting to straighten herself again when Luzier surprised her. Perfectly timed, he threw a left hook and punched Dantés right in the face.

"Hey!" Keithan cried.

His dad reacted the same way while the Aramises gasped. Caleb rushed to Dantés, who staggered backward. Yet she shook her head and managed to quickly straighten herself. She didn't bother rubbing her cheekbone. She simply stared back at Luzier with menacing eyes despite the man's fist energy pulser now pointed at her chest.

Keithan turned to Luzier, furious. What was the guy's problem with Dantés? Keithan wanted to hit him so badly, probably just as much as Dantés also wanted to. Luzier's malicious smile made it worse. It made Keithan hate him even more, especially when it showed how much Luzier was enjoying all this.

Once again, the man pointed the pulser at Keithan.

"Let's go, kid."

Keithan hesitated and looked at everyone else over Luzier's shoulders.

"Are you deaf? *Let's go!*"

"Keithan ..." Marianna said with a trembling voice.

Keithan noticed her eyes filled with tears. He wanted to assure her it'd be all right. He didn't need to say the words, though. He could sense she wanted to tell him the same thing.

Luzier placed his free hand on Keithan's shoulder and forced him to move. The two of them stepped out of the workshop with the energy pulser pressed against Keithan's back, all the while Luzier savored his victory in silence.

CHAPTER 24

Alexandria had never felt so much anger as she felt right now. It felt like it was burning her inside while she, Caleb, and the three Aramises helplessly watched Keithan leave the hangar with Luzier. The Daedalus Project in Keithan's hands, as well as Luzier's plans with it, seemed secondary to her now. Even the pain in her swollen right cheekbone didn't concern her at the moment. Still, Alexandria knew her anger was nothing compared to the agony Keithan's dad was experiencing. Just seeing the man suffering from being unable to help his son—his only son—was more than enough reason for Alexandria to fight her anger and frustration. Moreover, to channel them into the strength she required to figure out a way to get Keithan back.

"This isn't happening," Caleb said in a low, trembling voice. "H-how could I have let Luzier take him?"

He was facing the hangar's entrance, yet he seemed to be staring at nothing. Mrs. Aramis, unable to suppress her tears, held his right arm in support. Fernando and Marianna stood behind them, staring in shock out the hangar's entrance.

Almost in a flash, Alexandria recollected everything that had happened today so far. It didn't matter the different angles she tried to see everything, a common factor remained constant: Pegasus succeeding in every single plan it had secretly set in motion.

Not in everything, Alexandria then realized. There had been one exception: the MA-7 robot. It had failed to take the Daedalus Project to steal a Sky Phantom. No doubt Luzier could use another unit to take the Emmeiseven's place, but at least all the Sky Phantoms remained grounded and hidden now. Of that, Alexandria was certain.

"It's not over yet. There's still hope," she said, instantly puffing up her chest and turning to Caleb and the Aramises. "I swear to you—to all of you—I'm going to get Keithan and Mr. Aramis back safe."

"How?" Fernando asked.

Alexandria failed to answer right away.

"I … don't know yet, but I'm not letting Luzier and Pegasus Company get away with this."

"Maybe this will help," Marianna said. In her hand lay her round hover camera.

Alexandria frowned. "Is it still recording?"

"Never stopped," Marianna said. "I snatched it from over my shoulder and kept it in my hand when I saw Luzier's fist energy pulser. It might not seem like much, but it'll help expose Luzier as the villain he is, not as the victim and casualty everyone probably thinks he is."

This time, Alexandria raised her eyebrows. "Quite a smart move, Marianna."

Clear on what she needed to do now, she looked down at her left forearm and swiped her index and middle fingers over the black sleeve, turning on its integrated flexed screen. She started typing on it.

"What are you doing?" Caleb asked.

"Getting the help we need."

Alexandria pressed the Send key on the flexed screen before raising her gaze again. "Everyone, come with me."

"Huh? Where to?" Fernando said.

"We're meeting with the rest of the Legion. Marianna, make sure you don't lose that hover camera."

Alexandria considered the risk she was about to take, but she knew what she had to do. She would have to explain herself to Colonel Lanzard and deal with the consequences too.

She noticed the look of deep confusion that had returned to

Keithan's dad and Mrs. Aramis before she marched out of the hangar with them. Yet she tightened her jaw at the sight of Fernando's and Marianna's slight smiles, which the two teens exchanged between themselves before proceeding to follow her too.

She knew what those smiles implied: Fernando and Marianna were now looking forward to seeing the Legion's secret base.

A hexagonal glass module with metal frames stood at approximately twenty feet outside the Aramises' hangar. Keithan recognized it immediately as the same module that had shuttled him and his dad to Colani's airship last night. This time, however, four of the Pegasus spheres accompanied it. All the while, the rest of the drone armada remained floating over the entire airfield, the majority protecting both Colani's airship and the air carrier that had the giant winged stallion bust at its front.

"Watch your step," Luzier said as Keithan climbed into the shuttle with the Daedalus Project.

Just as it happened the first time he'd been in it, Keithan hesitated when he saw the Pegasus service robot that piloted it. He decided to stand opposite it, just in case. No way was he looking forward to getting into trouble again with another robot.

The shuttle's glass door closed after Luzier stepped inside, and the robot activated the propulsors. Then the shuttle started ascending with the four spherical drones following around it in perfect synchronization. The intense afternoon sunlight rested on the shuttle's glass walls despite the air carrier's broad shadow that still covered half of Ramey Airport.

To his left, Keithan gave one last glance at Hangar H11. He sighed as it became smaller in the distance. He couldn't help wondering if he would ever see his father and friends again.

Somehow Luzier must have perceived what he was thinking, for he said, "Relax, kid. You'll get to see them again if you cooperate."

To Keithan's surprise, Luzier lowered his fist energy pulser and tucked it into his leather racing jacket. Following that, the man rested both hands on the metal railing in front of the glass, still facing Keithan.

"So that Aramis girl," Luzier said with an unexpected casual tone despite his still-expressionless face, "is she your girlfriend?"

Keithan bit his tongue and tensed his grip on the Daedalus Project. It was all he could do to hold his anger toward the impertinent comment.

"What does that have to do with anything?" he dared to say.

Luzier shrugged. "Just doing some friendly conversation to help you loosen up."

Friendly conversation? Up until now, Keithan had perceived Luzier as a man of very few words. Now, for some reason, Luzier was acting like a completely different person—a people person. Friendly, instead of acting as coldly as he always projected himself before the cameras. Even the man's sky-blue eyes seemed to have softened. His radiant arrogance, however, which currently stood out by that annoying smile of his, was the only thing that hadn't changed about the man's well-known persona, and it repulsed Keithan the most, as it showed how full of himself Luzier was.

Keithan decided to keep his mouth shut this time, but Luzier, who wasn't done, said, "You make a cute couple."

The comment couldn't have sounded more taunting and out of place. It made Keithan want to jump on the man and punch him in his supermodel-like face. He settled for simply rolling his eyes and looking away to the sight outside. The ascending glass shuttle had just flown over the airport's main runway and the pond at approximately two hundred feet high in the direction of the Pegasus airship.

Unfortunately, the silence that followed Luzier's comment was short-lived when the man spoke again.

"All right. Pay careful attention," he told Keithan. "I need you to do exactly as I say and nothing more once we arrive at Colani's airship. If you do that, no harm will come to you. And you have my word, once my mission in all this is complete, I'll make sure you return to Caleb and your friends. Do you have any questions?"

Keithan wanted to tell him he had about a hundred, but he settled for one in particular. "Yeah, about Caleb."

Luzier blinked several times; clearly he hadn't expected that. "What?"

"My dad's name. How do you know it?"

Luzier threw his head back slightly.

"You asked if I had any questions," Keithan insisted. *And I know you won't tell me more details about the whole plot against the Sky Phantoms.* "I'd like to know that at least. You called my dad by his name also back at Mr. Aramis's workshop, but I remember last night you left in a hurry, right before Colani could introduce my dad and me to you. So how could you possibly know my father's name?"

This time Luzier chuckled as if faking his amusement, yet he didn't answer. Instead, he turned to the view beyond the glass behind him, which now showed the growing shape of the embellished white airship.

He couldn't escape Keithan's gaze, though. Keithan stared at him from the glass's reflection, and it now revealed something he had never seen Luzier show before: a slight inner turmoil. Had something Keithan said pushed a button in the man?

It didn't take long for Luzier to notice Keithan staring back at him through his reflection, which was why Luzier shook his head. He raised his chin again as if regaining his confidence and said, "Get ready to board."

The shuttle made a smooth landing on the platform at the bottom of the airship's envelope. Two men in uniforms received them and proceeded to anchor it.

"Where is he?" Luzier asked them just as he stepped out.

"He'll be meeting you at the conference room," one of the men said. He gave Keithan a weird look, most likely wondering why Keithan was there.

Keithan proceeded to follow Luzier into the airship's envelope while still forced to carry the Daedalus Project. They were passing beneath the forward ballonet, which like a balloon within a much bigger balloon, contained the air used to make the airship ascend and descend.

Keithan stared at it while Luzier led him down a series of narrow catwalks with ornate golden railings. These snaked within the composition of curved beams that formed the inner structure of the airship's envelope. Most of the catwalks stretched on the same level and disappeared beyond small hatch doors, while others led to either higher or lower ones through connecting aluminum ladders.

Finally, Luzier led Keithan to a doorway on the left. Past it, the two appeared in the room where just last night Keithan and his father had dined with Captain Colani. Keithan recognized it by the collection of robots that stood on black pedestals between arched gilded columns at either side of the room. The wide round table at the center was no longer decorated with the golden cloth and fancy dishware, silverware, and glasses. Instead, it held nothing more than a hologram of the entire Pegasus racecourse plagued with innumerable tiny dotted lights, which Keithan figured represented the swarm of spherical drones spread throughout Puerto Rico. And at the far end of the table, Keithan saw Giovanni Colani.

"Keithan?" said the Pegasus CEO, looking from Keithan to Luzier. "What are you doing here?"

Keithan exhaled in disappointment before he halted in front of the table. "Captain Colani. I can't believe I thought you weren't involved in all this."

He expected the bearded man to sneer or respond with sarcasm, but strangely, the captain's face showed fear.

"You've got it all wrong," he told Keithan. He tensed his arms, which were settled on the armrests of his high-backed chair, and when Keithan narrowed his eyes, he noticed why: Colani's wrists were tied to the chair's armrests.

Keithan turned to Luzier and gulped, yet Luzier looked past him as a man entered the room.

"Good. You made … it," said the man, stopping dead in his tracks when he saw Keithan.

Keithan only had to glance at Colani again to understand. The new figure in the room was the true mastermind behind all this, and it was none other than Drostan Luzier's senior advising aeroengineer.

No longer did the man look like Luzier's silent shadow as Keithan had perceived him every time he'd seen the two together. The man, whose snow-white mustache resembled a handlebar, looked much more surer of himself than Luzier. Worse still, he looked much more mysterious, not just because of his gray-and-white lab coat and the black smart glove on his left hand, but also because of his eyes, which he always kept hidden behind red-lensed glasses. Now, however, his eyes remained hidden behind bloodred-lensed goggles, which were perched on the bridge of his nose since they had no temples.

"Care to explain what that boy is doing here?" the man asked. His Dutch accent, Keithan noticed, was much heavier than Luzier's.

"Relax, Jeroen. He's just insurance," Luzier said.

"Is that so? The son of the legendary Adalina Zambrana?"

"The perfect hostage to guarantee our safe escape," Luzier clarified. "It was sort of a last-minute idea."

The man called Jeroen placed both hands inside the pockets of his lab coat and paced toward Luzier. "Are you lying to me?" he asked.

Luzier stared back at him with his hands behind his back. "Why the blazes would I do that?"

"Oh, I don't know. Perhaps because it seems too convenient, considering the connection between the two of—"

"Perhaps it would be wise to remain focused on what we need to do, Jeroen, like moving on to our next phase," Luzier said, cutting him off and raising his voice. "As you can see, not only did I bring Keithan, but I also brought the Daedalus Project. The MA-7 robot at Aramis's workshop failed to take it and carry out its mission."

"I did notice," said Jeroen, glancing at Keithan and the jetboard with a slight smile that tilted his mustache. "No matter. I was prepared in case something like that happened. What matters is that you brought it. So we will get to use it after all, and very soon."

Keithan looked back and forth from Luzier to Jeroen, analyzing the relationship between the two. Were they really working together, or did each one have his own true agenda hidden from the other? He glanced at Colani from the corner of his eye and wondered if the captain was wondering the same thing.

"Now, let's move on to our next phase, shall we?" Jeroen said. He held out his gloved hand and tapped his fingertips together, making a small neon-green hologram appear over his palm. He started tapping on the hologram with his other hand. Then, raising the back of his glove closer to his mouth, he spoke into it.

"Air Carrier One, this is General Luzier. Report."

"General Luzier?" Keithan turned to Drostan in shock. "He's your—"

"Keep quiet," Drostan cut him off without looking at him.

"General Luzier, this is Air Carrier One. Proceed," a voice said from a speaker on Jeroen's smart glove.

"Prepare to welcome the Pegasus airship before departure," Jeroen spoke into his glove again.

"Roger that, General. Flight deck will be ready to receive you."

Seeing Jeroen communicating with the air carrier suddenly gave Keithan an idea.

My wrist communicator! He lowered his gaze and saw it half hidden beneath the left sleeve of his leather racing jacket. He could contact Dantés and his friends if communications had been reestablished at Ramey, send them a message or a live feed. He only needed a chance to try it.

Jeroen turned off the hologram on his smart glove and raised his gaze again.

"Well, let's get ready to leave," he said, turning to Drostan. "Bring Colani and the boy. They will want to see this."

"Sir?" Drostan interjected. "I think it would be best if I take Keithan to a safer location. Keep him locked—"

"Nonsense," Jeroen insisted. "The boy is our guest."

"Let Keithan go, Jeroen," Colani interceded. "He's just a boy. He has nothing to do with this."

His words didn't seem to make any difference. If anything, it seemed to amuse Jeroen more. Keithan would have sworn the old man was smiling slightly behind his handlebar mustache.

"I'm sorry, Colani. It seems you still feel like you're in some kind of position to give orders—"

"This is *my* airship!"

"*NOT* anymore!" Jeroen thundered. "*I* am in command now, and don't you forget it!"

Keithan jumped when Jeroen pounded his right fist on the round table. The hovering hologram of the racecourse flickered. As for Colani, Keithan saw him swallow his anger while still staring challengingly back at Jeroen.

Jeroen straightened himself. "Don't you dare question my authority again," he told Colani, now in a soft but still-menacing tone, "or I will toss you out of this airship myself."

And with that, he turned around to Drostan.

"Leave the Daedalus Project here and bring the boy with us."

"Where?" Drostan asked.

"To the bridge."

Fernando and company had just arrived in front of the unidentified hangar that he and Marianna knew belonged to the Sky Phantom Legion. They were panting since they hurried to get there soon after they saw Keithan leave with Luzier on the flying glass shuttle. Yet while the others felt the pain in their legs, Fernando felt it in his arms since out of impulse, he'd pushed his wheelchair all the way there instead of turning on its custom motor.

At least they didn't have to wait long in front of the hangar. They were expected at Professor Dantés's request. The large front door was opening upward to let them in when Fernando shouted, "Look!"

Everyone looked upward in the direction Fernando was pointing. The Pegasus airship was ascending, and its dangling mooring lines were retracting into the envelope.

"No!" Marianna said before covering her mouth with both hands.

"We're running out of time," Fernando said.

"Don't worry," Dantés told them. "The Legion is not letting it out of their sight. So come on. We have to hurry."

But Fernando and the rest didn't move. They couldn't stop staring at the airship as it continued ascending like a balloon that a child had lost hold of. It was impressive how, despite the airship's huge size, the thing looked dwarfed by the massive air carrier. It was now nearing the carrier's altitude, but it looked like it was going to continue going higher.

"Guys, we need to keep moving," Dantés insisted behind them.

Keithan felt the entire airship's structure shaking. That, along with the loud hissing of compressed air traveling through the numerous pipes above him, gave him the feeling of being inside a living, breathing—and flying—mechanical monster. It didn't scare him in the least, though. What did scare him was that he didn't know where the airship was heading, that is, until he arrived at the bridge, located at the nose of the airship. Jeroen was at the front while Drostan brought up the rear with Colani, who now had his hands cuffed behind his back.

On the bridge, which Keithan thought looked like a blend between a ship's bridge and a luxurious hotel lobby, stood a wide round window with golden framing that revealed a top view of the air carrier's flight deck. The thing out there was mainly one giant platform, almost half the size of Ramey's main runway, with a tower at its front where the giant stallion bust protruded.

Keithan gaped. "We're landing on that?" he murmured.

"Yes, we are," Jeroen said with pride. He halted at the end of an elevated observation post in front of a railing that gave him a complete view of the rest of the bridge below him. "Airships, you see, have speed and altitude limits due to helium levels, pressure, and strong winds. Therefore, by anchoring and securing this baby to the air carrier, we'll be able to have a swifter and safer journey."

Everyone inside the bridge was now gazing out the window while the airship descended toward the carrier's flight deck.

Keithan reached for his wrist communicator, hoping not to draw attention to himself while still pretending to be looking out the window. He slid his index finger over its digital screen, and as soon as the key appeared, he pressed and held the number five. He also muted the communicator's speaker and glanced around him. Nobody seemed to have noticed what he was doing.

There was a thud, and the floor trembled, making everyone standing stumble. The airship had landed. A chorus of deep mechanical whining outside soon followed, along with several heavy thuds that made the walls tremble.

"General, anchoring arms are being attached to the envelope," reported a female voice at the bridge.

"Good," Jeroen responded aloud. "Get ready," he then said over his shoulder and in a lower voice to Drostan, Colani, and Keithan. "We are about to commence our voyage to find the Sky Phantom Legion."

Oh no. Keithan dared to glance again at his wrist communicator. It was still dialing. *C'mon, c'mon, c'mon!*

"Anchoring complete," said the same female voice at the bridge. "We're ready for departure."

"Excellent," said Jeroen and Drostan simultaneously.

"Contact the carrier's bridge," Jeroen added, raising his voice again. "Tell it to set a course for Arecibo."

What? Keithan almost burst out aloud in surprise. Arecibo? Did Jeroen think the Sky Phantoms' secret base was there?

"This is absurd, Jeroen," said Colani, who now stood next to Keithan and Drostan. "The Sky Phantom Legion? That's nothing but an urban legend."

"Is it?" Jeroen challenged. "Then how do you explain the attack against our flying spheres during the invasion?"

Colani couldn't come up with an explanation.

Next to him, Keithan dared to look down again at his wrist communicator.

Yes! The mini screen now showed him the call time counting, along with the letters "AD"—Professor Dantés's initials. Yet no sooner than he saw this did a pale hand grab his communicator.

"Bad form, Keithan," Drostan said.

Keithan froze, all the while hoping against all hope the professor had picked up the call in time to have heard Jeroen Luzier reveal the airship's destination.

CHAPTER 25

Alexandria rushed Caleb and the Aramises to keep up with her. She only wished they'd stop being so distracted by everything they were seeing along the way. Unfortunately, it was impossible, as Alexandria had just brought them to the Sky Phantoms' secret base at Mona Island. More than that, to get there, she'd taken them through the underground tunnels beneath Ramey Airport before shuttling with them at supersonic speed inside two capsules that ran through pressurized glass tubes deep underwater.

Now they were moving down the maze of dimly lit narrow tunnels deep inside Mona. Moisture covered the rock walls all around them, and dripping water echoed. Also following Alexandria was Agent Brave Gala, who like the other Sky Phantom agents they passed by, didn't seem to approve of having unexpected civilians inside the top-secret base.

"You really think it was a good idea to bring these people here?" Gala whispered while trying to keep up with Alexandria.

"I had to," Alexandria replied without slowing her pace and still looking straight ahead. "They know too much already, so we'll have to take care of that after all this is over."

She didn't need to explain herself more. She trusted Gala knew what she meant.

"How much further?" Fernando asked behind them over the echoing sound of his wheelchair's motor.

"Not much," Alexandria told him.

The tunnel curved left, and just as Alexandria turned, she ran into Lieutenant Colonel Lanzard.

"Whoa! There you are," said the colonel. He glanced at the rest of the group behind Alexandria and Gala. "You do realize the consequences of having these people here, right?"

"I do, sir, but that's not important at this moment."

"You're darn right it's not important at this moment," Lanzard raised his voice. "The Pegasus airship has been anchored to the air carrier at Ramey. The two are now headed to the center of Puerto Rico with the flying spheres."

"They're headed to Arecibo, Colonel," Alexandria said quickly.

Lanzard flinched. "What? How do you know?"

"Keithan is inside the airship."

"What?!"

"He contacted me through his communicator a few minutes ago, but the call was dropped."

"What on Earth is Keithan doing inside—?"

"*Colonel*, everything you need to know is in here." She pulled out Marianna's sphere camera from one of her pockets and handed it to him. "You can look at it later, but right now we need to figure out a way to get on board that airship as soon as possible."

Lanzard gave her a questioning look. Meanwhile, everyone else stared at the two as if not sure what to expect.

Lanzard shook his head. "All right. You come with me to the control room—just you, Agent Venus. Agent Gala ..."

Gala stepped forward. "Colonel?"

"Take the civilians to my office. Wait for us there."

"Um, Miss Dantés?" said Caleb Quintero before Alexandria held up her hand.

"It's all right. Go with her," she told him, already leaving with the lieutenant colonel. "I'll be there as soon as I can."

She and Lanzard hurried down the tunnel to the control room in the direction Lanzard had come from. On their way, Alexandria did her best to summarize everything that had happened at the Aramises' hangar with the Daedalus Project, including William Aramis's involvement, Drostan Luzier's faked death, and of course, Keithan's kidnapping and unexpected call from the airship.

"So the voice you heard during Keithan's call ..."

"It was from someone named Jeroen," Alexandria said. "A general, apparently. I heard Colani in the background say the name."

"And that Jeroen was the one who gave the order to fly to Arecibo?"

"Yes, sir. The call dropped after that. I fear Keithan was caught using his communicator."

They had just reached the control room, and as soon as they walked in, they found out things were about to get worse.

"Oh no." Alexandria gaped.

She and Lanzard were now staring at the giant holo screen projected at the other end of the room. It showed an aerial view of the black air carrier with the Pegasus airship moving toward Arecibo over Puerto Rico. More than that, it showed the air carrier and the airship surrounded by innumerable dots, which was obviously the swarm of spherical drones. Worse still, the other two carriers that had arrived on the island were moving in the same direction, and they were bringing with them the rest of the flying sphere armada that had spread all over the island.

"Now that's a smart move," Lanzard commented, placing both hands on his waist while staring at the giant holo screen.

Alexandria turned to him. "Why do you say that?"

"Isn't it obvious? They're moving deeper inland to protect themselves. They know no one will dare attack them while they remain above land. Can't risk more of those flying spheres—worse still, one of the carriers—crashing on top of civilians."

Lanzard started marching down the raised walkway that stretched to the center of the control room. Alexandria hesitated before following him.

"Zoom out the image," Lanzard ordered aloud. "I want a clear visual of all military ships and aircraft that have responded to the invasion."

Right away, the image on the giant holo screen zoomed out to show a full view of Puerto Rico, Mona Island, and several miles of the Caribbean Sea and the Atlantic. Following that, small lighted circles started appearing within thirty and forty miles around the island of Puerto Rico.

"Oh my ..." Lanzard trailed off at the sight of the many military naval ships popping up.

He and Alexandria, now standing in front of a digital console at the center of the room, couldn't believe what they were seeing. There were over a dozen craft on the nearby waters surrounding the entire island of Puerto Rico.

"That's quite a massive fleet," Alexandria commented without blinking.

"Colonel," a technician called aloud from one of the workstations on the left, "all ships have been identified as U.S. Navy. One carrier, three amphibious assault ships, three cruisers, five destroyers, three littoral combat ships, and two unmanned underwater vehicles."

Lanzard shook his head in disbelief. Alexandria could tell he was having a hard time figuring out a way to deal with the Pegasus carriers and their drone armada.

"I don't get it," Lanzard said. "What does Pegasus want?"

Alexandria came up with an idea while still watching the holo screen.

"Zoom in on the air carriers," she said aloud.

"What are you doing?" Lanzard said. Alexandria ignored him.

The image zoomed in again on the carriers. Alexandria leaned forward to the digital console in front of her and the lieutenant colonel. She started tapping on its projected keyboard. The next second, a glowing line appeared in front of the carrier that had the Pegasus airship attached to its top.

"Agent Venus, wha—?" Lanzard started to say but stopped when he understood.

The new line showed a possible trajectory of the air carrier. It stretched eastward from the front of the craft and through the south of the city of Arecibo.

"Oh … no," Lanzard muttered.

It was clear now where the carriers and the spheres were headed. Alexandria, Lanzard, and everyone else in the control room could see it on the giant image: a white concave area, 305 meters wide in diameter, and isolated by mountains.

Alexandria straightened herself and tightened her jaw. "They're headed to the Arecibo Radio Telescope."

Keithan expected Drostan to either smash his brand-new wrist communicator or step on it to break it, but the guy did neither. He simply forced Keithan to hand it over and put it on his own wrist.

"Let's see if she dares to call back," Drostan told him.

Now out of ideas, Keithan remained biting his tongue while staring with frustration at the impressive view outside the bridge's wide circular window. The landscape below, bathed in the yellow and red of the afternoon sunlight, seemed to be the one moving along with the clouds in the sky. Next to Keithan, Colani also stared out the window without saying a word.

"Twenty minutes to reach Arecibo, General," reported a crewmember.

"Good. Maintain current speed," Jeroen ordered.

He and Drostan now stood side by side, focused on a group of holo screens projected on the left side of the bridge. Close to a dozen in total, the screens showed different local and international news channels' broadcasts of the air carrier and the airship as both continued flying slowly over Puerto Rico with the sphere armada.

"Would you look at that?" Jeroen said with pride, loud enough to get Keithan's and Colani's attention. "All eyes are still on us."

"Sure," Keithan said bitterly. "What else would you expect after sabotaging the grand Pegasus Air Race to cause terror all over Puerto Rico?"

Both Jeroen and Drostan looked at him over their shoulders with raised eyebrows.

"A small price to pay," Jeroen said nonchalantly.

"*Small?!*" Colani burst out. "Are you serious?"

"If you look at the bigger picture, yes," Jeroen said.

Keithan shook his head. "That's pure madness!"

Right away, he regretted having opened his big mouth, for his comment brought a very uncomfortable silence to the room. Worse still, it made Drostan shoot him the most penetrating glare so far. Keithan would have bet Jeroen's gaze was just as penetrating if not for the man's red-lensed goggles. Yet it was Jeroen's handlebar mustache that brought a chill down Keithan's spine when, unexpectedly, it tilted upward.

"Well," Jeroen said, "sometimes madness is exactly what we need to dare to accomplish what we truly want. I mean, look at this!" He turned momentarily to the holo screens again and stretched his arms to the sides. "Only by causing terror was I able to keep the full attention of many as we embark on our journey to expose one of the greatest secrets in the history of the world!"

"*Per favore,*" Colani said, unimpressed. "The Sky Phantoms? The greatest secret in the history of the world?"

Keithan did his best to keep a straight face while struggling with the urge to reaffirm Jeroen's words.

Jeroen, on the other hand, chuckled at Colani's comment. "Oh, it's much, *much* more than that, Colani. You'll see. Everyone will see. There will be no secrets today. I guarantee that. Unless ... my partner in crime here intends to say otherwise."

He turned to Drostan.

Drostan, taken by surprise, didn't reply. Yet his sudden flared nostrils showed Jeroen had stepped over the line between them.

"What?" Jeroen told him with a shrug. "Why not start with *your* deep secret? There shouldn't be any reason for you to keep it any longer. Would you prefer if I reveal it?"

Drostan still didn't say a word. Instead, he shot Jeroen the same glare he'd shot at Keithan a few minutes ago. That, however, only seemed to make Jeroen enjoy the moment more.

"Amazing!" Jeroen went on. "I can't believe it. Even up close, Colani and the boy still fail to see it."

Keithan, completely perplexed about what was happening, looked back and forth from Jeroen to Drostan.

Then Drostan responded. "You're right. There will be no secrets today."

He reached for his long blond hair and pulled it off to reveal a mane of light-brown hair that reached his lower back. Following that, he reached for his eyes and removed what turned out to be sky-blue contact lenses.

Still, Keithan didn't recognize who Drostan really was. He tilted his head and wrinkled his nose while still staring at him. The man's perfectly chiseled face still looked unique. His real eyes, however, honey in color, looked somewhat familiar, which, along with the smirk Drostan was now showing, reminded Keithan of another legendary air racer.

Suddenly, Keithan's eyes widened, his mouth dropped open, and his chest tightened as if it had been turned to stone.

Meanwhile, Jeroen stared at Keithan and Colani with an impish glee slightly visible on his face despite the goggles and mustache hiding most of it.

"Wow. It's like a soap opera in the sky," he commented with a chuckle. "Meet the true greatest air racer that has ever lived—back from the dead. Colani, your favorite air racing champion. Keithan, your—"

"*Mom?!*" Keithan cried.

CHAPTER 26

So many different feelings came to Keithan in that moment that he didn't know how to react. He wasn't sure if he wanted to believe what had just been revealed to him, either. Drostan Luzier, the famous air racing champion Keithan had come to despise and, at some level, envy, wasn't real. The guy wasn't even a man in disguise, but a *woman*, and not just any woman …

Mom?! Keithan stared at her, flabbergasted. Her skin was no longer tanned as he remembered, but everything else about her matched the image he had of her in his mind.

"Adalina?!" said Colani, also having a hard time believing it. "Milady Adalina Zambrana? Th-that's impossible! Why …?"

"How?" Keithan added, fighting back tears.

His mother seemed to be about to explain herself when one of the crewmembers at the bridge announced aloud, "General, destination sighted up ahead."

It made everybody on the bridge except Keithan turn to the wide circular window.

"Ah, finally!" Jeroen said before turning to his two guests again. "Well, as interesting as this special reunion has turned out to be, I'm afraid it will have to continue later."

"No!" Keithan exclaimed.

"Don't worry, young man," Jeroen insisted. "I'm sure your mother will explain herself in good time, but right now, she and I have more urgent matters to take care of down at the air carrier. Therefore, I'm going to need you and Colani to wait in a more secure room."

Keithan didn't care. He needed an explanation now while he continued struggling to make sense of the moment.

"Mom," he said, finding it hard to get the word out, "please … don't. Whatever the reason, it's not worth it."

He couldn't take his eyes off her. Despite that, Adalina didn't show the slightest hesitation and said, no longer in her Dutch accent, "It is, Keithan, and I have to."

And with that, Adalina turned away. She didn't even wait for Jeroen and marched out of the bridge.

Keithan took a step forward as if to go after her, but he immediately contained himself and turned to Jeroen instead. The man now had a small hologram hovering close to the smart glove on his left hand and was typing something on it with his right.

"There we are," said Jeroen, raising his gaze again at Keithan and Colani. "I just ordered two security robots to escort you. Oh, and Colani, keep in mind that I reprogrammed them so they only respond to my command codes and my voice, just in case you planned on having them help you. Here they come."

The sound of metal steps ascended from the bridge's entrance. Just as Keithan and Colani turned around, two bulky robots with sleek white-and-gold coverings and faceless heads that had nothing but a round red lens at their centers halted in front of them and grabbed them by their arms.

"No! Let me go! *Mom!*" Keithan shouted, but to no avail.

The two security robots dragged him and Colani out of the bridge and down several narrow passages and catwalks. All the while, Keithan fought to loosen himself. The robots didn't slow their pace. Keeping their one-lensed heads straight and facing ahead, they continued forcing Keithan and Colani to move until they ended up in front of a familiar white door with a golden ornamental frame.

"Is that …?" Keithan started to say.

"My designing room," Colani replied.

The robot holding Keithan pressed the panel next to the door, which slid to the side. Meanwhile, the robot holding Colani removed the captain's cuffs from his wrists. Subsequently, the four of them went through the doorway.

Just as Keithan remembered, the small windowless room was shaped like a dome, aside from being completely covered by concave panels that had numerous tiny projectors on them. But there was someone else already there, a man clad in an old khaki jumpsuit that, like his calloused hands, was stained with grease. Yet his face was what caught Keithan's attention more, for not only was it bruised with a black eye and stained with dried blood, but Keithan also recognized him right away.

"Captain Colani ... *Keithan?*" the man said.

"Mr. Aramis!"

"Quick! Both of you, shut your eyes!"

"What?" Keithan said.

"Shut your eyes tight! *Now!*" Mr. Aramis insisted.

Keithan and Colani did as they were told, right before a burst of white light took over the whole room. It was so intense Keithan could still see it through his eyelids. It even forced him to cross his arms in front of his face to block it. The next second, Mr. Aramis threw himself at him and Colani, who had no time to react, and fell on their backs.

Both Keithan and Colani cried out, feeling the weight of Mr. Aramis now on top of them.

Keithan opened his eyes again and saw the three of them now lying outside the designing room. Mr. Aramis jumped back to his feet, though with some effort, and hurried to help Keithan stand up.

"Come on! We gotta get out of here!" he told them. "That light won't affect the robots for long!"

He and Keithan hurried to help Colani stand, and together the three of them started running down the narrow passageway.

"We need to find a place to hide," Mr. Aramis said at the front while still on the move.

"My office," Colani said. "Quick, head to the second doorway to your left."

Past the doorway, Colani guided them to a set of ascending staircases and a long hanging catwalk.

"Now turn right. Head for that opening," Colani said.

This time, they appeared back at the conference room where Keithan had found Colani tied to the high-backed chair. Mr. Aramis, however, stopped abruptly halfway to the doorway at the other end of the room.

"What the—? My jetboard!" He was now staring at his invention, which lay next to the round table that still projected the racecourse. "How did it get here?"

"There's no time for that, sir," Keithan said before turning to Colani.

"*Seguimi.* We're almost there," said Colani, now taking the lead.

He and Keithan were already moving again. Mr. Aramis, on the other hand, hesitated. He was about to pick up his jetboard but was forced to leave it behind at the ascending sound of metal footsteps behind him.

Colani led them to another gilded-frame door to their left and said, "Giovanni Colani."

That was all it took for the door to open.

"Hurry! In here!" he said. He locked the door behind him as soon as they were inside.

Finally, they were able to catch their breath. Keithan looked around and took in the luxury of the office. Simply put, it was an impressive combination of two different and far-apart periods: classical Renaissance and high-tech mid-twenty-first century. Attached to the walls stood shiny modern shelves decorated by golden ornaments and filled with awards of all shapes and sizes. They were accompanied by white modular furniture, which was also decorated with an elaborate pattern of golden ornaments. These, however, were built in weird organic shapes and oriented toward a wide black wood-and-gold desk from which several small holo screens were being projected. And right behind the desk stood a small version of the bridge's window, showing nothing but an orange sky.

"Whew! I … can't believe … that worked," said a panting Mr. Aramis.

"What exactly did you do back there in the designing room?" Keithan asked him while bent forward with his arms resting on his knees.

"Not much, really. I just made all the holo projectors there create one bright sphere of light, potent enough to mess up the robots' optic systems for a few seconds."

Keithan looked at Colani. "Do you think the robots will find us?"

"Most likely, but don't worry, we'll be safe here," Colani answered. "That door can only be opened by my voice command. Plus, it's reinforced." He turned to Mr. Aramis. "And who are you, sir?"

"Oh! He's a friend," Keithan said.

"William Aramis," Mr. Aramis said. "It's an honor to finally meet you, Captain, though I wish it were under better circumstances."

He offered a hand to shake Colani's. The captain looked reluctant, yet he accepted the hand.

"He's the one who created the Daedalus Project," Keithan told Colani.

"I apologize for doing it without your knowledge," Mr. Aramis added. "Drostan Luzier and his senior advising aeroengineer tricked me into believing that you, Captain, had approved and funded it. Unfortunately, it all turned out to be a lie."

"How did you end up here?" Keithan asked him.

"Emmeiseven attacked me last night inside my workshop, knocked me unconscious when I discovered Luzier and Jeroen's true intentions hidden inside Emmeiseven's memory. Sometime later, I woke up and found myself locked inside that designing room back there. Drostan and his senior advising aeroengineer must have done it to stop me from warning the authorities."

Colani took a deep breath. "Well, it seems you don't know the half of it," he told Mr. Aramis.

"What do you mean?"

"Drostan Luzier isn't who everyone thinks he is."

"You got that right," Mr. Aramis said.

"No. You don't understand, Mr. Aramis," Keithan said. "Drostan, he's ..." He tried but couldn't say it.

"He's actually Keithan's mother in disguise," Colani finished for him.

Mr. Aramis threw his head back. "What? That's absurd! She's—"

"Alive," Keithan assured him.

It took Mr. Aramis a few seconds to register it.

"You mean, all this time ... my meetings with Drostan, that was your mother?"

Keithan nodded vaguely.

Mr. Aramis shook his head. "*She* sabotaged my whole project?"

Keithan shrugged. "I'm afraid so."

"Gentlemen," Colani said, "perhaps it would be best if we remain focused on our current circumstances."

Colani headed to his wood-and-gold desk in front of the window.

"Holo screen on," he said, and a holo screen appeared over the glass desktop. "Access outer bridge's camera."

Keithan and Mr. Aramis moved next to Colani as a live feed appeared, showing what could also be seen from the bridge's window.

"Oh my ..." Mr. Aramis trailed off.

"Whoa," was all Keithan could say.

They were now staring at the famous Arecibo Radio Telescope. Best known worldwide for its important role among astronomers in the search of potentially dangerous asteroids—and extraterrestrial intelligence—it contrasted itself from the dense green mountainous landscape all around it. Mainly, it was a huge dish made of perforated aluminum panels. Three tapering concrete towers surrounded it and each one held the end of tense cables that kept a triangular steel truss platform with a metal dome and a receiving spike antenna, both of which were suspended hundreds of feet above the dish. But what got Keithan's attention more was the fact that there were three big black cables and what appeared to be a wire bridge connecting the front of the air carrier with the telescope's suspended platform.

"So that's what they're going to use to find the Sky Phantoms' base," Keithan realized.

"The Sky Phantoms?" said Mr. Aramis, looking more confused now. "Is that what all this is about?"

"I'm afraid so," said Keithan, still staring at the live feed. He narrowed his eyes and noticed several tiny figures moving inside the platform.

"Could you zoom in on the image?" he asked Colani.

The captain did, and immediately Keithan spotted his mother among the figures. She and her companions, some of which appeared to be robots, were standing on the girders of a bow-shaped track from which the metal dome and the spike antenna, which was pointed downward, were mounted on. Suddenly, the entire thing began to rotate.

"They're repositioning it," Colani said.

"Why isn't anybody doing something to stop them?" asked Mr. Aramis, frustration clear in his tone.

"There's gotta be something we can do," Keithan thought aloud.

"Just the three of us?" Mr. Aramis said. "We don't stand a chance. Unless there's someone on this airship we can trust."

"Well, not necessarily some*one*," Colani said.

He looked like he was deep in thought. He stood at the center of the office, staring down at what appeared to be the outine of a hatch door visible on the scarlet carpet.

"I think I know where we might find some extra hands to help us ... if I can figure out a way to access them from here first."

—(-o-)—

Right at the base of the radio telescope's west tower, two black vehicles with twin spherical tires skidded to a halt without anybody noticing. Their side doors swung upward, and a special team of six Sky Phantom agents came out. Each agent, among them Alexandria Dantés and

Brave Gala, was fully clad in black armor and a tight hood that included communications headgear. In addition, each one wore a waist harness, a backpack, and a grappling gauntlet.

The six of them hurried to the foot of the tapering tower while the two vehicles took off and disappeared into the surrounding forest. Alexandria led the group to a caged ladder that rose to the top of the tower. The bottom stood behind a closed gate, but that didn't stop them. All it took was one laser shot to break the gate's padlock. Then, one by one, the Sky Phantom agents began to climb. Halfway up, Alexandria could see the canopy of the surrounding forest below them, but she and her comrades still had a long way to go. And the higher they got, the stronger she could feel the wind challenging her climbing speed.

Once Alexandria reached the top, she took a moment to take in the unbelievable sight. It was like gazing at something out of a dystopian science-fiction world. Hundreds of the Pegasus flying spheres overcrowded the sky all around the radio telescope. Worse still, many of them seemed to still be protecting the three giant air carriers like sentinels.

Alexandria took out a pair of digital binoculars and turned her attention to the triangular truss platform suspended over the gigantic radio dish.

"I can make out three, four … no, five. Five figures on the platform," she reported to her companions who waited below her on the ladder. "Two of them are robots."

Yet it was the man in the white-black-and-gold racing uniform who made Alexandria tighten her jaw.

"Drostan," she said.

She could see him on one of the girders of the platform, but there was something different about him: his hair. It was no longer blond; it was brown and longer. Was he pretending to be someone else now? Alexandria frowned in confusion.

She attached her binoculars back on her waist and moved to one of the suspension cables anchored at the top of the tower. Behind her,

Agent Gala and the others finished climbing up to join her.

"Everybody ready?" Alexandria asked.

"Yes, Captain," the team replied.

Alexandria proceeded to remove a pulley from her waist harness and attach it to the cable in front of her. Once secured, she jumped off the tower and started sliding down the cable as if it were a zip line. Gala went right behind her, then the rest.

No doubt somebody would spot them going down the cable, straight toward the platform, which was why Alexandria dared not slow down. Close to twenty feet away from the platform, however, one of the figures there spotted them coming.

"We have company!" the man shouted just as Alexandria reached the platform and released herself from the cable. He stood on a beam lower than where she had landed, and before he could make a run for it, Alexandria dropped on top of the man and knocked him unconscious.

"Gala?" Alexandria called out, quickly pressing her earpiece while glancing at the higher beams.

"Right here, Captain!" Agent Gala responded.

She had already reached the platform and was now on her knees, taking off her backpack and opening it. The four other agents had just landed, laser handguns drawn to give Alexandria a hand with their opponents.

Their laser shots burst in sparks on the white steel framework while their enemies returned fire with pulsing charges that shook the entire platform. The exchange slowed the Sky Phantoms' advance, but it also slowed their enemy from heading back to the wire bridge connected to the air carrier.

"Graw!" a voice cried in the distance.

"One down!" Alexandria heard one of her comrades report through her earpiece. Meanwhile, she continued trying to get closer to Drostan. She could see him hiding and firing pulsing charges in her direction.

"Watch out!" shouted one of the agents.

Alexandria looked up just as a figure shot past her from above. It was one of the Pegasus robots, which had dropped from a girder. The thing barely moved its legs and arms while it fell as if it knew it was not worth it. Then—*CRASH!*—it smashed against the dish below, breaking like a tiny plastic toy.

"Three left," Alexandria murmured. She raised her gaze again and saw Drostan now making a run for the wire bridge connected to the carrier.

"Somebody give me some cover!" she shouted to her team. She didn't wait for confirmation. She dashed after Drostan, gracefully moving on the girders but careful not to lose her footing.

Drostan also moved gracefully on the steel girders as he continued his escape. He jumped from one to the other like a cat. Then he jumped off the ledge of the platform and landed about ten feet below on the wire bridge.

It might have been an impressive stunt to anyone else, but not to Alexandria, for she had no choice but to do it too. And so, at the same ledge where Drostan jumped off, she did the same but with more impulse.

"Heyaa!"

She landed on the bridge with such force it made the whole thing sway like an angry snake. It even made Drostan lose his balance and grab on to the cables, which made him drop his fist energy pulser. He managed to regain his footing, but before he could start running again, Alexandria raised her laser handgun again and shouted.

"Freeze!"

Surprisingly, Drostan obeyed.

"Sky Phantom team, report," Alexandria said into her communicator while keeping her laser handgun pointed at Drostan.

"All clear, Captain Venus," responded one of the agents. *"Enemy party has surrendered up here. The platform is ours."*

Alexandria sighed. "Good. Agent Gala, what's your status?"

"Just got inside the maintenance room, Captain," Gala reported. *"Ready to connect to the antenna."*

"Copy that." Alexandria then addressed Drostan. "Put your hands up and turn around—slowly."

Once again, the famous air racer obeyed.

Alexandria did her best to calm her breathing. Nevertheless, she remained fully under control and with her weapon steady. She didn't dare blink while Drostan turned to face her.

They were only ten feet away from each other, which was more than enough for Alexandria to get a good look at him. Still, nothing could have prepared her for what she saw next. She wasn't staring at Drostan anymore. The man before her looked different, and strangely, somewhat familiar.

Alexandria frowned. "Who are you, really?"

Drostan, still with his hands up, just smirked.

"Who *are* you?" Alexandria insisted louder, now holding her weapon with both hands.

This time, Drostan responded. "Look deep into my eyes and you'll see."

Not only his words, but the way he said them too—without his Dutch accent—took Alexandria by surprise. Even weirder, Drostan's voice no longer sounded masculine. Alexandria tried to match it with the man's new light-brown hair and honey eyes.

Suddenly she realized who she was really staring at, and this time it was she who froze.

—(-o-)—

Agent Gala knew time was against her and her team, yet she took a few seconds to study what she was staring at inside the antenna's maintenance room. In front of her, in the middle of the mechanisms that rotated the antenna and the dome, stood a floor-to-ceiling machine where the three black cables that extended from the Pegasus air carrier had been connected. This was how the bad guys had been able to reposition the antenna, and most likely how they would be able to send a signal and/or receive one from the air carrier.

Therefore, the first thing Gala did was plug her handheld data pad into the machine.

"All right. Let's see what you people at Pegasus are really up to with this thing."

She was already working her magic on the data pad.

One of her comrades dropped behind her from a hatch door. "Need any help?"

"I'm good," Gala replied without looking at him. "Just need to hurry and ... got it! I'm logged into its computer!"

Her excitement, however, was short-lived when she saw what was on her data pad. It was enough to tell her what Pegasus was using the radio telescope for: to send and receive a signal to what appeared to be a cloaked GPS satellite in space. And that was just the beginning. The signal was currently locked on the western part of the North Atlantic Ocean, marking three particular locations that triangulated a fourth and much bigger one at the center.

"Oh ... this is *not* happening."

Gala's next step should have been reporting it to Captain Venus, but due to the urgency of the matter, she tapped the flexed screen on her left sleeve to contact who really needed to be warned.

"Phantom Base," she said, holding her sleeve close to her mouth, "this is Agent Gala."

The reply was almost instantaneous. *"Agent Gala, this is Lieutenant Colonel Lanzard. Go ahead."*

"Colonel." Gala swallowed hard. "Pegasus has managed to use the Arecibo Radio Telescope to locate the Sky Phantoms' bases, and they have a lock on them ... on all of them."

Several yards away from the antenna's maintenance room, Alexandria remained with her laser handgun pointed at a ghost. She was still trying to process who the figure in front of her actually was.

"H-how is this possible?" she said. She struggled to stop her laser gun from shaking.

Adalina Zambrana didn't bother to explain. She simply remained with her hands up and her gaze fixed directly at Alexandria.

"Does Keithan know?" Alexandria dared to ask.

Adalina flashed her a sneer this time, which was more than enough for an answer.

Three loud, deep horn blasts coming from the air carrier made both of them jump.

"Whoa! I guess that's my cue to head back to the carrier," said Adalina, now stepping backward.

"Stay where you are!" Alexandria demanded.

"Really? You might as well shoot me now because there's no way you and your team are taking me with you."

"Come on, Adalina! Why are you doing all this?"

The two of them jumped again at the sound of another set of three horn blasts.

"You'll see," Adalina replied aloud while still moving backward. "The whole world will see before this day is over, when your entire Sky Phantom Legion pays for what you people did to me."

"What we—? What are you *talking* about?"

This time, Adalina ignored Alexandria. She looked over her shoulder at the air carrier and gave a nod. Seconds later, the wire bridge they were standing on went taut, and so did the three black cables connected from the air carrier to the antenna.

The carrier was moving away from the radio telescope.

Alexandria lost her balance and grabbed on to the bridge's wires. Adalina, on the other hand, managed to stay on her feet and took the opportunity to dash in the carrier's direction.

"Stop!" shouted Alexandria, yet the sound of tensing cables made her look behind her toward the suspension cables holding the platform. She spotted the other Sky Phantom agents and the men from Pegasus they had disarmed holding on to the steel girders.

"Head for the carrier! Now!" Alexandria shouted to them and made a run for it.

Already, Adalina had disappeared through a small opening in

the carrier.

Then—*SNAP!*—one of the cables connected to the carrier broke loose.

Alexandria staggered and looked back at the truss platform.

"Gala, get out of the maintenance room!" she ordered through her communicator while still running. "That thing's not going to hold much longer!"

"*On my way, Captain!*" Gala's voice said.

SNAP! SNAP!

The other two cables that had been connected to the carrier broke loose too. Alexandria staggered once again. Shockingly, the bridge still held on, though now it was stretched to its fullest, which allowed her to keep running. Alexandria knew it would break at any moment. And just as she thought it, a loud set of metallic snaps rang through the air. This time it came from the suspension cables of the radio telescope's east tower.

Then the entire triangular truss platform flipped over. The bridge broke free. Alexandria dropped her laser handgun and grabbed the bridge's wire handrail right before it sent her swinging downward.

Screams of terror behind her followed, along with the clank of metal, and the entire truss platform hurtled 450 feet down with her team and the men from Pegasus.

"*Nooooo!*" cried Alexandria, yet her cry wasn't heard due to the crashing sound of the platform when it smashed against the giant dish below.

Rage took control of her while she held on for dear life from the dangling bridge. The air carrier was now taking her away from the radio telescope and higher into the sky.

"Bring her up!" someone shouted from above. It made Alexandria look up, and there, at the top of the dangling bridge, she saw Adalina and two other figures looking down at her.

No way was Alexandria going to allow them to capture her. She regained full control of herself and pointed the gauntlet on her right forearm upward, firing a tiny grappling hook from it. The hook shot past the opening where Adalina and the other figures stood. It trailed a reinforced thin line from which it was attached and continued to the top of the air carrier. The hook ended up striking a metal panel, and instantly its magnetic power activated, locking it in place. Alexandria wasn't sure it was safely secured, but with no time to check, she pushed herself off the bridge. At the same time, she pressed a button on her gauntlet, which started retracting the grapple line and pulled her up with full speed.

All Adalina and her companions could do was watch Alexandria ascend to the air carrier's flight deck. It happened so fast they didn't even have time to shoot at her.

Soon, Alexandria reached the ledge and pulled herself up. She hid behind a stack of fiberglass crates, where she finally got a chance to catch her breath. Meanwhile, she gazed at what was left of the Arecibo Radio Telescope as it became smaller in the distance.

"Phantom Base, this is Agent Venus, over," she said, holding her wrist communicator close to her mouth.

"Agent Venus, report," responded the voice of Lieutenant Colonel Lanzard.

Alexandria took a moment to shut her eyes to control her emotions. "Colonel, my teammates ... they're gone."

"Say again, Agent?"

"My teammates, Colonel, they're—"

An incoming call interrupted Alexandria. She looked at the flexed screen on her left sleeve, and her eyes widened.

It was Keithan's phone number.

"Agent Venus?" Lanzard called.

Alexandria hesitated.

"Agent—?"

"Stand by, Colonel," she said and quickly pressed her flexed screen to switch the call. "Keithan?"

The voice on the other end, however, replied with a chuckle. "You wish."

It was Adalina.

"If you've hurt Keithan in *any* way—!"

"You better start worrying about yourself, Alexandria. You're not leaving this air carrier alive."

"Perhaps, but I'm not going anywhere until I make sure Keithan and William Aramis get out safe and sound."

"Yeah, right."

"Dare to prove me wrong? Come and get me. I'll be ready."

Alexandria hung up.

Adalina couldn't help but snort at Alexandria's last comment. Nevertheless, she took the woman's words seriously. She could tell Alexandria was fearless, even when the odds were against her.

Next to Adalina, General Jeroen Luzier seemed to be thinking the same thing about the Sky Phantom agent. He'd listened intently to the whole conversation, keeping his hands tucked inside the pockets of his lab coat, his face expressionless. His eyes, as usual, were hidden behind the red lenses.

"Is she going to be a problem?" he asked.

"Not at all," Adalina assured him. "I'll take care of her. Everything can continue as planned."

"Good, because you're going to like this...."

Jeroen turned on the spot and extended his arms to the sides, gesturing to the big holo screen hovering in the middle of the dark room they were in.

"Behold what our cloaked satellite orbiting within the exosphere found! The exact location of each of the Sky Phantom Legion's secret bases! Turns out there are three of them that seem to be serving as outposts enclosing a much bigger base. One here in Puerto Rico, as we already suspected; another on the southeast coast of the United States, in Florida; and another in the Bermuda Islands."

Adalina stared at each of the locations marked on the map that was projected on the holo screen.

"Well, I'll be damned," she said. "They form the infamous triangle."

"That's right," Jeroen said with a smile. "And who would have thought? At its very center is our final destination. As Americans would say, the mother lode. The headquarters of the Sky Phantom Legion."

CHAPTER 27

"**L**adies and gentlemen, it is now 4:37 in the afternoon, and we are continuing our live coverage of the atrocious, unexpected attack on the Caribbean island of Puerto Rico. I'm Rebecca Knight reporting for Channel 2 News, and just a few moments ago, the Arecibo Radio Telescope was destroyed when one of the invading Pegasus air carriers ripped out the telescope's suspended antenna and dropped it on the dish. The images, as you can see, are quite disturbing. We've been informed there were people on the antenna when it happened, so we fear there may have been casualties. This adds up to the terror everyone in Puerto Rico has been experiencing today. A sad and tragic turn of events, you might say, when today was supposed to be a day of celebration with the famous Pegasus Air Race.

"What you are currently seeing on screen is the entire Pegasus Company armada. It appears it is finally leaving the island. The three air carriers, looking like three dark flying pegasi with their winged stallion busts at their fronts, surrounded by the swarm of spherical drones, are leaving via the north coast together. We don't know where they are headed. However, if you focus on the background, you'll see U.S. Navy ships positioned in open sea at the Atlant— Wait a minute … This just in. We have confirmation that U.S. Navy ships surrounding the island are moving to meet the Pegasus's armada in battle. Yes, U.S. Navy ships surrounding the island are following course to meet the

Pegasus's armada in battle. Ladies and gentlemen, stay with us for more details while we continue covering this and more as it develops...."

Four feet away from the holo screen, Jeroen continued watching the breaking news with his chest raised. He was enjoying every minute of it, as all eyes were still on his armada. He imagined feeling the intense fear of all the people on the island, a fear he had placed upon them like a shroud. Yet he knew all that would fade soon, for now Puerto Rico and its people were being left behind.

But Jeroen no longer needed their fear. A new battle was approaching over the Atlantic Ocean, and Jeroen couldn't wait for it to begin.

"Are you sure we are ready?" asked Adalina next to him.

"Oh, yes," replied Jeroen, turning around. "Now, come."

"Where?"

"Back to the airship's bridge. If I'm going to lead in a battle, I want to do so in style ... and in luxury."

——(·O·)——

More than a dozen men and women in the Pegasus uniforms had been ordered to the flight deck of the leading air carrier to search for Alexandria with fist energy pulsers drawn. Bulky humanoid robots like the ones Alexandria and her late team had fought back at the radio telescope were also involved in the search. Even a few of the spherical drones could be seen flying very close to the flight deck, scanning it. Yet not one of them had found a trace of her.

"Maybe she already managed to sneak inside the carrier—or the airship," Alexandria heard one of the men say to another.

"Maybe," the other said, "but none of the security cameras in either craft has spotted her."

Alexandria remained completely still behind a group of pipes. She did her best to keep her breathing silent. The two men were approximately six feet away with their backs toward her. Past them, she could see a great part of the flight deck and the Pegasus airship.

Suddenly, she spotted two familiar figures out there. One was

Adalina and the other the man with the red-lensed goggles and handlebar mustache who used to follow Adalina every time she went out in public disguised as Drostan. Strangely, the man was now the one in the lead.

That must be Jeroen, Alexandria thought.

She followed the two of them with her gaze while they marched toward the anchored airship. They seemed to be in a hurry, and they picked up their pace when they reached a mobile staircase that led to an opening at the airship's gondola. At the top of the stairs, Jeroen turned around and shouted, "Everybody to your battle stations!"

All the people out there immediately stopped the search and hurried to get back inside the moving air carrier through different hatch doors. Seconds later, klaxons started to sound all over the place to alert the rest of the crew.

"Battle stations," Alexandria murmured, realizing with dread what was about to happen.

She felt the urge to go after Adalina and Jeroen, but an incoming call held her.

"Agent Venus."

"Colonel," Alexandria responded in a whisper.

"We fear we've just figured out the enemy's next destination. Based on their current direction, they are headed to our main base."

"What do you mean, sir? Mona Island?"

"Worse. Our main headquarters. And that's not the worst part. Our ... superiors have just contacted us. They're going to take matters into their own hands."

Alexandria gulped. She understood what that meant. She looked back at the airship and focused again on her priority: finding Keithan and Mr. Aramis, and somehow, no matter the cost, getting them out of there safe before it was too late.

—(-o-)—

The klaxons' rhythmic wailing outside could still be heard while Jeroen and Adalina marched down the narrow corridors and catwalks of the

Pegasus airship. Adalina knew they should have been inside the air carrier instead, where they would be much better protected, but Jeroen insisted they had nothing to worry about.

"Trust me," Jeroen told her. "The spheres will protect the carriers and the airship during the battle, and we have more than enough of them to do the job."

They were entering the conference room when a man in a Pegasus uniform appeared from the doorway at the other end and halted in front of Jeroen and Adalina.

"General, we have a small problem," he reported.

"What is it?" Jeroen asked.

"Colani and the other two hostages locked themselves inside Colani's private office. We can't find a way to get them out."

The man kept his distance, as if uncertain of how Jeroen would react. Yet Jeroen simply took a deep breath and huffed.

"I really don't have time for this," he said.

"Sorry, General, but I thought—"

"I'll take care of it," Adalina said. "You just focus on the upcoming battle."

Jeroen nodded. "All right. Make sure they don't interfere with our plans. Oh, and make sure you keep that thing close to you." He pointed to the Daedalus Project, which still lay next to the round table at the center of the room. "You're going to get your chance to use it near the end of—"

But Jeroen didn't get to finish the sentence. Adalina shouted, "Watch out!"

She threw herself at him just as a large mechanical arm swung over their heads, knocking out the man next to Jeroen. It was one of the Pegasus robots from the pedestals. Humanoid but with a bulb-shaped torso, short legs, and heavy forearms like those of a gorilla, the thing had come to life and launched itself at them. And it wasn't alone. One by one, the rest of the collection of robots came to life and stepped down from their pedestals. They were moving toward Adalina and Jeroen.

"Get out of here! Go! *Go!*" Adalina shouted to Jeroen. She blocked the robots from reaching the general. "Get to the bridge and lock the door! Don't let anyone in!"

Jeroen managed to rush through the doorway at the other end of the room. Immediately after that, every door slid shut and locked.

"What the—?" Adalina started to say while looking around as the robots enclosed her. She reached inside her uniform to pull out her fist energy pulser but then remembered she had dropped it back at the hanging bridge over the radio telescope. There was no way she could fight her way out of this. She had no choice but to raise her hands in surrender.

She expected the robots to stop there, but one of them surprised her from behind when it grabbed her arms and forced her to drop on her knees.

"Argh!"

"Would you look at that," said a familiar deep voice with an Italian accent. "Guess the general forgot to reprogram these robots to respond only to his command codes and voice."

Colani appeared, climbing out from a secret opening on the floor. He held a small data pad in one hand. Behind him, also coming out of the opening on the floor, were Keithan and William Aramis. The three of them came to stand behind the eight robots now surrounding Adalina. They stared directly at her. The expressions of satisfying victory were clear in Colani and William. Keithan's was something completely different, though. He wasn't smiling at all, but his deep look said it all.

The boy had every intention of confronting her right there, right now.

CHAPTER 28

K
eithan would have never imagined seeing his mother the way he saw her now: as a villain. Worse still, as a great disappointment after having looked up to her all his life. No longer could he see in her the legendary air racing champion he and so many other people had come to admire, and it hurt like a heavy stone in his chest.

He kept his deep gaze fixed on his mother. Yet he couldn't ignore the ring of intimidating robots around Adalina, especially when he, Colani, and Mr. Aramis were also locked inside the room with them.

"Are you sure they won't turn against us?" Keithan asked Colani.

"Not these ones. Otherwise they would have done so already," Colani assured him.

Even so, Keithan kept his distance. The eight robots remained unmoving while the one that had forced Adalina to her knees remained holding her arms behind her.

"You're going to explain to me everything about you right now," Keithan told his mother.

Adalina couldn't help hissing. "Now is *really* not the time for that, Keithan. A battle is about to happen, in case you haven't heard."

"All the more reason to tell me now, if we don't survive," Keithan said. "You owe me. You owe all of us here an explanation for everything you've done. So start by telling us why you faked your death and remained hidden in disguise all these years until now."

Adalina poked her tongue into her cheek. Then she said,

completely calm, "Fine. I'll tell you. I faked my death nine years ago because I needed to escape from the people who turned me into the horrible person I never wanted to become."

"What?" said Keithan, wrinkling his nose. He hadn't been expecting something like that.

"Which people are you talking about?" Mr. Aramis dared to ask.

"The Sky Phantoms," Adalina said.

Silence hung in the air for a brief moment while Keithan, Mr. Aramis, and Colani exchanged perplexed looks.

"I don't understand," Keithan said. "The Sky Phantoms are the good guys. Their job is to protect the sky and the world."

"Ha! You wish. You all wish. The Sky Phantoms are monsters who manipulate others to do their terrible work for them in secret."

"What exactly did they do to you?" Colani asked Adalina.

"They turned me into a mass murderer."

Keithan, Mr. Aramis, and Colani froze.

"And afterward," Adalina went on, "they erased my memory so I would continue my life as if nothing had happened."

"A mass murderer?" Keithan repeated in a low voice.

"Hold on," said Mr. Aramis, shaking his head. "How could you possibly remember what you say the Sky Phantoms did to you if they erased your memory?"

This time, Adalina hesitated. "I'm … not sure."

Keithan narrowed his eyes. Like Mr. Aramis, he could tell something about what his mother was telling them didn't make sense.

"You're lying," he told her.

"I'm not," Adalina countered with a tone of assurance. "The Sky Phantoms did make me murder hundreds of people. They did erase my memory afterward, and for years I had no recollection of any of it until one day, I don't know, something just clicked in my mind. I began to get these weird dreams, pieces of information that seemed somewhat familiar. Dreams of me piloting a super-advanced fighter aircraft and doing something terrible with it that involved the death of many. Eventually, I figured out those dreams were actually memories, but I didn't know about the Sky Phantoms' involvement until I met Jeroen."

"What do you mean?" Keithan said.

"He knew what the Sky Phantoms had done to me, how they had manipulated me into committing the crime. And he was the one who found me and revealed it to me."

"And how did he know?" Keithan asked.

"Because he was the only survivor of what I did," Adalina answered.

Keithan swallowed hard.

"So all this is about revenge?" Colani asked.

"And about stealing the Sky Phantoms' highly advanced technology, of course," Adalina said, still staring at Keithan. "Jeroen already had a plan to seek revenge against the Sky Phantom Legion, but he needed the resources to carry it out. That's where I came in. Having a common goal against our enemy, I offered him access to the resources he would need to build his armada."

"*My* resources!" Colani snapped at the realization. "You infiltrated Pegasus—my company!"

"Yes, I did."

Adalina complemented her response with a slight smile that showed no remorse.

"To go through with it, I knew I was going to have to leave my former life behind. So in the grand Pegasus Air Race of 2046, the one that took place in Italy, I faked my death by crashing my aircraft right after flying it through the finish ring and winning the race."

This time, Keithan tightened his jaw. His fists were turning white while he clenched them. He couldn't believe how his mother explained herself as if she were telling a meaningless story. The news of his mother being a mass murderer was still shocking, and so was the thought that it was the Sky Phantom Legion's fault and that because of that, she and General Jeroen were seeking revenge. But all that still didn't infuriate Keithan as much as the real reason he was so angry at her.

"So, because of all that, you decided to leave Dad and me," Keithan asked, feeling the weight of his own words.

He took a deep breath, holding his burning emotions, feeling his eyes water but still not looking away from Adalina.

"You were my mother. Didn't that mean anything to you? More than anything else?"

That seemed to hit Adalina hard. She didn't dare to respond this time. Her confidence seemed to have vanished off her face, and now she couldn't even hold Keithan's gaze. But that only lasted a few seconds before she looked him straight in the eyes and said, "Not after I found out the truth about myself. And trust me, Keithan, it was worth it. So don't bother calling me Mom anymore."

She might as well have punched him in the chest with all her might, taking the air out of his lungs, for that was exactly how her words felt to Keithan. His heart seemed to compress. No longer could Keithan hold back his tears, and he felt them run down his cheeks before they dropped onto the royal red carpet.

"All right. That's enough," Mr. Aramis said, putting a hand on Keithan's shoulder.

"I agree," Colani added. "You're going to pay for the crimes you have done today, Adalina, including sabotaging my company. But first, we have Jeroen to take care of."

Inside the airship's bridge, General Jeroen remained leaning forward with his hands resting on a golden ornamental handrail that arched in front of the flying crew's workstations. He was gazing out the window, which now showed him three tiny shapes in the distance, floating on an endless expanse of sea that he could only see in blood red through his goggles. The shapes, Jeroen was sure, were some of the United States Navy ships, and his air carriers were heading straight in their direction.

"Maintain an altitude of twenty thousand feet," he ordered aloud. "And full speed ahead."

"General, we are receiving a message," reported a crewmember.

"Let me hear it," Jeroen ordered.

"This is the United States Navy," said a sharp male voice amplified through every speaker in the bridge. *"Hold your course, or we will be forced to open fire on you. I repeat, hold your course, or we will be forced to open fire on you. Acknowledge."*

Jeroen remained silent but with a smirk.

"General?" asked the previous crewmember, gazing up at Jeroen over his shoulder.

"Continue onward," Jeroen said while still looking out the window. "And all weapons ready on the three carriers."

"Cancel that order!" shouted a deep voice that surprised everyone on the bridge.

The voice even made Jeroen jump and turn around before he found himself facing the twin barrels of a fist energy pulser in Giovanni Colani's hand.

"How did you get—? *Oh.*"

Jeroen got the answer at the sight of Keithan and Mr. Aramis, who were climbing out of a secret hatch on the floor, right behind Colani.

"Cancel that order, Jeroen," Colani said, deeply serious.

"I'm afraid I can't do that at this point, and you could benefit from it."

"Really? How so?"

"General!" suddenly shouted one of the crewmembers. "They've fired!"

"What?" Colani exclaimed.

"That's how," Jeroen replied, completely calm.

He turned around and stepped aside to let Colani and company look out the window. In the distance, a thin trail of smoke had appeared, growing upward from one of the tiny shapes that floated on the sea. But it was also growing in width, making it obvious it was coming straight in their direction.

CHAPTER 29

Keithan gasped with bulging eyes at the sight of the incoming missile. The thing was flying insanely fast, and like a flash, it brought the horrible memory of the moment he'd almost died earlier today before the *d'Artagnan* was blasted out of the sky. The big difference now was that there was no way to escape, no way to eject. The missile was about to strike the air carrier and the airship, and there didn't seem to be anything that could stop it.

Strangely, Jeroen gazed at the incoming missile as if it were an insignificant object in the sky. Keithan feared the man was actually enjoying its approach.

Jeroen took a moment to type something on his smart glove before raising his gaze again.

"Wait for it," he said.

About a dozen flying spheres appeared from every side of the bridge's window. They shot past the air carrier and headed straight toward the missile. Halfway, they started shooting laser bolts at it nonstop.

"Aaaaand …" Jeroen added with an ascending tone.

BOOM!

The missile turned into a ball of fire in front of the spheres.

"The battle begins!" Jeroen cried, fully excited.

Just as he said that, all the Navy ships visible in the distance responded with full firepower. But Jeroen and his armada were already one step ahead. In response, hundreds of the metallic spheres appeared before the air carrier to form a protective wall at the same time they returned fire.

Some of the spheres exploded, but as soon as it happened, other spheres replaced them and continued firing. Their explosions were constant, and they sounded like popping popcorn from inside the bridge, accompanied by the zapping sound of their laser shots.

"Stop this madness!" roared Colani over the noise. He pointed his energy pulser closer to Jeroen, though it didn't seem to intimidate the general in the least.

"Stop this? Are you mad?" Jeroen told him. "Our counteroffensive is the only thing protecting us from—"

"I don't care! Stop it *now!*"

Still, Jeroen didn't comply. Keithan, along with Mr. Aramis, who kept Keithan behind him, watched the confrontation, paying careful attention to Colani's fist energy pulser.

"You may shoot me, Colani, but that still won't stop the carriers from continuing their course." Jeroen opened his arms challengingly to the sides while staring back at the captain. "My entire crew will continue following my orders whether I'm alive or dead."

"Yeah? Let's put it to the test, then."

Colani fired.

Jeroen staggered backward.

"Gawh!"

Some of the crewmembers turned around, but Colani quickly pointed his fist energy pulser even closer to Jeroen, letting them know he meant to shoot him again if necessary.

"Now will you reconsider?"

Jeroen took a deep breath while pressing the flesh wound on his right shoulder and looked back at Colani.

"Never," he responded through gritted teeth.

An explosion outside, much closer than expected, shook the entire airship. Keithan and Mr. Aramis staggered, and so did Colani and Jeroen, who grabbed the gilded railing of the elevated observation post.

"Hear that?" Jeroen said teasingly. He straightened himself and looked from Colani to Keithan and Mr. Aramis. "That, my friends, is the introductory symphony of today's final battle, which will mark the beginning of a new era. Just you wait and see what will come out of this."

"War?" Keithan asked challengingly.

"War, my dear boy, is only the means to the cause, and the cause— my cause—is to push the world to an era of more technological innovation and advancements."

"You will not!" Colani fumed. "Not with my company. I may have built Pegasus for those same reasons but *not* through war."

"And *that* is your biggest limitation!" Jeroen shot back. "You have innovated with your inventions but not enough, Colani. You don't dare to push yourself to the limits because you lack the push itself: a crisis! Think about it! A deep, impacting crisis can provide that if it can be controlled. And that can only be achieved when mankind itself creates crises with purposes. Such crises can push technology forward, force all the wild geniuses like you and me not just to want to invent but also *to need to invent!* And if there's one thing history has taught us, it's exactly that. World War I, World War II. The Aerial War of the 2020s, for crying out loud!"

Once again, the airship shook as a result of another explosion outside. Keithan regained his footing and looked out the window again to witness how more of the spherical drones continued being shot down. Yet the air carrier and the rest of Jeroen's armada continued flying forward.

"Look out that window, gentlemen!" Jeroen said aloud with complete confidence. No longer did he seem to care about the wound on his shoulder. "The future awaits us! Think of all the new offensive and defensive technology this event will inspire people to invent: weapons, giant fighting robots, drones, shield generators, super-advanced fighter aircraft, new ways of detecting enemies and hiding from them. The possibilities are endless, and the Sky Phantom Legion, with its highly advanced secret technology, holds an important key to all that, which is why I'm after them. I tried to accomplish this fifteen years ago, but I was defeated in the most brutal way before I could cause such a crisis."

"What are you talking about?" Colani said, slightly lowering his fist energy pulser.

"A well-known pilot, manipulated by the Sky Phantoms to do their bidding, annihilated my entire army of nearly a thousand men with one swift stroke. One. *One* pilot. Can you believe that?"

"My mother," Keithan murmured.

"That's right," Jeroen said. "So excuse me and your mother for wanting a little payback since then."

At this point, Keithan could only see Jeroen as nothing more than an incredibly insane genius who was willing to stop at nothing to accomplish his goal.

"I already lived through one war to learn the hard way that none of this is worth it for the sake of progress," Colani told Jeroen.

"Ah, yes. The Aerial War. But you can't deny the great technological innovations that came out of it, especially in the field of aviation," Jeroen insisted. "If anything, you should be grateful for it. After all, it led you to build your company. Am I right?"

Keithan hated himself for thinking it, but Jeroen was right on that one. Worse, Keithan could tell Colani knew it too, and couldn't deny it. The horrible battles of the Aerial War had indeed changed the world in the first half of the twenty-first century, especially by revolutionizing the way people flew today. More than that, it had inspired Colani to create Pegasus Company. The entire world knew it too. The end of that war had even motivated the captain to create the famous air race to prove that the technological advances in the aviation industry could be put to better use rather than for war, especially those made by Pegasus.

Colani shook his head and raised his fist energy pulser toward Jeroen again. "You and Adalina have sabotaged my company. You've tarnished its image and mine for your crazy scheme. Regardless of whether or not I let you live, I am still going to make you stop all this right here."

A strange moment of silence followed inside the bridge. For some reason, the zapping of the spherical drones' laser firing had stopped outside along with the constant explosions of incoming fire. It made Keithan and the others turn to the window again.

"What's going on?" Jeroen asked his crew.

"They're retreating!" shouted one of the crewmembers.

"What?" Jeroen and Colani chorused.

"All U.S. Navy ships, even the ones behind us, are retreating, General."

Confusion was evident on the entire bridge while everyone struggled to make sense of what was happening.

"Are they allowing us to continue our course?" Jeroen asked.

Before anyone could answer, a clanking sound, like that of a pinball ball that had dropped on the floor, broke the silence in the room. It made Keithan and the others around him look down. There, on the floor, they saw a black sphere about the size of a tennis ball with a blinking red light. It rolled before stopping at Jeroen's shoes.

Keithan had no idea what it was, but Jeroen did.

"No!" Jeroen cried just as the little sphere made a buzzing sound. Then every single electronic equipment in the room went dead.

"*Nooo!*" Jeroen cried, enraged.

Everybody became a silhouette. The only light that could still be seen came from the window. Not a single computer or holo screen was working now. Even Jeroen's smart glove and Colani's fist energy pulser seemed to have gone dead.

Right then, Keithan felt a hand fall on his shoulder and pull him backward. Mr. Aramis was pulled in the same direction too, and like Keithan, he didn't have time to react. The two of them staggered backward.

"Into the hatch!" the stranger behind commanded in a whisper.

"*What?* Let me—!" Keithan struggled to say, but the stranger didn't let him finish. It forced Keithan down the hatch before doing the same to Mr. Aramis.

The stranger dropped through the hatch last and locked it.

"It's me! It's me, Keithan!" said the stranger with a familiar British accent.

"Professor Dantés?" Keithan said.

"Dantés?" Mr. Aramis repeated.

"How did you—?"

"I'm getting you out of here," Dantés cut Keithan off. She started pulling him by the arm, but Keithan held her back.

"No! We gotta go back for Colani."

"What? No. We don't have time for that. I gotta get you two off this airship."

"Wait. *You* caused that up there?" Mr. Aramis interrupted.

"It was a small EMP bomb, which released a short-range, electromagnetic pulse to shut down all power inside the airship."

"What about the air carrier?" Mr. Aramis asked.

"It wasn't that strong. Couldn't risk making the whole thing plunge into the sea. Otherwise we would all be dead by now."

"Whoa! Hold on," Keithan said. "That little ball shut down all the power in the airship?"

"And it won't last long. I'm sure Jeroen and his people will manage to restore the power soon," Dantés replied.

"Could that thing knock out robots too?" Keithan asked.

Dantés nodded. "Why?"

Keithan and Mr. Aramis exchanged looks of dread in the dim light of the hidden corridor. Then Keithan turned to Dantés again.

"We gotta get to the conference room. Now."

It took some effort on Keithan and Mr. Aramis's part, but after a few challenging minutes, they managed to find their way back to the conference room. Dantés went up first to make sure it was safe. She, Keithan, and Mr. Aramis found the eight robots still there, forming a circle where they had been guarding Adalina. But just as Keithan and

Mr. Aramis had feared, Dantés's EMP bomb had shut down the robots' power too, which had allowed Adalina to escape.

And still that was only the half of it; Keithan and Mr. Aramis realized it at the same time.

"Oh no," Mr. Aramis said, looking around the room.

"What's wrong?" Dantés asked, yet it was Keithan who answered.

"The Daedalus Project. It's gone too."

CHAPTER 30

I gotta find her, and I gotta stop her, was all Keithan could think of in that moment. He knew what Professor Dantés and Mr. Aramis would say, which was why he didn't bother to tell them. Instead, he headed out to the balcony to his left, where he was sure his mother had escaped.

"Keithan, get back here! Someone could see you!" Mr. Aramis told him.

But Keithan approached the golden railing anyway. He leaned over it and looked at the flight deck below from side to side, searching for any sign of his mother.

"I found her!" he shouted.

He could see her far at the front of the flight deck. She had just dismounted the Daedalus Project, which up until now Keithan hadn't seen hovering and with its wings open.

"I'm going after her," Keithan said, unable to keep it to himself any longer.

"What?" cried both Dantés and Mr. Aramis from inside the conference room.

"Keithan, we're getting off this airship and the air carrier right now," Dantés said. "We need to get to one of the escape po—"

"No. Not yet," Keithan insisted.

"Not yet? Keithan, the Sky Phantom Legion is planning a massive counterstrike against the whole Pegasus's armada!"

"It's not Pegasus's armada," Keithan corrected her. "It's Jeroen's."

"It doesn't *matter*! We have to leave before the armada reaches the center of the triangle!"

"What triangle?" Mr. Aramis interrupted.

Dantés huffed. "Just … trust me, guys. This airship, the air carriers, the flying spheres, they're all going to be taken care of—and not in a good way."

Keithan couldn't stop himself from looking back outside toward his mother. She was carrying the Daedalus Project under one arm, its wings folded again. She was about to enter a metal hatch. Desperate, Keithan turned his gaze down to a big stack of fiberglass crates beneath the airship. The highest of the crates was close to ten feet below the balcony.

I can do this, he thought.

"Uh-oh!" Mr. Aramis said.

Keithan glanced over his shoulder and found the lights at the conference room had been turned back on, along with the hologram of the racecourse on top of the round table.

"That was sooner than expected," Dantés said. "They're gonna come after us any moment now. Let's go!"

Still, Keithan remained on the balcony.

"It's now or never."

And so he climbed over the railing and held on from the other side.

"Keithan! *No!*"

Mr. Aramis and Dantés rushed in his direction, but it was too late. Keithan let go and dropped.

"Keithaaan!"

Keithan rolled forward to break the fall just as his feet hit the highest crate. The stunt led him to the edge, and he almost fell on his back on a lower crate.

"Whoa!" he cried, stopping the roll in time.

He went on to climb down the stack of crates. As soon as he reached the bottom, he ran to the metal hatch he'd seen his mother hurrying to. He had to fight against the battering wind, which was so strong because of the altitude that it didn't allow Keithan to run as fast as he wanted to. At least there wasn't anyone out there. Soon Keithan reached the hatch and closed it behind him.

A descending ladder took him to a dimly lit corridor with pipelines that covered the low ceilings. An enclosed spiral staircase appeared next. Keithan moved quietly, careful not to bump into anyone and get caught. He had no clue where he was headed. All he knew was that he was moving down the air carrier, hopefully in the same direction his mother had gone.

Heavy machinery and indistinctive voices gradually became louder while Keithan continued down a tunnel made of riveted steel walls. The sounds made him slow his pace. At the end of the hall, Keithan reached an opening that led to a balcony from which he was able to see where all the noise was coming from.

"The cargo bay."

Keithan had a full view of it from where he stood. He felt like he was staring at the belly of a man-made beast. The cargo bay looked much longer than a soccer stadium. It was crowded with an almost infinite conglomeration of stacks of crates and levels after levels of overhead conveyors that extended to the far end. Hundreds of metallic spheres hung from these conveyors like Christmas tree ornaments. But as if that wasn't enough, crewmembers, along with Pegasus robots and long mechanical arms, were also there moving all over the place. Many crewmembers could be seen high on hanging catwalks and on fixed scaffoldings. Some of them kept busy inspecting and fixing a few spheres while others charged, attached, and detached them. All the while, more spheres continued flying in and out of the cargo bay through the wide opening at the far end.

"No wonder those things can keep flying and firing for hours."

He approached the railing in front of him, and miraculously, he spotted his mother descending on a hovering platform. She was still holding the Daedalus Project under one arm. The platform was taking her to the lowest level of the cargo bay.

Keithan quickly looked at either side of the balcony for another way down but found none. He would have no choice but to use the platform too.

Maybe nobody would notice me, or at least not in time to stop me, he thought.

He watched the crewmembers and the robots spread throughout the cargo bay. They all seemed deeply immersed in their duties. Then he looked at his mother again. She was marching fast down the cargo bay when an amplified voice with a Dutch accent was heard all over the place.

"Attention, all crews at the three air carriers. This is General Luzier. We are approaching our main enemy's coordinates. I repeat, we are approaching our main enemy's coordinates. Man your stations and make sure all weapons are ready. Over."

Jeroen's words sent a chill down Keithan's spine, but Keithan shook it off, set his jaw, and took a deep breath to gather his courage again. Now, more than ever, he was clear he was running out of time.

—(-o-)—

Having lost all power in the airship bridge may have been a minor setback of a few minutes for Jeroen and his crew, but at least it had allowed them to disarm and apprehend Colani again. Two of Jeroen's crewmembers now held the Pegasus CEO while Jeroen kept the former captain's fist energy pulser pointed at him.

"Should we lock him inside the designing room?" asked one of the men holding Colani.

"No," Jeroen replied. "I want him to witness everything."

He placed the energy pulser inside his lab coat and turned to face the window again.

"Keep watching, Colani. The legendary Sky Phantoms are about to reveal themselves big time, only to be exposed once and for all. You see, while they try to stop us during the upcoming battle, a few of my spheres will record the whole thing. And once it's all over, I will transmit it to the rest of the world and reveal who the Sky Phantoms really are and what they can do."

Jeroen waited for Colani to come back at him with a pointless comment in an attempt to frustrate him. Surprisingly, Colani remained silent behind him.

"What's our current distance?" Jeroen asked aloud.

"Ten miles, General," responded one of the technicians below the command post where Jeroen stood.

"Good," Jeroen said under his breath.

Staring out the window, he and everyone else on the bridge could still see nothing more than the open sea mirroring the orange sky with the last rays of dusk. Jeroen was sure his enemy was out there, well hidden from plain sight with its unique and much desired stealth technology. The anticipation was becoming too much for him, making his heartbeat accelerate and his breathing become deeper. Any moment now, he would see the Sky Phantoms with his own eyes, and he couldn't wait to crush them just like they had crushed his armada fifteen years ago.

And then his new era of war would commence against the rest of the world, finally pushing progress and innovation to its maximum!

"Sir!"

"I see it," Jeroen said, leaning forward over the gilded railing of the elevated observation post.

Something in the sky had just become visible over the horizon. It had appeared out of thin air. And it looked alive, for its amorphous gray-and-purple shape seemed to be growing as if it were blossoming.

"What is that?" asked one of the technicians.

"It looks like ... a cloud of some sort," another said, though not sounding too convinced.

Jeroen grinned. "It's them. The Sky Phantoms."

"Sir, that looks nothing like fighter aircraft," another technician said.

"Trust me. It's them," Jeroen reassured him.

He raised his smart glove, which he'd managed to get working again, and slid his index finger on his palm. A small hologram appeared on it, and he typed on the hologram with his other hand.

"The moment of truth, Colani," he said over his shoulder.

He tapped the Enter key on the hologram over his smart glove. Instantly, an entire squadron of over a hundred flying metallic spheres reappeared in front of the window, forming a protective wall, ready for the showdown Jeroen had been dreaming about so much for so long.

Keithan still couldn't believe how lucky he had been. Even after having sneaked to the lowest level of the cargo bay, no one had noticed or bothered to go after him. Now Keithan remained with his palms against a metal hatch, standing on his tiptoes and peering through the glass of a rectangular porthole. He could see his mother on the other side. She was alone inside what appeared to be a small private cargo hold that had nothing but a few fiberglass crates. She was putting on some protective gear on her arms and legs. A shiny black helmet that matched her gear lay on the floor next to her. And several feet behind her, unattended and resting close to a big pair of closed doors on the floor, lay Mr. Aramis's Daedalus Project.

She's flying away, Keithan thought.

Adalina straightened herself when a holo screen appeared in front of her. It displayed a live image of Jeroen. Keithan figured this was his chance to make a move. He exhaled, carefully turning the wheel on the hatch, and pushed. Incredibly, the hatch didn't make a sound, which allowed Keithan to sneak into the small cargo hold without being noticed. Meanwhile, Adalina listened intently to Jeroen.

"They have just revealed themselves in front of us," Jeroen was saying. "Are you ready?"

"Just finishing putting on the gear," Adalina answered.

"Excellent. Remember, don't hesitate. Fly into the base with the jetboard and leave with one of the Sky Phantoms. I'll take care of the rest."

"Understood."

"And for goodness' sake, Adalina, smile. We're finally going to have our revenge."

"I'm not smiling or claiming any victory until my mission is complete," Adalina said stiffly.

Not too far behind her, Keithan continued moving quietly toward the jetboard. He passed over the big double doors on the floor to get to it. He picked it up and turned around, yet he only managed to take one step when the double doors opened abruptly downward in front of him. A loud gust of wind blew in.

"You *just* can't stay out of trouble, can you?" Adalina shouted over the noise of the wind.

Great. Her too? Keithan thought. "Yeah! I hear that a lot!"

He turned around while keeping the Daedalus Project firmly gripped against his chest. He found his mother no longer accompanied by the holographic image of Jeroen, but instead close to the far wall, still holding the lever that had opened the double doors.

"Put the jetboard down," Adalina said.

Keithan didn't move.

"I'll give you a chance to escape, but you're running out of time." Adalina started pacing toward him. "Head back to the airship, find Mr. Aramis, and get inside one of Colani's escape pods. Just leave the jetboard here."

"Only if you come too," Keithan challenged.

He could see the inner turmoil in his mother's gaze. It was enough for him to be sure she had no intention of hurting him. Despite that, Keithan could tell she was becoming irritated.

"I have a mission to accomplish. I'm setting things right!" she growled.

"But you are my *mother!*"

"I *never* was!"

Keithan froze. The words struck him as if Adalina cast a powerful spell against him. They seemed to have even silenced the howling wind coming through the opening on the floor. Had he heard right? Adalina's deep gaze, however, showed she had meant every word.

"How else do you think I can feel no remorse for everything I've done, especially to you?" Adalina sighed. "A real mother would never have left you."

A shadow suddenly shrouded her face like an eclipse. It made her straighten up and look over Keithan's shoulder before she finished her thought.

"And speaking of which."

Frowning and completely confused, Keithan dared to look over his shoulder. Standing before the doorway of the hatch door where he had sneaked in, Keithan found whom Adalina was referring to …

Professor Alexandria Dantés.

"*You!*" Keithan said almost without a voice. He couldn't believe it. How *could* he? Dantés? Professor Dantés, aka Sky Phantom Agent Venus, his …?

"Step aside, Keithan," was all she said while looking straight at Adalina with menacing eyes.

"Yes, Keithan. Step aside," Adalina said with a malevolent smile. She didn't bother to take the Daedalus Project from his hands. Instead, she forced Keithan aside without even looking at him and marched around the floor's opening in Dantés's direction.

Dantés was already marching toward her. The closer the two got to each other, the faster they moved. Soon they were charging. Then …

Adalina sprang forward. "*Eeaahh!*"

So did Dantés. "*Eeaahh!*"

Both women collided in the air and hit the ground. The impact should have knocked out at least one of them, but the battle between Adalina and Dantés was just getting started. Both women grabbed each other's wrists and wrestled while rolling on the metal floor. Neither one noticed they were moving toward the floor's opening. Only Keithan did, and so he dropped the jetboard and rushed to the lever on the wall. He managed to flip it upward in time for Adalina and Dantés to roll on top of the big double doors. There, Adalina pinned Dantés between her legs, but Dantés managed to release one of her hands and punched Adalina beneath her rib cage.

"*Argh!*" Adalina fell to the side.

Dantés quickly jumped to her feet and turned to Keithan.

"Get that jetboard out of here!" she yelled. "And get to an escape pod!"

Keithan hesitated.

"Now!"

Right then, Adalina surprised Dantés from behind with a chokehold.

"Don't you dare grab that jetboard again!" Adalina warned Keithan. She dragged Dantés backward, out of the floor's double doors, and tightened her grip around Dantés's neck to show Keithan how serious she was.

Dantés struggled to free herself. Despite turning purple, she kept looking at Keithan, warning him with her eyes not to intervene and just leave.

Keithan nodded and ran toward the jetboard.

"I *said*—!" Adalina started, but Dantés bent down and threw her over her shoulders, making Adalina fall flat on her back. She tried to get back up, but Dantés forced her to turn sideways by holding Adalina's left arm in a lock.

Once again Adalina cried out in pain.

"Keithan!" Dantés called out.

Keithan was about to pick up the jetboard but raised his hands instead, almost reflexively, when he saw Dantés toss something small in his direction with her free hand. He caught it; it was his wrist communicator! Dantés had taken it off Adalina's wrist.

"Now *go!*" Dantés commanded.

This time Keithan didn't hesitate. He quickly put on his communicator and picked up the jetboard lying in front of him.

"Keithan! Get ba— *Argh!*" Adalina roared while still trying to free her arm.

"Stop it!" Dantés growled at her. "What happened to you? You were a good person—a hero!"

"*You* happened!" Adalina roared. "You and your legion ruined my life!"

She released a scream and swung both legs around Dantés's, locking her ankles together and bringing Dantés down. Dantés hit the floor hard, and Adalina punched her in the already-swollen side of her face.

Adalina jumped to her feet, free at last.

Keithan only had to make eye contact with her to know she would be coming after him. He would have been scared to death earlier today if he'd been forced to fight her, but not now. She was nothing more than a villain to him now, and he knew what he had to do.

Just as Adalina launched herself in his direction, Keithan did the first thing that came to mind. He picked up the black helmet Adalina was planning to wear, which lay on the floor near him, and threw it with all his might toward the lever at the wall behind him. Again, a gust of wind blew into the cargo hold the instant the big double doors between him and Adalina dropped open.

Adalina stopped dead in her tracks mere inches from the edge. She had to raise her arms out to her sides to prevent herself from losing her balance.

"*Wait!*" she shouted in horror.

Finally, Keithan had the upper hand. He stood across the opening from her, holding the Daedalus Project over the edge.

"It's over, Adalina!" he said aloud. "You're not winning this time!"

He glanced at Dantés, who still lay on the floor, though she was staring at him too a few feet behind Adalina. And so, taking a deep breath, Keithan jumped off the air carrier with the jetboard.

"NOOOOOO!!!"

The two women's screams were drowned out by the wind, which roared in Keithan's ears like an enraged beast. It flapped his cheeks and his clothes as if it wanted to rip them off. But still, that was the least of Keithan's problems. He tried to stop spinning out of control with the jetboard while he fell. More than that, he tried desperately to get the thing under his feet.

"Come on! Come on! *Come on!*"

Dizziness started to overcome him, for the sea and the sky looked as if they were the ones spinning around him faster and faster. He managed to slip his left foot into the jetboard's back foot mount and reached out with his hands to lock it. He tried his other foot immediately after that and—CLICK—locked it into place on the front foot mount.

"Yeaaah!"

He craned his neck, well aware he wasn't out of trouble yet. He was falling upside down, the sea rushing up to him. Arms flailing, Keithan bent his knees and arched his torso, straightening himself.

Everything he'd learned and practiced about skydiving at Ramey Academy flashed before his eyes. But what good was any of that now without a parachute? Falling like a sky surfer with the jetboard attached to his feet, Keithan faced his last challenge: figuring out how to turn on the jetboard. The thing had no button or switch, at least not one that was visible.

Keithan glanced at the rushing sea below. He was going to hit it in less than a minute.

"How the blazes do you turn on?" he cried, looking again at the jetboard.

He was just starting to regret jumping off the cargo hold when a hand grabbed his left shoulder.

"What the—?!"

Keithan looked up and gasped. It was Adalina, upside down and holding on to him. She reached out with her other hand and pulled herself closer.

"Are you *crazy*?" Keithan shouted. Did she intend to take the Daedalus Project from him in midair?

Keithan tried to push her away, but Adalina managed to keep a firm grip on him. She pulled herself further down, still upside down, till she reached the jetboard.

"Don't! *Don't!*" Keithan cried in panic.

Adalina grabbed his left foot. She was going to release it from the back foot mount—or so Keithan thought. She forced him to turn it clockwise. The Daedalus Project came to life with a whine and a vibration, and the curved wings flipped open to the sides from underneath.

"Pull up!" Adalina shouted.

Keithan frowned. He definitely had not been expecting that.

"Fly! Like you've never flown before!"

And with that, Adalina let go.

There was nothing Keithan could have done to help her. Everything happened so fast. Adalina was lost from sight almost in the blink of an eye, and Keithan had no choice but to get ready to save himself. Falling at terminal velocity, he bent his knees, reached for the jetboard's nose with both hands, and pulled with everything he had. At the same time, he pushed down on the rear of the jetboard with his left foot to raise its front.

"Come on! Come … *ooonnn!*"

Then—*SWOOSH!*

He was flying! He was rushing upward like an eagle with his hands extended to the sides in the same angle as the jetboard's wings, leaving the sea and his tiny shadow farther and farther below him.

"*Woo-hoo!*" Keithan howled.

All panic dissolved as a rush of relief and exhilaration took over him. It was the greatest feeling ever! No longer was he fighting the wind. He was riding it with the jetboard and feeling it flowing, cold and moist, through his whole body! The deeper he pressed the rear foot mount, the more thrust the jetboard gave, and he could control the wings by angling his feet.

He continued ascending as fast as his body allowed it. The excitement of the flight, however, was short-lived when Keithan arced sideways and got a full view of Jeroen's entire armada from the rear. But there was something else beyond it in the sky, Keithan noticed, something much bigger—and threatening. It was a massive dark cloud, the strangest and scariest one Keithan had ever seen. It looked alive, blossoming smaller clouds from its center, which seemed to make the whole thing grow. More than that, it was manifesting what Keithan could only make out as a frightening show of thunderclaps and bright purple lightning from deep within.

And Jeroen and his armada were headed straight in its direction.

Keithan, who had become an insignificant silhouette flying in the now-dark sky, couldn't look away from the terrifying scene. Then it hit him: That monstrous cloud was no natural phenomenon. It was the Sky Phantom Legion's doing. *It has to be!* Keithan thought, remembering Dantés's warning about the Legion's plan to deal with the armada.

"This is it!" Keithan said, transfixed.

"This is it!" cried Jeroen with the widest of grins. "Fifty spheres recording, and all spheres at the front ready to give our enemy hell!"

His crew on the bridge didn't seem to share his enthusiasm at the moment, though. Instead, it remained silent while staring transfixed at the morphing dark cloud outside and the strange weather readouts on the radar screens.

"Don't let that thing intimidate you, people," Jeroen went on encouragingly. "This is what we prepared for! This is our moment!"

But despite his confident pep talk, there were no cries of agreement, only a warning from Colani, who was still being held by Jeroen's men.

"You're already doomed, Jeroen. We all are," Colani said in a low, trembling voice while also staring out the window.

"Ha! In your dreams," Jeroen responded over his shoulder.

Holding his smart glove with his palm up, he tapped the holographic key hovering from it to make his spheres commence their attack. Yet Jeroen neither saw nor heard any of their laser shots. And an instant before he realized what had happened, his overconfidence dissolved, and terror took complete control of him.

"No," was all he managed to say, right before he saw his enemy attack.

Keithan screamed and crossed his arms in front of his eyes at the unexpected flash of an intense purple-and-white light that shot out from the large morphing cloud. A shock wave accompanied it, so strong it sent Keithan careening backward in the air. He would have been knocked off the jetboard if not for the foot mounts' locking mechanisms, which kept his feet secured. Still, Keithan had to put up a fight to maneuver with his whole body and regain control.

It was soon afterward that he witnessed all the flying spheres in the distance drop from the sky like dead flies. At the same time, long purple energy bolts engulfed the two air carriers at either side of the one with the Pegasus airship attached at its top. Then the two massive vessels went down too. Keithan gasped and watched them fall in slow motion till they plunged into the raging sea, bows first and raising huge splashes.

How and why the lead air carrier remained in the sky, Keithan did not know. Yet he had a strong feeling it was going to suffer the same fate of its former companions at any moment. Dantés, Mr. Aramis, and Colani came to Keithan's mind, and at the horrifying realization of their fates, he braced himself to fly toward the air carrier.

He had just pushed the jetboard's throttle to the maximum when the unthinkable happened again: the air carrier and the Pegasus airship vanished before Keithan's eyes!

"Oh my— No ... *no!*"

Keithan stopped pressing the rear foot mount, making the jetboard decelerate. The only thing he could see in the sky now was the sinister cloud. It was no longer lighting up from the inside or making thunderclaps. Instead, it was shrinking, and fast, as if it were being swallowed by an invisible wormhole in midair, till it disappeared and Keithan was left alone in the middle of nowhere under the night sky.

"Okay, now I'm really scared."

He was barely able to see himself, and he had no clue of what to do next.

Then came the second flash of intense light.

CHAPTER 31

K eithan opened his eyes with a fright. For a moment he thought he had woken up, only he didn't feel like he had been sleeping or unconscious. On the contrary, he felt fully awake—disoriented but fully awake. It was a strange feeling, as if somebody had paused his life and then suddenly pressed "Play" to keep it going.

Was that what happened? Keithan wondered.

He looked down, expecting to see his feet still attached to the Daedalus Project, but he saw they were no longer mounted on it. The jetboard wasn't even anywhere on sight, and the dark sky and the sea were gone too.

Instead, Keithan found himself standing in the middle of his bedroom at number one, L Street, in Ramey, Aguadilla. His wrist communicator showed it was 9:21 a.m., Sunday, May 2. The day after the Pegasus Air Race.

"How is it possible?" he said, looking carefully around him. Was this a dream?

The sunlight coming through the concave window opposite to his queen platform bed illuminated the room. Everything there looked exactly the way Keithan had left it yesterday before having left for Ramey Airport. The laptube on his desk in front of the window, the small pile of dirty clothes on one side of the bed—which he'd promised his dad he would wash after the Pegasus Air Race—even the numerous vintage editions of *Fast in the Sky* magazine that lay scattered on the floor. The imposing figure in black who stood before the closed door, however, was not supposed to be there, and Keithan jumped with a shriek at the sight of it.

"You're not dreaming, kid. This is your real bedroom," said the figure who happened to be Lieutenant Colonel Lanzard.

Keithan narrowed his eyes. "And you?"

Lanzard snorted. "I'm real too. Just here to make sure you're all right." He folded his arms and paced toward Keithan. "Do you remember what happened to you last night?"

"Last night?" Keithan said. "I was flying a moment ago with the Daedalus Project in the middle of nowhere—"

"That was fourteen hours ago," Lanzard corrected him.

Keithan's jaw dropped.

The lieutenant colonel was now moving around him. "I have to admit, kid, you have really impressed me with your bravery and recklessness. Flying into the very center of the Bermuda Triangle, getting a glimpse of who's hiding there, and still being alive ... you're lucky they didn't erase your entire memory."

"They?"

"The *real* Sky Phantoms."

Keithan wrinkled his nose. "W-what?"

"The ones I report to," Lanzard explained. "The very same ones you encountered at the triangle and who, um ... are not from around here, so to speak."

"Huh?"

Lanzard seemed to choose his words carefully. "Let's just say they're from far, *far* away, if you take my meaning."

Keithan couldn't help staring at the lieutenant colonel, completely confused. Then he gasped.

"You mean they're—"

"They're here to help," Lanzard clarified quickly, "as they have done in top secret for a very long time, and we intend to keep it that way. That's all you need to know."

Keithan shook his head. "W-why are you telling me this?"

"Because you helped them—us, the entire Sky Phantom Legion, by stopping Adalina from accomplishing her plan with the Daedalus Project. We could have stopped her, but there was a chance we could have failed too. We thank you for that. And figuring we owed you, we decided—after careful deliberation, I must add—not to erase your memory, but only as long as you promise to keep the existence of the Legion secret. You think you can do that?"

Keithan nodded quickly, though he wasn't sure if he did it out of determination or out of fear of having his memory erased.

"So you found out about Adalina?" he then said.

Lanzard nodded. "Your mother explained everything. Your real mother."

"Dantés," Keithan said in a low voice, as if to convince himself by mentioning her last name. "Is she all right?"

"She's safe, and we took care of everybody else that was inside the air carrier and the Pegasus airship. Jeroen and what remained of his crew will never be free again. Our special Sky Phantom agents inside the Bermuda Triangle will make sure of that."

"And Colani and Mr. Aramis? Don't tell me you—"

"They're safe. They weren't captured. However, they won't remember what really happened. We couldn't allow it."

Keithan gave a deep sigh of relief. Dantés, Mr. Aramis, and Colani were safe. That was enough for him.

Lanzard had turned his attention to the small collection of aircraft models on top of one of Keithan's drawers.

"Well, now. You think you are ready to get back to your normal life?" he asked. "You shouldn't have any problems with that."

"What about you and the rest of the Legion?" Keithan asked. "I mean, after everything that happened yesterday."

"Oh, we managed to cover our tracks from the rest of the world," Lanzard said. "We always do."

He had picked up a racing aircraft model that had a fleur-de-lis decal and the number 18 on either side.

"Is this …?"

"Mom's— I mean, Adalina's former racer, the *Milady 18*," Keithan said, scratching the back of his head.

"Hmm." Lanzard continued looking at the model in his hands. "All your life you thought you were following your mother's footsteps."

Keithan sighed and shrugged. "Guess I was kidding myself."

Lanzard placed the model back in its place. "Maybe not. Still, my advice: Don't try to be anyone's shadow, Keithan. Just be yourself."

He headed to the door, but before opening it, he turned to Keithan one last time.

"See you around, kid," he said, "but hopefully you won't see us."

And with that, Lanzard shut the door behind him.

Keithan remained in the middle of his room, staring blankly at the door, deep in thought. He would need time to make sense of everything Lanzard had just revealed to him. Yet he couldn't help wondering at the moment how the lieutenant colonel had gotten into his house.

Does Dad know?

The question made him shake his head, and in seconds, he was out of his bedroom and hurrying to catch up with Lanzard.

"Colonel, wait!" Keithan called as he reached the living room. "Colonel Lanzard?"

"Who?"

Keithan looked to his right in surprise. "Dad!"

Caleb Quintero looked up at him over his shoulder from the red faux-leather sofa. "Who's Colonel Lanzard?"

"Uh …"

Keithan turned left and could have sworn he saw the front door close without making a sound.

"Is everything all right, son?"

Keithan sighed and turned back to his father. Just by staring at his expression, he could tell the man was oblivious of what had just happened. The Legion had taken care of him too.

"Yeah," he finally said. "I thought … Never mind."

"Well, come take a look at this," his father said. "They're talking about what happened yesterday. Every news channel is covering it."

Keithan raised his gaze toward the holo screen projected in midair, opposite the sofa. The screen was divided into six viewports, each one showing a different news channel. The enhanced viewport at the center, however, was the only one with the audio on, and currently, it showed Channel 2 News's field correspondent Rebecca Knight addressing the viewers.

"… Finally, it has all come to an end," the woman reported. "Last night, U.S. Navy ships took down all three air carriers and the entire armada of flying spheres somewhere over the Atlantic while they were trying to escape. As far as we know up to this point, there was only one survivor: the CEO of Pegasus Company, Captain Giovanni Colani, who was rescued in an escape pod in open sea. Colani was believed to be the principal subject of the sphere attack throughout Puerto Rico while the Pegasus Air Race was still going on. However, he is not likely to be charged since, according to confirmed sources, the true masterminds behind the attack turned out to be former air racing champion Drostan Luzier and his senior advising aeroengineer, Jeroen Luzier, who also turned to be Drostan's father."

"Whoa!" said Keithan's dad, leaning forward.

"Whoa," imitated Keithan, faking his surprise.

"Luzier, as many of you may already know, was killed during the sphere attack after crashing in a mountainous area deep inland in Puerto Rico," the reporter continued. "As for Drostan's father, Jeroen, nothing is known about his whereabouts. It's believed he was inside one of the air carriers when they were shot down from the sky.…"

"Man, it's like something out of Hollywood," Keithan's dad commented.

"I know," Keithan added. *And you don't even know the whole truth.*

"So how are you holding up?" his dad then asked, momentarily muting the holo screen. "You know, after what happened with the *d'Artagnan?*"

"You know about that?"

"How could I not? Don't get me wrong. I should ground you

for making me almost have a heart attack, but you sacrificed your aircraft to save that young air racer's life: Oliviera. You're a hero, Keithan."

Keithan felt his face turn red. So it turned out his dad remembered some of the other things that had happened yesterday, though not exactly the way they had really happened. But how much, exactly?

"Where were you when that happened?" Keithan asked, testing his father.

"With the Aramises. Don't you remember?"

"Oh. Right." Keithan tapped the side of his head with his palm. "Speaking of the Aramises, I better go see how they're doing."

He started moving backward, toward the door.

"Um, Keithan ..."

"I won't be long."

"Son, you're not gonna be able to enter the airport," his dad insisted. "The whole place remains closed until further notice."

Still, Keithan was already at the door, but no sooner than he opened it than he stopped. Right outside, mere inches from him and about to press the doorbell, he found Alexandria Dantés.

"Wow," said Keithan, only to realize too late how indiscreet his reaction had been at the sight of the woman's swollen purple right cheekbone "I-I'm sorry. I didn't mean—"

"It's all right. I know how ugly it looks," Alexandria said with a crooked smile that seemed to hurt.

"Professor Dant— *Wow*," said Caleb as he stopped behind Keithan. "Are you all right, Professor?"

"Yeah. It's no big deal. Sorry for showing up here unannounced, Mr. Quintero. I was hoping I could talk to Keithan in private if it's all right."

"Oh. Sure. Please, come in."

Keithan shot his dad a look, wanting to oppose, but it was too late. It was clear he wasn't going to get out of this one.

—(-O-)—

The terrace at the back of the house ended up being the best spot for Keithan and his mother to talk in private. They could feel the warm tropical breeze there, which swayed the areca palm trees as well as the dwarf palmettos that stood behind the pool beyond the terrace. The breeze, however, forced Alexandria to gather her hair in a ponytail. Meanwhile, Keithan sat and waited for her to begin talking. Alexandria seemed to be about to speak, but instead, she pulled out a folded piece of paper from one of her pants pockets and handed it to Keithan.

"What's this?" Keithan said.

"Open it."

Keithan did and found himself staring at an old photograph of a man and a woman, probably in their early twenties. They were leaning their heads against each other and holding hands in front of a sunflower field with a bright clear sky in the background.

"It's the only evidence I have of your father and me," Alexandria said, making Keithan look up at her in surprise. "I was nineteen when it was taken, your father twenty-one."

"Didn't you have digital pictures back then?"

Alexandria shot him an annoyed look. "I've kept it in printed form on purpose, to keep it untraceable."

Never in a million years would Keithan have imagined seeing something like this. His flight professor and his dad? In love? Alexandria didn't look much different in the photograph than she did now except for her light-brown hair, which was much longer now. His dad, on the other hand, looked much more different, with long dark hair covering his ears and barely the slightest evidence of a stubble beard yet. More than that, Keithan could see the man looked much happier and full of life in the photograph than he looked nowadays.

"I don't intend to give you all the details, Keithan, only that it just didn't work out between your father and me ... mostly because of my double identity, which I could never reveal to him."

"So was it your decision?"

Alexandria lowered her gaze. "Yes. Believe me, Keithan, leaving your father shortly after finding out I was pregnant with you was the most painful thing I have ever done in my life. That and leaving you in his and Adalina's care soon after you were born."

"Why?"

"I … just wasn't prepared to be a mother."

There was a short moment of silence.

"And that's still only half the story, isn't it?" Keithan said. He looked again from the photograph to his mother.

"I'm afraid so," Alexandria replied. "Your father and Adalina's so-called 'marriage' wasn't real. The Sky Phantom Legion fabricated it to help Adalina after something horrible she did the year before you were born."

"The massacre," Keithan said, remembering what Adalina and Jeroen had revealed inside the Pegasus airship.

"How do you know about that?"

"Adalina mentioned the Legion manipulated her into doing it and that the Legion had her memory erased because of that. That's the reason she resented all of you."

"No," Alexandria said quickly. "Adalina did it out of her own free will to stop her father's madness. She wasn't involved with the Legion in any way until after what she did. Keithan, she alone saved the world fifteen years ago and prevented what would have been a second aerial war, but at a terrible price. Her actions were too much for her to bear afterward, especially considering that she thought she had killed her father too."

"So that's why the Legion erased her memory."

"Had it partially altered—and upon her insistence," Alexandria corrected him. "Adalina didn't want to have any memory of what she'd done. She didn't even want to have anything to do with the Legion even though she was invited to join, but as you know, she was a well-known air racing champion, not a fighter pilot. Therefore, once the Legion agreed to help her, I was assigned to make sure her memory was altered, and by turning her into a mother—your mother—we changed her life for the better, or so we thought, until she somehow got her memories back."

"And what about Dad?" Keithan said. "Did the Legion have his memory partially altered too?"

Alexandria swallowed hard and nodded. "That was my call, and I don't regret it. It was the only way I could help your father forget about me and what we'd had. I didn't want him to suffer."

Her gaze now seemed to be fixed past the sloped glass doors separating the terrace from the living room, where Keithan's dad remained, still watching the news. Curiously, her eyes showed something Keithan had never seen in Alexandria before: longing.

"I know it's a lot to take in after everything that has happened," Alexandria said while still looking past Keithan, "but you deserve to know ... son."

Son. The word sounded weird coming from her. Despite that, for some reason, Keithan no longer found it easy to remember Adalina calling him that when she had played the role of his mother. All the memories of him as Adalina's son also seemed hard to remember now, as if they had been nothing more than a very odd dream.

Deep in these thoughts, Keithan stood up and gave the photograph back to his mother.

"So all my life you never actually left," Keithan said. "Adalina was right. A real mother would have never left."

Alexandria smiled and placed both hands on his shoulders, turning him around to face the living room. "Nor would a real father."

Just as Keithan's dad had mentioned, Ramey Airport remained closed until further notice. It even continued to be under maximum security by the National Guard. Yet that didn't stop Keithan from entering it, and all thanks to his awesome and well-connected mother who managed to pass him through the two security checkpoints without any problem.

Keithan held on tight to Alexandria's waist from behind while she drove her hoverbike down the airfield. All around, he could see airport staff and robots still cleaning the scattered debris of Pegasus spheres, as well as more staff in the distance dismounting what remained of the race's grandstands.

Alexandria drove to the residential hangars at the east side of the airport and stopped the hoverbike right in front of Hangar H11, which had its main entrance open.

Keithan dismounted. "Thanks for the ride, *Mom*," he said while handing her the helmet.

"My pleasure, *son*."

Alexandria shot him a smile that, like Keithan's, showed she was still trying to get used to this new way of addressing each other, at least in secret.

She was about to put on her helmet when Keithan threw his arms around her waist. He did it out of impulse, and he didn't care. He gave himself to the moment, feeling her warmth while she hugged him back. To Keithan, it felt like the warmth only a mother can give to her children, that warmth Keithan had thought he would never get to feel again.

They held each other for almost a whole minute before Keithan stepped back.

"I better go," he said, clearing his throat.

"Of course."

He watched his mother put on her helmet and take off. It wasn't until she disappeared in the distance that he turned around and headed into Hangar H11.

The Aramises were gathered near the far end, close to the entrance of Mr. Aramis's workshop. As usual, Laika was the first to notice Keithan.

Woof! She ran up to him, and Keithan bent forward to meet her. Try as he might, he couldn't stop the excited golden retriever from licking his face.

Fernando turned his wheelchair. "You're right on time!"

Keithan straightened up and continued toward his friends. He couldn't help locking eyes with Marianna on his way, though. Of all of the Aramises, it was she who Keithan had wanted to see the most. He had to fight the urge to hurry up to her as he remembered she would most likely have no recollection of what had really happened yesterday.

"What's going on?" Keithan said instead when he reached everyone.

Fernando reared his wheelchair to reveal his dad holding the awesome jetboard upright.

"Oh!" Keithan said.

"Dad finally revealed it to us," Marianna told him.

"It's the top-secret project he'd been working on for Pegasus!" Fernando said, beaming.

Keithan did his best to stare at the jetboard as if it were the first time he was seeing it.

"Wow! That … is really cool."

"It is, isn't it?" Mr. Aramis said.

"Can you believe it?" Fernando told Keithan, still excited. "It's a whole new awesome way of flying!"

"Show Keithan how it works!" said Mrs. Aramis, just as excited.

Her husband placed the jetboard on the floor, reached for the rear foot mount with both hands, and turned it clockwise. In response, the jetboard, already with its wings open to the sides, powered up and rose from the floor.

"Whoa!"

Everybody stared at the humming jetboard, which now hovered two feet off the floor. Keithan only wished he could share how it actually felt to fly that thing, to feel it under his feet and move freely in the sky with it.

Just then, he felt Marianna lean closer and whisper in his right ear, "Thanks for bringing it back, by the way."

"Yeah. No probl— Wait. What?" Keithan flicked toward her. "How do you—?"

"We know," Marianna told him, still whispering. "Dantés convinced the Legion to only take care of Mom and Dad's memories. That way

Keithan Quintero and the Pegasus Air Race

you don't have to keep the secret to yourself. Still, she warned us not to reveal anything of what really happened to anyone else—ever. The Legion will be keeping a close eye on the three of us."

Keithan turned to Fernando, who was clearly aware of what Marianna had just revealed and winked at him while still pretending to be surprised by his dad's invention.

Keithan wanted to say a thousand things, but with Mr. and Mrs. Aramis there, he had to continue playing along too.

"So that's the Daedalus Project?" he ended up saying instead.

"Oh, no," said the four Aramises simultaneously.

"No, no, no, no. This is just the main piece of the whole thing," Mr. Aramis added.

"What?"

"The Daedalus Project is much, *much* bigger than this!" Mr. Aramis went on explaining. "It was all supposed to be revealed yesterday."

"But it's still going to be revealed," Mrs. Aramis said.

"It is?" Keithan said.

"Oh, yeah. The whole thing is gonna be announced to the rest of the world," Mr. Aramis reaffirmed.

Keithan, still puzzled, could only ask the obvious questions.

"When? And where?"

Six Months Later

Ramey Airport
(Aguadilla, Puerto Rico)

EPILOGUE

SHOOM! SHOOM! ... SHOOM! SHOOM!
It was the sound of the horizontal light streaks that flashed between black pauses on the giant holographic screen. They seemed to keep the audience in a trance. Then a low motorized humming took over, and the image changed to the close-up side view of an unusual and never-before-seen aircraft flying steadily at top speed. The camera zoomed out. The audience oohed. Louder oohs and gasps followed when everybody saw that the aircraft was much smaller than it had appeared to be at first. Much louder oohs and gasps soon followed when everyone saw the aircraft was not being piloted from inside a cockpit, but rather ridden by a figure clad in a black-and-white racing uniform and a matching helmet while standing on top of the thing as if it were a surfboard—a flying, winged surfboard!

"Coming next year," a deep, dramatic voice announced, "the future we have been waiting for ... Inspired by a mythological Greek legend ... and brought to you by the creators of the most famous air race in the world...."

By this point, the rider on the jetboard was facing the camera, arms stretched to the sides, knees bent, and still flying steady and fast. Then three more figures appeared from behind—also on jetboards.

"Pegasus Company proudly presents ..."

And right at that moment, the four figures froze just as a checkered pattern hover ring rushed toward the one at the front, enclosed it, and a surprise title appeared below it with a date:

THE
DAEDALUS
AIR RACE
SUMMER 2056

The entire audience spread throughout the airfield burst into thunderous applause and cheering. Their excitement intensified seconds later at the sight of a familiar figure who appeared on the stage below the giant holographic screen. A spotlight illuminated the figure, highlighting his gold-embroidered white suit and peaked cap, which he held under one arm. There was no need to introduce him. Everyone knew who he was, and they had been looking forward to seeing him after months of absence: the CEO of Pegasus Company, Captain Giovanni Colani.

"Thank you! Thank you!" Colani exclaimed over the applause and cheering that didn't die down. The audience was even giving him a standing ovation. It took nearly two minutes for Colani to be able to speak again.

Colani raised his chest. "Wow! It feels so good to be back on stage, and to finally share with you this amazing new event! An air race definitely unlike any other you have ever seen before—at least in real life. It is a dream come true, people! A dream that, curiously, was inspired by a fictional invention that dates back to the ancient times of Greek mythology, when a man with such an imagination and skills in craftsmanship created two pairs of wings for himself and his son so they could escape from a dangerous labyrinth where they had been imprisoned. For those of you who don't know, that man's name was Daedalus. And just like Daedalus, a man from *our* time came up with a similar but much better invention. Let me be clear; I'm not talking

about myself. You will meet this man soon. But first, I must ask …"
Colani lowered his voice and gave the audience a mischievous look
while rubbing his hands. "Would you like to see that invention?"

The response was instantaneous: deafening, excited cries.

Colani threw his head back and laughed. "Then, ladies and
gentlemen, boys and girls, I give you the main piece of what led to
creating the Daedalus Air Race … the Daedalus racing *jetboard!*"

Right next to him, a trapdoor opened, and a platform rose out of
the stage, carrying the real thing—sleek and streamlined—and shown
on the giant holographic screen for the world to see.

"And let's welcome to the stage its designer, *William Aramis!*"

William appeared from the right side of the stage, wearing what
could only be described as a million-dollar smile. He was dressed as he
had never been seen before, with a shiny black suit, white shirt, and
black shoes. He looked so elegant even with his long curly gray hair,
which only grew from the lower back of his head, and which was always
tied in a ponytail. William waved at the audience while he paced toward
Colani. The two shook hands before they turned their attention to the
jetboard.

"So, William, care to share about our new *belleza* here?"

William, all red and sweaty as he did his best to not look nervous,
adjusted the tiny microphone attached to his suit and spoke. "Well, this
here is the official jetboard model that has been specially designed and
standardized for the future Daedalus Air Race. It can exceed a speed
of two hundred miles per hour. It's very maneuverable too since its
wings can rotate in mid-flight. Because of that, it can only be flown by
well-trained air racers."

"Oh, I bet," Colani said while the audience applauded.

"And, um, I could go on and on about how great this jetboard is,"
William continued, "but simply put, this thing here is for flying at a
whole new level."

More applause followed.

"I'd like to add," said Colani, turning again to the audience and the
cameras, "this jetboard, along with the Daedalus Air Race, is clear proof

of the real aims and values of Pegasus Company, which is to show through innovation and air racing how technology can be used for good, not for war. Of course, we can't deny we have faced people in the past who have tried to prove me—us—wrong, people who believe war is the best way to push technology forward. What they have failed to understand, however, is that war should never be the answer at the cost of freedom, stability, and peace. No, the best way to push technology forward, my friends, is through science!"

That last statement made the people in the audience stand up and applaud louder in agreement.

"Science has always been our path, especially Pegasus's path," Colani went on. "Science also for the sake of innovation, and most importantly, for humanity's well-being and progress. And so, with the all-new Daedalus Air Race next year, William and I, and all of Pegasus Company, hope to introduce not just a new and amazing way of flying and air racing, but also an era that reflects a fun and better future, one that we can actually look forward to!"

The cheers and applause intensified.

"But enough talking!" Colani clasped his hands together. "I'm sure you all are eager to see a live demonstration of this jetboard, right?"

Shouts of approval resounded all over the place.

"What do you say, William?"

William looked back at the side of the stage where he had come from. "Oh, I have the perfect person for that."

"Keithan, that's your cue!" Fernando announced from behind the black curtain at the left side of the stage.

"Almost ready!" Keithan replied over his shoulder. He buckled the last strap of his emergency parachute harness and was about to do a quick overall check of his gear when he noticed something was missing.

"My helmet. Where is it?" he said, looking around him.

"I have it!"

Keithan turned on the spot and found Marianna hurrying up to him with the helmet in her hands.

"Sorry! I was just giving it one final touch. Here."

Keithan took the metallic-orange-and-silver helmet and immediately saw the new design Marianna had painted on its back. It was a light-blue triangular shield with the number eighteen in black at its center.

"I figured you'd like to keep using Adalina's racing number, for luck. You wouldn't be here if it hadn't been for her, you know."

Keithan smirked while he held Marianna's gaze. Unable to control himself any longer, he stepped forward and met her lips, eyes closed, and breathed in deeply. For that short moment, he put everything aside: his mix of nervousness and exhilaration at the anticipation of what he was about to do, his focus on everything he'd learned about the jetboard and what he'd practiced with it, even the fact that there were people around him and Marianna staring. All of that to remind himself of how much she meant to him over everything else.

Their kiss would have been longer if not for Marianna, who pulled away and cleared her throat before she gestured for Keithan to turn around. Keithan did and saw why she had reacted that way.

Fernando was staring at them, slightly exasperated in his wheelchair a few feet away.

"Now *that's* my cue to leave," Keithan said, snickering.

Marianna could only smirk.

Blushing, Keithan turned to Fernando again. "Ready!"

Fernando rolled his eyes. He then put on his communicator headset and showed Keithan the data pad in his hands.

"Stay focused," he told Keithan. "I'll be monitoring you and the jetboard from here. "Now, *go!*"

"*Now*," Colani bellowed, "let's welcome to the stage a young and rising star who so happens to be the son of the late and legendary air racing champion Adalina Zambrana—and the youngest competitor in the Daedalus Air Race next year. Ladies and gentlemen, boys and girls, I give you our flyer, *Keithaaan Quinteeerooo!*"

Hearing his name, as well as the excited cheers and applause of the audience, made the hairs on Keithan's arms and the back of his neck stand on end. Still, Keithan managed to remain fully under control as he appeared on the stage and waved at everybody. He even spotted his dad and Mrs. Aramis not too far away at the front row, waving back at him.

"So, Keithan, are you ready?" Colani asked.

Keithan didn't answer. Instead, he brought his wrist communicator close to his mouth and activated the device's voice-recognition power-up synchronizer. "Engine on."

And right in that instant, the jetboard in front of him came to life, rising two feet off the platform. It was all it took to get the audience even more excited.

Now grinning, Keithan put on his helmet, slid down its tinted visor, and gave Colani and Mr. Aramis two thumbs up. He proceeded to attach the oxygen hose dangling from his chest to the helmet's jaw guard and finally climbed onto the hovering jetboard and locked his boots into each of the foot mounts.

"And here we go," Keithan murmured to himself.

"All systems go," he heard Fernando through the helmet's integrated communicator. *"Good luck!"*

"And have fun," Keithan reminded himself.

He pressed the rear foot mount and took off.

All eyes and hover cameras followed him as he gained speed and altitude over the audience. Three hover rings already waited for him in the sky over two hundred feet, and one by one, Keithan flew through them. The first by making a half loop upward and passing through it upside down. The second one by flying sideways, and the last one, which hovered horizontally, by shooting through it from below.

"Woo-hoo!" Keithan cried. He kept his arms to the sides and raised the jetboard's nose for a steep climb.

Never had he felt so free, so alive, and so happy as he realized at that moment that this was the beginning of his new life as an air racer. Not at all as he had dreamed about since he was a little kid, but much better.

Soon he was past the first thousand feet, still climbing and heading straight toward the clouds. By now the cameras would most likely be able to capture him only from a distance. It was then that Keithan spotted two blue-and-white flames flanking him. Had it been the first time he had seen such things, he would have been scared, but Keithan knew well what they were, and so he looked to each of them and saluted. He was also sure one of those blue flames had to belong to his mom's invisible and highly advanced fighter aircraft, and that made him feel safe.

His mom, the secret Sky Phantom agent, was true to her word. She and the Sky Phantom Legion would continue keeping an eye on him. But more than that, on the rest of the sky as well to make sure every flyer like him could be free up there. Always.

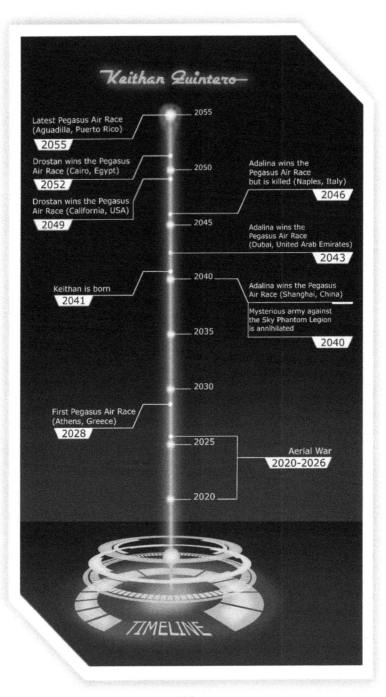

Keithan Quintero

Latest Pegasus Air Race
(Aguadilla, Puerto Rico)
2055

— 2055

Drostan wins the Pegasus
Air Race (Cairo, Egypt)
2052

— 2050

Adalina wins the
Pegasus Air Race
but is killed (Naples, Italy)
2046

Drostan wins the Pegasus
Air Race (California, USA)
2049

— 2045

Adalina wins the
Pegasus Air Race
(Dubai, United Arab Emirates)
2043

— 2040

Keithan is born
2041

Adalina wins the Pegasus
Air Race (Shanghai, China)

Mysterious army against
the Sky Phantom Legion
is annihilated
2040

— 2035

— 2030

First Pegasus Air Race
(Athens, Greece)
2028

— 2025

Aerial War
2020-2026

— 2020

TIMELINE

Acknowledgments

This book and its prequel turned out to be much more than a fun story to write. They became the essence of a journey full of fun experiences that involved meeting some interesting people I would like to thank. First and foremost, I would like to thank my best friend José M. Campo (Chema), who not only shared with me his knowledge and passion for science fiction and architecture but also taught me to never stop being creative and doing what I love. He had such a strong influence in me that the character of Mr. Aramis, along with his eccentric inventions, ended up being almost a mirror image of Chema. I would also like to thank my good friend and pilot Germán Trujillo for taking the time to explain to me some of the aviation terms and rules about flying. More than that, for giving me an exclusive tour inside an airfield during the initial phase of the first book. To my dear friend Arturo Rivera, I thank him for inviting me to those unforgettable first trips to the famous aviation museums in Washington, D.C., and Virginia, which inspired me while I was brainstorming the background of the future of flying that I ended up creating in the books.

To my friend Alexandra Rodriguez; I would like to thank her for the support and constructive feedback she gave me during the development of the first book. Also, I must not forget Michael Báez, Carlos Sánchez, and Abraham Colón: the three musketeers who provided so much support, especially by giving me feedback during the initial stages of each book's first draft. Another person I would like to give proper thanks to is Ricardo Correa, Communications and Public Relations Officer at the Arecibo Observatory, for helping me get permission to use the famous radio telescope as one of the locations in this book. To Andros Martinez, for doing the amazing illustrations for the covers of both books. And last but not least, I would like to give my biggest thanks to all my readers for whom I am so grateful. You were the ones who motivated me the most, and that is something I will cherish forever.